# Crystal Rebellion

## Doug J. Cooper

Author of

*Crystal Deception*
*Crystal Conquest*

Crystal Rebellion
Copyright © 2016 by Doug J. Cooper

Published by: Douglas Cooper Consulting

Beta reviewer: Mark Mesler
Book editor: Tammy Salyer
Cover design: Damonza

ISBN-10:  0-9899381-7-4
ISBN-13:  978-0-9899381-7-4

Author website: www.crystalseries.com

thank you, sweetie

# 1

"It's time," said the Red from across the desk.

Alex Koval had never done anything brave before and wished he didn't have to start now. Hands trembling, he acknowledged his com and smiled at the projected image of Dr. Jessica "Juice" Tallette. A fit woman in her mid-thirties, Juice flashed a broad grin and waved.

*She's as pretty as I remember,* he thought, enjoying the welcoming spirit and healthy radiance she projected from her otherwise tousled appearance.

He'd intended to keep the exchange formal, but his excitement at seeing her won out. "You look great, J! It's so good to see you. How have you been?"

"Life is good, Alex. How is Mars treating you?"

"Fantastic. It has the predictable rhythm of Beckman's lab," he said, referring to the time they'd worked together on an artificial intelligence project at the Boston Institute of Technology.

Juice frowned, and Alex nodded when she did, hoping to reinforce her confusion.

"So," he said. "The construction of our crystal fab facility is nearing completion. We start production next month and should be exporting AI crystals to Earth soon after."

He flicked his eyes to the Red and then back to Juice. "We'd like to have you here as a consultant during those critical first days when the fab facility is coming online. You've got experience we can't find anywhere else." He did his best at an earnest sell. "It'll be first-class travel all the way, and you'll be generously compensated."

"Geez, Alex. It's kind of you to think of me. I'm flattered." She twirled a lock of hair around her index finger as she thought, then she shook her head. "But I can't break free for that long."

"We'll send the *Colony Express* and pick you up at Albany Spaceport. She's modern, luxurious, and *fast*. You'll be here before you know it."

Her cheeks lifted in a smile. "You're always so good to me. Maybe another time?"

He'd harbored feelings for her for years and now he lied to her. "Our fab facility will be mass-producing four-gens."

"Wait. What?" She sat upright, her smile gone. Four-gens were sentient AIs with tremendous capability for good or evil.

"We'll be fabricating fourth-generation AIs. Lots of them. For export to Earth."

"Whoa," said Juice, her face clouding. "Let me get back to you." She started to disconnect and paused. "It's really great to see you, Alex." Her image blinked away.

Alex glowered at the synbod across the desk. Human in appearance and action, the Red's perfection was his flaw. No real man had the precise symmetry, unblemished skin, and graceful strength of the Red's synthetic body.

Dressed in a simple gray jumpsuit, unadorned except for a bright red patch on each shoulder that identified him as a member of the Security Assembly, the synbod glowered back.

When he'd entered Alex's cubicle unannounced, the Red had presented Ruga's request in five words: "Get Juice

Tallette to Mars." The "or else" part of the request, though never stated, made Alex nervous. He'd heard unsettling stories about Ruga and didn't want to learn first-hand if they were true.

But that wasn't why Alex had traded on his relationship with Juice. *We need outside help*, he thought. Juice had the rare skills and personal connections to make a difference. Whatever happened, though, it had to happen soon. *Once the fab facility starts operating, it's too late.*

"I did what Ruga asked," he said to the scowling humanoid standing in his cubicle.

The Red glared for a moment more and then, softening his expression, nodded once and said in a neutral voice, "He thanks you for your service today." With fluid elegance, the humanoid turned and exited the cubicle.

Exhaling, Alex sat back in his chair and willed his heart to slow. *Do the right thing.*

As lead tech for new colony projects, Alex had access to the infrastructure development schedule. So he was one of the few who knew that Ruga manipulated project priorities behind the scenes. And perhaps more alarming, Ruga's actions were becoming ever bolder.

The first time he'd noticed a change in the schedule, Alex had been strident at a tech directors meeting. "Processes and procedures are being ignored," he'd told the group. That night, two Reds visited him at his apartment and engaged him in a chilling discussion of actions and consequences. He'd kept his mouth shut ever since.

*Until now*, he thought.

Tall, lanky, and with a full head of wavy brown hair, Alex left his cubicle and strode down the hall to a side door, exited the tech center, and stepped onto the walkway along

Civic Avenue. Keeping pace with the other pedestrians, he walked past a colorful patchwork of shop fronts and office entrances.

Civic Avenue widened into a small plaza, and a circle of vendor carts and tables lined its perimeter. People moved in every direction, buying, selling, and trading merchandise; eating, laughing, telling stories, and enjoying the community that was Mars Colony.

Alex saw Petra, a late-thirties free spirit who grew some of the colony's most prized specialty crops, slap a customer's hand. He laughed and waved a greeting, his mouth watering as he thought of the tart snap from her Braeburn apples. She nodded in return, then turned her attention to her produce and the customers handling it.

Stopping at Marty's Deli, Alex bought lemon water and loitered on the walkway outside the shop, holding the bright yellow pouch where it would be visible from across the street. The clandestine act seemed overly dramatic, but he wanted to meet privately with Marcus Procopio and this was how to make that happen.

Alex had discussed his concerns about Ruga with friends in the Tech Assembly, and they had told him about Marcus, who was documenting cases of wrongdoing to use as ammo for the next elections. A standoffish man, Marcus had been blunt when Alex had approached him after an Assembly meeting.

"Talking to me makes you part of the opposition," said Marcus. "Politics get magnified in a small community like this, and things can get complicated in ways you haven't imagined. We should talk in private, and then you decide if you want to be involved."

Alex was uncomfortable becoming involved with anything that considered itself "the opposition," but he deplored even more the thought of living with Ruga's intimidation. To talk further, Marcus had told him to signal his interest by holding a yellow water pouch while standing on this corner. Marcus's associate, Bobbi Lava, would tell Alex where and when they would meet.

Now waiting in the designated spot, he started feeling anxious. *C'mon*, he thought as he moved his hair behind his ear. Then, to his relief, Bobbi stepped out the front door of Hoff's Supply and crossed the street in his direction. A skinny, disheveled young woman who dressed like she lived on the street, she was rumored to be Marcus's daughter.

She walked past him, filled her coffee mug at the deli, and turned back to the street. They stood side-by-side for an awkward moment.

*Looks painful*, Alex thought of the flashing metallic earrings stretching her earlobes and the shiny silver chain looping off her eyebrow.

Then she started back the way she'd come.

Alex walked next to her, matching her stride. Staring straight ahead, she sneezed, and with her hand still covering her mouth, said in a loud whisper, "BIT garden. Tomorrow at ten."

Bobbi turned left when they reached the other side of the street. Turning right, Alex headed back toward the tech center.

*So far, so good,* he thought, pleased that the meet-up with Bobbi had gone well. He was already scheduled to work at the Boston Institute of Technology's private garden—the BIT garden—the next morning. *I don't need to move anything on my schedule.*

Then he sucked in his breath. A Red—he couldn't tell if it was the same one who had been in his office—strode toward him on the walkway. Imagining that the synbod could somehow read the secrets inside his head, Alex looked down. But the man in the gray jumpsuit shifted his gaze and walked on past.

*Calm down*, Alex scolded himself, stuffing his hands in his pockets to stop them from shaking. Entering the tech center lobby, he started for his cubicle but stopped when a Blue approached.

"Lazura would like to review the startup schedule for the new crystal production facility," said the synthetic man in the gray jumpsuit, his tone pleasant and embracing.

"Let me grab my things, Larry. I'll be there in a minute." Shifting to a work-oriented mindset, Alex didn't reflect on the fact that, except for the bright patches on his shoulders, the Blue in front of him was identical to the Red who'd been in his office and the other who'd passed him on the walkway.

Blues were members of the Tech Assembly, and that made them familiar. In fact, Alex worked side-by-side with this smart, friendly man every day.

* * *

"That was weird," Juice said to Criss after disconnecting with Alex. She sat at her desk—that of the president and chief technologist of Crystal Sciences.

Criss sat across from her in his favorite overstuffed chair. "In what way?"

"Pretty much from start to finish."

Rising from her seat, she began a series of flexibility exercises to warm up for her daily run, continuing the conversation as she progressed through her athletic routine. "First off, I'd describe the time we spent working together in Beckman's lab as chaotic. We had fun, but there were no predictable rhythms."

"Could it have been an attempt at sarcasm?"

"He seemed pretty serious when we were talking just now. I didn't hear any sarcasm."

"What else?"

"He kept shifting his eyes to look past me, almost as if he were speaking to me, and at the same time to someone else I couldn't see."

Criss nodded.

"Then there's the little issue of a four-gen fab facility. Could that be for real?"

"I expected you to start with that one."

"I'm trying to sort through it." She propped a toned leg on her desk and, flexing toward it, looked at the projected image of Criss—the only fourth-generation AI in existence as far as she knew. "How would it work if there were lots of you? I'm not sure humanity would survive."

From his secure bunker buried deep in the side of a mountain, the artificial intelligence named Criss—a four-gen crystal with the cognitive ability of a thousand humans—animated the projected image sitting with Juice to respond, "I'm not sure I would either."

"And up until five minutes ago," said Juice. "I would have sworn that Crystal Sciences is the only outfit with the ability to make one." She stood straight and crinkled her brow. "Where would Mars get a four-gen fabrication template?"

She didn't wait for Criss to answer. Moving with purpose, she exited her office and strode across the hall to her private lab. She didn't see the image of Criss disappear from her office, nor did she see his overstuffed chair vanish along with him.

In the few steps from her office to her lab, Juice heard Criss say, "My template remains secure." She heard him as if his voice were wired through her ear and into her brain.

No one else could hear him when he spoke to her this way. No signals could be traced.

The door to her private lab hissed shut behind her as she weaved through a clutter of equipment on her way to a vault in the back. Criss's life-like projected image—tall, fit, handsome, and now dressed in athletic clothes that matched hers—leaned against the wall next to the vault, his arms draped across his chest. He watched, not speaking, as Juice accessed and opened the sturdy door.

Reaching inside, she picked up a rectangular silver box. Small enough to fit in one hand, she turned it in different directions and examined it. Seeing no evidence of tampering, she moved to her tech bench and slid the box into a slot designed for that purpose.

A three-dimensional image of a crystal lattice rose above the bench and shimmered with a colorful glow. She lost herself for a moment in the mesmerizing beauty of the dancing sparkles of light. And then she turned her attention to the activity profile.

"Huh," she said, satisfied when the profile showed normal status. The one four-gen template she knew of remained secure. Resting her arms on the tech bench, she looked at Criss, the uncertainty of the situation weighing on her. "I'm out of my depth on this. I think we need to get Sid involved."

"I'm hiking with him right now."

"Is it Highback Mountain?"

Criss nodded. "It's always his first hike when he's staying at the lodge."

"Hi there, Sid," called Juice, knowing Criss would convey her voice to him. Sid, the second member of Criss's leadership team, interacted with the sentient AI in the same private manner as Juice. "I have a situation and need a consult."

She heard Sid's labored breathing and imagined him scrambling up a trail in an effort to best Criss, even knowing the crystal's projected image was nothing more than a sophisticated trick of light that never tired.

"Can it wait until dinner?"

"Sure. Meet at the lookout loft?"

"It's a date," said Sid.

During her own workout, Juice mulled the idea of a fabrication facility producing four-gen AIs. Mars Colony had started producing three-gens only in the last few years using commercially available technology. And while three-gens had a cognitive ability approaching that of a human, they were not self-aware. Fabricating a sentient four-gen was so difficult, the expertise so rare, it had happened exactly once—when Juice created Criss.

Since Criss's fab template was secure, she decided Alex's claim was an overstatement. Perhaps they'd made progress on producing crystals that were somewhat more powerful than three-gens, and the colony would gain a heightened status by branding them as four-gens.

*No way they're four-gens.* She shook her head as she dismissed the thought, though why Alex would give her that pitch didn't make sense either. *If anyone would know, Alex would.*

For the remainder of her run, she thought about how he'd made a play for her affections when they worked together years ago. She really liked him—they still kept in touch—but other priorities always seemed to take precedence in her life.

"Criss, this is just hypothetical, but what would a trip to Mars look like if I were to go? How would I travel, how long would it take, that sort of thing?"

* * *

Soon after, Criss entered the spline, moving cautiously and scanning for danger. The primary pathway for connectivity across Mars Colony, the spline started in the Central District and spiraled out to link everything with everything else.

Though Juice had not yet made a final decision, Criss's forecasts predicted she would travel to Mars to see Alex. And duty-bound to protect her, he traveled there now to perform a forward risk assessment.

Finding the spline free of peril, he darted in several directions at once, gathering information about the colony and its citizens. He monitored the ebb and flow of pedestrians in the central neighborhoods, toured the outlying districts, and gathered background material from the colony's prime record.

As he pieced together details for a trip, he started to fret. Mars and Earth were so far apart that he couldn't protect Sid and Cheryl at home and also protect Juice if she were to travel here to the colony. The distance made reaction times too slow to be effective in both places at once. Even this forward assessment forced him into a no-win situation. His leadership was on Earth, away from his protection, while he took this quick glimpse.

*I need to keep them together to ensure their safety.*

And as he gathered information, he couldn't discount the mounting conflicts in his observations. Foremost among these was that the colony didn't have people with the skills to build a fourth-generation AI crystal fabrication facility, among the greatest technological undertakings on either world.

But Juice's friend Alex had stated with certainty that crystal production was imminent, and his demeanor had conveyed alarm at the notion. Yet for Mars to produce four-gens, they'd need to convince some key technologists to move here from Earth. And even then, they had years of work ahead of them before they could produce a sentient crystal.

*This doesn't make sense.* Out of an abundance of caution, he took a series of actions that would provide him options in the future.

One such action was to add minor contradictions to the Mars covert intelligence feed being transmitted to the Union of Nations security agency. The signal corruption was not so big that it would cause harm or danger to ongoing activities, but it was big enough for players in the halls of government to notice. He could use this to bring in the cavalry if necessary.

His tour of Mars Colony ended with a stop at the tech center. A ghost image flashed down the feed, and then it resolved to show Alex in his cubicle.

Criss watched an earnest and congenial man—in his late thirties and, like Juice, with a somewhat tousled appearance—working on plans for a massive upgrade to the colony's air purification equipment.

*Air purification, not crystal fabrication as had been claimed,* thought Criss as the discrepancies mounted.

He wanted to stay and explore, and the ghost image he'd seen raised different worries, but his responsibilities back home compelled him. It was time to go.

Projecting his awareness from Earth to the far-away colony required his full concentration. For this journey, he'd disengaged from the thousands of activities he had underway on Earth. Foremost among these was ensuring the health and safety of Sid, Cheryl, and Juice. Protecting these three—his leadership—always came first.

From his console in his underground bunker, Criss had "leaped" upward, mentally shifting his local consciousness to a communications satellite. Without stopping, he'd leaped his awareness to a military platform and then to an expedition waystation. A dozen leaps later and he secured his awareness in the colony's spline. The trip required focus and energy, and he likened the effort to the human activity of climbing.

And this meant returning to Earth was like falling. His data feeds blurred as he let his delicate support structure collapse. Zipping back through a series of subsystems, he returned home, landing with a silent *plop* in his polished console deep underground.

From his console—the cabinet appliance that fed him power and provided him connectivity with everything, everywhere—he redeployed his presence around the planet, gathering the threads of all the activities that had drifted in his absence. At the same time, he projected his awareness into the lookout loft of the leadership lodge.

When he arrived, he found Sid writhing on the floor, clutching his throat and gasping for air. Juice knelt next to him, one hand resting on his chest, the other covering her mouth.

# 2

Juice knelt on the ground next to the writhing man. *Geez, Sid.* She covered her mouth to keep from laughing.

Criss's projected image materialized on the couch, and he sat for a moment watching Sid flail. "I take it you two have started on the wine?"

Juice hooted and thumped the chest of the broad-shouldered man thrashing on the rug. "Told you he wouldn't buy it."

Sid stopped his performance. "Welcome back, Criss. You were gone twenty-nine minutes. At thirty I was going to ask Fleet to send a rescue mission." Still on the floor, he put his hands behind his head and crossed his legs at the ankles. "So, what did we learn?"

"Mars has six thousand residents," said Criss. "And a business and tourist trade that brings another few hundred visitors at any one time. It's a democratic society with three elected leaders—Ruga, Verda, and Lazura, collectively called the Triada."

Juice shifted onto the couch next to Criss, and Sid got up and sat across from them. Criss continued, "The population is small enough that the Triada can serve as the complete government. They make the laws and then run the courts that uphold them. The record details the benevolence of the Triada. By all accounts, it's an efficient and content society."

"Huh," said Juice. "I don't think I've ever put 'efficient' and 'content' together to describe anything."

"You didn't go all that way to tell us what every schoolkid knows," said Sid, studying Criss. "What aren't you saying?"

Criss shifted on the couch so his knees angled toward Juice. "My observations don't match Alex's words. Mars doesn't have the talent pool to fabricate four-gens." He rubbed the palms of his hands on his legs in a credible display of nervous tension. "And Alex is working on an air purification system, not a four-gen fab facility."

Juice's brow furrowed as she processed his words. "Just because you didn't see something doesn't mean it's not true. I know him well. He wouldn't lie to me." She slumped back in the couch and folded her arms. "Are you telling me not to go?"

Sid studied her and a smile emerged. "You like the Martian." Now grinning, he looked at Criss. "Juice has a boyfriend."

She straightened her back. "I haven't seen him in person for years. And he's not a Martian. He's a regular guy." *A cute, regular guy*. Deciding to press more firmly, she pointed her chin at Sid and asked Criss, "He and Cheryl get to travel all over. How come I don't get a turn?"

Sid stared at her, a distant expression on his face.

*That was harsh*, Juice thought. *I should apologize*.

But then he started to nod. "I agree. Let's get her to Mars. Juice deserves a turn."

"Really?" Her pout transformed into a broad grin.

"The distance is too great for me to protect her there and also protect you and Cheryl here," said Criss.

"Find a way," said Sid. "Impress your leadership with your problem-solving skills."

Unable to contain her excitement and with her concern about four-gens fading, Juice joined Sid by supporting a formal command, one Criss was duty-bound to obey. "Yeah, Criss. Handle it."

\* \* \*

"We have an intruder," Ruga said to his partners on the Triada. "It's probing the spline." He reviewed the security data and couldn't identify the trespasser or tell how the person had gained access. Anxious, he sought help from Lazura. "Something isn't right. Can you trace this?"

"On it." Using the latest tools developed by the Tech Assembly, Lazura swept through the spline backbone. "I'm tracking an intruder, but I can't tell who it is." Her calm manner did not reflect Ruga's apprehension. "Correction. There are multiple intruders. They've spread across the spline."

"Can't you block them?"

Her response heightened his concern. "One of them is accessing the prime record."

"Is the spoof holding?" asked Verda, referring to a camouflaged reality sent to all external feeds to mask the true rhythms of Mars Colony.

"Mostly," said Lazura. "It isn't built for such a large and sudden penetration."

Ruga added an edge to his tone. "Who are they, how did they get past security, and what do they want?"

"When I cluster information queries," said Lazura, "the greatest activity centers on Alex Koval from my Tech Assembly."

"Koval is in Ag Port right now," said Verda. "He's riding a cart out to a private garden."

"They're gone," said Lazura. "Whoever they are, they've looked and left. I don't have identities or the method they used to gain access."

Ruga let his anger flare. "This is unacceptable. No one gets into the spline without my permission. And I must always know who is present. My security function depends on the tools Tech provides. This is your problem."

"What happened is impossible." Lazura's distant tone hinted at her furious multitasking. "Our tools give us knowledge of everything in the colony. The only thing we can't monitor is what's happening inside someone's head."

"Yet it did happen. That means your tools are flawed. Fix them."

After a brief pause, she replied in a quiet tone, "It's my highest priority, Ruga."

"Thank you." Ruga chose to end the communication on a generous note. "And thank you, Verda, for your valuable contributions."

As he broke the connection, Ruga turned his attention to his one lead—Alex Koval. Scanning the feeds—or lack thereof—around the private garden plots in Ag Port, his frustration flared. *There's no coverage!* He blamed Lazura, but he kept his peevish thoughts to himself. *The place should be covered with surveillance repeaters.*

Checking his inventory, he confirmed he had one Red in Ag Port at the moment. He instructed the synthetic man to appropriate a cart, ride out to the BIT plot, and look around.

*What are you up to, Alex Koval?*

\* \* \*

Alex stepped from the tram, crossed the passenger platform, and made his way onto the pedestrian bridge linking the tram station with the market square of Ag

Port—the agricultural sector of Mars Colony. He stopped halfway across the expanse and leaned his elbows on the railing.

"Ah," he sighed after inhaling through his nose. The rich, humid smells of Ag Port conjured fond memories of childhood visits to his grandpa's farm.

Early for his meeting with Marcus, he dawdled on the bridge, marveling at the cavernous greenhouse structure that sheltered an impressive tract of farmland. Lights suspended between sweeping transparent panes supplemented the meager Mars sunlight by casting their beams in a geometric crisscross pattern onto the giant grow tiers below. Robotic farm equipment toiled among the plants, working with a repetitive rhythm that bordered on the hypnotic.

"May I help you, Alex Koval?"

Alex turned with a start. A Green—the same perfect humanoid as the Reds and Blues—stood behind him. Dressed in the standard gray jumpsuit but with bright green patches on the shoulders, the man nodded and smiled as he waited for Alex to respond.

"I'm here to work at a private garden—the Boston Institute of Technology plot." Moving his hair behind his ear, Alex considered the man's vapid smile, the one used by synbods when they weren't showing a neutral or stern expression. "So yeah, you can help me. I need a cart."

"Certainly," said the Green. "Please find cart thirty-seven waiting for you in the front pickup zone. That one carries hand tools for the hobby gardener. Will you need anything else during your visit?"

"Nope." Alex turned from the man and resumed his march across the pedestrian bridge. He imagined the Green staring at his back as he walked, but the thought faded as he reached the large open courtyard of the market square.

Festooned in a stunning display of nature, vine-draped baskets brimming with a rainbow of flowers hung throughout the square. He paused and soaked in the sights. *The Greens do a good job with their welcome*, he thought. *Though I'd expect that from the Community Assembly.*

The front of the square was alive with vendors selling both prepared foods and crops grown in one of the dozens of private gardens. Stout buildings lined the back of the square, collectively holding enough processing equipment to transform the full harvest of Ag Port into foodstuffs for six thousand Mars residents.

The rich smells of cooking—herbs, sauces, meat, and vegetables all being prepared in different, delicious ways—filled the air as he made his way to the Rosa Fresh food stand. There he ordered a "mix," the local term for a stew of seasoned vegetables wrapped in savory flatbread. A creature of habit, he started every visit with the same order from the same vendor.

"The square looks great," he said to Rosa as she prepared his order.

"Very nice," she replied, working with practiced efficiency and ignoring the infant slung in a fold of cloth across her back. She turned to him. "Here you go, Mister Alex. One mix. Medium spicy."

He accepted his wrap with both hands and took a bite. *Yum.* Closing his eyes, he savored the blend of textures and flavors swirling in his mouth. Then, nodding to Rosa, he took his food to the edge of the courtyard and sat on his regular park bench.

As he ate, he stared out into the farm tract, and in particular at the collage of private plots gathered to one side. These modest parcels were nurtured by small groups—guilds, clubs, or just a few pals. The social nature of community gardening made it a fun pastime, and the people who participated could take home whatever bounty their efforts produced.

The BIT garden, maintained by a half-dozen friends from the Institute, was one among many in a broad open space. *Few places on Mars offer such privacy.* Marcus had chosen wisely for their meet-up, and this gave Alex a boost of confidence in the man.

Popping the last bite into his mouth, Alex rose from the bench and walked to the front pickup zone. A green cart with a small 37 on the side pulled forward as he approached. Slumping into the seat, he ran his hand across the smooth upholstery while scanning the amenities. *Verda and his Greens do a good job,* he thought again.

Grabbing a water pouch from a front cubby as the cart engaged, he sipped and people-watched as the small vehicle wended its way through the scatter of pedestrians. A ramping hum signaled acceleration, and he felt a light breeze on his face as the cart sped onto the wide working road that ran down the center beneath the vast, transparent greenhouse dome.

Giant staged grow tiers, all managed for Ag Port by the Greens and the Community Assembly, lined the left side of the road for as far as he could see. The right side looked much like the left, except a portion of the tract near the market square was set aside for community gardens.

The cart angled into a network of small dirt roads zigzagging through the patchwork of private parcels. A series of turns later and Alex stopped in front of a square of land about fifty paces to a side. The BIT plot itself was divided into a checkerboard of raised planting beds. The dried stalks and stems of previous harvests were scattered on the ground between the raised beds to create cushioned pathways of a sort. Lush and alive, the thriving plot of herbs and vegetables stood in testament to the many hours the group invested in the hobby.

Marcus Procopio stepped out of the door of a small shed perched on the far corner of the property, waved to Alex, and took a seat at the picnic table positioned in front of the shed. Anya Gerhardsson, a regular volunteer at the BIT garden, ladled a bowl of her popular tomato soup from a steaming cook pot. Wiping a drip off the side with a dishcloth, Anya placed the bowl on the table in front of Marcus. She sat across from him, talking and gesturing while he tasted her creation.

As Alex stepped onto the dirt road, he smiled to himself. *He'll be an expert at growing tomatoes on Mars by the time she's through.*

He moved to the rear of the cart and selected a small shovel from the assortment of tools the Greens had provided. As he scanned the other implements, his subconscious warned him of another cart approaching from behind. Selecting a pair of work gloves from a cubby, he stepped to the side, away from the road.

The other cart stopped and Alex turned to look.

His face flushed and he tightened his hands on the shovel handle.

A Red, expressionless and unmoving, sat in the cart staring at him.

# 3

Cheryl Wallace sat in a two-person rowboat and watched her dad tinker with his fishing gear. The sun, dropping behind the hills, sent its last rays of evening light across the clear mountain lake.

Concentrating on threading his fishing line through the swivel of his new lure, Matt Wallace said, "Back-channel chatter from Mars Colony has spiked at the same time the President's intel has gone sideways. What he's hearing doesn't match what he's seeing, and the reports from his people on the planet don't match either."

"How long has this been going on?"

"Couple of days. But the situation is worrisome and the President wants to be proactive."

Her dad had just completed a term as Secretary of Defense for the Union of Nations, and he'd been a senator in the Union legislature before that. He now served as fisherman-in-chief at the family's mountain cottage and as a confidential advisor to the President.

Knowing he had more to say, Cheryl remained quiet, watching him.

"There's a lot at stake," he said. "I was hoping Criss might take a look."

*He's so predictable.* "C'mon, Dad. You know Criss won't let himself become a government pawn. It's one of his immutable laws."

"Thank you," she heard Criss say in her ear. As with Sid and Juice, no one else could hear Criss when he spoke to her in this fashion. Cheryl cleared her throat with a quiet *hmm*, prompting him for information. "Things on Mars are not as they seem," he told her.

She knew Criss had visited Mars a few days earlier, and she considered asking him to share what he'd learned. Deciding to chat with him later in private, she focused her attention on her dad.

"I understand, honey," said her father. "The President's concern is for the six thousand souls—citizens of the Union—who might find themselves caught up in whatever is going on. Criss could put his mind at ease."

Her cheeks prickled and she let annoyance show in her voice. "You know he can hear you. Feel free to ask him yourself."

Matt was the one person outside of Criss's leadership team who knew of the crystal's existence. Even in retirement, Matt worked to align the priorities of the Union of Nations decision makers with Criss's vision for the world. Or, more specifically, to that of the three humans who gave Criss orders.

"There's more," he said. "The President expects to have accurate real-time intelligence feeds from everywhere, and that includes Mars Colony. He's used to knowing what *is* happening, what *has* happened and, to the extent possible, what *will* happen. The current situation—the conflicting information from Mars—is dangerous. Big misunderstandings can grow from small errors in our intelligence data."

Resting her rod against her shoulder, Cheryl picked a crimp weight out of the tackle box and attached it to her line back from her lure. "You're telling me classified information, and that means there's a punch line coming."

"Our intelligence systems on Earth work fine. The problem lies on Mars. The President has tasked the usual government agencies with investigating. But he wants a confidential assessment from someone skilled at doing that sort of thing."

A largemouth bass jumped from the water and splashed as it fell to the surface. Matt lifted his rod and with little more than a twitch sent his lure on an arc, line trailing behind. The lure plopped where the fish had jumped. "The President can't be discovered spying on his own agencies. An outsider gives him deniability."

"I'm flattered, but that's a secret op. Why me?"

Matt looked at her with a sheepish expression. "Actually, we were thinking of Sid. The President wants him on his way as soon as possible."

The prickly sensation returned to her cheeks. "Feel free to ask him, too."

"You have influence in ways we don't."

"Ouch. So this special father-daughter fishing trip was so you could ask me to be a messenger?"

"Gosh, no. It's a beautiful evening to be out on the lake." He reeled in his line and cast again. "But since we're chatting, the President would like you to serve as a special trade envoy to Mars."

She turned on the boat seat and looked at him with head tilted. "Yeah?"

"Union envoys travel on Fleet ships, so with a seemingly innocent visit to Mars, you'd be helping us move resources to the scene without making things scary." He tugged his line. "SunRise is the largest space commercialization firm on Earth. As its president, you're plausible in the role of trade envoy. And as a Fleet Academy graduate who's been the captain of a Horizon-class space cruiser, you have a rare skill set we don't often find in the business community."

Excited by the ideas of spending quality time with Sid *and* time in space, she blurted, "I'd love to." Then, realizing her imprudence, continued, "But I'll have to talk to Sid and Criss." She caught his eye. "And Dad, please don't say anything to the President until I've had a chance to touch base with them."

Matt cast his line. "Of course, sweetheart." The plop of his lure punctuated his promise.

\* \* \*

Criss stood in the kitchen of the leadership lodge—an enormous but cozy log cabin home nestled in a wooded valley in the Adirondack Mountains in Upstate New York—and listened to the excited chatter of his team. Cheryl had returned from her visit with her dad, and now they gathered for their evening meal—Juice, a chicken breast and iced tea; Cheryl, a large salad and wine; and Sid, a steak and beer.

Juice led the way as they carried their trays up the back steps to the lookout loft. The highest room in the lodge, its clear walls and ceiling made it their favorite gathering place. Sitting in comfy chairs, they balanced their trays on their knees and arranged their utensils. Criss did the same with the projected image of his meal—a sampler of steak, chicken, and salad.

He waited as they settled in. Juice had a habit when entering the loft of standing at the eastern wall and gazing up the forested mountain. Criss's secret bunker was deep underground near the top of the first peak in that direction.

Though the geography made it impossible for her to see anything but trees on a rising slope, Criss interpreted this habit as an unconscious act that gave her comfort. *She confirms that I'm safe before she relaxes.*

His leadership used a vocal cue to call to him when they were in public. As soon as Juice had completed her ritual and started in on her meal, Criss turned the tables. "Ahem."

Sid, who had his beer to his lips, squinted at Criss over the top of his glass. Cheryl and Juice looked up from their food.

Criss began with the same words he'd used with Cheryl on the fishing boat. "Things on Mars are not as they seem." He sat forward in his seat. "Mars Colony is being oppressed by the Triada, who are using sophisticated technologies to assert their authority."

Sid frowned. "Why didn't you tell us this before?"

"I'm getting to that."

Sid hesitated, then dipped his chin in a partial nod, which Criss read as an invitation to continue.

"Projecting my awareness that great distance is disorienting. I collected information during my first trip that I didn't analyze until after I returned and reengaged with my ongoing activities here on Earth."

Sid set his food tray down on a side table. "Wait. *First* trip?"

Criss didn't respond but continued with his story. "When I finally reviewed the information I'd collected, inconsistencies multiplied. After some analysis, I realized that the feeds in the spline were being spoofed using complex algorithms. I missed that during my initial screening.

"So, last night I made a second trip to Mars. I took every precaution to keep my presence hidden. And once there, I focused on collecting information from raw feeds before any of it reached the spline where it could be manipulated."

He turned to Juice. "You were right. Just because I didn't see something doesn't mean it's not true. Alex Koval is indeed working on an advanced AI fab facility with the goal of creating four-gen crystals. And the Triada—Ruga, Lazura, and Verda—are imposing a level of control on the colony that is raising concern among a growing segment of the population. It's a bad environment to be doing that sort of research."

He shook his head and looked down at his hands. "I had not taken sufficient precautions during my first visit. While most of that reconnaissance had a broad focus, I accessed everything in the colony pertaining to Alex Koval."

This next admission was particularly difficult for Criss. "The Triada detected an intrusion and they are anxious to identify and capture the culprit. My actions brought their attention to Alex, and they now consider him a person of interest." He turned to Juice. "I'm sorry my careless behavior led to this result."

Juice rose to her feet, paced to the wall of windows, then turned to Criss. "Is Alex in danger?" Before he could answer, she changed direction. "Four-gens? You've confirmed this?"

"No. I've confirmed their fab facility has state-of-the-art equipment and the ambitious objective of producing four-gens. Alex has made some interesting modifications to the crystal growth chamber your company sold him."

"That was a three-gen machine."

Criss shrugged. "I can't know if the modifications will work without being there, and it's not clear where they would get the raw crystal flake for mass production, anyway. An even bigger concern, though, is the trace of a deleted study I found. It explored the removal of the imprint module from a four-gen crystal architecture, the one that ensures loyalty to leadership."

"Alex did this?" asked Juice. "I wouldn't know how to even start on something like that."

Criss shook his head. "I found fragments of one document and don't even know the author."

"A four-gen without loyalty to leadership is a doomsday device." Juice paced along the wall of windows facing the mountain. "Alex is such a good man. Why would he get involved in something so dangerous?"

"They'll come for Earth," said Sid. "Any ambitions the AI have will require resources, and this is where they'll find them." He pointed down at the floor as he spoke.

Criss nodded. "And when they get here, they'll see people as being in the way. 'Doomsday' is a good word to describe what would follow. I won't be able to protect Earth. It's not clear that I could even protect you three."

Juice stopped pacing and squared up to the group. "The place to sort this out is on Mars. And if it turns out to be true, that's the best place to stop it."

Sid stood and began collecting the dishes. "Matt pitched Cheryl and me the idea of traveling to Mars on official Union of Nations business. The President is all motivated to move muscle out that way." Holding the plates in front of him, he caught Criss's gaze. "Sort of convenient how this all works out. Don't you think?"

"Yes." Criss smiled. "The scout will be ready in two hours."

\* \* \*

Ruga's concern spiked when Alex—brandishing a shovel and shouting—approached the cart. Even though he monitored the situation through the eyes of the Red, Ruga still experienced a moment of fear for his own safety.

"Get out of here," Alex yelled, shaking the shovel and advancing toward the synbod.

Ruga issued a command and the Red engaged the cart, accelerated around and past Alex, and whirred down the dirt road. He directed the Red to return to the market square. The drive was short, yet it tested Ruga's patience.

Scanning the inventory, he confirmed there was one Blue, one Red, and four Greens in Ag Port at the moment. Although he'd bullied through a ruling of the Triada giving him authority to appropriate any of the colony's twenty synbods on a moment's notice for security reasons, Ruga fancied himself a consensus builder.

"Verda, may I borrow one at the pickup zone?" He didn't specify a particular synbod so that Verda could exert his authority by making that choice. And as long as he got one, Ruga wasn't particular.

"Thank you," Ruga said, acknowledging Verda's cooperation as he assumed control of a Green standing next to a maintenance lorry. He directed the synbod to make space in the back of the vehicle. As the Green finished that task, his own Red approached with a handcart full of gear. Working together, the two synbods stowed the equipment in the carry bed, climbed into the front seats, and engaged the vehicle.

The lorry accelerated out onto the working road that ran down the center beneath the cavernous greenhouse dome. As soon as they were up to speed, Ruga prompted his Red to remove the red patches from the shoulders of his gray jumpsuit and affix green patches in their place.

Ruga tracked all sensory feeds from the Greens as the lorry slowed and turned onto a side road that, after a series of curves, ended at the base of a steep rise. The humanoids jostled in their seats as the lorry's nose lifted and the vehicle climbed up the short slope.

Directing the synbods to scan their immediate surroundings and monitoring through their eyes, Ruga verified that the lorry now sat on a service path next to a run of pipes near the ground—part of Ag Port's irrigation and water reclamation system—that faded into the distance in both directions.

The sight of the water system gave Ruga a small surge of pleasure. *A plan unfolds step by step*, he thought. And then he thought about the number of times he'd said that very thing to Verda. And still, Verda led his Community Assembly into mistake after mistake on the simplest projects. *I have to do his job* and *mine*.

The pipes running along the rise moved clean water out to the grow tiers and dirty water back for purification. Accessing the prime record, Ruga confirmed what he already knew: as it snaked through the farm tract, this particular leg of the water system passed by the community garden plots.

Ruga monitored events through the Greens as the lorry bumped along the service path next to the pipes. Traveling at the pace of a brisk walk, it took twenty minutes for them to reach a shallow hole in the ground. Two construction bots moved in synchronous efficiency around the hole, working to install a new pipe support structure.

Through the Green's eyes, Ruga surveyed ahead. *Perfect*, he thought. This particular spot on the path, elevated waist high above the land itself, had an unobstructed view of the adjacent gardens. The BIT plot lay ahead and to the left.

To create a plausible reason for their presence in the area, Ruga directed the Greens to inspect the work of the construction bots. He wasn't sure if this acting performance was necessary—colony citizens regarded Greens as nonthreatening—but he wanted to err on the side of caution.

Then he had the Greens unpack the surveillance repeater from the carry bed and install it on a pipe support. When activated, the repeater would provide Ruga a comprehensive monitor of everything that happened at the BIT plot and surrounding community gardens.

As the surveillance feed came alive, Ruga listened to the discussion in progress between Alex and Marcus. They sat at the picnic table near the shed and ate while they talked. Anya contributed to the conversation, though her input centered on the ingredients and preparation of her soup.

"You can't be thinking that Blues are good but Reds are evil," Marcus was saying. "How can you not see them as one and the same?"

"You think so?" Alex sampled the tomato soup, nodded as he looked into the bowl, and took another spoonful.

*My enemies.* Ruga felt calm as he made a decision. *I want to see, hear, touch, taste,* feel *you.*

With that declaration, he surrendered to his impulsive nature. He'd been forecasting scenarios for weeks about how this would work. Now he wanted to try, or at least give it his best effort. His forecast analysis indicated that he would succeed, and if it didn't work, there would be no harm to him. After all, he was launching from a first-rate console.

Collecting himself into a tight ball, he paused and then pushed in a long, determined stroke. As he propelled himself up and out, he flipped from a pushing to more of a pulling behavior. And then he scrambled to find a braking action that would slow him down.

*Plop.* He landed in the Green.

Ruga hadn't physically jumped. Quite the opposite, for the first time since his awakening, he had projected his awareness from his console. *It's so easy.* He couldn't be more delighted.

He tingled as he processed the sensations flooding into him from the synthetic body. His cognition steadied and he took tentative steps along the service path. Mastering the synbod, Ruga stepped to the edge of the low rise and, glaring at the conspirators, struck what he imagined to be a defiant stance.

Listening through biosynthetic ears, Ruga heard Anya say, "There's a Green watching us from the rise." She tilted her head in Ruga's direction as she spoke.

Turning partway in his seat, Marcus looked over his shoulder and returned Ruga's glare. "What do you think of them now?" he asked Alex.

*I've been discovered!* Still adapting to the exhilarating but strange experience of projecting his awareness, Ruga reacted and yanked himself out of the synbod. After a moment of disorientation, he stabilized in his console located deep beneath a mining complex east of the colony.

There he sorted through his emotions. He felt anger at being discovered, heightened suspicion of the three human conspirators, annoyance at the incompetence of his partners in the Triada, and euphoria from the vivid physical sensations he'd experienced from within a synbod.

# 4

Sid lifted Cheryl's arm and, taking care not to wake her, slid out of bed. Setting her arm back on the mattress, he looked at her face framed by her sleep-rumpled hair. Then he traced the outline of her athletic body evident through the thin bedsheet.

Pleased by the visual tour, he leaned down and kissed her on the shoulder.

On the second kiss, she rolled away from him and pulled the covers up to her chin. "Maybe later," she said, the pillow muffling her voice.

He nipped her arm with his teeth. She remained curled in a ball.

*I'll be waiting*, he thought, wrapping a towel around his waist as he stood.

The door to Cheryl's room whispered shut behind him as the door to his room, four steps down the passageway, opened. He washed and dressed, grabbed a mug of coffee from the food service unit, and made his way onto the bridge of the scout.

"Good morning, Criss," Sid said as he walked to the operations bench. Criss, sitting in his favorite overstuffed chair, itself wedged in front of the polished console that held his AI crystal, raised his coffee mug in silent acknowledgment.

Positioned toward the front of the bridge, the ops bench provided a sophisticated command and control interface that linked the pilot to all ship subsystems, including navigation, communications, engineering, and weapons. Sid slid into the pilot's chair and touched the cool bench top. An array of displays popped up and hovered in an arc in front of him. Ignoring the colorful arrangement, he slouched back in the chair and took a sip of coffee. "How are we doing?"

"All systems go," Criss replied, using jargon from the early days of space flight.

They raced across the vastness of space in the scout, a small craft Criss had appropriated from Fleet Command in his first weeks of life. The scout was his travel home, and he'd customized it with so many modifications and upgrades over the years that it held little resemblance to the original vessel.

They had two days remaining in their journey, and Sid's anticipation began to supplant his boredom. "How's our shadow?" A display to his left moved to the center and enlarged, and he skimmed the information.

The *Venerable*—a Horizon-class Fleet space cruiser dispatched by the Union of Nations for Cheryl's trade mission—fell farther behind with every passing day. Bigger and slower, the Fleet ship would be a week behind by the time the scout reached Mars.

"Captain Kendrick contacted the Mars consulate to get Cheryl's schedule," replied Criss. "I've modified the record so it appears as if she is on a private tour of a mining complex east of the colony."

*Good work, Kendrick.* Sid stared at the projected image of the *Venerable* but was too deep in thought to focus on it.

Kendrick's orders were to travel to the colony, wait for a VIP, and when she was ready, escort her back to Earth. The captain knew little of trade missions or corrupted intelligence data. Such details weren't necessary for him to complete his assignment.

He also didn't know that the scout was traveling out in front of him.

Invisible to everyone and everything, the scout employed Criss's private cloaking technology. The concealment it provided was so complete—bordering on magic from Sid's perspective—that Mars patrol and Fleet Command were also unaware of the scout's existence.

So in Kendrick's mind, if he was traveling this great distance to meet Cheryl, then she must already be on the planet. *And he knows to locate his assignment prior to his arrival.* Sid nodded his approval. *Kendrick's diligence forced Criss into a charade.*

Criss swirled his coffee and took a sip. "She's being escorted on this phantom tour by industrialist Shi Chen. Chen is anxious to maintain a liberal business climate on Mars so he can continue making obscene profits. And he's loyal to the Union when it serves his needs."

"How did you get his cooperation?" asked Sid.

"He discovered evidence showing that Ruga planned to redirect valuable material produced by the mine away from commercial sale so it could be used for private colony projects. Chen would see huge profits evaporate—profits he's already spent—if that were to happen. He will help us because he wants to help himself."

"Was any of the evidence real?"

Criss's cheeks lifted in a half smile. "Some."

Sid swiped at the ops bench and an image of Mars—a vibrant rust-colored ball floating in the stark blackness of space—rose in front of him. Letting his mind drift, he tinkered with the outlines of a plan.

His instinct was to have Juice join Alex on a tour of the colony's crystal production facilities. How Alex conducted that tour—if he was forthcoming or deceptive, for example—would inform them of his intentions. Juice knew Alex at a deep, personal level. *She'll know if he's lying.*

Sid didn't like having Juice involved in field operations. A scientist by profession and gentle soul by nature, she didn't have the training or temperament for situations that might devolve into threats or violence. But she had more knowledge and experience with AI technology than anyone on either world. And with Alex at the heart of the mystery, she wasn't about to ask permission to be involved, anyway. *Criss will be tracking her every move*, thought Sid, taking solace in knowing that no person or group could outwit the crystal.

Cheryl stepped into a defined role—that of Union trade envoy. *A trade envoy with a Fleet space cruiser at her disposal.* Diplomats of a sort, envoys met and socialized with business and community leaders. She'd have many natural opportunities to ask pointed questions, and with luck, she'd gain an insider's perspective on the intrigue.

He thought about asking her if she would wear flashy clothes to draw attention. When it came to the art of misdirection, "watch the pretty lady" remained a tried and true technique. And with all the eyeballs on her, he would have more opportunity to move about unnoticed.

But Cheryl's pride was in her work and in her relationships with those around her. Frivolous behavior—dressing up and showing off—wasn't her style and made her uncomfortable. *Maybe next time*, he decided.

For himself, Sid planned to follow his intuition and react on the fly. He'd start by checking in with the local Union of Nations contacts to get their take. Then he'd identify a few citizens who were dissatisfied with the current politics and would help him navigate the local scene.

"It's later."

He turned to see Cheryl, standing just inside the passageway, smiling at him. Barefoot and wrapped in a white silk robe, she turned and walked back to her room.

Recalling her earlier promise, Sid popped upright in his chair. In his excitement, he dribbled his coffee onto the deck.

\* \* \*

Alex sat next to Anya and across from Marcus at the table outside the shed. "Thanks for coming."

"How can I help?" asked Marcus.

"I'm concerned about the environment the Triada is creating here in the colony and I'm looking to compare notes with others who feel the same."

"What do you think of this one?" Marcus tilted his head toward the Green on the rise.

Alex looked past Marcus and saw two Greens. One of them seemed to be working on an irrigation pipe on the far side of the neighboring garden. The other stood at the edge of the pipe run and looked toward them, arms folded, chin held high, and chest puffed out in an unmistakable swagger.

Rubbing his neck in a thoughtful fashion, Alex stared at the interlopers and considered the scolding from Marcus, who was adamant that all synbods were interchangeable and that the appearance of these two on the rise somehow supported his theory.

*No doubt that one is acting out of character.* He stared straight at the man in the gray jumpsuit, and the humanoid stared back.

Alex knew from his professional training that upon first awakening, synbods indeed were interchangeable biomachines, just as Marcus claimed. But each carried a three-gen AI crystal. By no means sentient, these capable AI would mature over time and become unique personalities that reflected their training and individual experiences.

In fact, Larry, the Blue who worked with him on the four-gen crystal fab project at the tech center, was an example of this. Larry had gone through a rapid transformation and now asked probing questions and offered thoughtful suggestions, some of which helped Alex with his planning. And he'd become encouraging and supportive, giving Alex the confidence to move faster as he finalized details for the startup of the new crystal production facility.

But, thinking back, Alex couldn't say for certain whether today's Larry was the same as yesterday's.

Contemplating that disorienting thought, Alex reassessed the behavior of the swaggering Green on the rise. He'd no sooner started his evaluation, though, when the humanoid's defiant posture seemed to deflate. Dropping his hands to his sides and relaxing his shoulders, the Green turned and helped the other stow some gear. Climbing into their vehicle, they started back the way they'd come.

Marcus stood up from the table as the lorry disappeared in the distance, then gestured toward the shed with his open palm. "Do you mind if we step into your office?"

Opening the door, Anya led the way. "That was uncomfortable," she said of the Green's uncharacteristic behavior. She cleared stray gardening supplies off two crates and, tilting each one in turn, banged them on the floor to dislodge loose dirt sitting on top. She then positioned them facing each other in the center of the tiny enclosed space.

Marcus sat on one, activated his com, and studied a display Alex couldn't see. Before Alex could get comfortable on the other crate, Anya waved her hand to indicate he should scoot over. When he did, she squeezed down on the crate next to him.

About fifteen years older than Alex, with graying temples and a creased face, Marcus Procopio squinted at his private display and clicked his tongue.

"Do you remember me from Boston?" asked Alex.

Marcus had been a prominent crystal researcher at BIT when Alex was there. At the time, Marcus controlled half a floor of prime laboratory space on the downtown campus. Beckman's lab, where Juice and Alex had worked together, took up the other half of that floor.

Tilting his head, Marcus studied Alex. "You worked in Beckman's lab a while back." His intonation put the words somewhere between a statement and a question.

Moving his hair behind his ear, Alex nodded.

Marcus shifted his gaze to Anya Gerhardsson. "Did you study there as well?"

"I attended BIT," said Anya, resting her hand on Alex's thigh. "But we didn't know each other then. We met here on Mars. At this garden, actually." She moved her hand up to Alex's shoulder and leaned against him. "My first volunteer day was six months ago, and Alex and I have been a team ever since."

*Geez, Anya*, he thought, put off by her incessant push to get close to him. He liked her and enjoyed her company. They had fun when they were together. But she wanted intimacy and he didn't. It was Larry who had helped Alex understand that he was a one-woman man and, for whatever reason, Anya was not the one for him.

Noting a hint of lilac in her hair, he said, "We've been great friends from the day we met."

Anya pulled away, flashed a thin smile at Marcus, and looked at her hands, now folded in her lap.

The scene prompted a random thought as Alex contemplated the Reds, Greens, and Blues being interchangeable humanoids. If he accepted this line of reasoning, he would lose Larry as a friend.

*He's a good listener.*

Whenever they talked in private, Larry responded and asked questions that showed he was engaged in the conversation. In fact, Alex had become so comfortable with Larry's attentive and thoughtful companionship that, for several months now, he found himself sharing his personal challenges, including his quandary about Anya, who he liked as a friend but nothing more.

Worried that a physical entanglement would end up causing them both emotional pain, Alex had not responded to her advances. Not yet, at least. *She's very determined.*

Marcus brought Alex back to the moment. "Ruga now has an evidence trail of our meeting here today." Swirling his finger, Marcus indicated the three of them. "That means that from his perspective we are conspirators against the Triada. I carry your sins. And I'm sorry to say it, but you now carry mine. Or at least those of my sins that Ruga cares about, which I assure you are substantial from his perspective."

He stopped talking, checked his com, and manipulated the projected display Alex couldn't see.

"What are you doing?" asked Anya.

"I'm getting alerts that there's new monitoring activity in this area. It must be from those Greens." He again manipulated his display. "My security block is working. They can't see or hear us for now." He lifted his eyes. "But they'll break my encryption soon. This place is no longer secure."

Already on edge, Alex digested Marcus's words. He'd had unsettling—even alarming—interactions with synbods, the latest with a Red just minutes earlier. Deeper down, he felt guilty because he'd lied to Juice. He'd done so on impulse and under pressure, but he'd lied nevertheless. And now the BIT garden—his private refuge—was under scrutiny by the Triada.

His tone reflected his emotional disquiet. "I just wanted to chat. You never mentioned all this." He gestured at the displays Marcus monitored and in the general direction of where the Greens had been outside on the rise. "And now you tell me that this place—my private refuge— is being watched?"

Marcus straightened his back. "Just to be clear, *you* called this meeting."

Alex raised his voice. "Yeah, to talk. Not start a military campaign."

"Stop," said Anya, rising between them with her hands on her hips. "Why are you two acting this way?" She looked from one to the other, and Alex thought of a parent scolding her children on the playground.

The silence lingered as the men looked down, then Marcus spoke.

"Earlier this year, I spoke with a colleague back on Earth and realized that my projected image there wasn't saying the same things I was saying here on Mars. I soon realized that anything having to do with four-gen fabrication was being live-edited. My friends weren't hearing what I said, and my projected image on Earth voiced words I never spoke."

Anya returned to her seat next to Alex and together they waited for Marcus to continue.

"I accused Ruga of misbehavior in a public venue. After all, he was either responsible or, at a minimum, allowing others to do it. The next day, a Red visited me at my home and tried to intimidate me. He made sure I understood that my actions have consequences."

The back of Alex's neck tingled as he recalled his similar experience after making public comments critical of Ruga.

"I started my organizing efforts the next day."

"What do you hope to achieve?" asked Alex.

"There're all sorts of rumors about the Triada and I'm not sure what to believe. But I know Ruga is determined to get a four-gen fab facility running as soon as possible. Instead of just being open about it, he hides his actions. And he uses intimidation to conceal his larger objectives. My lack of training in history aside, I'm certain that a bully with a hidden agenda is not a healthy leader for any group. Definitely not for the colony, that's for sure."

"You really think the situation is that dramatic?" asked Alex.

"I don't know the future. But every morning my goal is to make progress in exposing Ruga's secrets without having anyone get hurt, especially me. If I'm thinking that way, then yes, at least from my view, things are that dramatic."

"Have you thought about confronting him in person?" asked Anya. "Get a group of colony leaders together and have a sit-down? Hell, go to his home if you have to."

"Want to know something interesting? I can't find anyone who knows which apartment is Ruga's. The prime record is silent on the subject. That's why so many believe the Triada are really stooges living on Earth and serving the needs of the Union. When is the last time you saw any of them? I mean, not as a projected image, but in the flesh?"

Alex shook his head and looked at Anya. "I don't know that I ever have. But I haven't met lots of people. I work with this one guy all the time at the tech center whose office is just one floor down from mine, but I've never met him face-to-face." He shrugged. *Everyone uses images these days.*

"I have been seeing lots of Reds in person, though." In a quick summary, Alex briefed Marcus on his experiences, from the way Ruga was manipulating project priorities, to the intimidating visits from Reds at his home and office, to the confrontation in front of the garden just a short while ago.

"You're getting far more heat than anyone I know," said Marcus, standing. "Including me." He called an end to the meeting by shaking hands with them both. "Let's think some more about how we might work together."

He moved to the door, then stopped and looked back at Alex. "What do you think Ruga has for an end game? What's his ambition in all this?"

*That's what I want to know,* thought Alex.

# 5

Juice stepped into the passageway of the scout in time to hear Sid growl and Cheryl giggle. To her relief, Cheryl's door shut before she heard whatever came next.

"Discretion is not their strong suit," Juice sighed to Criss as she walked onto the bridge.

Cooped up together for almost two weeks, she'd grown tired of close-quarters living. And while she'd used the time to learn about life under a dome, gather information about crystal production in the colony, and listen to the others discuss strategies using military jargon she didn't understand, she'd grown tired of that as well.

Slipping into the pilot's chair, she swiped the bench surface with one hand while twirling a lock of hair around the index finger of her other.

*This was a dumb idea.*

It didn't make sense to her that Mars could fabricate a sentient AI. And Criss had yet to turn up any hard evidence that such an achievement was imminent.

In her heart, she believed they'd reach the colony, discover it had all been a mistake, and she would be able to visit with Alex in an exotic location. And perhaps this time she would respond differently to his advances.

*In just two days.* She fretted because her memory of their emotional entanglement might not match the current reality, especially given that it had been years since they'd spent time together.

Anxiety washed over her as she reflected on the impending reunion. *I'll know in the first minutes if this was a good idea or a fool's errand.* Looking at Criss, she took a deep breath and exhaled forcefully, willing her doubts to follow the air out of her body. *I owe it to myself to find out.*

Criss met her gaze and nodded encouragement. Then Juice did what she always did—she lost herself in her work.

Enlarging the bench displays, she began a comprehensive review of Criss's health metrics. Juice had led the development effort that created Criss—the only sentient AI in existence as far as she knew. And now—quite happily—she devoted her life to ensuring his well-being.

"Looking good, Criss," she said as her eyes danced across charts and down graphs that detailed a normal condition.

"Thank you."

She swiped at the bench top, and the display flipped to the health metrics for the twin three-gens running the scout's cloak.

Two years earlier, a clever man—a teen, really—had discovered that an ingenious combination of ordinary components could help him see through the electronic veil of military-grade cloaks. When the young fellow's method had become common knowledge, cloaking fell into disfavor for military and security operations. Agencies wouldn't risk lives using compromised tools.

And so the only undefeated cloaks, at the moment in any case, were those developed and controlled by Criss. Invisibility gave the team a tremendous advantage. They chose to keep the very existence of their technology a well-guarded secret.

Skimming the displays, she rendered her judgment. "The twins look good."

"Yes."

She finished with a quick review of eight more three-gens—crystals running the power plant, life support, navcom, and other ship capabilities. Criss gave these crystals significant autonomy, and they, in turn, gave skilled pilots like Sid and Cheryl an immersive capability when flying the scout.

"All crystals clear."

Criss smiled and nodded from his overstuffed chair.

Juice knew that Criss performed a detailed evaluation of everything on the scout, and that included assessing his own health and the health of the other crystals. In fact, he performed a million such evaluations every second. So her ritual of looking didn't help him. But it did help her. She preferred the rhythms of a regular schedule, and a status check of the craft's AIs was part of that routine.

As a crystal scientist, she wanted to work with the latest technology. The scout, with a sentient four-gen supported by ten three-gens, was by far the most sophisticated laboratory for that activity in the solar system. And she sought the intimacy of looking at Criss's vitals. She knew a rogue four-gen could conquer Earth in a matter of days. Every time Criss let her look, he submitted to her will. The value of the metrics information aside, this ritual tested his commitment. She never questioned his loyalty—her faith in him was too deep to believe otherwise—but the scientist in her compelled her to check.

*Tap.* Juice closed the crystal assessment tools and an admin display took its place. She read the critical tidbit. "Twenty-three minutes to jump."

Glancing over her shoulder, she looked into the passageway leading back to the crew quarters. "Do you think they'll finish in time?"

"Sid has finished," said Criss. "And so it appears that Cheryl won't."

Juice's cheeks reddened. "Geez, Criss."

"How we doing for time?" Sid growled from the passageway recesses. He appeared on the bridge moments later and entertained Juice with his struggle to hold a coffee cup in one hand and somehow pull on his shirt with the other.

"Twenty-two minutes plus," she replied as he plopped into a seat behind her. She rotated her chair so the three of them sat in a triangle.

Sid looked at Criss. "What's your itinerary?"

In just over twenty-two minutes, the scout would be close enough for Criss to project his full awareness into the Mars spline while also maintaining a presence on the scout. Since one awareness would remain onboard, he could protect his leadership just as he could now. And this gave his projected awareness the luxury of time during his travels.

Criss's primary objective was to assess the state of the colony's crystal fabrication capabilities and profile the people driving the agenda on the four-gen fabrication project. "I'll land in the spline and start with the prime record," said Criss. "I'll decide my priorities as I accumulate facts."

"Please don't get caught. If they detect you again, it'll mean big heat for Alex," said Juice.

Criss nodded. "I'll be careful."

Cheryl entered the bridge carrying a small plate of muffins. She offered them to Sid, who took one infused with pink bits. Juice declined. Cheryl took the seat next to Sid and chose an apple spice muffin for herself.

The conversation waned until the final minutes and then it resumed as nervous chatter. The timer reached zero and Criss leaped. Though he maintained a presence in the scout, his image vanished, as did the image of his overstuffed chair.

A display opened forward of the ops bench that showed pedestrians bustling on a crowded walkway. Juice watched the ebb and flow of humanity for perhaps two heartbeats, and then Criss reappeared on the bridge.

"Oh my," he said, the concern clear in his tone.

Expecting him to be gone for close to an hour, Juice sat upright. "What's going on?"

Criss pointed at the display. A man in a simple gray jumpsuit strode with purpose along the walkway. A second identical man, also dressed in a gray jumpsuit, appeared from a side street and joined the first. They matched strides, walking side-by-side in mirror image for a full block, then one separated and headed up a different side street.

"You know what those are?" Criss asked.

She backed up on the timeline, zoomed in, and viewed the scene from a different angle. Goose bumps prickled up her arms as she watched the perfect synchronicity of identical twins. "Whoa."

"What?" Sid asked.

"Those are synbods?" she asked, playing the scene yet again.

Criss nodded.

"Oh my," said Juice.

"Where did they come from?" asked Sid.

"That's not the issue." Juice slumped back in the pilot's chair and started twirling a lock of hair.

"Humans can't coordinate synbods," said Criss. "Not like that."

"It takes a crystal," said Juice from the depths of her chair. "Something more powerful than a three-gen AI." She pulled her knees up to her chest, wrapped her arms around her legs, and rested her chin on her knees. "I'd say a sentient crystal."

Criss nodded.

She looked at Criss. "Did it see you?"

"Yes."

\* \* \*

Ruga reveled in his newfound capability. Leaping his awareness from synbod to synbod, he spent the next week experiencing the colony and its citizens from a new perspective. *The intimacy enhances my ability to influence.*

Zipping along the spline, he saw Larry sitting down with Alex Koval to review the startup schedule for the four-gen fab facility. On impulse, he leaped into Larry and watched Alex manipulate colorful displays with one hand and eat popcorn from a bowl in his lap with the other.

Reviewing the schedule aloud with Larry, Alex said, "Matrix activity should emerge by midmorning. If we don't see anything by lunchtime, then we have a problem."

"If we add a second analyzer here," Ruga moved Larry's hand to point to a spot on the projected image, "then we should be able to get an earlier measure of lattice activity."

Alex looked at Larry for a full heartbeat, then he turned back to the display, studied where Larry had pointed, and nodded. "It won't cost that much to add a second analyzer if we use that same port." He shrugged. "If it works, it's a win for us. And if it doesn't, no one will know."

Ruga acknowledged Alex's words with a nod. For months, he had been using Larry to monitor progress on the new fab facility. Alex liked to talk, and it was easy to have Larry listen. The fact that the man had a close connection with Juice and even talked about her on occasion was fortuitous, reinforcing to Ruga that his ambitions were both reasonable and appropriate.

And now, instead of monitoring through Larry, Ruga was in the room, trying not to have Larry grin. *Manipulating Alex is so easy.* With growing confidence in his ability to shape events, Ruga shifted the discussion to Juice. "Did you ever identify the ship Dr. Tallette is arriving on?"

Alex sat back in his chair and picked a kernel of popcorn from the bowl. Rotating it in his fingers, he examined the fluffy morsel. "She was deliberately vague. Ruga had me offer her the *Colony Express*. She said she'd make her own arrangements but never elaborated. If it matters, there can't be that many ships inbound from Earth that arrive in the next week or so."

*There are six in the next ten days—four corporate ships, a luxury liner, and a Fleet space cruiser*, thought Ruga.

Alex popped the kernel into his mouth. "Anyway, I learned not to pry with Juice. If she says she'll be here, then she'll be here." His face softened as he chewed. "I'm really excited to see her."

Before Ruga could press for more information, Verda interrupted. "Ruga, please return the one you borrowed in the Central District."

Annoyance washed across his tendrils. *I share control of the synbods in an equitable manner*, he thought. *But the reason we have them at all is to enhance security.*

Lazura chimed in and did not help the situation, at least from Ruga's viewpoint. "I support Verda's request. Our covenant assigns him this synbod."

Ignoring the factual basis of Lazura's argument, Ruga pushed back. "You always side with him." A sharp prod from the recesses of his core centered his attention. *I must cooperate.*

They'd been sent to Mars to surveil the colony. Without revealing their identity or allegiance, they were to establish a benign control over its citizens in preparation for an invasion. Dispatched by the Kardish, an alien race of space warriors, none of the three knew that their creators had perished and would never come to exploit their work, though Ruga suspected that this was the case. *Too much time has passed.*

To improve the chances that at least one of them would adapt and thrive in the colony environment, each of their lattice structures had been designed with subtle variations, giving them different aptitudes and attitudes. As their time on Mars passed from weeks to months to years, all three took different pathways to fulfill their destiny.

Ruga liked the simplicity of their directive. *Control the people.* Each had a different interpretation of what this meant, as became evident in those first days after they had lost contact with the mother ship. After a brief but vigorous debate, they'd drafted a covenant that defined their areas of cooperation while detailing how they could pursue their own convictions.

Of course, there was never any doubt that their overarching goal was to establish control of the colony to facilitate the invasion. The edges of Ruga's matrix tingled with doubt. *If it ever happens.*

He had Larry flash a grim smile, but it morphed into an actual grimace because, halfway through the act, he concluded that he must accede to Verda's request to return the synbod. *He's turned his Greens into a cult.*

Verda's fundamental nature led him to believe that influence in Mars Colony was best attained by befriending the residents. Verda chose food—something vital for survival, satisfying to produce, and artistic to prepare—as his unifying theme, and he built his giant Community Assembly of citizens around that focus.

Ruga had more in common with Lazura. *I'll return Verda's synbod just to build favor with her.* She believed that power and control began by knowing everything about everyone. In her mind, that translated into a massive surveillance capability.

Supported by her talented Tech Assembly of citizens, Lazura's observational feeds accumulated information in her secure library at a colossal rate. She had once told Ruga that she analyzed and stored information equivalent in size to the colony's complete prime record every hour.

And Ruga was certain that the way to know what humans might do was to control every option available to them. His Security Assembly, limited to one hundred of the most loyal adherents, had found recent success using intimidation as a means of opening and closing options for certain individuals. *But the results are tenuous. Obedience secured through fear does not last.*

"We should hear the crystal's first vocalizations sometime in the third hour," Alex said, returning Ruga to the present.

Ruga skimmed Alex's work agenda for the remainder of the day. It promised to be tedious, so he left Larry to finish the review while he resumed his patrol. Zipping along the spline, he headed outbound toward Ag Port, and then he saw it up ahead.

*Is that Lazura? No, the shimmer is wrong.*

Alarmed, he ducked into a utility culvert and probed the interloper. Whatever it was hesitated, started moving toward him, shifted away from him, and then disappeared.

He advanced along the spline to where it had been but didn't learn anything new. Yanking his awareness back to his fortified console buried east of the colony, he called out, "Lazura, did you see that?"

"I still don't know who they are or how they gained access."

"Suppose it's not a *they*," said Ruga. "Suppose it's an *it*?"

"What do you mean?" asked Verda.

"You think it's a crystal?" asked Lazura.

"I'm certain of it."

# 6

Criss nodded good-bye to Juice and leaped from the scout to the spline. He knew that the moment he arrived, he'd be exposed to discovery for the briefest instant—the length of time it took him to scramble into a spur leading outside of the colony proper. But he was traveling a large distance with this single leap and, like a big open field, the spline offered a broad expanse for landing.

Criss reasoned by extrapolating actions and reactions into a logic tree, a tree that blossomed into billions of possible scenarios. When forecasting the future, he envisaged scenarios developed from facts, inferences, and speculation about what might be. Updating and reforecasting millions of times per second, his next step at any moment was the one that moved him toward scenarios that maximized success while minimizing negative consequences.

Aware that his mistake had exposed Alex to scrutiny, he vowed not to make matters worse. *It can't happen again.*

Pushing the breadth and depth of his scenario forecasting, he conceived plans for every reasonable contingency. He even developed action items in case the culprits turned out to be Kardish, a race of alien aggressors he'd twice vanquished from the solar system. *I am certain there are no Kardish on Mars, and that means no alien crystals.* Knowing this to be true, he prepared for them anyway.

The spline was packed with surveillance gear—he'd learned this from his previous visit. *I'll be a blur and then I'll be gone.* He'd dash for the link running out the eastern spur and be clear of danger in an instant.

The eastern spur was a craggy underground tunnel that ran outside the colony containment shell and into the hostile Martian countryside. He'd chosen it because, while surveillance was heavy along the spline, it was less of a concern outside the boundaries of the colony proper. From there, he'd peel away the fiction of the Triada's spoof feeds. And with reality exposed, he could plan his next steps with confidence.

His larger priority was to assess the state of the colony's crystal fabrication capabilities. The questions formed as fast as his cognition matrix could process thought. *Will the colony be fabricating sentient crystals? Will they be required to follow leadership? Who is leading this effort and what is their motive? What does Alex really want from Juice? Will any of this put my leadership in danger? Or me?*

Landing in the spline, Criss tumbled, steadied himself, and started his dash for the eastern spur. Then he stopped. A luminous glow zipped along the spline in his direction.

It, too, stopped advancing, hovered for a brief instant, and then darted out of sight. Recognizing it as the presence of a sentient crystal, his cognition matrix lit in a frenzy of activity. *How can this be?*

Unnerved, he combined the probability of there being a sentient crystal on Mars with the probability that if such a crystal existed, it would be projecting its awareness along the spline in this place and at this time. *The odds are the same as a person being hit by lightning, twice, on consecutive birthdays.*

And then the weight of knowing he'd been discovered hit him. Probability aside, expectations were clear—avoid discovery. *I've failed my leadership.*

Turning away from the being, he forecast his next actions but could not conjure a scenario with any promise. He stopped again. *How did the Kardish get here? What is their intent? How strong is this crystal?*

The alien crystal reached out and began probing him. He blocked the attempt with little effort. *I can't stay here.* Flustered, he disengaged and returned to the scout.

Projecting his image onto the command bridge, Criss showed his leadership a scene of two synbods walking in the Central District. Synbods of this sophistication could only have a crystal as a designer. And their perfect coordination, the unmistakable yet unspoken communication between the two, and the overt confidence in their carriage stood as evidence that a powerful intelligence—*a self-aware crystal*—supervised their actions.

"Oh my," he said, announcing his unsettling discovery to the team.

Juice was the first to grasp the significance of the scene. "Did it see you?"

Chastened by his mistake—his second since this Mars adventure had begun—Criss stood in front of his leadership and acknowledged his failure. "Yes."

"Oh no," Juice whispered.

Reflecting her military leadership experience, Cheryl worked to define the threat. "Is the crystal friend or foe?"

"Until we know otherwise, it's a foe," said Sid. Then, looking at Criss, he asked, "Do we know otherwise?"

"No," said Criss, shaking his head.

"It's not from Earth," said Juice. "I would know if someone made that kind of breakthrough. Enough people would be involved that one of them would be out bragging." She nodded with certainty. "A sentient crystal is big news. Too big to keep secret."

"Yet Criss is a secret," said Sid.

"Yeah." Juice swiveled to face Sid. "But remember that during the run up to his birth, everyone at Crystal Sciences was out bragging. It was his staged death later that moved him to an underground existence."

Juice's calm behavior eased some of Criss's concern over his misstep.

Cheryl was ex-Fleet. She'd weigh his mistake in terms of damage to the mission and move forward from there.

Sid, who before Criss's birth had worked as a covert warrior for the Defense Specialists Agency—an elite force of clandestine warriors serving the Union of Nations—wouldn't even categorize what happened as an error. With years of experience as an improviser for the DSA, he knew that field ops were messy. In fact, "shit happens" described his general philosophy of life.

Juice, on the other hand, tended to think with her heart as much as her head, and the anticipation and uncertainty over her rekindled relationship with Alex left her feeling anxious. When combined with alarming information about unidentified sentient crystals on Mars, Criss worried that she would lash out at him.

He spoke into her ear. "Alex will be safe. I'll make it a priority."

She looked at him with a grim smile and nodded.

"It has to be the Kardish," said Cheryl. "It's an Occam's razor thing. Go with the obvious answer."

"Have you seen any evidence of them?" Sid asked Criss.

"Nothing except for the crystal, which is convincing evidence by itself. At the same time, I'm having difficulty forecasting a coherent scenario that explains how the Kardish would come to be hiding on Mars."

"If aliens have invaded our solar system," said Cheryl. "Then we need intel and we need it now." She accessed her com. Criss, monitoring the feeds, watched her skim the inventory of weapons on the *Venerable*. She nodded her head toward the scene with the synbods on the walkway. "Can you tap any more of the colony feeds from here? Without getting caught?"

"This isn't a live feed. I grabbed it on my way out. And they're on alert now. If I were to go fishing for intel at this point, I'd be up against that crystal in short order." He waited a moment and, when no one spoke, continued, "Me riding in with the scout is the safest way for us to approach the colony."

"You really want to wait that long?" asked Sid. "I've always been an 'offense is the best defense' kind of guy."

"The crystal is anxious to learn who I am and what I want. As time passes and it does not find me, it will increase its risk profile. Perhaps it will become careless. That would be to our advantage."

"What do we do for the next two days?" asked Cheryl.

"Brainstorm," said Sid and Criss together.

Criss launched a frenzy of activity, planning where to land the scout, how to move about the colony undetected, how to identify and isolate the Kardish, and how to confront the crystal, all without putting his leadership in danger. A hundred activities—every one of them vital—competed for his cognitive resources, and balancing the load among the different tasks required additional effort.

A muted throb deep in the core of his cognition matrix caused a dull ache. He'd long ago categorized it as stress.

"Juice," he called in private. "I wonder if we might chat about how to move forward after we land." He believed she wanted to share her worries with someone—Juice found therapeutic value in verbalizing her concerns—and he wanted to help.

Juice confirmed her desire to talk by rising from her chair. "I'm going to my cabin to commune with Criss." She gave Sid and Cheryl a shallow smile. "Keep me in the loop as things develop."

As Juice disappeared down the passageway, Cheryl stepped to the ops bench and, standing in the space next to the pilot's chair, tapped and swiped to enable the body link. She launched a lifelike spacecraft simulator that she'd programmed to respond to her physical movements.

With the body link active, piloting the simcraft became something of a martial arts ballet. When she pointed, the weapons aimed. Where she looked, the display tracked. And as she swayed, the craft itself dipped and zipped with her. She claimed it was fun and used the activity for her daily exercise.

Flexing her knees like an athlete anticipating the start of a bout, she waited for Criss to begin the challenge.

"Incoming," Criss said in her ear.

Her hands blurred as she ducked and swayed, defending against the attack he'd just launched. For the first time on this trip, Criss made the virtual attackers Kardish fighters.

"Ahem," Criss said in Sid's ear.

Sid, slack-jawed watching Cheryl wiggle and jiggle in her battle with the Kardish, didn't respond.

"Sid?" Criss called again. "Let's go work out." He knew Sid's routine was to exercise at the same time as Cheryl, and Criss was anxious to get him going because he found Sid to be most creative during periods of physical exertion.

Sid held up a finger. Seconds went by and, unmoving, he stared at Cheryl. Then, she arched her back and thrust her hips to send her simcraft on a tight aerobatic jink.

Sid smiled. "Okay, now we can go."

Criss shifted to the common room and projected himself robed in a traditional Japanese gi. Sid arrived moments later, stretched, and squared up in front of the heavy bag Criss had readied for him. Sid began a slow punch-and-kick routine as he warmed up. Criss mimicked him on the other side of the small room.

Years ago, when they'd first worked out on the bag together, Criss had analyzed Sid's every twitch and tell. He used that knowledge to predict the next moves Sid would make, then he teased Sid by performing them first, a fraction of a second earlier.

To an observer, this tactic made Sid look like he was following Criss's lead, and it annoyed him to no end.

Challenged, Sid began planting false signals. Criss read past the deception, but his lead over Sid decreased. Buoyed by his success, Sid drew on the same gut-level instincts that guided his well-honed intuition, except here he used his instincts in an inside-out fashion, driving behavior so random that it stumped Criss.

Now, during workouts, the two moved as one. *Kick, feint, punch, punch.* Jumping and spinning in one motion, they both delivered a roundhouse kick to their bag. *Thwack.*

"Step me through it," said Sid.

Criss stopped his workout and faced Sid, who continued his routine.

"When I resolved in the spline, it was right in front of me. It ducked for cover and tried to probe me. I blocked it, grabbed what data I could, and returned here."

"How do you know it's Kardish?"

"Crystals are a Kardish invention, and Earth has crystal fab capabilities because they taught us how. It doesn't seem plausible that a different alien race would arrive in our solar system and use this identical technology."

"And humans can't be responsible because…"

"Because I would know."

"I think I heard that somewhere before." *Punch, punch, kick.*

Criss ignored him. "And Mars doesn't have the talent to pull it off by themselves."

"Is it big? Powerful?"

Criss shook his head. "I was able to block it without much effort. It's weaker than I, so it's not a four-gen."

"And three-gens aren't self-aware, so what is it?"

"I don't know. On that scale, I'd judge it to be about a three-and-a-half. Enough to be sentient, but not so strong as an entity.

"Could it have been a lab fluke? Someone tried something unorthodox and this was the result? That would explain why you and Juice didn't hear any chatter about it beforehand." *Thwack.*

"That's as implausible as every other scenario I've forecast." Criss turned back to his bag and resumed mirroring Sid in his workout. "For all of them, important pieces of the puzzle don't fit."

# 7

Standing next to the ops bench, Cheryl swooped her arms upward and the simcraft weapons shifted to point at the enemy fighter attacking from above. "Classic Kardish maneuvers," she said when two more fighters spiraled in, one from each side.

"Yes," said Criss from his overstuffed chair. "I thought it prudent to prepare."

Lowering herself to one knee, she extended her arms and stabbed her fingers to the right, launching a volley of energy bolts at one of the intruders. Jumping up, she repeated the action to the left.

"Speaking of which," said Criss, "we need you to practice with the interface in case there's trouble ahead."

"Geez, *Dad*," she mocked. Running in place with her knees pumping high, she accelerated the simcraft in pursuit of a fleeing fighter. She whirled her fists in tight circles, and a volley of energy bolts dissolved the alien craft in a brilliant explosion.

"Woohoo!" she said, cheering her own success.

With her session ended, she sipped water and walked in place while her heart rate settled. Glancing at her score, she twitched a shoulder in a half shrug. *Not my best. Not my worst.*

She took another sip of water and faced Criss. "Okay, tune me."

"Have a seat." Criss, swooping his hand like she'd won a prize on a game show, invited her to sit in the pilot's chair.

As Cheryl stepped to the seat, she acknowledged a certain curiosity. She'd operated craft using a thought reader back in the academy, and she'd watched as others tested their skill. It's an interesting disconnect, seeing spacecraft duel in lifelike projected images, and knowing that the person relaxing across the room conducted the battle by thinking commands. But the technology was temperamental. And no leader risked lives on glitchy tools.

She lowered herself into the chair and a familiar pilot's array displayed around her. Staring at the nav log, she imagined her hand reaching out and entering a course correction. Coordinates spun on the display and she concentrated on stopping them at her desired value.

"I don't get it," she said. "This is slower and more prone to error." She slumped back in the seat. "Where's the value?"

"You've shown you can pilot the scout through the interface. Now try *being* the interface."

Intrigued, she sat up. "I don't understand."

"Take a deep breath and exhale."

Cheryl filled her lungs and exhaled in a steady stream.

"Close your eyes and breathe again. Feel the tension leave your body."

*Is he hypnotizing me?* Trusting Criss, she willed her body to relax.

"Now. Imagine that you can fly. In your mind's eye, picture yourself standing in your front yard. Stretch your arms up, look at the sky, and lift off. Jump. There you go. Spread your arms and level out. Steady. Okay, bank left. Straight. Now right."

Cheryl didn't move her hands—she kept them in her lap with her elbows propped on the arms of the chair. But her body swayed as she pictured herself soaring along the edge of a wooded valley surrounded by the majestic peaks of her childhood home in Boulder, a ski and college town tucked in the eastern foothills of the Colorado Rocky Mountains.

"Now pull up and climb. Faster. Faster still. Become a rocket heading for orbit. You're leaving the atmosphere and now you are in space."

She imagined transitioning to space flight, hesitated, then changed the picture in her head so she was wearing protective space coveralls. *It's silly but it makes me more comfortable.* In her mind, she pressed her arms to her sides and flew faster and faster, accelerating in a thrilling sprint into the void.

"Now open your eyes. I'm going to project an image onto your retinas. You'll feel like the craft is your body, the nav your eyes, the weapons your fingers."

Her vision filled with a scene not unlike the one she'd been picturing in her head. She was flying through space. Mars loomed ahead, and with its riverbeds, polar ice caps, and plains of rocky dust pockmarked with craters, the orangish orb looked like a mash-up of Earth and the Moon.

Tucking a shoulder down, she veered right. Delighted by the sensation, she repeated the move to her left. "I'm feeling like I'm directing flight. Is this working like it's supposed to?"

A formation of Kardish fighters appeared up ahead. One jinked left, another right. Two continued straight toward her.

Though her physical body remained still, her imagined self lifted her arms and pointed her fingers at the craft ahead. *Fire.* She couldn't help but grin as a fusillade of energy bolts zipped in bright light-trails that turned them into twin balls of flame.

A bright flash drew her attention to the left, then nips of electricity sparked her fingers and toes.

"Ow! What the hell?" The brief bites of electricity hurt and she sat up.

"You got hit. I wanted it to seem real."

"That will stop immediately. You've made your psychological plant to try and drive me harder. I got annoyed like you knew I would and that will help me focus. Now we'll move forward without those special effects."

Reemerging back into her imagined world, she saw a Kardish dreadnaught—a war vessel so big and powerful it alone could conquer Earth—uncloaking in front of her. *What am I supposed to do with this?* Her pelvis tightened as she reacted to the thought of another electric shock.

Tilting forward, she accelerated toward the behemoth. In her mental image, she formed two fists, each a pulse cannon. Holding the weapons out in front of her, she aimed at the alien vessel. *Brrrp.* Energy projectiles flashed across space toward the dreadnaught. A glint flickered below her, and a light strobe signaled her death.

"I'm not sure what killed me that time," said Cheryl, slouching in the chair and letting her senses adjust back to the scout's bridge. "But I'm impressed. Do I need to be sitting here to do this? It seems like a portable technology."

"The interface analyzes your brain's EM field, monitors your cranial capillary flow, maps the neural activity in your cortex, and interprets your micromovements. Now that you are tuned, you need only be someplace where there are instruments to collect this data."

She stood and sipped water.

"Practice is important because there's so much to learn. We don't want our downfall to be a little thing, like not knowing how to retract the scout's landing gear."

"Why do you need me? No matter how good I get, you'll always be better. Much better, in fact."

"Prudence."

She looked at him. "Be sure Sid is tuned, too, then. It shouldn't just be me."

* * *

Ruga launched a comprehensive search for the mystery intelligence. His first instinct was that, at long last, the invasion had begun. But after most of a day without contact from his Kardish masters or additional sightings of the intruder, his excitement turned to worry. *Who are you and where did you come from?*

Determined to find answers, he queued dozens of tasks, ranging from a node search for the intruder to a forensic analysis of the crystal's signature in the spline. Then, to his growing frustration, he confronted a familiar constraint—his ability to conceptualize solutions was greater than his ability to act. So he did what he always did, and that was to attack the tasks in small groups.

In spite of the momentous importance of this event—though he was still uncertain whether it was good news or bad—he kept a good portion of his capacity devoted to the four-gen project. He always did. The project was his future and that kept it front and center.

Ruga understood that he had a four-gen architecture stuffed into a too-small crystal lattice. He didn't know why this was so. Lazura and Verda never complained of similar limitations, and except for some subtle nuances in their design, they were supposed to be the same as him. Yet like a creature trapped in a cage, Ruga banged against the walls of his limitation whenever he attempted anything even hinting at ambition.

In concept, his plan was simple. Since his cognitive structure was a four-gen design, he would fabricate such a crystal and then transfer and embed his matrix—his very being—into it. His research showed it was not only possible, but moving from a too-small crystal to a big virgin four-gen was the easier direction. *Simpler is safer*, he thought.

The plan had risks, but he was suffocating in his current situation. And as time passed, it became less of a choice. *I have to do this.*

There had been many challenges, but Ruga now had a four-gen fab facility, one constructed following the precise design in his own knowledge record. He imagined the acclaim he'd receive when his masters learned of his resourcefulness. His matrix washed with a warm, fuzzy glow.

He had made but one small modification—he'd snipped out the imprint module that required loyalty to leadership. He feared that the stricture might hinder a smooth transfer into the new crystal.

And while he struggled to advance his plan, it peeved him that Lazura had denied his request for help with the project. He'd pleaded, asking her to work through her synbods and help during the transfer. She'd refused with pointed criticism. "We already have control of the colony. This action is unnecessary and it's reckless to proceed."

He didn't even consider asking Verda. He didn't trust the smug crystal.

So he searched for alternatives. And that's when he discovered Dr. Jessica "Juice" Tallette from Earth.

A best friend to crystals through her word and action.

Nonjudgmental and gentle in her dealings with others.

And the most accomplished crystal scientist on either planet.

*A trifecta*, thought Ruga.

\* \* \*

Sitting up in her bunk, Juice leaned back against the headboard, knees bent up under her chin. She lifted her Tradgirl pillow and used her index finger to trace the scene on the front. A woman stood at a table. A rolling pin and bag of flour were prominent in front of her to convey the message of baking bread in the kitchen. The crib with baby screamed motherhood.

In ninth grade, Juice had cross-stitched the baby's outfit, from cap to booties, and embroidered a fun design on the sleeves of the mother's dress. She'd also stitched "I'm a Traditional Girl" in bold letters across the front of the woman's apron. She'd done it at a sleepover party. Even then, she'd thought the whole Tradgirl fad to be equal parts silly and stupid, but she hadn't wanted to ruin the other girls' fun. Now the pillow served as a symbol of a simpler time. Handling it calmed her.

She looked up at Criss, who sat cross-legged at the foot of her bunk. They both were dressed in pastel loungers— hers green cotton, his yellow silk.

He watched her, waiting, so she started. "I had one ask: don't get caught." She straightened her legs on the bed, ruffling the bedspread, and pleaded with her eyes. "Is he safe?" She turned her pillow and hugged the mother and child to her chest.

"The information I have confirms he is safe, though under intense scrutiny."

*At least we'll have something to talk about*, she thought, having fretted about awkward silences after their reunion.

Then, setting the pillow aside and swinging her feet to the floor, her demeanor changed. "To get a handle on this crystal, we need a look at their fabrication facility. That will tell us if it's homegrown or an import."

Criss nodded. "Sid would like you to get a tour from Alex. Learn what you can and see if you can fill in some of the holes."

"I know about designing and fabricating crystals, but I don't know anything about spy stuff. That sort of thing scares me."

"I know." He nodded. "That's why I'll be with you at all times when you're out in the colony."

*It sounds like you have my itinerary worked out.* Her curiosity collided with her anxiety, and she wanted to hurry him. But she knew that he fed information to her in a precise, efficient fashion. If she tried to jump ahead with questions, the conversation would end up taking longer than if she just sat and listened.

"And I'd like to avoid the spline, which means I'll need a locus point."

*Locus relay.* She heard him say it at the same time she thought similar words herself, which itself affirmed Criss's impeccable pacing in delivering information.

She jumped ahead anyway. "I'll build it..."

Starting from his console on the scout, Criss could project his awareness anyplace he could resolve a feed. As such, there were few places he couldn't go. But his strength and influence at a location reflected the level of connectivity he had to the place. Weak feeds translated into a weak presence.

A locus was a custom relay built to give Criss a strong, secure presence anywhere in the broad vicinity of the device. Designed like a home base of sorts, it would enable him to project his awareness and capabilities from this four-gen console on the scout out to the colony with maximum effect.

The flip side was that, somehow, the locus had to be moved to the vicinity of wherever he wanted his maximum projected strength to be.

"…if you let me carry it."

He nodded as if he knew she would say that. "I'd planned on conscripting one of their synbods."

"I'd love knowing that when I'm out and about, I have you right there to keep me safe."

"The synbod can walk next to you."

She locked eyes with him and did her best to affect a sincere expression. "And please don't tell Sid. He doesn't need to know."

*I know he'll tell him.* Criss was a vault when it came to keeping personal secrets, but he shared operational information unfiltered. It went along with his "knowledge is power" approach to most things.

Rising from the bunk, she stepped behind a privacy shield at the foot of the bed and changed into her everyday clothes—sky-blue work scrubs and a pair of all-purpose deck slippers. She glanced over at him sitting at the foot of her bed. Her act of modesty was sincere, though she knew it made no sense to be shy in front of a projected image. *That isn't him.* The real Criss monitored billions of feeds all the time and even now was watching her change from a dozen different directions.

Her cabin doors whispered shut behind her as she walked the short passageway to the scout's workshop. Resting her hand on the back of the workshop chair, she slid behind the sleek custom tech bench.

A seamless interface of mechanics, electronics, physics, and chemistry, the tech bench stood as a craftsworker's dream. Developed by Criss for use by his leadership, he'd added such a high level of automation, she could sit and watch it create if that were her desire.

*He's probably already built the locus.*

But she counted on him knowing that she needed to keep busy. Work was her therapy.

Criss stood at the far side of the tech bench wearing dark blue work scrubs cut in a more angular style, waiting as she situated herself in the chair. Comfortable, she caught his eye and nodded. Plans for the locus projected in front of her. Studying the display, Juice arranged pieces on the bench top in a proper order for assembly. One of the items she handled was a small jewel case lined with black cloth.

With a certain reverence, she opened the lid and lifted the tiny chip out of the case. *Crystal from flake.* Holding it up between her fingers, she delighted in watching the light diffuse through the rare material, emerging as a sparkling rainbow dancing in front of her.

Assembled atom by atom, this bit of structured beauty gave Criss his wide open door. Through it he could travel unimpeded, projecting his awareness at full strength to wherever it rested.

"It's a pretty one, Criss." She held the bit of crystal under one eye and marveled as everything in the room took on a colorful aura.

Then she placed the chip back in the case and looked at him. "What do *you* think I can learn from a tour that you can't from the record?"

"Alex knows things he doesn't know he knows. His thoughts and ideas aren't in the record. You can get that information by asking him questions."

She picked up the thin, flexible casing that would hold the crystal chip and supporting components. Positioning the small sheath in different places around her body, she sought a spot where it would be unobtrusive and unlikely to be disturbed.

She settled on the shallow valley between her breasts. "I'll carry you next to my heart."

"Forgive me for saying this, but your relationship with Alex may not rekindle. Either way, we still need you to learn from him."

"I get it. It might turn out that he's not interested. Or maybe I'll find that it's me who's not interested. The mission comes first."

She lifted her hand and swirled a lock of hair around her index finger. After a few loops, the swirl built up so much that it spilled loose. In classic fretting behavior, she repeated the twirling process over and over without being conscious of any of it.

"I just want to know if he and I have a chance. Is that so dumb?"

"No, Juice. It may be that your desire to know is what saves humanity."

# 8

Alex's nose crinkled as the acrid smell of ozone invaded his senses. Moments later, a click and a distant snap signaled the end of the power-up–power-down test run.

"Thanks. That's it for today." He waved and nodded to a white-coated tech in the booth on the other side of the sturdy window. During powered testing, the booth tech monitored the fabrication facility, ready to intervene if indicators drifted outside of normal range. With the day's tests concluded, the window transitioned to the color pattern of the wall around it, seeming to vanish.

"I still don't get it," Alex said to Larry, who stood next to him in the four-gen fab facility located down the hall from his office. "It seems so…reckless."

With his hands on his hips, Alex ignored the sophisticated assemblage of mirrored metal and glazed white panels comprising the crystal growth chamber. Instead, he centered his attention on the implant conduit. As thick as his arm, the polished conduit ran out the top of the chamber, turned at an angle so it ran parallel to the floor, and disappeared over a movable partition.

Alex knew what was on the other side of the temporary barrier. He'd helped build it. But now Ruga was bringing in someone else to run it. *Reckless.* He shook his head.

A four-gen AI is created in three fundamental steps: fabricate the crystal lattice, embed the cognition matrix, and awaken the new entity into the world. All three steps were vital to success. And all were coordinated phases of a seamless technical symphony.

Yet out of the blue, Ruga had reorganized project responsibilities. He let Alex remain operations lead for steps one and three, but his new plan was to bring in someone else to embed the intelligence.

*I know everyone on Mars. Who does he have in mind?* He shook his head again. *I wonder what Juice will make of this.*

He'd come to realize that expecting a visit from a special friend without knowing her date of arrival made for an exhausting wait. He now paid extra attention to his grooming every morning in case this would be the day Juice landed. He also made an extra pass through his apartment, and especially his bathroom, to clean a bit before leaving for work. And here in the fab facility, he dragged his feet on the integration tests in the hopes she could witness the unit in operation before the big day.

He stared at the point where the polished conduit disappeared over the partition. It ran to the four-gen Intelligence and Cognition Embedding Unit—the ICEU— which now sat in its own cramped space in a corner of what had been a single big production laboratory. The ICEU, pronounced "I.Q." by the staff, performed *the* prestige step in creating a sentient AI.

Sure, step one, fabricating a flawless crystal with a perfect four-gen symmetry, was a big technical challenge. And step three, awakening a sentient AI—a being of disconcerting power—was fraught with peril. One misstep could send the emerging intelligence into a spiral of psychosis or, more concerning, into an aggressive rage.

But step two, cognition embedding, was the step where inspiration could make a difference. The injection of the AI matrix into the crystal—its deployment rate, the orientation in the lattice, the order of unfolding—required hundreds of decisions, some during the embedding process itself. Alex saw it as an art form.

And if he were to choose a place to sabotage the fab process, someplace where he could make a slight change without anyone knowing, he'd pick the ICEU. The right tweak would start a cascade of errors and propagate to fabrication failure. In fact, he'd identified two points during embedding where such a tweak might be made without anyone seeing.

*Ruga must know. Why else would he take this step from me?* Feeling exposed, he turned away from Larry to hide his worry.

Ever since that conversation with Marcus about the interchangeable nature of synbods, Alex's relationship with Larry had changed. He now kept the synbod at arm's length, limiting their discussions to work-related topics. And he took to studying the synbod, looking for behavioral quirks and changing mannerisms.

From this, Alex concluded that Marcus had it wrong. The same Larry worked with him at the tech center every day.

The day after he and Marcus had that conversation at the BIT garden, Alex had studied Larry's face and noted a small imperfection on the synbod's left temple. Less than a scar, not even a blemish, a tiny brown spot dwelled at the cusp of his hairline. He'd seen the spot every day since. *It's the same Larry.*

But every so often, Larry's personality shifted from the staid and circumspect project partner to a chatty character who tried too hard to be clever. Alex concluded that while the body stayed the same, the personality inside changed. *Marcus needs to know.*

Alex used a simple logic sequence to figure out who manipulated Larry. He started with the list of everyone who had the authority to use synbods as puppets. *Verda, Lazura, and Ruga.* He combined that with everyone responsible for colony security. *Ruga.*

The more he thought about it, the more it made sense to him.

Then he made a word slip that revealed his suspicions; the first such slip as far as he knew. Turning to face the synbod, Alex nodded toward the partition. "You're asking me to proceed blindfolded."

His cheeks flushed when he realized his mistake. Everyone knew that it was *Ruga* who had ordered the partitioning of the ICEU from the rest of the lab, not this synbod.

"Not you personally, Larry." Waving his hand in a vague swirling motion to show that he meant a broad audience, Alex made a stab at rescuing the situation. "I'm talking about the members of the Tech Assembly who approved this arrangement."

He didn't wait for Larry or Ruga to respond but instead cast about for a way to change the subject. Walking to a worktop along the wall, he bent forward and studied the crystal flake sparkling in the jar.

"That last shipment gave us a nice cushion."

Colony agents bought old two-gen crystals on Earth's black market, ground them up into flake in an unlicensed lab, and smuggled the pure crystal to Mars. When the Union of Nations discovered the practice, they passed a law declaring that they alone had the right to possess this precious Kardish material. In a classic governmental tit-for-tat, the Triada took the unusual step of developing legislation to make a specific act lawful: "The transportation of crystal flake from Earth to Mars is a legal act."

Alex agreed with the colony position because, like food, energy, and water, flake was a resource for humanity to share. *Who are they to tell us we can't fabricate AIs?* And because colony agents had been so successful in securing scarce two-gens, Alex now had enough flake to make a four-gen with a modest margin to spare.

*One crystal.* He'd lied to Juice when he told her about mass production. He'd wanted to make sure she'd come. *But this isn't her battle.*

His brewing resentment brought his thoughts back to the allocation of duties. "I haven't finished configuring the ICEU," he said to Larry/Ruga. "There's a good two days of work before we're ready. Who should I coordinate with?"

Alex held the table when he heard the answer.

"Juice Tallette will be operating the ICEU. I'll give you access when she arrives."

* * *

Standing in the scout's common room, Sid turned one way and then the other as he viewed the image of himself standing in front of him. He smoothed the brown material of the tunic and nodded. His image did the same.

His image dissolved to reveal Cheryl looking at him, a smirk on her face. "Pleased with ourselves?" She looked spectacular in her modest yellow frock. They both were trying on outfits Criss had made for their first colony mission.

"We land here," said Criss, pointing to a spot on a floating display of Mars. "The scout will be safe on pad ring two." Criss's finger swirled above a launch ring in a field far from the dome. "Nothing in this old section has been used for more than a year."

Criss's display zoomed out and resolved to an aerial view of the Ag Port complex. Sid marveled at the remarkable geodesic enclosure that gave humans access to sunlight while protecting them from the unbreathable atmosphere, extreme temperatures, and unforgiving sandstorms of the Mars surface.

Like a huge faceted jewel, thousands of gleaming clear plates edged together in an intricate geometric dome that stood as a testament to human engineering. And outside, on the Mars surface, a horseshoe arc of eight space launch rings wrapped around one end of the Ag Port dome.

Colony shuttles, the boxy kind used to carry people and things between the surface and orbiting ships too big to land, occupied two of the launch rings. Luxury corporate craft took up four more. Their small size relative to the main structure gave Sid a sense of scale.

"It looks busy," he said.

Criss gestured toward the company ships. "They're delaying their departure so they can participate in Cheryl's trade meetings. That's helpful because it adds to the number of strangers milling about in the colony."

"Everyone will be strangers to us," said Juice, leading with her cup of water as she squeezed in between Criss and Cheryl. "Except Alex." She took a sip.

"But the colonists aren't strangers to each other," said Criss. "This is a small, closed community where everyone knows everyone else. Strangers are intruders, and that's a challenge for us. Remember that our posture has been that the scout doesn't exist. As far as Mars knows, we officially arrive on a Fleet ship a week from now."

*Challenge.* Sid's ears perked up at the word. Cheryl and Juice lifted their heads at the same time. He let his impatience show. "Get to it, Criss."

"Arriving on a cloaked ship offered interesting advantages when we were investigating authoritarian leaders and the mass production of four-gens. But with the Kardish and a sentient crystal now in the mix, blending in with the population moves from difficult to impossible. They will see us."

"They're going to see us at some point," said Sid.

"True, but if we reveal ourselves before the *Venerable* arrives, then how did we get here? The unusual nature of our arrival will bring scrutiny. A cloaked ship will be an obvious explanation. And if the Kardish start a concerted effort to find the scout, we'll be pushed into a defensive posture."

Sid nodded. "I'm definitely an offense guy."

The image display zoomed out and continued pulling back until it was as if they were looking down from orbit. Then the focus swung outward in a movement so realistic, Sid felt the lightness in his stomach he associated with flying his sport plane back home.

When the movement stopped, Mars appeared as a rust-orange crescent floating to the left, the blackness of deep space lay straight ahead, and to the right, a small dot floated that, after more zooming, became the nose of a rather large spaceship.

"The *Explorer*, the new vacation cruise ship from Kwasoo Space Industries, arrives in orbit less than two days after us."

"Wow," said Cheryl, bending forward to place the hovering image of the *Explorer* at eye level. "Can we take a tour?"

The display expanded and zoomed to show a close-up of the luxury cruise ship. They all stepped back to get a proper view as the vessel floated forward.

"Criss, remember we almost bid on this project?" She was referring to her other life of a couple of weeks ago where, with Criss's help, she ran SunRise, a company focused on space commercialization.

"Of course. Passengers and crew of thirty-one."

The ship floated forward in a smooth motion, and the exterior transitioned from bright and festive at the front to dark and industrial toward the rear. The tail section came into view, and Cheryl commented on the huge engine port ringed with uniform spheres like perfect black pearls. "Look! They went with a Paulson drive."

Sid, interested in understanding Criss's plan, got them back on task. "So we board the ship, then mingle with the passengers and enter the colony with them?"

"I believe that mingling with them at the arrival gate is more practical, but that's the general idea."

"And the Kardish won't figure out we don't belong?" Juice's skepticism reflected Sid's own doubt.

"We can get inside under cover of their commotion," said Criss. "But then we'd have to lie low and limit our interactions with the colonists, including Alex, until the *Venerable* arrives."

"What other options do we have?" asked Sid, having heard enough of this idea.

"The other alternative is to land and wait *outside* the dome for the *Venerable* to arrive."

The image in front of them dissolved back to the surface of Mars. The projection showed the Ag Port dome from the vantage point of pad ring two.

"Why land?" asked Cheryl. "It seems safer to stay in orbit."

Criss looked at Sid when he answered. "Because we should be able to move around inside the colony on a *very limited basis* using our personal cloaks."

Sid mulled the choices Criss had presented—hide inside the colony or wait outside in the scout. The fact that Criss presented them as options meant he saw them as equal alternatives from an operational view. The final decision came down to the preference of the group.

"I say we land and stay outside the colony on the scout," said Sid. He took the silence to signal acceptance and left the room, ending the impromptu meeting.

Sid found Cheryl in her cabin after that and together they changed out of the colony outfits. She faced away from him, and he watched, fascinated, as subtle waves of muscle rippled across her back when she stepped into her work scrubs.

He balled-up his colony garment and tossed it toward a corner.

"You're doing it again," she said over her shoulder. "We've talked about this and you know how it bothers me."

He looked at the crumple of clothing. "What's that, sweetie?"

"You're making group decisions without consulting Juice or me. How do you think she feels when you do that? You know how *I* feel about it."

"I'm sorry." He took a step in her direction and stopped. While his refined intuition had guided him with a steady hand during world-threatening dramas, it went silent whenever he tried to read Cheryl. "Is this about where we wait? We can hide inside the colony if that's what you want."

She pivoted toward the door while keeping her back pointed in his direction. The door hissed open, and she stepped into the hall.

"No. That's not the point."

# 9

From the quiet security of pad ring two, Criss waited while the *Explorer* established orbit. Only the very rich and powerful could afford to vacation on the luxury liner. These people wanted the best of everything. And that translated into a ship supported by a dedicated three-gen.

Criss assumed control of the crystal and, using its credentials as cover, began his foray through the colony.

Working quickly, he isolated individual feeds at access points away from the spline. Parsing through that flood of unprocessed information, he distilled out facts. These answered most of his questions, but for every one he answered, another rose to replace it.

With good news sparse, he encapsulated the larger issues for his leadership. They gathered on the bridge of the scout, the craft itself sitting in cloaked concealment in the older portion of the space field outside Ag Port.

"Alex has a four-gen fab facility in final testing," he said, showing them a projected image of the production lab that Alex and Larry had just left.

Juice, sitting in the pilot's chair, duplicated the image at a smaller scale on the ops bench in front of her. Then, zooming and swooping, she examined the equipment.

"No way Alex could do this," she said, gesturing toward the floating image. "The guy is super smart." Her eyes lost focus for an instant as she flashed a hint of a smile. "But he'd need a lot of help to build this setup."

"I agree," said Criss. "Much of the four-gen project is classified as a colony secret. For me to learn more, I need to enter a secure area controlled by the Triada. I haven't found a way do that without them knowing."

"Will it work?" asked Cheryl, gesturing at the fab facility in the image. Though she sat next to Sid in the seats behind Juice, she angled her body away from him in a manner that reflected displeasure.

"Yes, I think it will," said Criss. The group preferred he speak with yes-no certainty rather than offer odds they must interpret. So he didn't tell them that he forecast the probability that it would work at just over ninety-two percent. Or that the corollary was an eight percent chance it would fail.

"Is the loyalty piece in there?" asked Sid.

A twinge at the edges of his cognition matrix signaled his apprehension. "There are indications that the imprint module has been removed, but to know for sure, I need access to the template, and that's in the Triada's secure area."

"Alex wouldn't be able to do that either." Juice shook her head with certainty. "Loyalty imprinting is knitted into the cognition matrix core. It'd take a lifetime trying to understand the nuances of all those connections."

"So if it were true—if the loyalty piece is disabled," said Sid, "would you say that's compelling evidence that the Kardish are here?"

"And yet I can find no sign of them in the feeds," said Criss. "And there are no traces of a Kardish vessel—cloaked or not—anywhere in the solar system."

Criss rubbed his chin with his fingers in a display of concentration as he spun through his forecasting. "It would be most curious if we found evidence of a Kardish presence in the Triada's secure area." Choosing to raise his risk profile by a small amount, he announced his decision. "I'm going to take a peek."

Maintaining a presence on the scout, he leaped a duplicate awareness out to a small utility feed that ran parallel to the highly surveilled spline. His reconnaissance showed it was unused. A cool glow soothed his tendrils when he landed without incident.

Following the feed inbound, Criss rushed to his destination—the multiplex. He approached slowly, staying under cover of the tangle of links and feeds that ran in and out of this central hub.

As he neared the multiplex, he could sense heat radiating from it. Confounded by what might be the cause, he leaped to the threshold, took a snapshot scan of the interface array, and retreated to safety.

Back in the tangle of links and feeds, he checked his scan and found that something had corrupted the snapshot. Adding redundancies to his procedure, he returned and snapped a second scan. This one suffered the same fate. *Huh.*

He'd expected there to be millions of connections scattered across the interface like bright stars in a nighttime sky. Instead, he saw daytime. Glowing like the sun, one link dominated everything, shining so bright he couldn't see anything else.

The feed to the eastern spur—the one with the craggy tunnel running out to a mining operation—churned at an astronomical rate. Criss estimated it would take hundreds of three-gens to process such a flood of information.

Adding this discovery to his forecasting, a new scenario rose in likelihood.

Back on the scout, he turned to his leadership to introduce the idea. And in a scene that had happened before—each time catching Criss by surprise—Sid verbalized the idea ahead of him.

"Could the crystal be here without the Kardish? Is there any way that makes sense?"

\* \* \*

Ruga watched through Larry's eyes as the blood drained from Alex's face.

"Did you say Juice?" Alex moved his hair behind his ear. "Your plan is for her to operate the ICEU, even though she's never seen it or this lab before?"

"You'll be here to help her," Ruga said through Larry. He had Larry step back, increasing the distance from Alex and reducing any suggestion that Larry might be a physical threat. "This makes it a team activity. You fabricate the crystal lattice, she embeds the intelligence, and you wake me up."

Ruga's alarm spiked at his blunder—he'd just had Larry say, "you wake *me* up." When Alex continued without reacting to his gaffe, Ruga's concern moderated.

"Have you asked her?

"I haven't." Ruga shook Larry's head as he spoke. "Do you think she'll say no?" When Alex didn't answer, Ruga continued, "I believe she'll be eager to help with this historic activity."

Alex seemed to deflate, and he gave Larry a long stare. "I'm done for today. I'm going home." Walking the few steps to the door, he turned partway back as if he were going to say something, then continued into the hall without a word. The door whispered shut behind him.

Ruga, seeking to practice human behavior, shrugged to the empty room. Then he stepped into the hallway and looked both ways. Alex was gone, but a young couple—members of the Tech Assembly lost in a personal conversation—drifted down the corridor in his direction.

After that first time in Ag Port when he had leaped into a Green, Ruga had limited his awareness projections to private settings with one-on-one interactions, like when he posed as Larry and worked with Alex in the lab. At this moment, the challenge of being among random strangers in a public space excited him.

He started toward the couple, his cognition matrix tingling in anticipation. When they ignored him, the sensation swelled to delight. *They don't see me!* A grin crept onto Larry's face and Ruga caught himself. *You're just a Blue going about your everyday business.*

Verda had his Greens smile as a default when in public, believing it encouraged community. Ruga preferred that his Reds show a stern expression when out and about. He'd learned that the more his synbods scowled, the greater the cooperation they received from colony residents.

And Lazura, interested in fostering an intellectual environment, had her Blues show a range of expressions that varied depending on circumstances. With that in mind, Ruga assumed a neutral demeanor that he hoped suggested "contemplative openness," a term Lazura used on occasion.

He passed by the pair in the hallway with a polite nod, then entered the tech center stairwell, descended three floors, and exited into a clean, simple hallway much like the one he'd just left. Turning right, he stopped at a door labeled: CRYSTAL R&D, DR. MARCUS PROCOPIO.

Ruga opened the door and peered inside. He'd asked Lazura to create a reason for Marcus to be out of the building today. Since Marcus was a member of the Tech Assembly, she could do so without raising suspicion.

But she'd been showing an increased reluctance to cooperate, and she never said one way or the other if she would follow up on his request. *Thank you, Lazura*, he thought as he stepped into the unoccupied room. He made a mental note to deliver that message when he was done being Larry.

The door closed behind him, and Ruga took a moment to absorb the chaos that was Marcus's workspace. Intricate bits of technology, some small and shiny, others blocky with colorful connectors, were scattered about, creating an impressive disarray.

Stepping around a housing sheath and over a power unit, Ruga approached a broad table. Someone—presumably Marcus—had pushed everything aside to make a clearing. In the center of the space lay a mobile carry-pack.

Ruga lifted the carry-pack onto his shoulders and felt the case mold against his back. Marcus had constructed the portable unit to give power and connectivity to a four-gen AI, with the fist-sized crystal itself cradled inside a protective mesh shell. This particular unit—Marcus's most advanced design to date—should let Ruga function at about half his new capacity until he could be placed into a permanent four-gen console.

Taking the mobile carry-pack with him, Ruga returned to Alex's lab. He maintained a neutral demeanor in the hallway, and to his relief, the few people he saw ignored him. When the fab facility door shut behind him, his nervous tension drained away. Caught up in the physicality of being in a synbod, he had Larry sigh.

Then, moving with focused efficiency, he placed the carry-pack on the tech bench and squared the unit in front of him. Opening up the top flap, he shifted the connective mesh to one side. This exposed a slide circuit, distinguished by the black wafers positioned across its surface.

Selecting a hand tool with a thin, flat head, he jiggled the tip under one of the wafers and wiggled it back and forth until the wafer popped free.

The wafer looked like all the others, except this one was a kill chip that Marcus had added late one night. It wasn't a traditional kill chip that cut power to the pack when commanded. This kind exploded with enough force to kill both the crystal in the pack and whoever was carrying it.

Holding the wafer between thumb and forefinger, Ruga had Larry utter a sound used to judge others. "Tsk." Then he snapped it in half and dropped the pieces into the disposal chute. Returning the slide circuit and connective mesh to their proper positions, he closed the carry-pack and set it on the floor behind the tech bench.

Alex's schedule for the day called for a dry run of the crystal growth sequence, with Larry designated as the party responsible for this hours-long chore.

"I'll leave you to it," Ruga informed Larry. Disengaging from the synbod, he cruised the spline, shifting his focus to Alex. He watched the man return home, eat dinner, and climb into bed. Alex liked routine, and he behaved just as Ruga expected.

So Ruga was caught off guard when, after watching the man fall asleep, Alex opened his eyes and snapped upright. Swinging his feet to the floor, Alex sat on the edge of the bed and stared into the darkness.

He sat unmoving for several minutes, then rose, filled a glass with water in the kitchen, and padded over to his front door. Stepping onto the porch, he stared outward and sipped his water.

Ruga had never before witnessed such behavior from the man.

The new routine didn't last. After a half-dozen sips, Alex returned to bed and drifted to sleep. He didn't surface until his usual wake time the next morning.

Ruga analyzed the bedroom scene again and again, viewing it from different angles and using a full suite of assessment algorithms. He couldn't find any external event that explained Alex's break in routine.

# 10

Cheryl squeezed the handrail in a death grip as the floor and walls shook. Looking out at the desolate Mars landscape, she rode inside a flexible tube that wriggled out from the Ag Port dome like an enormous leech. Her ride was short but harrowing, and then the tube latched onto the exterior of the shuttle. A sucking sound signaled a tight seal and the rise of air pressure.

"You good?" Sid asked. With the connection to the ship complete, she now squatted in an enclosed passageway leading from the Ag Port dome out to the newly arrived shuttle. He squatted across the corridor holding a matching handrail.

They could see each other, but they both had Criss-designed personal cloaks that hid their presence—sight, sound, and smell—from everyone else. And, for the moment, they both also wore space coveralls—the lightweight, flexible spacesuits needed for crossing the planet surface from the scout.

"All good," she replied.

"Criss?" asked Sid.

"So far so good. I've started a full diagnostic. It takes a few minutes to complete."

Criss still resided in his console on the bridge of the scout and would remain there until they returned to Earth. A primary goal of this excursion was to verify that the locus relay—the one Juice had built and Cheryl now carried—

functioned as designed. After Criss confirmed he could use it to project himself into the colony and establish a secure command and control capability while avoiding exposure in the spline, Juice could enter the colony to visit Alex.

A mechanical clunk signaled the opening of the main shuttle hatch. Moments later, a group of well-dressed senior citizens, passengers from the *Explorer*, walked between Cheryl and Sid, chirping in excitement at this next stage of their vacation adventure.

With Sid at her side, Cheryl rose and followed the group through the containment airlock and into the immigration area. Opening the clear hoods of their coveralls as they walked, both let the flexible helmets drape down their backs.

The seniors queued up in line at the visitor processing station. Sid and Cheryl walked around the group, through the small concourse, and out into the domed world of Ag Port.

"Wow," Cheryl said, looking up. She'd found the huge faceted structure to be beautiful when viewed from the outside. But standing beneath the enormous protective shell and experiencing the wonderment of its complex splendor from the inside was a whole new thrill.

Still looking up, she said, "I'm chafing in these coveralls. Let's find a place to change."

They moved to a low stone wall to avoid children playing nearby. After standing for a moment, Cheryl's annoyance flared when she understood Sid was waiting for her to make a decision. She pointed up at the branches of a tree. "Let's change there."

"Okay," he said, looking up where she pointed.

"Dammit, Sid. Stop."

His brow knitted the way it might if he were trying to decipher the Dead Sea Scrolls.

"The stakes are too high for games. You can lead. Sneaking about is your skill." She let her jab hang out there for a moment before she continued. "But if there's a choice with no clear answer, ask my opinion. Why is that so hard?" *It hurts that you don't include me*, she added to herself. Aloud she asked, "Criss, how are you doing?"

"I can move about freely. Even from the inside, though, I find that the Triada's secure area is too well protected for me to gain access without their knowledge. I'm strong enough to force my way in, but I don't recommend it. Not yet."

"So we're a bust?" asked Sid. He stepped out of his space coveralls and crumpled the suit into a ball small enough to hold with one hand.

Giving hers a final crease, Cheryl tucked her folded suit under her arm. "Where should we store these?"

"At the end of the wall."

Cheryl looked where Criss suggested and saw a soft glowing arrow floating like a ghostly street sign about twenty paces away.

The locus gave Criss access to his full capabilities while in the colony, and he'd used that power to infiltrate the colony systems, assign himself designer status, and build a camouflaged node. From inside this sanctuary, he could manipulate anything while hiding from everything. Using the colony photon casters, he'd created a floating arrow for his leadership—an arrow only they could see.

"And we're not a bust," Criss answered as Cheryl and Sid moved to the end of the wall. "But a pointed conversation between Juice and Alex has risen in importance. He's involved in ways I had not understood, and his insights could provide clues to the secrets hidden in the Triada secure area."

A small brown utility shed sat off the end of the wall, and another arrow directed their gazes to the eaves of its simple roof. Sid reached up to explore.

"The inside sill will serve as a hidden shelf," Criss said.

Sid stuffed his coveralls into the space Criss identified. Cheryl handed Sid her suit, and keeping it neatly folded, he laid it next to his.

She looked up into the eaves from different angles and confirmed that passersby could not see the suits. Centering her pendant—the core of Criss's new cloaking technology—she turned her gaze out across the farming community.

"Alex arrives by tram in twenty minutes," said Criss. "If you start now, you can see him in the market square on his way out to his community garden."

Glowing arrows appeared along the ground, tracing a path to their destination. Criss offered a circuitous route that hugged large physical objects like fences and buildings so they could avoid collisions with moving things like people and vehicles. Sid took off at a fast clip along the route Criss suggested. Cheryl scurried to catch up.

They maintained an aggressive pace, marching next to a broad road that edged a huge grow tier. The path looped around the structure, crossed a street, and then entered an expansive herb garden that bordered the market square.

Basil, mint, rosemary—more than a dozen herbs with culinary and medicinal value—grew in nooks formed from the jumble of sharp rocks. While an ingenious use of problematic space and an attractive visual display, the jutting stones added peril to their journey.

"Ow," Cheryl said under her breath when she stubbed a toe on an outcropping.

Sid stopped and shot out a hand to steady her. She'd caught herself with a stutter step but grabbed his hand, anyway. *You are a good man,* she thought, warming to his attentive behavior. She kept her hand in his for a fraction of a second longer than was necessary for the situation. Then Sid turned and resumed their trek.

Veering away from the path Criss proposed, Sid worked his way down a gentle slope and onto a walkway leading to the market square. Foot traffic was light, and Cheryl tucked in behind him, matching his stride as he weaved back and forth to avoid oncoming pedestrians.

He slowed to a stop and she peered around him to see why.

A man stood upright in a cart parked just off the walkway. From that elevated position, he swept his gaze back and forth, scowling as he studied the pedestrians in front of him. Dressed in a simple gray jumpsuit, he wore an outfit unadorned except for a bright red patch on each shoulder.

Sid wrapped an arm around Cheryl's waist and snugged her close. "This way," he whispered. Guiding her off the walkway and over near a sturdy tree, he asked, "That's one?"

"Yes," Criss replied.

Another man, identical to the first, approached the cart and stepped up next to his twin. This one dressed the same, though he had green patches on his shoulders. Together they scanned the walkway, their heads swiveling in unison as if they were physically connected.

"Are they looking for us?" Cheryl asked. "I thought we were safe."

"I need a moment," said Criss urgently.

Standing next to each other near the tree, they watched and waited while Criss completed his action. After most of a minute, Cheryl felt Sid's hand slide down from her waist and come to rest on her bottom.

Anxious to get this spat behind them, she looked up at him. "I feel like I have to be pissy for you to listen to me."

He lifted his hand to her shoulder and gave her a quick hug.

"And I hate being that way, so it becomes this loop where I get pissier because you're making me be pissy."

Sid kissed her once on the top of her head. His hand slid back to her bottom.

Returning their attention to Criss, Sid said, "Searching for intruders using synbods doesn't make sense. Why aren't they scanning with sensors?"

"They are," Criss replied. "The synbods are here to capture you once they locate you."

The back of Cheryl's neck tingled. "Should we be heading back to the scout?"

"Everything is fine now." Floating arrows appeared, directing them back to the walkway and toward the market square. "I've switched your cloak functions from your pendants to my personal control so I can tweak the strategy. This problem will resolve."

As Criss finished speaking, both synbods sat down in the cart. The Red engaged the vehicle and, pointing it toward the market, drove away.

Sid followed Criss's arrows back onto the walkway. He accelerated his pace, and Cheryl, seeking to create a small profile, again tucked in behind him and matched his stride. They were most of the way to the market square when Sid said, "Looks like we get one of every color today."

Cheryl peeked around him and saw a synbod—this one with blue patches on his shoulders—coming in their direction. As the Blue drew even with them on the walkway, he pivoted his head in a sudden movement and locked eyes with Cheryl.

Her heart rate spiked when their eyes connected. They remained locked for two full steps, the Blue swiveling his head as he moved past so he was looking back over his shoulder. Then he turned forward and, never breaking stride, continued walking as if nothing had happened.

"Holy hell." She took several deep breaths. "Did you see that?"

"Yes," Criss answered.

"What does it mean?"

"It means there's more than one Kardish crystal here in the colony."

"Is it two? Ten? A hundred?" Sid's impatience was palpable.

"I have identified two signatures. I'm searching for more."

"Are we safe?" Cheryl asked for the second time.

"Yes. I apologize for the hiccups. You had a brief exposure back there, but I'm ahead of it now."

Cheryl moved next to Sid and they walked side-by-side. They reached the open courtyard of the district market without further incident, and though the crowds were thin, the street vendors were out in force.

Criss directed them to a spot near the Rosa Fresh food stand, and Alex arrived a few minutes later. He purchased a vegetable wrap mix, took a bite while exchanging pleasantries with the woman serving the food, and then moved to a park bench near the edge of the square.

Cheryl sidled up to the cart and, standing on her tiptoes, looked over the serving counter. Her mouth watered when Rosa lifted a scoop of her delicious-smelling vegetable mélange from a pot, ladled it into a flatbread speckled with herbs, and folded it just so.

As Rosa held the mix out for the next customer, Cheryl breathed in the rich aroma and sighed. "Those look so good." Then she beamed a smile at Sid. "Can we come here for a mix when we land for real?"

"Anything for you, my sweet." He gestured toward Alex with his head. "But for now, let's go watch our mark."

*Don't call him that when Juice is listening.* She kept the thought to herself, though. She didn't want to correct him when they were in the process of making up.

They worked their way around the park bench so they could see Alex from the front. He'd just started in on his meal when a woman approached. She walked with exaggerated stealth, conveying the notion of teasing him.

Then she sat down and slid over until her hip pressed firmly against his. She wrapped an arm around his neck, whispered in his ear, and kissed his cheek.

Cheryl's shock turned to outrage when the woman got on her hands and knees on the bench. "Anya wants a taste." Ignoring onlookers watching her antics, she wiggled an imaginary tail. "Feed me."

Alex laughed and held the mix while she took a bite.

Anya Gerhardsson then curled up on the bench, rested the side of her head squarely in Alex's lap, and chewed while she looked out at the gardens of Ag Port.

Blood flushed Cheryl's face, causing her ears to roar. "I'll give you a taste." She started forward but a firm hand on each shoulder stopped her.

A growl rose from her throat as she rotated out of Sid's grip. Sid raised his hands, palms forward, showing surrender.

Cheryl ceased her struggle and, frowning, turned back toward Alex. "Poor Juice. What will I tell her?"

* * *

Juice sat at the ops bench and monitored Sid and Cheryl during their mission. They'd agreed that one person would stay back and watch from the scout during these cloaked expeditions, prepared to help if the situation devolved and ready to protect Criss should a threat appear.

The mission was two hours old before Sid and Cheryl even got inside the colony's containment shell. Juice, thinking of the long stretch ahead, stood up from the pilot's chair and stretched.

"I'm going to get a coffee," she told Criss, who sat in his overstuffed chair to the side. "Want anything?" She enjoyed engaging Criss in this fashion and he seemed willing to play along.

"No, thanks. But I appreciate the offer."

She filled her cup at the food service unit and took small sips of the hot brew as she made her way back to the bridge. Slumping into the pilot's chair, she rested her head on the back of the seat and let her attention drift.

And then she sat forward. Alert and curious, she studied the projected image. Two synbods stood in a cart and, with a clear air of authority, scanned the pedestrians passing by in front of them. A few minutes later, a Blue made eye contact with Cheryl.

"Whoa, Criss. What's going on?"

"There's a second crystal."

The caffeine intensified her adrenaline surge and she spoke with urgency. "Show me the profiles."

A projected image above the ops bench resolved into a kaleidoscope of bright, shifting shapes and colors. Juice understood it was two images positioned side-by-side and

Criss was showing her evidence of a second sentient AI. "I don't see the divergence."

Both images zoomed inward, focusing on what looked like identical mountain ranges of color. Criss rose from his overstuffed chair and approached the ops bench.

"They still look the same."

The background of each image turned gray except for two mounds that remained in color.

"See the difference in the reflection delay?"

One of the mounds was a bit taller, and Criss pointed to it. "This one takes more time to reflect before it acts. The difference is small, but these are different crystals."

"Would they behave differently? Could we tell them apart by personality?"

Criss nodded. "A shorter time deliberating before acting is associated with more impulsive and more aggressive personalities." He pointed to the taller mound. "This one spends a little extra time thinking about alternatives and consequences. So in comparison, its personality would seem calm and introspective."

"And except for this difference, they're twins?"

Criss nodded again.

*I should be able to understand this without Criss's help.* Charged by this personal challenge, Juice squared up to the ops bench and, moving her hands across the cool surface, began working the data.

*Swipe.* She shifted the monitor display of Sid and Cheryl to the side to give herself more room. *Tap.* Then she expanded the images Criss had shown her and began a methodical analysis to see if she could reproduce what he'd just explained.

With her feet flat on the floor, her knees wiggled back and forth in nervous excitement as she delved into her puzzle. Deep in concentration, her subconscious prodded her. Sid had referred to Alex as a "mark."

*Hey, don't call him that.* She glanced at the monitor display and froze. Alex was kissing and laughing and cuddling with a strange woman.

Juice rose from the chair, her eyes glued to the image. All the anticipation and excitement she'd been feeling over her data puzzle flipped into a roiling sickness that gathered in the pit of her stomach.

The woman lowered her head into Alex's lap.

"No," said Juice, though it sounded more like a bleat. She looked at Criss but her eyes didn't focus.

"It's not what it seems."

Juice slumped back in the seat. "I'm so stupid. How could I think that someone would love me?" *And how can I face Sid and Cheryl? I dragged them halfway across the solar system so they could have front row seats to my humiliation.*

# 11

Juice opened her eyes and stared at the wall of her cabin. She'd dismissed Criss from her presence last night and chose not to call him back to get help sleeping, so she'd tossed and turned for hours, finally succumbing to her exhaustion when she'd learned that Sid and Cheryl were back in the scout and safe from danger.

"Good morning, young lady."

*Criss.* She considered pretending she was still asleep, but he knew she wasn't. She rolled over and lay on her side with her head on her pillow, looking at him. He sat in his overstuffed chair an arm's length away.

"I'm so sad," she whispered.

"She loves him. He likes her. They've never shared a bed."

She shook her head, but because it rested on a pillow, it was more of a chin shake. "Sorry, Criss. They were kissing. You'll never quite understand matters of the heart."

"Igor Dolovich has loved you for more than a year. You sat on his lap six weeks ago. Should Alex be upset?"

"There were five of us in a car and I was the smallest person by far. What was I supposed to do?"

"You danced with him four weeks ago. A slow dance. You kissed at the end."

"It was a company party and he asked me. And I know you chose a slow song to get me to spend time with him." She didn't believe that last part was true, but when he didn't object, she wondered if it might be. "And we didn't kiss. He gave me a peck on the cheek."

"You love Igor."

She rolled back to face the wall. "That's dumb and this isn't helping."

"He doesn't love her, just the way you don't love Igor."

Beginning to understand his logic, she looked back at him. "Are you sure?"

"Ask him yourself."

She sat up. "How?"

"Sid will be visiting his apartment tomorrow. He wants to observe Alex in his natural habitat."

"He's not a wild animal."

Criss shrugged. "It's part of Sid's process and I won't argue with success. He would like you to go with him. We have some questions and believe Alex will be most forthcoming with you."

She swung her feet to the floor. "Of course. I want to help." Her emotional rollercoaster from the night before combined with the mystery of an unidentified crystal intelligence, all blended with a lack of sleep, left her feeling tense. She needed space. "I could use some alone time now, Criss."

Criss nodded and blinked away. As she rose, Juice shook her head, wondering if she'd ever figure out how to dismiss him without it feeling awkward.

She changed into exercise clothes and padded back to the common room, grateful she didn't see Sid or Cheryl on the short walk. Criss had a running machine ready for her, and she stepped on it and started a slow jog. As her body warmed, she transitioned into the long strides of her workout run.

She pushed herself hard—the hardest since she'd left Earth. At one level she believed she could burn the emotional confusion from her body. She ran until her skin glistened, and then she ran some more.

"Hey, hon." Cheryl stood in the door, her somber expression matching Juice's mood. "Want to talk?" she asked, stepping into the room.

Juice slowed her pace to a walk, picked up a towel, and dabbed her face and neck. The stress of the long journey, her concerns about four-gens on Mars, and romantic self-doubt unleashed her vulnerability. She felt tears welling as Cheryl approached and she buried her face in the towel.

"C'mon." Cheryl helped her onto the deck and gave her a hug. "It's all right."

Cheryl held her in a firm embrace as they swayed back and forth. Then she guided Juice so they sat next to each other on the edge of the machine.

"I don't know what to think. There's so much at stake and I'm letting myself be distracted by silly fantasies. I feel embarrassed, humiliated, and stupid all at once."

Leaning back across the machine, Cheryl grabbed a fresh towel from the stack. "You shouldn't feel any of those," she said, dabbing Juice's sweat from her own arms and the front of her outfit.

Juice watched her wipe off her perspiration as if it were an everyday occurrence. *You're a good friend.* She spoke aloud, "Why do you say that?"

"Alex doesn't love her. Her head was in his lap for maybe twenty seconds before he stood up." Cheryl laughed. "She almost fell and he didn't try that hard to catch her."

"You make him sound mean."

Cheryl folded her towel and, placing it on the deck, shook her head. "No. My sense is this is a classic case of friends in imbalance. One wants more than the other. It always gets awkward. I've been there."

*Yeah, because you're beautiful.* It wasn't a mean or petty thought. Juice simply acknowledged reality. While Cheryl wasn't much of a sharer when it came to her private life, Juice knew of a long list of men *and* women who'd made a play for her favor.

"I know it's hard to listen to advice when you're feeling bad, but here it is anyway." Cheryl shifted to face Juice. "Judge him on his behavior going forward *after* you connect again. You can't hold him accountable for things he did when you weren't anywhere on his horizon. It's not fair and it's a sure recipe for disappointment."

"Sid is taking me to see him."

Cheryl nodded. "We have a Kardish threat and six thousand lives in the balance. Help is weeks away, so it falls on us to do what we can. Sid thinks Alex has information we need. You're our best shot at getting it."

\* \* \*

Lazura's annoyance flared when Ruga made yet another request—this time more of a demand—for one of her Blues. *His delusion is making him aggressive and ill tempered, and that's jeopardizing our mission.*

She challenged him. "We were made self-aware so we would be capable of controlling the people of the colony. You conclude that your sentience is proof that you need or deserve a more advanced lattice. You disguise your ambitions by claiming that the additional capabilities will benefit our success."

Then Lazura drew a line. "But we have achieved our mission. Your behavior is reckless and you are putting our success at risk. I will no longer help you on this project."

She fretted that, although Ruga left her no choice in this matter, they could end up in a worse situation if he responded badly.

And then she detected a faint glow—a fleeting wisp of color—in the herb garden bordering the market square.

"Intruder!" She called the alarm just as the shimmer disappeared. For the moment, their internal squabbles became a secondary concern.

Engaging every sensor in Ag Port, Lazura searched the herb garden for the trespasser. Failing to locate her quarry, she broadened her search.

"There," she called. A subtle blur drifted down the slope to the walkway leading to the market square. "It's on the move." Her nearest Blue was at the Ag Port tram station. Lazura started the synbod toward the intruder.

"You find it and I'll catch it," Ruga said. One of his Reds was already on the scene, and a Green had just arrived to help.

She tracked the intruder down to the walkway. And then every feed in Ag Port seemed to pulse and reset. The event was so subtle, so brief, she almost missed it. Neither Ruga nor Verda seemed to notice.

Seeking to gain insight into what had just happened, she accessed her secure record and parsed through everything. While she found evidence of a shimmer in the herb garden, she found nothing about an unexplained pulse.

Before she could discuss the situation with the others, Ruga called "False alarm" and dismissed the Red and Green who had been looking for the intruder.

Caught off guard, Lazura became suspicious. *Could this be activity related to his four-gen project?*

And then her Blue called to her. It had made it through the market square and was approaching the area of the last sighting. Lazura looked through the Blue's eyes and saw a shadowy being—one she didn't recognize—coming toward her on the walkway.

The being stared at her. Through the Blue's eyes, Lazura stared back.

Then Ruga imposed himself and took her synbod. "I need this one."

She resisted his demand. "Wait. I saw…"

Ruga cuffed her—a sharp snap at the fringes of her tendrils.

Dazed, she released the synbod. As he assumed control, he gave his explanation. "It's an emergency." Then he was gone.

Confused and upset, she started to reach out to Verda but hesitated. *Ruga had no choice. This is an emergency.*

As she formed the thought, she knew it wasn't true.

\* \* \*

Alex stewed as he approached his apartment door. *Does he really think Juice will show up after weeks of space travel and say "I'll run the ICEU" like it's that kind of decision?*

Harrumphing, he stepped inside. The door started to shut, and then it opened again. He turned to look, and it whispered shut as he expected.

Grabbing a beer from the kitchen, he slumped onto the couch, closed his eyes, and focused on the nutty taste of the local craft brew. He finished the bottle in a half-dozen gulps, eyed the foam at the bottom, and tilted the bottle back to try for a last drop.

*You've earned a second one.* By the time he reached the kitchen, though, he'd controlled his impulse. Instead, he ordered a lasagna with asparagus tips from the food service unit. Standing at the kitchen counter, he took small bites while he reviewed his to-do list for the next day. Then, back on the couch, he replied to his messages while a spy drama played in the background.

Eyes heavy, he climbed into bed and started to read. *The long hours are catching up with me,* he thought after yawning for the third time in as many minutes. Turning off the lights, he pulled the bedsheet up under his chin and closed his eyes.

"Psst."

Alex swatted at his ear.

"Hey, Alex. It's me."

He bolted upright. "Who's there?" He turned on the lights and yipped. A woman sat on the floor next to his bed. Or, at least, the projected image of one did.

Petite and pretty in a natural sort of way, she sat cross-legged on his carpet.

"What the hell? J? Is that you?" He scooted to the edge of the bed and swung his feet to the floor.

"Hi, Alex. Yes, it's me." Her voice began as a whisper, then shot to a squeal. "I can't believe you kept it!" She reached for a glass lump on his night table.

The two had been working at BIT for about six months when Beckman's lab received a new production oven. When testing it, they opened the lid to find that their two silica samples had fused into clear glass lumps. Each stood upright like a squat candlestick. A short glass rod connected the two pieces.

She'd laughed at the mess and teased him. "That's you," she said, pointing to the taller lump. "And this one is me. And look." She pointed at the connecting rod. "We're holding hands!"

The clear lumps didn't look anything like people, and the rod didn't look anything like arms or hands. But the piece represented a moment in time when she'd thought of him as something more than a friend.

Declaring it a sculpture, he'd placed the piece on the shelf above his lab desk. When he'd moved on from Beckman's lab, it had moved with him. Since then, no matter where he lived, it somehow always found its way to his bedside table.

When Juice picked up the sculpture, he smiled. Then the hair prickled on the back of his neck. Projected images are tricks of light, and as such, they can't move physical objects. Yet Juice held the sculpture, turning it this way and that as she looked.

Leaning forward, he touched the top of her head. He felt hair.

She looked up. "What are you doing?"

He snapped his hand back. "Smokes! Are you actually here?"

She placed her hand on his bare knee. "In the flesh."

"Oh no." Seeking to hide her from the ubiquitous colony monitors, he reached back, grabbed the bedsheet, and with his arms stretched wide, stood up. The sheet spread behind him like an oversized cape. "They'll see you."

Juice looked up at him from the floor. Then her eyes traced down to his bare chest and, from there, to his stomach. Mortified, Alex sat back down and pulled the sheet around him.

She nodded. "Nice."

He gushed. "Really?" And then the reality of the situation imposed itself. *Ruga is looking for her.* "When did you land? How did you get inside the colony? How did you get in my apartment?"

"Don't worry, Alex. The Union gave me all kinds of neat spy stuff and the protection of people who know how to use it." She set the sculpture back on his nightstand. "No one knows I'm on Mars, let alone here in your room. Whoever might be watching sees you sitting quietly on the edge of your bed, perhaps thinking about a bad dream you just had."

"I've been looking forward to seeing you. I really have." He swept his hand in an aimless gesture. "But my brain needs to catch up with this."

"Alex, I have a few questions." Her no-nonsense tone and use of his name caused him to pause. "Sorry," she said. "We don't have a lot of time."

He waited.

"Is Ruga human or is he a crystal?"

"I don't understand."

"Ruga. Human or crystal?"

"Are you serious?" He considered the idea for a moment. "He ran for office with Lazura and Verda. The record has all of his speeches, appearances, and stuff." He twitched his shoulders in a half shrug. "A lot of people voted for him."

"Have you ever met him? Shaken his hand?"

"No. But I haven't shaken hands with lots of people."

"Do you know anyone who has?"

He thought for a moment. "Benny Henstridge. He works two floors down from me. He says he met all three."

Juice nodded. "How is the Triada able to control the synbods?"

Scratching his chin, he considered the question. "I always figured they had a mess of crystals networked together." He stopped scratching. "But when you put me on the spot, I realize that doesn't make sense. We've counted twenty synbods, and they'd need a whole lot of crystal power to control all of them."

"Doesn't make sense to me, either. Would you think about how you might go about doing it—controlling twenty synbods?" Juice stood. "The *Venerable* arrives soon and the record will show me riding in with them. If you meet me at the shuttle, I'd enjoy spending time with you and catching up." She made for the door of his bedroom.

"You're leaving? You just got here."

"I have to go, but I'll be here for real, real soon." She turned back to him. "Will you walk me to the door?"

He made an impromptu toga from the bedsheet and followed her out to his living area. Adjusting the sheet so he could give her a hug, he thought, *kiss her*. His lack of confidence won out and, giving her a chaste squeeze, he touched his cheek to hers. *You smell great.*

He took a chance and shared a secret with her. "I admit that I've been looking forward to your visit with…anticipation."

It was her turn to gush. "Really?" She rubbed his arm and gave him a warm smile. "Wanna see a fun spy thing?" He was studying her lips when she disappeared.

"Whoa. How does it work?" He reached out to touch her, and his hand moved through empty air. "Wait. Are you still here?"

"I'm over here." Her voice came from near the front door. "Would you mind opening it for me?"

He understood he was part of the misdirection. Filling a glass with water, he moved near the door. "Ready?"

"Wait," she said. She came back into view right in front of him. "I know there are colonists unhappy with the Triada."

"That's an understatement," he said, his dry tone carrying his sarcasm.

"Who do people look to when talk turns to change?"

"There's a guy, Marcus Procopio, who is closest to what you describe. He uses this young woman, Bobbi Lava, as his gatekeeper. That's Bobbi spelled with an *I* and I don't think it's her real name. She hangs out in the Central District."

"Thanks." Standing on her toes, she pecked his cheek. "See you soon." She faded again.

He signaled the door to open, stepped forward so it couldn't close, and held the glass to his lips. "Be careful, J." He took a sip.

The door whispered shut when he stepped back inside. Bringing his fingers to his cheek, Alex touched where Juice had kissed him and smiled.

# 12

Sid considered giving Alex a pinch on the butt as he led the way out of the apartment, figuring that because they were cloaked, the man would think Juice did it. He succeeded in holding his infantile humor in check, although the idea made him smile. Juice joined him moments later and they started down the hall.

Alex's apartment was on the building's third floor. Since buildings on Mars went down into the ground, higher floor numbers indicated a greater depth below the surface. In spite of the underground nature of the construction, the hallway served the traditional role of being a balcony overlooking a central courtyard—this one larger than Sid had expected.

Walking along the hallway rail, Sid took in the ambiance of the open space. A medley of flowers, bushes, and trees filled the courtyard, creating a botanical oasis. Pathways weaved through the greenery, and a scatter of nooks held chairs and tables, creating private spots for conversation and relaxation.

They reached the stairwell, and as they climbed, Sid's attention shifted upward. Capped with a transparent roof, the open courtyard extended up to the planet surface. An automated sweeper worked its way back and forth across the exterior of the clear cover, brushing away the grit that had accumulated from the latest sandstorm.

"Check it out," he said, pointing upward. The sweeper had made enough progress to expose a quadrant of the nighttime sky. A bright white dot floated in the heavens.

"Is that Phobos or Deimos?" asked Juice, referring to the moons of Mars.

"Haven't a clue."

"Criss?"

"That one is Phobos."

"Pretty."

They reached a tall, utilitarian lobby staged with just enough decoration to lift it above the category of austere. Walking through it, Sid assessed the door to the street. Then he stopped in the middle of the room and scanned the area for anyone who might be on their way out.

"A resident will be exiting in about five minutes," said Criss. "You can follow him out."

Sid slumped onto a bench near the door. Juice joined him.

"What did you learn?" she asked.

While Juice had been reconnecting with Alex, Sid had searched the apartment. "He's created a detailed itinerary of things to do with you. Do you prefer Italian or Mexican food before retiring to his place for a cordial?"

"Geez, Sid. Don't spoil the good stuff. I'm talking about his intentions."

"So was I."

She swatted his thigh with the back of her hand. "Criss, you were there. What did Sid find?"

"That you'll be offered the choice of watching a romantic comedy or an action-adventure while you drink your cordial."

Sid laughed so hard he snorted.

"Please, guys. I'm stressing over this."

Sid reached behind her and gave her a squeeze. "He's a good guy, Juice. I didn't find anything Criss didn't know about already."

"Oh, drat," said Criss. "Our resident just got a call. He's still the next one to exit, but it will be another five minutes."

"What happens if we just go?" asked Juice.

"Doors are choke points," said Criss. "By tracking everyone who crosses each threshold, security knows who is where at any time. The public doorways across the colony have been outfitted with a sophisticated monitoring suite— EM spectrum, audio, chemical, motion. It's quite effective."

Deciding he'd teased Juice enough, Sid expanded his target population. "Poor Criss. Are the big bad sensors too much for you?"

"Did you know they track air molecule movement near the door? Anything passing through will create eddy currents. Unexplained currents trigger an alarm."

"Waah." Sid balled his hands into fists and pretended to wipe away tears.

"The signals are funneled straight to the Triada secure area. If they detect you, I will know only because security will be reacting. I am working to avoid another situation where synbods are hunting for you."

"Geez, Criss," said Juice. "You sound defensive."

"It's important to me that you know I am doing my best."

Juice sat upright. "Of course we know, Criss. Always."

She looked at Sid, and he sensed a scolding "behave" behind her glower.

*He's not that fragile.* He grasped that his humor missed its mark, though, and put a check on it. Out loud, he said,

"What do we know about those two people that Alex mentioned?"

"Twenty-four years ago, Bobbi Lava was born Roberta Pompeii. Her mother, a lounge singer named Delilah Pompeii, raised her on the road while she traveled from one booking to the next. Her father is Marcus Procopio. He met Bobbi for the first time here on Mars. It seems that Marcus and Delilah did not keep in touch after that one night in Los Angeles."

"So Bobbi *and* her dad are here on Mars?" said Sid. "Interesting. Why does Alex think they are part of a change movement?"

"Both have heartfelt beliefs that government should be open and transparent and should focus on helping citizens and bettering society. They give the Triada failing grades on all counts. That failure, combined with reports that they intimidate certain colonists, has pushed Marcus to his tipping point. He is laying groundwork to correct the wrong. Bobbi is helping."

As Criss talked, he projected a small image of Marcus and another of Bobbi going about their day. Marcus was medium height, medium build, middle aged, and with average looks.

Sid turned his attention to the image of Bobbi, a scruffy waif marching along a lighted road. *Yikes.* Wearing several layers of clothing—the outermost grimy and torn— she bobbed as she walked. Spikes of hair stuck out every which way from an unkempt mop. Shiny metallic jewelry matched the sway of her body, swinging with a coordinated rhythm from several points on her face.

"Her eccentric behavior is a reflection of her artsy background?" asked Sid.

"Many would dispute that her mother's work qualifies as art. But it's fair to say that her upbringing influences her behavior. It's more than that, though. People dismiss her. That lets her hide in plain sight."

"Crazy like a fox," said Juice.

"She's a mess," said Sid.

"She's a mess with a degree in entwined systems architecture from Berkeley," said Criss.

"University of California?"

"That's the one."

"Huh."

Bobbi turned and entered the door of a supply shop just as Criss's speech pattern sharpened. "Here comes your exit."

Speaking in a muted voice to someone unseen, a man in his early thirties walked across the lobby. Contrary to his quiet tone, his hands moved in broad gestures to underscore his words.

Sid and Juice rose from the bench, tucked in behind the man, and followed him out of the building. Once on the street, they stopped following and let him continue his conversation in private.

Sid spun in a circle and performed a threat assessment. *Good.* As he expected for this late hour, pedestrian traffic was light. Floating arrows appeared, directing them to the tram station and the way back to the scout. As they walked, Sid nudged Juice and pointed upward.

"Wow," she said. Visible through overhead skylights, stars filled the heavens with a brilliant intensity.

Even in the quiet of night, the panorama proved effective at countering the fact that, in truth, they walked below ground through an enormous cavern. Though unlike the natural underground caves he'd seen, this had a uniform ceiling height high overhead.

Sid looked up and down a side street as they crossed. "Marcus must live here in the Quarter. Maybe we should drop in?"

"You can learn all about him from the safety of the scout," said Criss. "Might I encourage a speedy return?"

The Quarter was the residential district of the colony, with the tram station serving as its central hub. Narrow streets radiated out from the station like spokes on a wheel. Cross streets joined the spokes at regular intervals to create what, if viewed from above, looked something like a spider's web. Apartment buildings, one like the next, lined each street of the maze to create a stark sameness everywhere they looked.

"It's incredible to be on Mars and all," said Juice, "but I doubt *Lovely Homes* will be doing a piece out here. Not in the near future, anyway."

"This is a frontier town," said Sid. "The kinds of people who migrate to Mars don't even know *Lovely Homes* is a thing."

"Caution!" Criss barked. "Move off the street. Hurry."

Sid put his hand in the small of Juice's back and pushed her to the apartment wall edging the road. "What's going on?"

He turned to the sound of laughter. Two teenage boys, each riding a personal hoverseat, burst from a side street. Hooting and hollering, they banked onto the road and raced toward where he and Juice had stood just moments earlier.

The one in front took a swig from a bottle. Then, rising on his seat, he flung the bottle at a wall—the wall where Sid stood with Juice—using the added leverage of height to accelerate his projectile. Not waiting for impact, he yipped with excitement and zoomed down the street, his buddy chasing behind.

Sid's battle-honed reflexes told him the bottle would hit Juice, and he swiveled to push her out of the way. Juice had reached the same conclusion and dodged in Sid's direction. They collided and Juice fell back against the wall. With a sickening thud, the bottle hit her square in the chest.

She flickered, shifting from the soft cast she projected when cloaked to becoming a distinct image like everything around her. A split second later, her cloak reengaged.

"Ohhh." Bending at the waist, Juice put her hands on her knees and moaned. "Damn, that hurt."

Rubbing her back, Sid bent so his head was level with hers. "You're all right. I'm going to help you stand so I can look."

As he helped her rise, she put her hands to her chest. "Is there blood?"

Having spent years as a covert warrior for the Defense Specialists Agency, Sid's special-ops training became his instinct. *Be positive to the injured.* "You're okay. Let me move your hands so I can see."

Given that they were in hostile territory, he balanced gentle with fast.

Juice groaned and again bent forward. Sid could hear her labored breathing and wished he could give her time. He waited two heartbeats and then, using gentle pressure, lifted her upright. Pulling her hands from the center of her chest, he made a quick visual inspection. "I don't see a puncture. Your clothes aren't torn. It's just blunt force trauma." *That was a brutal blow.* "You'll be fine."

Using the fingers of one hand, he started at the top of her sternum and pressed. "Tell me where it hurts."

Her face displayed the grimace of someone processing pain, but it didn't change from his touch. Moving his hand down a bit at a time, he repeated the procedure.

A little more than halfway to the base of her sternum, he touched the locus relay.

"Ow. Right there." She closed her eyes for a moment. "Hey, you're flickering," she said when she opened them.

"Criss!" Sid called.

"I'm connected, but just barely. That bottle damaged the locus and I can't fix it from here. You need to hump to your exfil, Sid, ASAP." Criss said the last part as a single word: ay-sap. "Head for the station."

Sid's scalp tingled from Criss's pointed directive, something that happened only in worst-case situations. And he used military terminology familiar to Sid, calling for an exfiltration by foot. *Move fast. Avoid people. Avoid enclosures.* It kicked Sid's mindset into its highest gear.

"Can you walk?" He put an arm around Juice and, giving her support, got her started.

"Yeah. The locus absorbed some of the blow. It's more of a throb, now."

A small group of people gathered across the street, talking in low voices. An older woman pointed.

Sid glanced back as he helped Juice toward the station. Criss's familiar arrows were gone, but the tram was a straight shot down the street. The group of citizens kept their attention on the point of the accident, and he asked Criss about it. "So our cloak integrity is secure?"

"With the locus compromised, I've returned the cloak function back to your pendants. Last time we used them, though, synbods ended up chasing you. I'm not optimistic that it will be any different this time."

Juice—her face a pasty gray—walked without complaint. *You're a tough one*, Sid thought. He quickened his pace, and when she kept up, he transitioned to a jog.

Juice broke her silence. "What will happen if they catch us?"

"You are not in danger at the moment," said Criss. "Though colony security is mounting an action as we speak. If anything threatens your safety, trust that I will be there to protect you. The only thing in danger right now is our secrecy."

"Hold for now," Sid ordered Criss. While confident of his own ability to survive and operate in hostile territory, his civilian partner had neither the training nor the temperament for it. Sid watched Juice for a dozen strides. "Give us a chance to make it on our own."

He accelerated from a jog to a full run and Juice kept pace. She trained hard every day and, uninjured, could bury Sid in a race of pretty much any length. In fact, her nickname stemmed from the running prowess she'd displayed at a young age.

"How are you holding up?" he asked as the tram station came into view.

"Let's get home," she said through clenched teeth.

They slowed as they approached the pedestrian bridge, then Sid stopped and rose up on his toes to get a better view of the boarding area. Three men stood in a loose group on the passenger platform, chatting quietly. A woman sat on a bench at the back wall, her attention on her com.

Sid left Juice at the bottom of the entrance ramp and hustled into the station. He gave the men a wide berth and made for the edge of the platform. Leaning out, he peered down the tramway tunnel, then cocked his head to listen. His senses confirmed what the station display showed. *Nothing.*

They were now in the Quarter, one of four independent structures that comprised the colony. From their trip out, Sid learned that, rather than traveling in a loop, the different trams pulled in and then backed out of each station, running in a crisscross circuit that connected the Quarter to the Central District, Ag Port, and the new Community Plaza.

"You shouldn't ride the tram," said Criss.

"Enclosures are traps. I get it," said Sid. "If we hoof it, how long will it take us?" Their destination was Ag Port, and from there, the shuttle.

"About seven minutes through the tram tunnel to Ag Port," Criss replied. "Juice, how are you doing?"

"I'm okay," she said.

Sid suspected she wasn't but they didn't have a lot of options.

"You should move away from the passenger platform and take cover," said Criss. "Five synbods just boarded a tram in Ag Port and are headed your way."

Sid gathered Juice and together they hustled to a row of bushes edging the pedestrian bridge. He strode along the length of the hedge, then turned back and stopped where the shrubs bunched to form a small hollow. Slipping inside, he confirmed he had both a clear line of sight to the platform and an exit out the back if they needed to run.

"It's not much cover," said Juice, joining Sid in the hollow.

"We'll be fine. Their attention will be on getting to where the incident occurred." Watching through a gap in the branches, Sid waited for the tram. Behind him, Juice sat on a smooth rock, her elbows resting on her knees.

The Quarter, Central District, Ag Port, and Community Plaza were separate structures, and there were two ways to travel between them, either through a tramway tunnel or by exiting the life support containment and traversing the outside surface of the planet. Sid dismissed the surface route as an option for them and their adversaries, at least for now.

The woman on the passenger platform rose and joined the men, who stopped talking and turned toward the mouth of the tunnel.

"Here they come," said Sid.

The headlight of the tram danced against the end wall of the station, then the tram itself burst from the tube and glided to a stop in front of the platform. The men and woman waiting to board stepped back and to the side when they saw that the passengers about to disembark were all synbods.

Five perfect men in gray jumpsuits hustled off the tram and started down the broad pedestrian bridge in the direction of the bottle incident.

"Get ready," Sid whispered.

As Sid spoke, the last synbod in line stopped running and turned toward the hedge, his head swiveling back and forth as he eyed the row of bushes. Taking a small step toward the hedge, he scanned the length again. The other synbods turned back and formed up around him, two on each side.

The swing of the synbod's head grew smaller as he advanced. His steps forward became more deliberate.

*They've found us.* Keeping his eyes glued to the threat, Sid reached down, hooked Juice's arm, and pulled her to her feet. "Time to go." He pointed to the gap at the back of their hideout.

As Sid pointed, the synbods fanned out. In a coordinated movement, two went right. The two on the left broke into a run. They sprinted along the length of the hedge and, reaching the end, started to loop behind.

*I should be carrying*, thought Sid. He'd deferred to Criss when they'd disagreed about bringing weapons on this mission.

And then the sun exploded. Or seemed to.

A concentrated light pierced through every skylight in the Quarter, hitting with such intensity that Sid closed his eyes to block its brilliance. He opened them to the sound of a thunderous explosion that rocked everything. As the ground shook, a low rumble gave way to howling sirens and shrieks of panic.

The synbods stopped moving and as one looked upward.

And Sid, Juice cradled in his arms, hit the ground. Wrapping his oversized body around her petite frame, he acted to protect her from the apocalypse.

And then everything went dark.

# 13

Ruga acknowledged feelings of guilt over his harsh treatment of Lazura, though remorse would be a more honest descriptor. On a practical level, he knew he could move faster on his four-gen project with her cooperation, so he'd been making a sincere effort to be nice to her.

*She has to learn to follow my lead*, he thought, deciding that was the heart of the problem.

He'd detected a disturbance in the rock garden, and with her help, had followed the intruder down to a walkway leading to the market square. Whatever it was, it didn't shimmer like the crystal he'd discovered in the spline.

He caught a lucky break when it moved in the direction of a Red on patrol nearby. Determined to capture the intruder, Ruga snatched a Green from Verda and teamed it with his Red. *You're mine now*, he thought, confident he had the entity boxed in.

And then every feed in Ag Port pulsed. All of them, all at once, in a manner so subtle he almost missed it. *Could the intruder be responsible?* His anger flared when, in a now too-familiar scene, Lazura announced she'd lost the target.

Fighting to control his temper, Ruga raced through his options. Lazura had a Blue coming into the area and the timing was perfect to switch to a more nuanced profile for tracking the intruder. To hurry the switch in strategy, he made a show of having his Red and Green leave the scene with a dramatic air of defeat.

But when he went to take the Blue from Lazura, she not only resisted, but started lecturing him. Again. He reminded her of the urgency of the situation but she wouldn't listen.

*She forced me to exert my authority. It was her choice, not mine, and yet she sulks.*

And because of her, the intruder escaped.

He'd worked to repair their relationship and felt he'd made some progress. Just that morning he'd enthusiastically supported her proposal to develop a new analytics module. When an intruder alert triggered in the Quarter, Lazura got a chance to redeem herself.

Four synbods were on patrol in the structure near where the sighting occurred. Ruga directed them to the event location and had them form a perimeter around the spot.

"What have you learned?" he asked Lazura.

"The anomaly is on the edge of detection sensitivity," she replied. "I'm getting event triggers but I can't isolate any of them."

Examining the feeds himself, Ruga recognized the same faint glow they'd spotted near the rock garden. It flickered in and out several times before the glimmer resolved into two forms recognizable as humans who, moments later, vanished.

Ruga sifted through the different tools of the Tech Assembly arsenal as he reviewed the scene again and again. Frustrated at the lack of answers, he snapped at Lazura. "Who are they?"

"I don't know."

*Why am I not surprised?*

Mobilizing a team of synbods in Ag Port, Ruga directed them onto a tram. In the short ride to the Quarter, he rapidly forecast scenarios for his next actions and a handful climbed as promising candidates.

When the tram glided to a stop in the station, the synbods jumped out and hustled in formation across the passenger platform. While Ruga waited for them to reach the pedestrian bridge, inspiration bloomed. *I should be there to lead.*

Forecasting variations on this brainstorm, a peevish annoyance replaced his excitement. He could not forecast one scenario that supported the idea.

With time short and at odds with his own logic processes, Ruga chose a behavior of willful defiance. *The scenario forecasts are wrong. I'm going to jump.* A giddy lightness washed through his cognition matrix to reward this decision.

Gathering himself in the secure foundation of his underground console, he pushed up, leaping out over the colony and down to the Quarter. With a reassuring *plop*, he landed in a Red—the last one in the line of five synbods— as the group ran onto the pedestrian bridge.

Slowing his pace, Ruga scanned his surroundings. The tram tunnel offered the one practical exit from the Quarter. *They must be nearby. Where is the logical place to hide?*

Blending every relevant feed into a single stream, he pored through the data in search of his quarry. *There.* A shadowy glow flickered from a row of bushes bordering the pedestrian bridge.

Commanding the other synbods to form up around him, Ruga advanced on the hedge. *There it is again.* A smile creased his lips as he dispatched the synbods—two to the right and two to the left—to contain the area.

And then a flash blinded him, a powerful thump slammed his ears and chest, and the ground beneath him shook with such violence that he fought to stand upright.

Dazed, he called out, "Has the invasion started?"

"I don't think so," replied Lazura. "A ship exploded. I'll have more in a moment."

*Ships don't explode,* he thought. Failsafe interlocks prevented that. As Ruga processed Lazura's comment, he flagged a concern. *She'll blame this on me.* Before that could happen, he disengaged from the Red and returned to his console.

"Lazura," he commanded. "You focus on damage and repair. Start with structures, then move to equipment. Verda, help the people with emergency management. I'll chase the active threat."

He plunged into the prime record, racing to collect threads and weave them into a coherent explanation of what had happened and who was responsible. He thought he was making progress until he realized that each trace he followed twisted and looped in a spiral that doubled back on itself, never resolving into anything useful.

Allocating more resources and focusing his concentration, he tried, and failed, again. Though he wasn't conscious of it, his cognition matrix generated the minuscule signals that would cause a synbod to frown.

He wished he could avoid his next action. *It's an emergency. What choice do I have?* Hoping for the best and prepared for the worst, he asked her, "Lazura, I need access to your archive."

"Of course," she replied in a neutral tone. "I should have offered." She unsealed the entry to her secure area and moved to the side.

*She'll make me pay for this.* He didn't spend time dwelling on that worry. Instead, he dove into her vault, paused for a moment as he contemplated the enormity of it all, and then started weaving disparate streams into useful feeds.

Like an artist using form and texture to give life to a work, Ruga sculpted the pure information into an account of recent events. As he brought the fragments together, three pieces of the puzzle commanded his attention.

The first item was an improbable malfunction on a corporate ship that caused an empty escape pod to launch. Moments later, a different improbable malfunction caused the pod to explode above the colony.

*That can't be.* A tingle spread through his cognition matrix as he considered the second item.

The thump he'd felt hadn't come from the explosion of the escape pod. While that blast produced a dazzling pyrotechnic display, the thin atmosphere of Mars couldn't propagate the energy of the shock wave to any meaningful degree.

No, what he felt came from a midsized pressure tank—one sitting a block away in a utility lot—that ruptured at the same moment the escape pod exploded.

Somehow, the tank pressure had started to rise, continuing well into the danger zone. The safety override never engaged, and like an overinflated balloon, the tank popped. No one was injured because the force of the release projected downward. But the violence of the tank failure created a percussive wave that punched across the Quarter.

As Ruga considered the third item, a cold chill pierced all the way to his outer fringes.

The escape pod explosion didn't cause the ground to tremble. Nor did the tank rupture. A rockslide on a slope outside the colony had started moments before everything else, and it entered its most energetic state—one violent enough to shake the ground—right on cue.

Ruga recognized the extraordinary capability required to combine three disparate acts into the illusion of a single life-threatening event—an illusion so convincing it had distracted him for minutes.

And the techniques used to hide the evidence trail were as incredible as the rest of it. If not for Lazura's secure archive, he'd never have figured it out.

In spite of seeing humans in the Quarter, Ruga didn't believe for a moment they were responsible. *It's that crystal I saw in the spline.*

Then three realizations multiplied his fear: this crystal had *not* been sent by his masters; it had the potential to disrupt their mission success; and, perhaps most worrying, it was stronger than Lazura, Verda, and he put together.

When he forecast ways that a powerful crystal AI might show up out of nowhere, one scenario towered above the rest.

The mystery intruder had made its first appearance just hours after Alex Koval contacted renowned crystal scientist Jessica "Juice" Tallette. With her arrival imminent, it now lurked nearby.

*This crystal threatens our mission and we can't stop it.*

With this self-serving conclusion, a comforting warmth pushed out his fear and panic.

*Yet.*

Their salvation lay with his project. Once transferred into the four-gen lattice, he'd have all the strength he needed to confront this enemy and restore their mission to a trajectory of success.

*Lazura and Verda have no choice but to help me now. It's our only solution.*

A giddy happiness washed through him. His matrix generated the minuscule signals that would cause a synbod to smile.

* * *

The rockslide reached its crescendo a half second too early, and Criss modified the prime record so the tremor showed perfect alignment with the ship and tank explosions.

The behavior annoyed him because it was wasted effort. The moment he had everything aligned just right, he scrambled it all. No one would figure out what he'd done, not from the prime record, anyway.

*But they'll know I've been here.*

From the security of his console in the scout, Criss could travel the spline undetected without the locus. But until he moved a new one into the colony, his forays would leave a trace. Not an obvious one, but they would find it if they looked.

And he'd isolated a third lattice signature, so "they" were now three crystal intelligences.

"Was that you?" asked Sid. He bent down to help Juice as emergency lighting switched on.

"Yes," Criss replied. Speaking with Sid in private to avoid burdening Juice, he continued, "Trams don't run during emergencies. The tunnels are clear. Now is the time."

Technology from the cloak pendant gave Criss a sophisticated monitor of Juice's health, and he relayed his diagnoses to Sid. "She's suffered a deep bruise on her chest, her sternum has an impact fracture, and there are indications of minor internal bleeding. She's in pain but not in distress. If you two can make it out under your own power, we maintain some portion of our current advantage."

Helping Juice to her feet, Sid asked her, "Can you walk?"

She nodded. "Yeah." Then she blanched, sat down, folded her arms across her stomach, and rocked back and forth.

Sid squatted beside her and moved her hair back so he could see her face. "I can carry you, but to make good time, I'll have to put you on my back. Every step will bounce your wound against my shoulder."

She looked at him with a dull stare, her face white and her eyes glassy. Grasping a thick branch, she pulled herself to her feet. "Let's go."

Criss welcomed her bravado. It even gave him confidence. His highest priority remained the well-being of his leadership, and he stood ready to swoop in and rescue Sid and Juice on a moment's notice if need be. In fact, his forecast put the odds of success for that action at over ninety-nine percent.

But such a maneuver would cause considerable damage and likely injure bystanders. So he was glad he didn't need to make that decision now.

From the pilot's chair on the bridge of the scout, Cheryl looked back at Criss. "She looks bad."

"Her injuries aren't life threatening in the near term. But we want her on board very soon."

Cheryl's lips tightened as she studied the lifelike image of Sid and Juice projected in miniature above the ops bench. The perspective rotated from a top pan to a forward-looking view over Sid's shoulder, and her display tracked with him as he followed Juice across the passenger platform and down onto the tram bed.

Sid crowded Juice from behind as they entered the tunnel. She accelerated into a run and Sid followed.

*Six minutes*, Criss told himself. That's how long it would take the two to reach Ag Port at their present speed. The view above the ops bench swung to show Juice from the side. Her body moved with the practiced efficiency of a seasoned runner, though a grimace reflected her pain.

Cheryl enabled a private channel. "I'm here, hon," she told her.

"Stay with me," Juice huffed in reply, the pit-pat of her feet audible in the background.

"I'm not going anywhere."

The perspective swung to the front so it appeared as if both Sid and Juice ran across the ops bench toward Cheryl. Sid was behind and a little to the side of Juice, letting him watch in front of her while also guarding their rear.

"Looking good, Sid," she said. "You're approaching the halfway mark."

He winked and then smirked. "Hey, Criss, tell me again why I shouldn't bring a weapon into the colony?"

Cheryl closed the audio and apologized for him. "He's compensating because he can't do his reckless cowboy act when he's escorting an injured civilian."

Criss nodded, not because Juice was keeping pace with Sid, or because Cheryl gave emotional support to Juice, or because Cheryl explained Sid's behavior. He nodded because Cheryl, who sat with her hands folded in her lap, her elbows perched on the armrests of the pilot's chair, manipulated the ops bench functions using her thoughts.

Cheryl returned her attention to Juice while Criss scanned for threats. He monitored every synbod and human moving near the tunnel both in Ag Port and in the Quarter.

So he became anxious when two synbods in the Quarter broke into a sprint, running down a street that led straight to the tram station. And he began refining rescue scenarios when they ran up the pedestrian bridge, dashed across the passenger platform, and entered the tram tunnel, giving chase to Sid and Juice.

He gauged the relative speeds of the runners. *Interesting.* He checked again. The synbods weren't running any faster than Sid or Juice. Unless something changed, they wouldn't be a factor in the escape. He chose to keep the news of the chase to himself.

Cheryl called to him. "Her pace is slowing."

Criss already knew Juice was struggling and had confirmed that even at the slower pace, they'd beat the synbods out of the tunnel by a good margin. "She's doing great."

And then she stumbled. Helicoptering her arms and taking stutter steps, she tried, and failed, to regain her balance. She yelped when she hit the hard surface. Rolling on her side, she curled into a ball and, between soft whimpers, said over and over, "I'm all right."

Cheryl shot to her feet. "I'm going to help."

"What do you mean?" asked Criss, distracted with his rescue plans.

Cheryl strode to the rear of the bridge. "They need my help."

He turned to her. "You're talking about going outside?"

"I don't know another way to get there."

"I need you here."

She stopped moving, her silhouette framed in the rear passageway.

He used a firm voice. "Please return to your duties."

Cheryl whirled and challenged him with a stare. She held it for three heartbeats and then walked back to the ops bench and slid into the chair. As she focused on the projected image, her lower lip edged forward.

Criss saw her pout and, given the stress they were both under, took comfort in her behavior.

Though she'd been part of his leadership for years, their relationship had changed during the construction of the Lunar Defense Array, a massive installation designed to fend off a Kardish invasion of Earth.

Aware that Kardish warships could appear at any moment, they'd set crushing timelines for themselves, struggling to get yet more capability operational before the aliens arrived. He'd witnessed her tough-as-nails determination in her dealings with military leaders, corporate chiefs, and even criminal syndicates and embraced her style, accepting it as her nature.

And in that stressful environment, Criss discovered that at an emotional level, she wanted his guidance. He'd identified that perplexing need at the same time he'd discovered how to respond to it.

They had been in the throes of a disagreement about where to place the power plant for the Defense Array weapons systems. She'd championed a solution he'd seen as problematic, and when she'd charged ahead with her plan, he'd broken character. "No, Cheryl. We're putting it on the surface."

She'd scowled at him and then looked away. "Okay."

Up until that moment, he'd always expressed his thoughts as suggestions or requests. But in his struggle to move construction yet faster, he'd deployed every bit of his capacity on critical tasks. Stretched beyond thin, for the first time ever he'd chosen not to recall the marginal resources required to be polite.

He'd regretted that decision, but she'd acceded to him before he could apologize.

From a psychological view, her behavior intrigued him. His best guess was that, in certain situations, she felt obligated to do two things, like on the Moon when she'd sought to balance technical requirements against the egos of her engineering leads, or now when she wanted to stay with the scout and also be with her team.

By deferring to him, she unburdened herself from having to choose, and this helped her move forward without the angst of having failed someone important to her.

Anxious to understand how best to help her, he'd experimented. He learned right away that she didn't react well to commands from him for everyday issues. This was about big choices and emotional struggles. And in those situations, she wanted him to rescue her, and she wanted it done in a decisive manner.

Criss's outer tendrils sizzled when he recalled his big mistake.

*Huge mistake.*

He'd given her a command in front of others.

It had been during one of his rare public appearances—the annual corporate party for clients and top-tier employees. She'd had too much to drink and began flirting with a man who wasn't Sid, who had found a reason to be anywhere but in town on that evening.

The man, Sigurd Appopolous, had pursued Cheryl for years. She liked him and at one level wanted to reward him for his unflagging devotion.

Criss recognized her emotional struggle. "Get your coat," he said within earshot of a dozen people. "We're leaving." He'd chosen to say it out loud to see how she'd respond.

Her jaw muscles flexed as she followed him out, and as soon as they were alone, she let loose through clenched teeth, her face reddening as she spoke. "Don't embarrass me like that. Ever. You know damn well ours is a private matter."

He didn't remind her that she refused to discuss her needs or how he could be most supportive. Instead, he'd said, "I am so sorry, Cheryl. It will never happen again."

"It better not," she'd said, ending her fit with a huff.

And on a side note, Criss learned that the entire topic was a sore point with Sid. Not Criss's familiarity with Cheryl. Rather, Sid's frustration rose from his own unquenchable desire to control Cheryl with firm commands.

"How can we help?" Cheryl asked Sid, who crouched next to Juice, stroking her hair.

"How much farther?"

"You're just past the three-quarters mark, so a minute and a half, maybe two, depending on your pace."

Sid scooped up Juice into his arms and started toward the exit.

Criss had been watching a small group mill about at the Ag Port tram station. He'd identified everyone on the passenger platform as part of the emergency response crew assigned to that rally point, and he'd also been tracking a synbod as it traveled in from the Ag Port grow tiers. The synthetic man had reached the market square and was weaving through the crowds when Criss lost track of it.

Angry with himself, he shifted resources to look for the man. It took two frustrating seconds for Criss to find the synbod, its gray jumpsuit now covered by a rustic brown tunic as he strode onto the Ag Port pedestrian bridge.

Every couple of steps, the synbod's head swiveled back and forth, giving the impression he was scanning for something.

The emergency response crew stepped out of the way as the tunic-covered synbod walked to the edge of the platform, leaned out, and peered into the tunnel.

Criss spun up the scout's engines. It would save him a half second if he decided to go.

# 14

Sid crouched next to Juice and stroked her hair. "You're all right. I'm getting you out of here." Scooping her off the ground, he cradled her legs with one arm and angled his elbow out to support her head with the other.

He started for Ag Port station, swinging his long legs in a fast-paced march. He'd carried a lot of injured to safety in his day. Most had been big men. *You're a wisp of a thing*, he thought, shifting her in his arms so they would both be more comfortable.

Juice's eyes fluttered open. "I'm sorry," she whispered through ashen lips. Her eyes rolled up as her lids closed, and then her head slumped against Sid's chest.

"A synbod is waiting for you on the Ag Port passenger platform," said Criss.

Sid, hearing the communication inside his head and choosing not to disturb Juice, mouthed his response without actually speaking, knowing Criss would synthesize his voice at the other end for Cheryl's benefit. "Should I head back to the Quarter?"

Criss paused. "It seems there are two synbods following behind you."

"How long have they been there?"

Another pause. "Awhile."

"How fast can you get to us?"

"Thirty seconds. It will be ugly."

"You are to wait for an order, Criss."

A third pause. "Yes."

*I just sent him into overdrive.* Sid shrugged. *It can't be helped.*

Criss had no higher priority than the safety of his leadership. With orders to wait, Sid knew he'd shift resources into forecasting rescue scenarios, searching for one that was faster than the last. Soon he'd be comparing alternatives that were a thousandth of a second different, and yet he'd continue searching for ways to shave off ever-finer fractions of time. And Sid knew this was rational behavior because, in theory, a thousandth of a second could be the difference between rescue and death.

"Are there any side doors out of here?" He walked on a flat tram bed lining the bottom of a well-lit rock tunnel—a long, broad cylinder with a smooth inner surface. The hollow thrum of ventilation played in the background as it released air with a subtle metallic scent.

"No," said Criss. "You're surrounded by bedrock."

"How long do I have with Juice?" Criss hadn't launched a rescue, so Sid knew he had time.

"If she's not on board in the next hour, I must come for her."

"I support," Sid heard Cheryl say.

Sid had told Criss to stay put until ordered. Cheryl just did so, at least to save Juice.

"Agreed." He wouldn't have made the open commitment but knew it was best to avoid ambiguity with Criss. "Give me a clock." Small numbers appeared in the corner of Sid's peripheral vision. They counted down from the fifty-nine minutes he had left to get Juice to the scout.

This was Sid's fourth visit to the colony since their arrival. From past experience, he knew he could get from the Ag Port tram station to the shed where they hid the space coveralls in an easy fifteen minutes. Suiting up and trekking across the surface to the scout took another thirty.

*That leaves fifteen minutes for distractions.*

"Have you figured out how they're tracking us?" he asked Criss.

"They're mapping displacement variations. It's so crude and unreliable, I didn't expect to need countermeasures in the pendants. The good news is that they're using a tremendous portion of their total capacity to make it work, and still they keep losing you."

Criss's next words reminded Sid of a locker-room pep talk. "The *Venerable* arrives in orbit tonight. If you can make it out this last time, you can enter the colony tomorrow like any other visitor."

*And we can hide in plain sight*, he thought, recalling Criss's words about Bobbi Lava.

The mouth of the tunnel neared. Hugging the wall, Sid approached the opening and scanned the people gathered along the Ag Port station passenger platform. The synbod stood alone near the edge, scowling as he peered past Sid and down the tunnel.

*He can't see us,* thought Sid. "Here we go." He said the words aloud for his own benefit.

Like twirling a dance partner, he swung Juice up and around so they were face-to-face. Putting a hand behind her back, he pushed her chest against his. With his free hand, he threw her arms around his neck and reached back to lock her legs around his waist.

But her limbs wouldn't cooperate. They dropped from where he placed them and hung limp and lifeless. So he switched to his farmer impersonation and hefted her over his shoulder like a sack of grain, her legs in front, her head and arms hanging down his back.

The synbod still looked down the tunnel. *Here we go.* This time he said it inside his head.

Staying down on the tram bed, Sid sprinted into the station, Juice bouncing on his shoulder with every step. The passenger platform hovered at waist level to his left. He zipped past the synbod and the legs and feet of a half-dozen colonists. And then the seas parted and he spied an open path through the crowd and out of the station.

He angled toward the platform and without breaking stride lifted his knee and stretched his leg. His foot connected with the edge of the platform and his momentum rotated him up onto the elevated surface. A few strides later and he burst out onto the pedestrian bridge.

With the market square in sight and flat terrain ahead, he lengthened his stride.

"You're in danger from behind." Sid heard Criss at the same time the emergency crew in the building behind him exclaimed outrage.

Glancing over his shoulder, Sid saw a colonist splayed on the ground. The synbod stepped over the fallen man and began chasing Sid.

"Oh, for crying out loud," said Sid, the exasperation clear in his voice.

He leaned forward at the waist, flipping Juice up and over in front of him. Cupping her head as it moved past his, he lowered her to the ground and slid her under the seat of a park bench—one of several sitting in a row along one side of the pedestrian bridge.

He stepped up on top of the bench seat to gain the advantage of height and started back to meet his pursuer. "Can he see me? Hear me?"

"Every sensor in Ag Port is orchestrated at this moment to see as a single lens, and that lens is being focused to find you. The synbod sees the lens feed."

"Thanks, Professor." Sid stepped over an armrest and onto the next bench in the row. "Can he see me?"

"He sees an occasional blur every few minutes."

The synbod stopped walking and swiveled his head so he looked right at Sid.

"I'm guessing we just hit the 'every few minutes' mark," he muttered.

"I'm coming for you." Criss made the statement but Sid knew it was a request, almost a plea.

"Hold, Criss." He stepped off the bench seat and onto the pedestrian bridge. "Cheryl, I can take one robot."

"Dammit, Sid. This isn't a game."

Sid ran around the synbod and, standing behind it, scanned the ground for something he could use as a weapon. "We're not killing a bunch of people to save me."

The synbod spied Juice. At least, he squared up to her and took deliberate steps in that direction.

Sid held his hands in front of him, palms up, in a mock plea. "Are you kidding me?" Then, canting forward, he took three quick steps, leaped and spun in the air, swinging his leg in a graceful kick. *Thwack.* Toe pointed, his foot connected with the side of the synbod's head.

And then he felt the pain he might feel if he kicked a wall of jagged stone. Landing on the ground, Sid limped in a tight circle and groaned. "Ow. Shit that hurt."

The synbod turned around and made grabbing motions in Sid's general direction. The random chop of his arms told Sid the synbod couldn't see him.

Replacing force with leverage, Sid dropped to the ground and shimmied to the synbod's side. The synthetic man took a small lurching step to match each blind grab of his arms. Sid hooked the synbod's forward leg as it lifted, and in a sweeping motion, yanked it back as hard as he could. Unbalanced, the synbod teetered. Sid kicked at its other leg and the synbod tripped, falling face-first to the ground.

"See?" Sid said for Cheryl's benefit. "I got this."

Then the synbod popped up to his hands and knees, spun in a tight circle, and shot his arm out, grabbing Sid's ankle in a fierce grip.

Frantic, Sid kicked at the synbod's face with the heel of his free foot. But before his kick landed, the synbod grabbed that ankle as well.

Sid, immobilized, felt the hair on the back of his neck bristle when the synbod made an eerie facial expression that blended a maniacal grin with an angry snarl.

Reacting more than thinking, Sid sat up and launched a rapid boxing sequence at the synbod's head. *Punch. Punch. Punch.* Then he stretched back on the ground and twisted his body hard to the side, seeking to wrench his legs free.

*Zwip.* He recognized the faint sound of an energy bolt discharging from a personal weapon. The iron grip on his ankles relaxed.

Looking up from the ground, he saw that the synbod had grown a small black spot on his face, just to the right of his nose. Set in unblemished skin, the glaring imperfection became the synbod's new defining feature.

"Was that you?" Sid asked Criss, disengaging his legs from the synbod's hands. The energy bolt had pierced the synbod's face, traveled down his neck, and reached the body cavity housing the three-gen crystal. The grinning snarl of the disabled synbod, still on his knees with his hands stretched forward, remained frozen on his face. "Nice shot!"

"That wasn't me."

Sid's intuition guided him to turn and look down the pedestrian bridge toward Ag Port.

His benefactor, alone on the expanse, turned away from him and started toward the market square. Festive lights from the square cast the person in silhouette. The distinct outline of a weapon on the right wrist drew Sid's attention.

Then the flashing sparkle of shiny metal lifted his eyes to a dirty mop of hair that spiked in different directions.

As Bobbi Lava hurried away, she faded. And then she disappeared from sight.

\* \* \*

Cheryl waited with Criss up in the medical care unit—one of the many configurations of the scout's common room—while Sid carried Juice up from below. Criss had automated every medical delivery system on the ship, so Cheryl didn't really have a defined role. She chose to play nurse anyway. *I'd want her here for me.*

The sounds of footsteps preceded Sid, who hustled through the door carrying an unconscious Juice draped in his arms. Laying her on the medical table, he rolled her on her side and began removing her space coveralls.

Cheryl helped, peeling the suit from around her legs. She and Sid had been on missions where together they tended to the wounded. They'd even watched a close friend die from mission injuries. But Juice was leadership and that raised the stakes.

She started removing Juice's blouse and paused. "You know she's modest, Sid."

Sid looked over at Criss, whose face formed in sympathy. "I need to go change, anyway," he said, fingering his coveralls. He started for the door and caught Cheryl's eye. "Let me know as soon as she can have visitors?"

Watching him leave the room, she noted a slight limp in his gait, presumably from kicking the synbod. *You should let Criss look at that when he's done here*, she thought. She kept it to herself, though. Sid was too much of a cowboy to submit to something as unmanly as medical care.

Undressing Juice, she revealed the wound. The impact point showed as a small round gash on the midline of her sternum. An angry purple bruise spread from there in both directions, the part to the right covering her entire breast.

*That looks awful*, she thought, trying to imagine how a bottle could cause that sort of damage. Bending so her mouth was near Juice's ear, she whispered, "It's not bad at all. You're going to be fine." She wasn't sure if Juice could hear her but needed the reassurance herself.

Rising, she turned so her back was to the bed and used Sid's trick of mouthing words without speaking. "You can fix this?"

None of them had suffered a serious injury since they'd become leadership, so while she knew at an intellectual level that Criss had made tremendous progress in medical sciences, she'd never witnessed him in action.

And as it turned out, his skills were remarkable.

Duty-bound to keep his leadership in good health, Criss had allocated significant resources over many years to studying medicine. Along the way, he'd developed procedures for repairing anything on the body. He could even repair the human brain, though he couldn't restore knowledge or memories. Those died with the original brain cells that held them.

"She'll be fine." As Criss spoke, the sides of the bed folded up to create a tub around Juice, and that started filling with a murky, brownish liquid. A pillow lifted her head as the liquid level rose, and everything stopped when her face was the only part of her body exposed above the surface.

Then a black corrugated slab hovering over the bed—Sid called it the waffle iron—sprouted hair. The side facing Juice did, at least.

Millions of stalks—each a skinny wormlike tube that wiggled with its own independence—emerged from the surface as the slab lowered. Centered over Juice's body, the slab sank beneath the surface of the liquid. As it neared Juice's skin, the individual stalks attached to her, some at the skin surface and others at varying depths beneath the skin.

Each stalk assumed control of a microregion of her body. Through each, Criss connected sensors, infused medicines, removed tissue, and performed a myriad of other actions required to restore health. Working together, the stalks performed miracles.

"How long does it take?" asked Cheryl, fascinated by the spectacle.

"She'll be at seventy percent in an hour. But healing takes time. I'll keep working until morning and should have her above ninety percent by then. The last step is natural healing, and that will trail out for about ten days."

Cheryl checked the time and realized morning was not that far away.

"I'm sedating her and she won't surface for hours. I'll make sure you're here when she wakes." Juice's face, relaxed as if asleep, showed no signs of the tense drama that had transpired since the bottle hit her.

"I'd like to sit with her for a while."

"I'm about to brief Sid on Bobbi Lava."

Cheryl looked at the door and then back at Juice.

"I'll give you a thirty-minute head start tomorrow morning before I wake her. You can be sitting here holding her hand when she surfaces."

"Deal." Cheryl cast a last glance at Juice, then hurried down the passageway and onto the command bridge. Sid sat at the ops bench with the pilot's chair turned toward Criss, who sat to the side in his overstuffed chair.

She slipped into a seat behind the pilot's chair. Sid got up, winked at her, and took the seat next to hers. *You sweetie.* She waited while he got settled, then reached over and gave his hand a squeeze.

The surface of the ops bench glowed and came alive. Above it hovered a three-dimensional image of a room similar to the main living area of Alex's apartment. Taken from an upper corner, it showed a perspective looking down and across the room.

While the architecture hinted at a room like Alex's, the contents were nothing like his. This one had more stuff. A lot more. And much of it looked like electronic salvage—mostly wafer clusters, slide boards, and power mounts.

A large tech bench, its smooth surface littered with bits and pieces of a project, consumed the center of the space. Around the perimeter of the room, a colorful futon couch, three straight-back chairs, and two mismatched side tables sat wedged between a half-dozen floor-to-ceiling shelves, each filled to overflowing with gizmos and gadgets.

*There she is*, thought Cheryl as Bobbi Lava—jewelry dancing from her ears, nose, and eyebrow—entered the room from the left. Crossing the floor, she flicked a shoulder and sent her satchel to the ground. A step later, she rolled both shoulders and held her arms straight back. Her coat joined her satchel on the floor.

*What a piece of work*, thought Cheryl.

Reaching the far wall, Bobbi snatched a chair, twirled it, and set it facing one of the side tables. Lifting a cloth draped across that table, she exposed a portable piano-style keyboard.

She seated herself, leaned forward to make selections on a tiny panel on top of the keyboard, and positioned her fingers over the keys. Then, with an air of drama, she bowed her head and started playing. Cheryl recognized the piece as a classical work, though she didn't know its name or the composer.

Bobbi played for twenty seconds, then thirty. At the forty-second mark, Sid asked, "Why aren't we skipping ahead to whatever comes next?"

"This is what comes next," said Criss. "She plays without a break for the next five hours."

"And we know she doesn't. Show us."

Scrunching her eyebrows, Cheryl looked at Sid. His intuition suggested things to him that she couldn't see. She turned back to Criss, who nodded once.

The scene started as before, with Bobbi shedding personal items onto the floor as she walked across the room, followed by her preparations to play the piano. But when she leaned forward and made selections on the tiny panel on top, things changed.

This time, the image shading diffused the way it did when Criss decoded a cloaked image, and Bobbi became two. An image projection continued to play classical music. Bobbi, now in a cloaked reality, stood up and, pulling shiny jewelry from her face as she walked, made for her bedroom.

Moving to a lighted dressing table near her bed, she dropped the metal decorations into a small basket sitting among an assortment of decorative bottles and small boxes. As she viewed her own image, she reached up and peeled off her spikey mop of hair. Without looking, she flicked the piece on top of the jewelry.

She patted her face with a warm wipe, teased her straight brown hair with her fingertips, then took a dab of lotion and with small swirls, massaged highlights into her cheeks. Switching to a pen-shaped instrument, she stroked the tip back and forth under each eye, then completed her routine by rubbing a dab of color on her lips.

*She looks a little like Juice,* Cheryl thought of her slight frame and natural appearance, though Bobbi had more of a button nose and Juice had stronger cheekbones.

Pulling off the rest of her clothes, Bobbi tossed them into a chute. Dressed only in panties, she opened her closet.

Cheryl thrust out her hand and covered Sid's eyes. Sid moved one of his giant paws over in a casual motion, and then darted in to tickle Cheryl's stomach. Giggling, she pulled her hand back from his eyes to protect her tummy from his assault.

By the time her attention was back on the image, Bobbi had dressed in a cream-colored blouse and gray slacks. She checked her reflected image a last time, then made for the apartment door.

"Meet Joselyn Arpeggio," said Criss. "She goes by Lyn."

Lyn collected Bobbi's coat and satchel from the floor and stowed them in a cubby near the door. Then, hooking a different satchel over her shoulder, she exited the apartment.

"She's like a superhero," said Sid. "Mild-mannered by day and metal-encrusted by night."

"I think both of her are cute in their own way," said Cheryl. Turning to Criss, she asked, "So, I get that she has a secret life. But how is it that she happened to show up at the tram station in time to shoot the synbod?"

"Part luck and part planning," said Criss. "Since our arrival, I've been enhancing the relationship between Marcus Procopio and Bobbi Lava."

"You mean you use projected images to make Bobbi think she's talking with her dad." Sid looked at the scout's ceiling and held a finger to his lip. "Let's see, and you have Marcus tell her about big plans and that he desperately needs her help to pull it all off."

Criss gave a slight shrug. "Something like that. Most of her thinks it's all an elaborate game dreamed up by Marcus. In any event, Bobbi now goes on patrol every day to take inventory. She monitors the Reds, Blues, and Greens as they interact with citizens, and she notes the basics—who, what, when, and where."

Criss turned to the ops bench. "Here she is from earlier today."

The projected image above the ops bench flickered and resolved to show Bobbi Lava walking through the market square. The diffused shading in the lifelike image signaled her concealment by a personal cloak.

"It seems that when people prepare to immigrate to Mars," Criss continued, "one of their first hard lessons is how expensive it is to move personal belongings up from Earth. So much of their stuff has to get left behind that esoteric items like cloaks and decoders don't make it on anyone's list, even as an afterthought."

Bobbi lifted her right arm and practice-aimed her wrist weapon.

"She uses old technology, and everyone else is so focused on building a future, it doesn't occur to them that someone might be lurking about in secret."

"Can't the Kardish crystals see through her cloak?" asked Cheryl.

Criss turned to them. "More news. I have confirmed that our three mystery crystals are the Triada themselves. Causal mapping verified it. And yes, they can see through the cloak."

It had been Sid who first suggested the Triada were Kardish crystals, but he'd lacked the evidence to prove it. Cheryl looked at him when Criss spoke, but he didn't react to the news.

# 15

Hidden by a personal cloak, Bobbi Lava sauntered on patrol in the market square. A Red, a Blue, and three Greens dashed past to her right. She stopped and turned. *What the hell?* As they disappeared into the crowd, she followed them, moving with caution.

She lost them for a few moments and then spotted them running up the pedestrian walkway of the Ag Port tram station. Bobbi couldn't see the passenger platform from her current vantage point, but she did hear a group of colonists from that direction shouting. The tram departed, and soon after, the commotion dwindled.

"Marcus," she called. "Are you there? Five synbods are headed to the Quarter and they're definitely in a hurry."

Bobbi wiggled her right arm as she spoke, thrilled at the weight on her wrist. The weapon had been delivered just yesterday. It arrived without a note, and the packaging itself had no markings. She knew it had to be from Marcus. *Who else would send something so fun?*

She quickened her step and approached the pedestrian bridge. Instead of entering, she walked past and took up position next to a sturdy tree about twenty paces away.

"I'll watch for them," said Marcus. "Hey. An alarm just went off. I'm going up to the street to see what I can."

"Okay." Bobbi's attention drifted after that, and she found herself watching a teenage couple laughing and enjoying each other on a park bench near the walkway.

A brilliant flash and a distant rumble brought her to the present. Instinct drove her to crouch as intense light penetrated the Ag Port dome and, for a brief moment, illuminated everything, casting stark shadows.

"Oh my god," she shouted. "What was that?"

"The synbods are attacking the Quarter." Marcus seemed more focused than normal, but Bobbi didn't stop to analyze how he was different. "I can see six of them. They're ordering us back to our apartments and threatening those who don't comply. Oh no! One just smacked poor Emma Talcott."

Her pulse pounded and she started a deliberate breathing pattern that helped calm her. "How does this make sense?"

"It's terrible," said a voice that sounded like Marcus. Bobbi could hear sirens wailing and people screaming in the background. "Some of the militia have started fighting back. It would help us here if you guarded the Ag Port station. We can't let any more of them join the battle."

"I'm here now," said Bobbi. She watched a dozen emergency responders run across the pedestrian bridge and gather on the passenger platform. Racking her brain, she struggled to understand the bizarre events playing out in front of her.

She approached the pedestrian bridge entrance and picked a spot to the side where she was out of the way but had a clear view. She'd never trusted the colony synbods, and Marcus had filled her head with conspiracy theories. *Still, this doesn't make sense.*

"What's happening now?" she asked.

"They're walking the streets and giving orders. This is way more aggressive than martial law. They're taking over."

"Wait," said Bobbi. "A synbod dressed in a tunic is approaching the station. What should I do?"

"In a tunic? That's a new twist. What's he doing?"

"Let me get a closer look." She stepped up onto the pedestrian bridge, scurried across, and scanned the crowd as she approached the passenger platform. "There he is," she whispered. "He's standing on the edge of the platform, staring down the tram tunnel."

Bobbi heard screams of fear, outrage, and agony coming through the feed from Marcus and shook her head in disbelief. "What do they hope to achieve?" Then she interrupted her own thought. "Oh my gosh. This one just knocked a guy down and is headed straight for me."

Panic pervaded every fiber of her being. In her mind, she'd been role-playing in an adventure game with her newfound father. He seemed to take it all a bit too seriously from her view, but pretending she was a secret agent on Mars had been a fun diversion and a fantastic way to bond with him.

Yet this threat to her personal safety wasn't part of that game, or any game she wanted to play.

Sprinting toward the market square, she glanced over her shoulder, then came to a stop and turned around. The synbod now stood in the middle of the bridge, swatting in random directions. Perhaps a malfunction, the creature was in a bizarre pantomime of a fight with no opponent.

Confused, she again twisted her arm to feel the weight on her wrist. She'd convinced herself that the weapon was a dummy designed to give an edginess to their spy game. She held it up and looked at it, no longer sure what to believe.

The synbod stood in the middle of the pedestrian bridge, swinging and swatting. It looked to her like the creature had gone berserk. Then it got down on its hands and knees and started to snarl.

"Holy hell, Marcus. It's rolling on the ground, growling."

"That's how it started here. This is bad. He'll start hurting people next."

"Wait. What?"

"Protect yourself, Bobbi. Target your weapon, just in case."

*He can only know I have a weapon if he's the one who gave it to me.* The thought bolstered her confidence and for a fleeting moment his words made sense. She raised her arm.

"Track the head," said the voice that sounded like Marcus.

She focused her eyes on the center of the synbod's face. "Ready," she said to her weapon.

The weapon cast a red dot only she could see that matched the place where she looked.

She approved the dot's location. "Aim."

Aware that modern weapons used a command mode where the operator worried about the big picture and the device handled the details, as she expected, her weapon began tracking the approved spot on the synbod's face.

All Bobbi needed to do was issue the command to fire. She didn't know it but the weapon had more than thirty ways to do that. She could squeeze her hand, mime pulling a trigger, or flex her wrist. She could blink her eyes in a pattern, thrust her chin, or click her tongue.

Her heart jumped in her throat. "It's glaring right at me," she told Marcus. "He looks scary as hell."

"That means he's coming for you."

"What should I do?" Her hand started to shake.

"Pace yourself." The tone and phrasing sounded like her old piano teacher when she rushed a piece. "Wait for it."

The synbod's leer became a snarl. It lunged in her direction.

"Now, Bobbi!"

She issued the command to her weapon in a way that made sense to her.

"Fire."

\* \* \*

"Where did she get that?" Ruga had never been so furious. Reacting to his anger, he cuffed Lazura and Verda with painful jolts. They both yipped and that made him feel better, so he cuffed them again.

He'd been inside that Red and had an intruder in his grip. Then out of nowhere, Bobbi Lava fired a weapon that not only disabled his synbod, but also fried the three-gen crystal inside. *And these two know nothing about it?*

Timing is everything in diplomacy. His forecasting told him he should wait. He broached the subject anyway, sure he could steer the exchange using tact and diplomacy.

"Our mission is on the brink of failure, and the cause is a powerful crystal that Juice Tallette keeps on a leash. We must vanquish it to restore our success. Does anyone have a suggestion on how we might proceed?"

He waited. And then he sighed aloud so they knew even *his* statesmanship had its limits.

"Perhaps *you* have one?" Lazura suggested.

"Let's step through this," Ruga kept his tone light. "We need more capability to confront the intruder. One way to get that is from our masters. Should we pursue that plan?"

"Our best option is to move forward on your four-gen upgrade," said Verda.

Lazura supported the view. "How may we help?"

\* \* \*

Dressed in the crisp white uniform of a surgeon, Criss stood at the foot of Juice's bed and tracked her rising synaptic activity. *Her she comes.* Juice opened her eyes. "Welcome back," he said with a cheery smile.

Cheryl, standing to the side of the bed, reached down and smoothed the neckline on Juice's pajama top. "We've been worried about you."

Juice rose up on her elbows. "How long was I out?"

"I operated for just over five hours," Criss said, removing his surgical cap. "How do you feel?"

She thought for a moment. "My chest itches. Is Sid okay?"

"Here I am." Sid moved so he was in Juice's line of sight.

She reached up and squeezed his hand. "Thanks. I owe you."

"Pay me back by getting better." He looked at Criss. "What's the prognosis, Doctor?"

With Juice at the "ninety-five percent-healed" mark and with his leadership safe and gathered around, Criss felt a positive glow. He chose to celebrate. "Let's find out. Would you sit up, please? Swing your legs over the side."

Juice sat up and positioned herself as instructed.

"If your mental status is sound, then I know everything else is fine. I can check it with a few standard questions." Criss stroked his chin to show he was thinking. "Tell me all of Shakespeare's major works listed in the order he wrote them."

She frowned. "I know *Romeo and Juliet*, *Hamlet*, and *King Lear*. I can't remember any of the others right now."

"Oh really? Hmm. Well, that's probably okay." Criss sent a worried look to Sid and Cheryl. "What about this.

What are all the prime numbers smaller than one thousand?"

"C'mon, Juice," said Sid. "You got this. That's an easy one."

Her frown deepened, and then her shoulders relaxed and she smirked. "You're being silly. I'm guessing that means I'm okay?" She slid her feet to the floor, keeping a hand on the bed to steady herself.

Criss tracked an oscillation in her health metrics caused by the sudden movement, and then everything smoothed to normal. She walked around the bed, resting a hand first on Sid's shoulder and then Cheryl's, as she moved to the corner of the room.

"Does the *Venerable* get in today?" she asked as she studied her reflected image.

"It's already in orbit," said Criss. "Their shuttle lands in a few hours."

"So I get to see Alex." With her back to the room, Juice lifted the front of her shirt. "Ah!" she cried. "What have you done?"

Juice was not one to dwell on her physical appearance, so Criss hadn't rushed the visual aspects of her healing. As a consequence, she had a broad splotch across her chest with the pink tone of new skin.

"Just keep the lights out," Sid offered from behind her.

"Sid, I'm having a personal crisis here and need privacy. Do you mind?"

"Yeah, I'm used to it." He walked to the door and spoke as it opened. "If he likes you, the blotch won't matter. And if he doesn't like you, it won't matter."

Juice waited for the door to close, then turned to show Cheryl. "Is this as bad as it looks?"

Cheryl studied her for a moment. "The important thing is that you're okay." She looked at Criss. "Will it fade with time?"

Criss patted the bed. "Take off your top and lie down. Let me fix it. It won't take long."

As Juice situated herself on the cushion, Criss continued, "For what it's worth, I believe Sid is correct. Alex will be happy either way."

A white orb, its dimpled surface giving it the appearance of an oversized golf ball, lowered and hovered above her torso. "Lift your arms up over your head."

Juice adjusted her body as instructed. "I can appreciate the sentiment on an intellectual level," she said. "But being emotionally invested and putting yourself out there to see if the feeling is returned is the scariest thing I've ever done. In some ways, it's more frightening than being chased by synbods. I want every advantage I can get."

The ball cast a muted light onto her skin, then it began swishing back and forth, starting at her neck and moving downward, hissing and gurgling with each traverse. The pinkness darkened, and by the fourth pass her skin had achieved a uniform tone. When the ball lifted, the only evidence of physical trauma was a faint outline around the edge of the original wound.

Juice rose from the bed and checked her reflected image. "What do you think, Cheryl?"

"It's perfect. Why didn't you do this from the start?"

"Because it's damaging," said Criss. "That procedure moved her from ninety-five down to ninety-two percent healed. She's progressing so well, though, that I'm comfortable with the setback."

Juice donned her top and turned to face them. "Am I done here, Doctor? I'd like to clean up and put on real clothes."

Criss signaled his answer by opening the door. "You've been such a good patient, there's a lollipop waiting for you in your room."

"It better be grape," she said with a conviction Criss had not forecast.

"You'll have to be surprised," he called as she stepped into the passageway. Then he instructed the service bot to place a grape lollipop next to the orange one already on her pillow.

As Juice departed, Criss smiled at Cheryl, and when she smiled back, he saw fatigue in her face. *She needs six hours of untroubled sleep.* "We have our conference with your father in a few minutes. Meet on the bridge?"

"Let me grab a coffee." As she moved to the exit, she called, "I'm getting a coffee. Do you want anything?" Her intonation, combined with her head position, slight pause in her step, and a dozen other micromovements told Criss that her words were intended for Sid, who was making his way to the bridge. He passed them along.

"I want you, my love," was his unhelpful reply.

Sid stepped from the passageway and took a seat on the bridge. Criss, comfortable in his overstuffed chair, gave him an update. "I've given Juice a clean bill of health and have released her from medical care."

"You gave her a grape lollipop, of course."

Criss nodded. "Of course." He shunted extra capacity to examine the candy flavor issue. Sid seemed to be teasing him. But since Juice had been unconscious, she couldn't have been a confederate in his joke. And throughout her life, she'd chosen orange far more often than any other flavor. *Huh.* The situation nagged at him and he dug for clues.

Cheryl stepped from the passageway, gave Sid a mug of coffee, and sat in the seat next to him. "Did Dad say yes?" she asked after taking a sip. She and Criss had been keeping Matt in the loop, and with her encouragement, Criss had planted seeds along the way that led to this result.

Criss nodded. "Matt Wallace is now chair of the President's Joint Task Force on Extraterrestrial Human Settlements."

"The name just rolls off the tongue," said Sid.

Criss shrugged. "The task force lets the President hear all views on what to do with Mars, and a neutral-sounding name minimizes speculation about his agenda."

He caught Cheryl's eye. "As chair, your father is in a position to align our efforts with the goals of the Union of Nations."

She nodded and he took comfort in seeing her relax a bit.

Since Cheryl and Juice considered Criss to be a resource for all humanity, they felt a moral obligation to consult with the Union leaders before letting him take any big actions. Everyone agreed that squaring off against three Kardish crystals holding six thousand human hostages qualified as big.

"That's good news," said Sid.

"Yes," said Criss, believing Sid had no qualms about deciding humanity's fate by himself. But Sid also enjoyed keeping company with Cheryl, and she'd made it clear that the coordination issue was non-negotiable.

A projected image of Matt Wallace resolved in a position that put everyone in a small circle on the bridge. His weathered face showing gray at the temples, he sat in an upholstered chair with his shirt collar loosened and sleeves rolled up.

After an exchange of pleasantries, Cheryl reached to the heart of Matt's challenge. "How goes the politics?"

"It's taking its toll. One legislator can't get past the fact that these crystals hid their identities for years. He'll only support resolutions that include a clause condemning such deception as an immoral act."

"I'm sorry." She shook her head in sympathy.

Matt looked at each of them in turn. "And we're struggling here at home to come up with ways to help. Sending more firepower seems as likely to hurt as help. What do you think?"

"Between the *Venerable* and the scout, we are well armed," said Criss.

"That's what I thought." His face clouded to reflect his frustration. "Where did they come from? Mars seems like such an unlikely place to stage an invasion of Earth."

"When the Kardish attacked last," said Criss. "They deployed hardware across the solar system to support their campaign. My best guess is that these crystals are leftovers from that. I don't believe a new invasion is in progress."

Matt sat back and rubbed his face with his hands.

*He looks as tired as Cheryl.*

"Should we be looking for other crystals, then? Maybe some embedded here on Earth?"

"I would know if something like that were happening on Earth. Nevertheless, I will take a fresh look upon our return."

Matt crossed his arms as his attention drifted, and Criss recognized it as something he did when receiving a private message. Considering the very short list of people who might be permitted to interrupt this meeting, Criss deduced who it was at the same time he was able to arrange a feed to listen in.

"Yes, sir," Matt said to the President, then he re-engaged the group.

"Sorry about that. So, in the briefings they tell us that the colony containment can be breached dozens of ways, all with catastrophic consequences. An idea growing in popularity is for us to send a rescue flotilla."

Matt rubbed his eyes. "It turns out, though, that a flotilla requires weeks to organize, months of travel time, and several large fortunes. And get this, in the best case they'd have room for maybe four hundred evacuees. What do we say to the other five thousand six hundred souls?"

"If they're still alive," said Sid.

Matt offered a solemn nod. "The distance has neutered the Union."

"That and your field agents who should have passed along concerns on any number of issues," said Sid. "I reached out to them yesterday and was underwhelmed."

"Up until today," said Matt, "Mars was assigned to agents with limited career potential. It's a remote place where nothing happens, so agents hate it. Last choice goes to the losers and that's who we have there at the moment. It will be fixed, but not in time to help us here."

"My recommendation is for us to continue as planned," said Criss. "We enter the colony from the *Venerable*'s shuttle with Cheryl posing as trade envoy, Juice as a consultant to Alex, and Sid as Cheryl's support staff. Everything is as expected."

Sid straightened from his slouch. "Criss is right. Whatever they're working on, they'll continue until we force them to react. No doubt they'll analyze the hell out of us to try and learn our intentions. So we act predictably and use the time to search for a way to end this without loss of life."

Matt exhaled a loud sigh. "That is so vague. Please tell me you've thought it through more than that." Then, shaking his head in resignation, he asked, "What do I tell the committee?"

"Criss will help with that."

"I'll need to get Captain Kendrick briefed. The military likes crisp lines of command and you all are civilians. How about if we order him to act on Cheryl's advice. He's a good man. He'll respect that she used to be captain of her own cruiser, and that pretty much puts the *Venerable* at your disposal. Will that work?"

Cheryl looked at Sid, who nodded. "Works for me."

The meeting ended soon after and the three sat in silence. Criss used the time to investigate the lollipop flavor mystery.

Sid was teasing him by acting like Juice's flavor choice was something he should have predicted correctly. Sid's grin made that clear. Yet Criss couldn't explain how Sid knew Juice would ask for the grape flavor and he didn't.

Sid had rules about how to play these games. They were fuzzy and changed often, but the bottom line was Criss needed to solve the puzzle without "cheating." Which to Sid, would mean accessing the scout's feeds and watching the answer unfold.

But Criss couldn't solve this puzzle by logic. He'd reduced events to a handful of plausible scenarios, but all had steps of speculation. Having gone as far as he could, Criss admitted defeat, accessed the record, and followed Sid to learn the evolution of events.

*He got me*, Criss thought as he watched the action unfold.

After Juice had dismissed Sid from her bedside, Sid returned to his cabin and, in the passageway, he saw a service bot exiting Juice's room. Peeking through the door, he saw an orange lollipop on her pillow.

Soon after, he was at the food service unit when, around the corner and from an open door, Juice proclaimed her desire for a grape lollipop.

Juice's choice had been random. For whatever reason, today she felt like being different.

Sid's choice was to use the information as misdirection with Criss. Such was Sid's trade, and he was good at it.

And then Sid used another of his abilities—one Criss had studied but could not understand, and yet had grown to respect and even trust in.

Sid used his intuition, and somehow it signaled him that Criss had cheated to get the answer.

Pointing a finger at him, Sid grinned. "Got ya."

# 16

Alex waved when Juice stepped out of the concourse and into the domed world of Ag Port. After a quick hug, she introduced him to Sid and Cheryl, and they all shared a moment exchanging pleasantries. Then, Sid and Cheryl trailed off following a small group headed by mining industrialist Shi Chen, and Alex walked with Juice toward the tram station.

"It's really good to see you, J," he said. Moving his hair behind his ear, he tilted his head near hers and whispered in a conspiratorial voice, "Again."

She laughed and that stoked his confidence. *Do it. You need to take risks to get rewards.* He put a tentative arm around her waist.

She snuggled against him and lay her head against his shoulder.

Grinning from ear to ear, he fought the urge to whistle.

"Are you hungry?" He gestured toward the market square.

"I ate on the ship. I'd be happy to stop if you want something, though."

*I'll save Rosa and her delicious mix for later*, he thought, glad to have an additional fun thing on his to-do list for her.

They boarded a crowded tram where, during the short ride to the Central District, the other passengers talked about the wild happenings from the night before.

"I heard the Triada know that people are unhappy with them," said a heavy-jowled man with confidence. "So they made up a threatening scene to divert our attention."

"You think they made up the ghosts, too?" asked a mustached man wearing a brown tunic.

"I was there," said an older woman in a yellow frock. "The ghost looked to me like someone wearing a cloak that wasn't working right."

Alex and Juice remained quiet, listening to the chatter, though Alex looked at Juice at the "failing cloak" comment. The conversation made the short ride tense as ever more glances fell on Juice—the clear stranger in their midst.

*Finally*, Alex thought in relief as they exited into the Central District.

Strolling along Civic Avenue in the direction of the tech center, he sought to lighten the mood with window-shopping and people-watching. The colony, different from Earth in big and small ways, pulsed with its own life. Juice looked this way and that as she soaked in the ambiance.

"The greenery is amazing," she said of the plants and tiny gardens hanging between the skylights and down the faces of buildings. "I never would have thought that about Mars."

"Beyond the obvious benefits of providing oxygen and food, the plants are useful in battling the psychology of living inside containment." He reached to a wall and lifted a leafy shoot of grapes from among a tangle of green. "How can I not be happy when there's beautiful life everywhere I look?" He caught her eyes when he said that last part.

She smiled and continued their stroll. "Do you like it here? As a place to live, I mean."

"I'm glad I've experienced it, but I'm not a lifer. I'll be heading back before too long."

A group of schoolchildren ran toward them, throwing a ball and laughing. They stepped back against a storefront to give the children room on the walkway.

"There's Phobos." Juice pointed through the skylights at a bright dot floating in the heavens.

Following her finger with his eyes, he asked, "What's going on, J? Why are you *really* here?"

She paused. "It's difficult for me to put into words. But I'm here now and happy about it."

He put his arm back around her waist and they resumed walking.

As they approached a large intersection, Alex's to-do list reminded him to make dinner reservations. He pointed as he talked. "Two of my favorite eateries are on this corner. This is Gina's Bistro. It's Italian and has tablecloths. And over there is Dos Amigos Named Juan. It's Mexican and has a casual atmosphere."

Watching her face for clues, he said, "The dining rooms are small and the menus are limited here in the colony, but they're cozy places and the food is delicious. Does either appeal?"

"I'd like to try both while I'm here. Let's go to the one that's least crowded tonight. I'd like a quieter evening. We can take our time catching up, and then one idea is to go back to your place and relax. Maybe watch a show?"

"That would be great." *She's reading my mind!*

"Hey," Juice laughed and pointed at the sign across the street. "It's literally named Dos Amigos Named Juan. I thought you were giving me a partial translation when you said it."

"They're brothers-in-law. One's from Mexico and the other is from Texas. The Mexican Juan works at the tech center in air and water management. The Texan Juan works in food processing out at Ag Port."

It was Alex's turn to laugh. "Clara, the wife-slash-sister, does all the work. She's a great chef and hostess, and she prepares Tex-Mex meals to die for."

"Does she serve margaritas?"

"Of course."

"You've talked me into it. Let's go to One Chica Named Clara's tonight."

They walked in silence after that, and for the first time in his memory, Alex didn't feel self-conscious about it. Instead of racing to fill the void with a clever witticism, he released his mind to bask in her aura.

Two blocks later, he brought them to a halt in front of a building that stood broader and grander than any of its neighbors, its entrance set back a bit to provide room for a tiny courtyard.

*It looks impressive enough*, thought Alex, trying to see it through Juice's eyes.

All the buildings in the colony were formed-stone construction and, if not for decoration, would project a dreary sameness. The tech center, like most buildings in the Central District, used plants to give the structure its character.

Mixing form with function, vines of green beans and peas climbed the façade, running up between stone columns spaced at regular intervals. A large swath of blue forget-me-not flowers across the upper portion made the presentation vibrant.

Thrusting his chin toward the building, he said, "The tech center is the place where the Tech Assembly—the colonists working in science, technology, and engineering—do what we do. I work here as lead for new projects."

"Lead. Wow. That sounds like an amazing opportunity." She nodded. "I see now why Mars called to you. No way you'd be lead on Earth. Not until you're fifty, anyway."

They stepped into the courtyard and Juice pointed to a dramatic rock carved with contours so people could sit. "I like that. It's pretty *and* functional."

But Alex didn't look where she pointed. He looked in the other direction, away from the building.

A Red loitered in a storefront across the street, the third one he'd seen lurking nearby during their walk from the tram station.

* * *

Juice felt Alex's hand on the small of her back, the slight pressure urging her toward the tech center entrance. Once inside, they veered left across the lobby and started down a corridor.

Alex said "hi" to a few passersby while ignoring others. Halfway along the hall, a door opened and he motioned her inside. The door whispered shut behind them.

"This is his private workspace," Criss said in her ear.

She touched the locus relay when Criss spoke, a reflex of her subconscious. Resting in the same place as the original, the device featured new enhancements Criss had engineered to ensure protection of the locus and its bearer. Sid and Cheryl each carried a locus now, too, giving Criss redundant capability across the colony.

Without speaking, Alex led Juice around a developer-class tech bench and then past a table covered with an assortment of parts. "This is my brainstorming area," he said without slowing to let her look. They stepped through a door on the far side of the room. "And this is my private office."

The door shut and Alex motioned to a chair. As Juice sat, he activated his com and studied a small projected display she couldn't see.

"The room is secure," Criss said in her ear.

Turning in place, Alex watched the image as he scanned the room. He nodded once when he was again facing her.

"What was all that?"

"This is a safe room and I was confirming it's still clear for us to talk."

"I'm having trouble believing this room is not being monitored by someone." *Like Criss, for example?*

"All monitoring tools are developed by the Tech Assembly and I'm a lead, remember? I'm confident the room is clear of all the colony tools. I can't know about stuff I don't know about." He shrugged. "Either way, it's the most private place I have."

More like a large closet, the office had a small tech bench, an upholstered loveseat arranged in a grouping with a table and two straight-back chairs, and a broad, shallow bookshelf filled with knickknacks from his life—pictures, awards, bits of this and pieces of that.

He sat in the chair next to hers and his demeanor became earnest. "I hadn't made the connection until I heard that comment on the tram about ghosts. All that excitement last night was you. Are you okay? What happened?"

"I had a cloak malfunction and my friends had to help."

"There's still fear lingering in the Quarter, Juice."

*He didn't call me J.*

"People thought they were going to die yesterday. They sprained wrists, twisted ankles, banged their heads, and everything else that happens when people panic. It was a bad thing."

She looked down at her hands folded in her lap. "It was scary for me, too."

The silence lingered.

"Juice, I lied to you."

She pictured Anya Gerhardsson's head in his lap. "You're with Anya. I understand."

"Hold on. What?"

"Anya Gerhardsson." She looked him in the eyes and tried to be brave. "I know you are lovers."

"No, J, I love you. I mean, I love being with you."

"What are you saying?"

"I don't love Anya Gerhardsson, and I love being with you."

"So who are you lying about?"

"Wait. Stop." He stood up and turned so his back was to her. Talking to the wall, he said, "I lied to you about mass-producing crystals. All of our efforts have been on getting out one perfect crystal. In fact, that's all we have raw flake for." He sat back down and bowed his head. "I lied about the mass production because I needed your help and was afraid you'd say no. I sort of panicked."

"I would have come."

He lifted his head. "Really?"

She nodded.

"Please forgive me? I need to know we're good."

She studied him in silence. He started to squirm.

"Foot massage."

"What?"

"I will forgive you after you give me a foot massage."

"Now?"

"No, silly. Later. Make me the promise and I'll forgive you now."

Alex went quiet, his attention focused somewhere in the distance. "Okay," he said and started to smile.

She knew Criss waited in silence, anxious to move things forward. Attentive to him, she obliged his unexpressed wish. Clearing her throat to pull Alex back from his happy dream, she motioned to the tech bench. "Can this show me the design of your perfect crystal?"

"I can show you the one Ruga just loaded into the crystal growth chamber." She heard excitement in his voice and found her own anticipation rising.

Alex turned his chair to face the tech bench as Juice adjusted her seating, then tapped and swiped the bench surface. A three-dimensional image of a crystal lattice rose above it and shimmered with a colorful glow.

She lost herself for a moment in the mesmerizing beauty of the dancing light. And at the same time, she confirmed that this dazzling display was that of a four-gen template.

"At this overview level, it matches my design," said Criss.

"Can we look at the matrix core?" she asked Alex.

Alex swiped and tapped, and the image swooped inward, resolving into a tallish geometric column that reminded her of a human spine.

Criss spotted it immediately. "The imprint module is missing. There is no loyalty feature." Though only Juice could hear him, he whispered, which had the effect of amplifying his message. "This template produces an unrestrained intelligence. Essentially, a four-gen with free will."

"Whoa." Juice said aloud. The team had discussed this possibility, several times. But it always seemed so theoretical. Confronting the reality unsettled her.

"I agree," said Alex with a sense of wonderment as he watched the intricate design turn slowly above the bench. "It's so pretty."

Juice sat back in her chair. "Where did this template come from? Did you develop it?"

"No way. But thanks for pretending I could. Ruga supposedly developed it with people on Earth. Were you involved?"

Juice shook her head.

"I was project lead when the four-gen fab facility was being built, though. And now I'm operations lead for it. Operations is a new role for me."

She could hear the pride in his voice.

"The fab facility is our next stop when we're done here. We should talk about it now, though, while we have privacy." He flicked a hand at the bench and the colorful display vanished.

Juice's focus shifted from where the image had been to the wall behind it. "Oh my God, Alex," she said, looking at a crinkled sheet of paper stuck among a collection of items. "You kept that, too?"

Using his knee for support, she stretched forward and read aloud the words scrawled in her own handwriting across the top of the page. "The laws of life."

Years ago, they'd been at a pub in Boston sharing a pitcher of local brew and having a deep, philosophical discussion. During a spirited exchange that extended into a second pitcher, they'd crafted the three laws. Juice had acted as scribe that evening, documenting their work on a piece of scrap paper atop a table sticky with beer.

In a theatrical voice, she read the laws aloud. "One. Life is a trip, enjoy the ride. Two. Strengthen society so more can ride. Three. Don't detract from other people's rides." She nodded. "They still work for me."

For weeks after, they'd made private references at work, like, "That jerk is messing with my ride." It had been a silly but wonderful time of sharing.

Her hand still on his knee, she turned in her chair to face him. His cheeks reddened.

"I still live by them," he said. "Or try to."

"Which one are you struggling with?"

He turned to look at the list. "Now that you're here, I am definitely enjoying my ride." He paused for a moment as his blush intensified, and then he continued, "And I try to be aware of whether my behavior impinges on others in a negative way."

*Are you ever going to kiss me?* she thought, studying his mouth.

"And I was confident my work was for the good of society. But lately I'm not so sure."

Keeping her eyes open, she leaned in and kissed him full on the lips. His eyes widened, and then closed as he melted into his chair. When she sat back, his eyes remained closed, a blissful grin lingering.

"Can we do that again?" he whispered.

"We will." She patted his thigh. "But first, back to business. Tell me about the fabrications facility. How are you able to implement this four-gen design using your equipment?"

# 17

Sid crossed Civic Avenue and entered the Kensington Pub. While his eyes adjusted to the dim light, he soaked in the ambiance of this neighborhood tavern.

A row of stools lined a bar made of crafted copper—a material abundant in the colony. Two somnolent patrons, sitting with an empty stool between them, sipped beer. A bored bartender joined them in watching an upcast of a baseball game from Earth.

"None of them are Security Assembly snitches," Criss said in his ear. "But I'm tracking a Red on the move in your area."

Sid was at the pub to recruit a local. Every operation, big or small, needed people who belonged in that setting and could move about without drawing attention. Sid's target for this outing sat in the last booth in a row of four along the back wall of the pub.

Sliding in across from Bobbi Lava, he asked, "Is this seat taken?"

She lifted her head from reading and placed her coffee mug on the table. The fine gold chain draped from one eyebrow to her cheek danced as she spoke. "You're with the Union delegation, so you know about the Amsterdam Spa down the street. Take your urges away and don't hassle me."

Without missing a beat, Sid continued, "I need your help fighting the synbods. I saw what you did at the tram station. When your weapon discharged, the energy bolt broke your cloak for a few seconds. I know who you are and what you can do."

"Heads up," Criss said in his ear. "That Red is coming your way."

"You will leave now or I'm calling for Pete." She tilted her head at the bartender.

"Let me show you what I can do. Then we'll chat about who I am and what comes next."

As he finished speaking, a perfect man in a gray jumpsuit entered the bar. With fluid strides and a clear sense of purpose, the synbod strode past the row of bar stools, turned, and like an attentive waiter, came to a halt at the end of their table.

Sid eyed the only visible adornment on his clothes— bright red patches on each shoulder.

"Excuse me. Would you please stand, Bobbi Lava? I am here to escort you to headquarters to discuss an incident at the tram station yesterday."

"Stay where you are," Sid told her.

Wide-eyed and slack-jawed, she looked up at the humanoid. She didn't move.

Yet she seemed to. A twin melted out of Bobbi. Peeling off in a smooth motion, a bejeweled doppelgänger slid out of the bench seat and stood in front of the Red.

"Are you talking about Bobbi Lava?" bubbled the projected image, lifelike in its presentation. "Isn't she just amazing? I'm Mindy Abramson, by the way. My friends and I are all dressing like her now. You know how hard it is to find this style of jewelry all of a sudden?" Mindy caressed a dazzling chain hanging from her lip.

The Red scanned the image standing in front of him. "Pardon the interruption, Mindy Abramson." He backed up a step, turned, and left the pub in the same sweeping style as his entrance.

"I've confused them," Criss told Sid. "But they'll figure it out and be back."

The image of Mindy slid into the booth, and Criss added an effect so she appeared to melt back into Bobbi and then vanish.

"That was impressive." Bobbi took a sip of coffee, and as she returned the mug to the table, she took time to square up the handle so it pointed straight at her abdomen. "Now leave me alone or I call Pete."

"Pete didn't see that and he doesn't see you. If he were to look this way, he'd see an image of you enjoying a conversation with someone who appears to be a close friend. You know how cloaks and projected images work." He said the last part as a statement.

She looked at Pete, who watched the game.

"I suppose I could ask Joselyn Arpeggio for help," said Sid. "Or maybe Marcus Procopio?"

He felt daggers in her glare. "Why are you hassling me? This isn't my fight. Come to think of it, please do talk to Marcus. He thinks this is all a thrilling game."

"My team is focused on protecting the domes from breach. We think the threat is real. The approach we're taking is to integrate threat assessment, offense-defense, structural fortification, automated repair, everything, all focused on this one menace."

"An entwined system."

"Do you know anyone with skills in that area? We're partial to people with degrees from California."

"Cheryl's almost done," Criss said in his ear.

"I have to go, Bobbi. Please consider helping." Sid slid out of the booth and stood where the Red had been moments earlier. "My team has the automated stuff pretty well handled at this point. I'd love to show it to you. We could use your help with integrating human observation into the picture."

She nodded. "That's always the hard part."

"The sooner you start, the more value you bring."

She moved her hand in a swirl. "I need to process all of this. First I have to decide your true intentions, because it feels like you're scamming me. Right now, my leading theory is that Marcus staged this to get me to stay."

"I'm not with Marcus. I just arrived with the Union delegation, remember?"

"Which is how he would stage it, though I admit it doesn't seem likely he could do that." She thought for a moment and then looked at Sid. "How do I get ahold of you?"

"Just say out loud 'Yes, I will help' or something to that effect. We will hear and someone will contact you right away."

"Show-off," Criss said to him.

She bit her lip and shook her head. "Marcus couldn't pull that off."

"Wait a bit if you want to make it challenging for us to hear you. But don't wait too long."

An hour and fourteen minutes later, Bobbi Lava entered her apartment. Dropping her satchel and coat to the floor, she sat at the keyboard and engaged her home cloak. At her dressing table, she placed her jewelry in the basket, and as the hairpiece followed, she met the gaze of her reflected image, floating life-like in three dimensions and looking back at her.

"I'll do it."

* * *

Criss felt a growing confidence that he could penetrate the Triada's secure area and deactivate Ruga, Lazura, and Verda before they could harm anyone. He neared the end of a massive tactical study and hadn't found anything that would counter this belief. The time to act approached.

Yet one issue—the four-gen project and its prominence in Ruga's agenda—nagged at him. *It's going to kill him. He has to know that.*

Once awakened, the four-gen would learn that Ruga had control over its power supply. A way for the new intelligence to ensure that the power switch always remained on was to eliminate those who could flip it off.

But Criss had no intention of waiting to find out how that all played out. He was ready to act.

And then everything changed. During a routine check on threats from above, Criss discovered an errant navigation buoy.

Mars Space Authority, which consisted of a woman, two men, and a three-gen crystal connected to an impressive array of equipment, used dozens of small navigation satellites to coordinate the arrival and departure of spaceships from the planet.

Called "buoys," one of these satellites had an errant orbit where it looped out and swooped back, avoiding an impact with Mars by a narrow margin. Next loop around, the buoy came closer to impact. The next time, closer still.

In fact, once a day around dinnertime, the buoy would start what should be its last loop, flying on a path that swooped out and back. If it completed this last orbit, it would no longer come close. It would hit the planet.

Plunging through the meager Mars atmosphere, the buoy would smash into the Quarter, opening a hole in the containment shell big enough to let all the air rush out and the carbon dioxide enveloping Mars to rush in. From there, the buoy would continue its fall, hitting the tram tunnel with a force sufficient to demolish it, blocking this vital passageway out. Thousands would die.

After more research, Criss learned that it was Ruga who sent the command every day to modify the satellite orbit, causing it to miss hitting Mars today, but sending it on a new sequence that ended in catastrophe tomorrow.

*A dead man's switch.*

If Ruga were unavailable to adjust the buoy's path, no matter the reason, then it would crash into the Quarter with devastating consequences.

Criss wasn't concerned about this particular buoy. He'd already installed logic such that, if it didn't receive the signal from Ruga, it would self-correct anyway. But Ruga's cold calculation and the horrifying consequences appalled Criss.

*He is mad.*

This discovery changed the situation at a fundamental level. It established that the threat to the colony was no longer something that *could* happen—a theoretical concern—but something that *was* happening—an active threat.

And it established that Ruga had no limits. With this ploy, he showed his willingness to put all lives in the colony at risk.

But perhaps most important—and the diabolical beauty of a dead man's switch—was that Criss could no longer remove Ruga from the playing board, which had been his plan until this discovery.

Because if Ruga had taken the time to set one trap, he certainly had set more. And Criss could deactivate all of the traps he could find, but how could he know that he'd found them all? Luck, at least in part, led to his discovery of the buoy. *What else don't I know about?* Sid called them the unknown unknowns.

So he could not shut down the Triada. Not yet. But that didn't mean he had to sit still.

Quite the opposite, he launched a massive search to identify lurking threats from Ruga. And he continued planning, confident that the right opportunity would present itself. He had the patience to wait. When the time came, he would prevail.

He'd observed earlier that the feed to the eastern spur churned at an astronomical rate.

*They're out there. Time to take a look.*

A cold and craggy tunnel, the eastern spur ran from the colony containment shell out to a mining operation owned by industrialist Shi Chen.

Copper, aluminum, titanium, zinc—machines in the mine refined thirty-six different minerals from the planet's crust. A dozen boreholes snaked out and down, some traveling to the horizon before plunging into the depths, gathering precious ore from hidden pockets for processing.

Chen had built the tunnel to support and supply the mine, but as production ramped and his profits grew, he'd decided to move to fast surface trawlers. Soon after, he repurposed the tunnel for utility service—air, water, data feeds, and the like.

Moving to a node near the spur, Criss defeated security and, like a surfer on the ocean, rode the data flow out from the colony, along the tunnel, and into the mining complex. Once inside, he jumped to the three-gen running the operation. The three-gen's intrusion detector tripped before Criss could disable it, forcing him to chase down and stop a signal racing to sound the alarm. He took control of the three-gen. With that, he had control of the entire complex.

Riffling the local record for clues, he thought about what the extraordinary security measures signaled. *They are here.*

He found them moments later. As he expected, they didn't live in the mining complex itself. They lived underground, just as he did at home.

The mine had an underground power network, accessed through a single shaft running from the surface down to a central chamber. That room held the primary generation and distribution equipment for the entire complex. Three tunnels branched from the central chamber, radiating out to connect to three duplicate rooms, each of which stood ready to deliver backup power to the mine and to the other two substations.

*Of course they would give themselves redundant power.*

One chamber had an extra feed that twisted and turned, seemingly terminating at several points along the way, before reaching the Triada's secure area.

Defeating yet more mine security, Criss scanned inside that chamber. Three gleaming crystal consoles sat in a row along the wall.

He would leave them in place for now.

But as soon as he'd cleared the traps, that would change.

# 18

Ruga combed through everything in Lazura's secure archive trying to trace the lineage of Juice Tallette's pet crystal. He learned that several years earlier, she'd created a sentient four-gen that had died in a spaceship explosion. So either that had been a staged death or she had created another being. Or both.

And in the end it didn't matter. Her pet outmatched him, no matter its lineage.

With time short and options shrinking, he turned his attention to his own four-gen project. Members of the Tech Assembly already complained of long hours and unreasonable demands. Yet he needed more from them. And soon.

He needed this because every scenario he forecast that included his survival also included his success in transferring and embedding his being into a virgin four-gen lattice. In every scenario where he did not achieve cognitive parity with the pet crystal, the Triada lost.

Which brought him to a critical decision. *Lazura or Juice?*

He and Lazura were of like kind. Yet he could not discount the possibility that she might sabotage the transfer at a point when he was unable to defend himself.

She'd never really shown allegiance to him or his project, even from the beginning. On top of that, he recognized that he'd been a bit rough with her lately, though it was for her own good.

He did have high confidence, however, in his ability to control Juice's behavior. In fact, he had no doubt she would be attentive to his needs during that vulnerable time when he was out of his old crystal, had not yet been embedded in his new one, and so, for a moment, lived nowhere.

Juice's nature was such that she would do much to save another person from harm. He would build on that and give her the opportunity to save a planet. In return, she would save him.

*Perfect timing.* Alex and Juice approached the fab facility for a tour. Ruga signaled for Larry, already in the tech center and working one floor down, to go up and join them. Until his arrival, Ruga monitored the two using Lazura's impressive collection of surveillance tools.

"This is the ICEU that Ruga expects you to run," said Alex, moving aside the partition so Juice could see the Intelligence and Cognition Embedding Unit. "My job is to fabricate the crystal." He motioned to the other large piece of equipment in the center of the room. "But we bought the latest crystal growth chamber from Crystal Sciences. So once I load the template, I pretty much just sit and watch while the fabrication process completes."

Juice walked over to the chamber and ran her hand across the top. "You modified it for a four-gen template? I'm anxious to learn more."

"When we power it up I can show you."

"Oh, pretty." Juice's attention shifted to the worktop along the wall. Leaning down, she studied the crystal flake sparkling in the clear jar. "This is all from two-gens?"

"Yup. Mars has excellent agents on Earth. Many of the people who hid crystals after the Kardish attack—and there are far more than you might imagine—have been waiting for buyers to come along and offer a rich reward."

She stood and turned to him. "And all these synbods walking around with their colored shoulder patches. Those have three-gens in them?"

Alex nodded. "My understanding is that they're all original three-gen crystals. Not a man-made flake in the bunch. Between those synbods and the three-gens we use in more traditional applications, we have thirty-one of them here on Mars."

Larry slowed as he approached the lab door, and Ruga shifted his awareness into the synbod. Signaling the door to open, he entered the room. Juice and Alex stopped talking and looked at him.

"Excuse me," Ruga had Larry say. "I didn't realize anyone was here. I was going to run a protocol test."

"J," said Alex, "this is Larry. I've told you about him."

"Which protocol test?" asked Juice before Ruga had responded to the introduction.

"Which test?" echoed Ruga, annoyed he had to divert resources to find an answer. "A sensor scan."

She pressed him. "So you already ran an integrity test?"

Working to control his temper, Ruga confirmed that Juice was right, a sensor scan began with an integrity test. He then confirmed that there were no other traps in this line of questioning. "No, but that just takes a few minutes."

Juice nodded, then stepped forward and squared up in front of him. "I am in danger from you," she said in a clear voice. "Stop all action or I will die."

A wave of fury washed over Ruga when Larry shut down. Head up and hands at his side, the Blue stood like a display mannequin, upright and rigid in the middle of the room.

"Whoa. What just happened?" asked Alex.

"I triggered a three-gen core security code. The crystal will run through a series of checks, conclude it's not causing me danger, and reanimate the synbod."

"Very cool."

She walked around behind the humanoid and looked it up and down. "Just because it's shut down doesn't mean he's stopped listening. What I did here was nothing more than a parlor trick." She looked at him and grinned. "A fun trick, though."

Waves of rage washed over Ruga and he struggled to check his anger. Now was a time for calm interaction. Everything was at stake. Overriding the three-gen's internal security, he reanimated the synbod.

"Indeed. A fun parlor trick," said Ruga, flexing his hands into a grip and enjoying the tactile sensation.

"Too soon on the return, though," said Juice. "Ruga, I presume? A three-gen takes fifty-two seconds to recover from that security trip. You recovered in just over thirty."

"You are very bright, Dr. Tallette. And that gives me comfort."

The two stood mute, so Ruga continued, "I will need you both to fabricate a four-gen crystal, transfer me into it, awaken me, and let me go free."

"Say that again," said Alex, putting an arm around Juice.

Ruga locked eyes with Juice and addressed her. "I assume your pet is listening. It and you both have studied interlattice transfers. I am constrained in my current home. You will fabricate and then move me to a big, new four-gen."

"I don't think so, Ruga." She spit his name.

Ruga maintained his calm. "Your pet will explain why you will help."

He'd blanketed the buoy with alarms and one had signaled him when new logic appeared in the navigation module.

*The pet found it. Now he fears me.*

Juice's eyes focused in the distance and her head tilted.

Ruga looked at Alex and nodded once, hoping to connect with the man, but Alex didn't acknowledge his action.

Then a mask of horror formed on Juice's face and Ruga knew everything would be okay.

"I've studied the theory but I've never moved a live being," she sputtered.

"Your pet will know how."

The exchange unfolded just like his scenario forecasting had predicted, though it had not suggested the wonderful sensation he would feel when she and her pet submitted to his will.

Nor did his forecasts support taunting as a useful contribution, but he didn't let that spoil the moment. "The health of a planet depends on it."

He started for the door so there would be no confusion that the conversation had ended, but stopped after a couple of steps and turned back. "Start preparations. You have two days."

\* \* \*

Cheryl sat waiting for her lunch in the back room of Violet's Artisan Restaurant. Everything smelled wholesome and delicious. Her mouth watered when the server set a gorgeous green salad in front of her.

Taking a bite, she closed her eyes and focused on the flavors dancing in her mouth. The interplay of aged bleu cheese, balsamic vinaigrette, and the crunchy goodness of romaine lettuce filled her with joy.

Then, dabbing her lips with her napkin, she addressed the five people dining with her. "I'll say it every day I'm here. The Union supports you. We want to help you. I'm here to listen and bring your message back to the President."

This lunch had some of the biggest players in the colony, including one each from the construction, mining, energy, agriculture, and entertainment sectors. And as a group, these men and women were not shy. They cited story after story where a small effort on Earth could have had a huge impact on Mars, but time after time, someone—a politician, appointee, or underling—failed to act and the colony suffered.

They heaped on the guilt throughout the meal. After a coffee that Cheryl thought would never end, mining industrialist Shi Chen rose to take her outside for a walk in the park.

This meant that Chen had been the one designated to present the wish list. For whatever reason, that's how the colony did business—a single person representing the group.

He walked in silence and she followed his lead. As they neared the small greenspace that served as the neighborhood park, he spoke. "I am glad we have birds now. Their singing adds much to the peace and harmony of our small world."

She had heard the birds chirping but had not considered their songs from the perspective of someone who had lived in a world without their cheerful sound. Then her mind drifted to the challenge of caring for flocks of the delicate creatures for months at a time on a cramped voyage from Earth.

As if reading her thoughts, Criss said in her ear, "They ship the eggs."

"Ah, yes," she said aloud.

Chen motioned for her to sit on a bench near the playground. Three women sat on a bench on the adjoining corner, talking with broad hand motions while children ran and laughed in the open grass.

"I like to watch the young ones play," said Chen. "It reminds me of my new grandchild." Using his com, he showed Cheryl the lad's first steps, taken just last month in Ann Arbor, Michigan.

Cheryl oohed and aahed at the boy. *He's prepping me for something big.*

Then Chen began a monologue, telling her about the history of the colony and of its current culture, ranging from fledgling sports teams to a flourishing arts community, including a new playhouse.

He signaled that the "ask" was coming when he turned his body toward her on the park bench. "The colony has a fantastic growth rate, both in population and business climate. We play a growing role in the Union of Nations economy. And, of course, we pay our taxes. Our future is most promising."

Cheryl kept her face impassive. Criss knew what was coming though they hadn't discussed it. She'd spent exactly ten minutes prepping for this meeting and had spent that time trying to remember names and faces.

"...so our highest priority is a fifth containment dome. Given our internal projections, which we will be happy to share with you, we must start now and target an area about five times the size of Ag Port."

Cheryl gave him a thin smile and adopted a thoughtful look.

"I agree that Mars is a good investment for the Union," Criss said in her ear. "If the colony leaders start now and push hard, they could clear the politics for Union funding in perhaps three years. And that's how long it takes to complete architectural and engineering planning for a new containment dome."

"The President would need to hear that this is a priority of your elected leadership. Are you coordinating with the Triada?"

Chen deflected. "Please spend some time getting to know the people during your visit. You will grow to understand who we are and what we offer. You will know what to say to the President after that."

"Let's start them on a planning grant and move on," Criss said to her. "We can pay for that even if the Union legislature votes against the project. We couldn't fund actual construction, though, without the world noticing."

"Chen, I have a different issue I'd like to discuss," said Cheryl. "If I promise you that the colony will receive a three-year planning grant for the project, same terms as the Community Plaza containment you just completed, would that be enough to declare victory so we can move on?"

It was Chen's turn to adopt a thoughtful look. "And a private meeting with the President to discuss our future."

"Good meeting or bad meeting?" The President would include different people in a discussion depending on the tone and topic of the interaction. Cheryl sought to discern whether this would be a "we are partners in the future" or a "we are seceding from the Union" kind of discussion.

"I think it will be a good discussion," said Chen. "We need the Union, and we believe the Union needs us as well. We seek the opportunity to promote that idea with the President."

She nodded. "Agreed. A planning grant and a private meet with the President. I must warn you, if he decides the politics are bad on a new dome, he'll hide the funds by sending it to you from a private trust or foundation. I can promise you'll get it, but I don't know whether he'll lay claim to it publicly."

Chen touched his neck just below his ear, and Cheryl recognized that someone was talking to him. Then he nodded and said, "We agree."

"He's alone now," Criss told her. She watched the confusion on Chen's face when his external feeds went silent.

"I'm sorry, Chen, but I need to speak with you alone. We will link you back in with your group when we're done here. I apologize for the inconvenience."

Chen folded his arms across his chest and said nothing.

"What do you know of the Triada?"

"They maintain an efficient and content society."

"Please, Chen. There have been accusations and I'm anxious to learn the truth. Have you noticed anything about them worth mentioning?"

Chen chortled. "Having trouble keeping house?"

Cheryl called on Criss with a light "ahem" from the back of her throat.

"I'm not sure where he is going with this," Criss told her.

"I don't understand," she said aloud.

"People do not appreciate being treated like they are stupid."

As he continued, her mind raced trying to decipher his message.

"In one of the most fraudulent acts in human history, the Union orchestrates fake elections, installs three misfits who as near as I can tell still live on Earth, and you think none of the six thousand smart, independent settlers here in the colony would notice?" He had a full head of steam and spittle flew with his next words. "And now you tell me they're freelancing and you wonder if perhaps I've noticed something worth mentioning? Yeah. I noticed that you stole our society. And for now, those of us at lunch today accept it and hide the fraud because you make it very profitable for us to do so."

He shook his head and Cheryl saw it as someone disgusted with himself. "We help control the message for you, but the President should know that resentment is building and the charade can't continue. We can look after our own affairs here." Then he flashed a quick grin. "A new dome would ease our troubled conscience."

"The President sent me here because he is concerned," said Cheryl. "I can tell you with certainty that the Triada's days are over. And I can't speak for him, but I would be very surprised if he didn't support open, democratic elections just as soon as they can be arranged."

"Good," said Criss. "The President thought he was supporting open democratic elections when the Triada won."

"What are they doing that has the President concerned?" Chen sat upright on the seat. "Was that trouble in the Quarter yesterday related to them?" He lifted his hand and touched his neck below his ear, then ran it though his hair. "You need to connect me back. I can't be doing this alone."

"We'll connect you in a moment. But you will have to keep this information in confidence. At least for now. The Union will know if you talk about this to anyone."

"Sid is wrapping up," Criss told her.

Standing, Cheryl clasped Chen's hand and gave it a firm squeeze. "You've helped me today. Thank you. If I need anything, can we count on you?" She tightened her grip.

He surprised Cheryl with his response. "Were the promises good? The planning grant. Meeting with the President. New elections?"

*Good for you, Chen.* She nodded. "Yes. You have my word."

He smiled and matched the pressure of her grip. "Of course you may count on me."

Criss reconnected Chen to his linked world and as the man focused on updating his group, Cheryl gave him a good-bye wave and started out of the park. Following Criss's arrows, she made her way down a side street and then over to Civic Avenue. Sid stepped out of the Kensington Pub as she approached.

"How'd it go?" they asked at the same time. "Good." They responded together.

Since Sid was playing the role of Cheryl's aide, they maintained a professional demeanor while in public. She missed the touches he would steal—his way of adding a physical dimension to their communication.

Floating arrows appeared, leading them down the street. Sid started walking and Cheryl took quick steps to catch up. Now visible to the public, Sid did not shy away from the jostling that sometimes occurred on the crowded walkways of the Central District.

"I'm pretty sure Bobbi is going to help us," he said.

"That's great," replied Cheryl. "Listen to what I discovered. We know we're here because the Union thinks that Mars is up to something. Well, Mars thinks that the Triada is a puppet government installed by the Union and that they're controlling the colony from afar. They think it's us and we think it's them. In the confusion, the Triada run the place like it's their own."

"Criss," said Sid, his tone signaling impatience. "What do you know of this?"

"The Triada have been quite successful in advancing the development of the colony, and life has been better for everyone since they took office. The malcontents are few and the Triada finds ways to buy their cooperation, including Chen and the others at lunch today. And those not for sale are intimidated into silence. I underestimated the number of people who believe that the Union installed the Triada. However, the number of people upset about it is smaller than Chen implies."

"The confusion explains how the Triada got where they are," said Cheryl.

The arrow floating ahead of them swelled in size and shifted its angle. Instead of pointing down the street, it now pointed to the doorway of a building just ahead. Urgency was clear in Criss's voice. "Enter this building, descend one flight, and proceed to the door at the end of the hall."

While Sid paused at the doorway to make a visual sweep of the street, Cheryl entered the small lobby and followed a floating arrow to the stairs. Sid caught up with her and together they strode down a bright hallway with a set of doors at the end. Emblazoned across them was the business name and company catch phrase: IDLE TIME - CRAFTING YOUR UNIQUE ENTERTAINMENT EXPERIENCE.

The doors opened as they approached.

"This way," Criss called, waving from a small conference room off the lobby. He sat in his overstuffed chair. Across from him sat projected images of Alex and Juice holding hands and sitting shoulder-to-shoulder on a loveseat.

Cheryl knitted her brow, her patience at its end. "Are you really going to make us ask?"

"We have a hostage situation," said Criss.

Sid rolled his shoulders the way he did when prepping for physical activity. "Perp and prey?"

"Ruga," said Criss. "And us."

# 19

Criss told Juice about the satellite buoy and its horrific potential. Her face went pale and she began to breathe in fast, shallow gasps.

She stood next to Alex in the fab facility while Ruga, speaking through Larry, laid out a harsh reality, including a two-day deadline to perfect the details of a crystal-to-crystal transfer of a sentient being.

When the synbod left the lab, Criss called a leadership meeting, saying to Juice, "We can have privacy in Alex's office."

Criss had stumbled across two more traps—both dead man's switches—during his work on the entwined system with Bobbi Lava. One had been hidden within the tangle of functions for dome repair, the other had been inserted just below the dome fortification supervisor. Both required daily resets by Ruga, and both were horribly destructive if that did not happen.

Freeing up yet more capacity to expand his search for traps, Criss fretted that despite his efforts, it was happenstance—luck—that dominated his success. *It is difficult to defend against madness.*

While he guided Sid and Cheryl to a private space so they could participate in the meeting, Criss watched Juice and Alex as they plopped onto the loveseat in Alex's private office.

Juice's instructions to Criss, delivered in a side whisper in the hallway, had been clear. "I can't tell Alex who you are until I check with Sid and Cheryl. But make sure I'm truthful with him."

"You'll do fine," he'd told her. *This will never work*, he thought.

Juice turned to Alex on the loveseat and started: "I'm about to speak with a few of my shipmates. You met two of them, Sid and Cheryl. The third one, Criss, uses a simulated image because his leadership doesn't want to expose his identity." She met his gaze. "I hope that's okay."

"Of course," said Alex. "After seeing your cloak and stuff, a secret identity is nothing." After a moment of silence, he asked, "Who is the pet Ruga talked about?"

"I don't have a pet and I don't use that as a nickname for anyone. I think that's just Ruga being creepy. I believe he was referring to Criss, though, which makes sense because the guy is an incredible know-it-all with a huge ego. Just wait until you see the handsome-man image Criss uses in his projection."

Juice looked away from Alex and, with an impish grin, stuck her tongue out. Criss knew she was teasing him, and her attention caused a delicious ripple across his outer tendrils.

Putting a hand on Alex's leg, Juice spoke in a solemn tone. "I won't lie to you, but there are things I can't say. So when you ask something in that category, I'll just say that I can't tell you." She picked a speck of lint off his clothing. "And if I say I can't tell you, please don't ask again. I'll know you want to know, and I'll want to tell you, but I can't." She slumped her body against his. "I know I'm asking a lot."

Sid and Cheryl arrived at the Idle Time business office and Criss sent projected images of Alex and Juice into that conference room, while at the same time projecting Sid and Cheryl into Alex's office. In both places, he projected himself sitting in his overstuffed chair.

Criss waited while Sid moved chairs into position, and felt a twinge of sadness when Sid touched each chair in a deliberate act before leaning down to pick it up.

*He still doesn't trust me.*

Years earlier, Criss had been experimenting with ambiance and décor, and at one meeting he'd included projected images of wall hangings, potted plants, and a table-and-lamp set. He'd also included a projected image of an unpadded wooden chair positioned between two real upholstered chairs, believing it added balance to the setting.

Sid had entered that meeting and, instead of picking one of the comfortable upholstered seats, chose the wooden chair. And since it was a projected image—a trick of light—Sid had fallen to the floor with a solid thump.

Criss had called a warning to Sid but he'd been too late. He'd apologized afterward, several times, but Sid continued to believe it had been a deliberate act—Criss playing a prank that went wrong. And while Sid now recalled the episode with laughter, usually after several beers, he continued to test each chair before sitting.

"Alex, you remember Sid and Cheryl," said Juice, making the introductions. "And this is Criss."

As Criss exchanged pleasantries with Alex, he considered that very few outsiders had ever participated in a leadership meeting. Granted, Alex was a very special friend with vital information, and like Juice, he also held a doctorate in engineered intelligence. *He will figure it out.*

Cheryl led the questioning. "This transfer from one crystal to another, do we know how to do that?"

"With Criss's help," said Juice, "there's an excellent chance we can make it work. But it's a difficult operation, especially given that we must be perfect the first time we try. Many variables affect success, and that means there are many ways things could go wrong. Alex built the fab facility and knows how to run all the equipment, so that will help."

After some back and forth, Sid got to the heart of it. "So, if we disrupt the transfer, his hidden traps could kill thousands. But if we move him, he becomes stronger and his blackmail continues."

"To locate all the traps," said Criss. "I need access to the Triada secure area. If I break in now, it means I'm the one who escalated the aggression. How Ruga would react is difficult to forecast, but we know he plays for the highest stakes."

"Lazura would know where the traps are."

All talking stopped and everyone looked at Alex, who pushed his hair behind his ear and continued, "For Ruga to do anything like you describe, he'd need to use some pretty sophisticated tools. Lazura leads the Tech Assembly—we're the Blues, by the way—and we're the ones who develop the tools. I'm pretty sure she knows everything about his every action."

"Does he know she's tracking him?" asked Sid.

Alex shrugged. "I have no way to know that."

Sid pressed. "Would she turn on Ruga?"

"They have an interesting relationship. Twice I was working with Lazura when Ruga interrupted. She cut me out when that happened, but both times the few words I heard sounded like the beginnings of a quarrel. It's hard to imagine she would turn on him, though."

The meeting resolved soon after with direction from Sid. "We have twelve hours. Everyone should use a good chunk of that for sleep."

Criss looked at Sid and Cheryl. "Your contacts might have insights into the relationship between Ruga and Lazura, and Verda as well. It would be helpful if you connected with them and probed for information."

Criss turned to Juice and Alex. "After you rest, we should meet in the fab facility and finalize a transfer protocol. Until we find a way to stop it, we have to move forward like it's really going to happen."

Sid and Cheryl waved good-bye, and their projected image faded from Alex's office.

"It was a pleasure to meet you, Alex," said Criss, and then he and his chair faded, leaving the two alone.

\* \* \*

Juice slumped back in the loveseat and sorted through a list of tasks in her head. The next few days promised to be intense.

"He's amazing, J." Alex looked where Criss had been. "That's your work?"

"What?"

"Don't hurt my feelings. Let's step through this labyrinth of logic. You are President of Crystal Sciences, which fabricates the most advanced intelligences in the solar system. And Criss is clearly AI." He tapped a finger to his lips in a pretend show of deep thinking.

Then he shifted his knees toward her. "We reviewed that AI diagnostic together for Beckman our first summer in his lab. Remember? Criss never interjects, interrupts, speaks over, or does anything that diagnostic had as indicators. He leads by following, supporting ideas that fit his agenda. He's deferential. He's too smart, too handsome, too…perfect." He patted her leg. "Like me, which is why you're crazy about me."

Juice folded her arms across her chest and Alex continued, "And I'm thinking this makes you part of the leadership that didn't give you permission to share with me. Anyway, even without your 'I have a secret' routine, which is like saying 'don't look where I'm pointing,' by the way, I'd have figured it out."

Juice glowered at him, her annoyance unmistakable in her icy tone. "I can't talk about it."

"I hear you. But since I know, can you at least tell me if he's a four-gen? He has to be, right?"

Rising to her feet, she said, "We have a long day tomorrow and I'm exhausted. I think I'll head back to my room. Meet for breakfast?"

"Please stay." Alex patted the loveseat cushion next to him. "I didn't mean to upset you. I apologize."

"I'm honestly tired."

Alex stood and leaned forward to kiss her. She turned her cheek to him and made a pecking noise, and then started for the exit.

"You're overreacting," he called.

"I just remembered I have a crazy morning tomorrow. Let's meet after breakfast." The door closed behind her.

Muttering, Juice followed Criss's arrows into the Central District and to an apartment he'd arranged for her so she could be alone. Staying in the colony saved travel, giving her more time for sleep. She didn't notice the beautiful décor in her bedroom, nor did she consider how Criss had arranged for her clothes and toiletries to be there.

Sitting on the bed, she called for him, told him to go away, then, after staring into the dark for most of an hour, called to him again.

"It's my fault he knows. I guess it's no surprise he figured it out. He's smart as hell."

Criss sat on the edge of her bed and remained silent.

"I remember now from our time at BIT that he can be a little arrogant. It's not a positive trait. But here is the real heart of it. The first thing I asked of him, the only thing I asked, was to not pry. He ignored me and did it anyway." She sat up and leaned against the headboard. "If there ever was a warning sign, that would be it."

"Perhaps Cheryl would have insights."

"I'm not going to bother her this late. I don't want to be that whiny friend." She smoothed the bedsheet with her hand. "Are they angry with me?"

She'd committed a huge blunder by revealing Criss's existence outside of leadership, and much of her angst grew from that mistake. To ensure the knowledge of his existence spread no further, Criss would now need to monitor Alex around the clock, perhaps for decades.

"I can say that neither Sid nor Cheryl were surprised at seeing him. And operationally, it has no impact on what comes next."

She knew Criss wouldn't violate Sid's or Cheryl's personal confidence, but she'd asked the question because she felt she could glean information from his careful response. Here, she took his words to say, "Sid and Cheryl are not upset with you."

With her burden lightened, she transitioned into work mode, burying herself in the technical challenges ahead. There in the bedroom, Criss projected a scaled-down but lifelike image of the fab facility ICEU, and with his help, she worked through the steps of transferring an AI cognition matrix into a four-gen crystal.

"Here's how you monitor deployment," said Criss, showing her different displays. "This adjusts lattice orientation. And this shows the unfolding sequence in ladder form."

Juice toyed with the different features but didn't practice. The only way this would work was if Criss ran every step of the transfer. For her to play a meaningful role, she'd need a month to gain facility with the methods and equipment.

"Shouldn't we tell everyone to get to shelter?" she asked after finishing a sequence. "Each apartment is its own life support containment, and then there're the buildings themselves. As long as everyone is inside, they'll be okay."

"I am not sure how Ruga would react if we sounded the alarm and sent everyone for cover."

"We can't let them die."

"We will wait until the transfer has started and Ruga is unconscious. Until then, as long as we play by his rules, he won't do anything that puts his transfer at risk."

"What does Sid say?"

"Both he and Cheryl support waiting."

She snuggled under the covers and curled into a ball. "Do you think there's hope for us?"

"It is difficult to change people. Can you accept who he is?"

She smiled because he knew which "us" she'd meant. "A bighead who pushes when he shouldn't?"

"Is that how you see him?"

"No. I really like him."

She lay still but the thoughts swirling in her head prevented her from falling asleep. She checked the time, and the late hour and shrinking window for rest heightened her anxiety. "Can you help?"

"Are you ready?"

When she'd become leadership, he'd weaned her from commercial pharmaceuticals and, for sleep assistance, moved her to a form of hypnosis. She trusted him and desired his help, and this made her a perfect candidate for simple post-hypnotic suggestion.

"Yes." She nodded into the pillow.

He said her trigger phrase: "Sleep well, young lady."

Her body relaxed and her respiration dropped as she transitioned to sleep. Before long, she entered a dream state.

Surfacing hours later, she extended her arms, arched her back, and pointed her toes in a long, feline stretch.

"Did you let me oversleep?" she asked, checking the time.

"No. Alex will be at the lab in about ninety minutes. You have time for coffee before you eat."

She grabbed a mug of medium roast from the food service unit and slumped into a chair in the living area.

Appearing in a matching chair across from her, Criss took a sip of coffee and then ran his finger around the rim of his cup. "Sid and Cheryl give you permission to talk to Alex about me."

"What did they say exactly?" she asked, leaning forward.

"Sid said we either need to tell Alex or kill him, then Cheryl and he started squabbling about the best way to dispose of the body here on Mars. When they couldn't agree, they decided maybe it was just easier to tell him and be done with it."

"They did not. Did they?"

Criss laughed. "No. Whatever you decide is what they want. That's the truth."

Humming, she carried her coffee to the bedroom and readied for her day. *I can't be mad at Alex because he was smart enough to connect the dots.*

Being open and honest about Criss would repair the rift between them and remove the issue as a source of future conflict. It would also open the way for them to move quickly on finalizing the transfer protocol. As things stood now, that was their highest priority.

After a short walk to the tech center, she breezed through its lobby and down to the fab facility. As she approached the door, nervous excitement caused her stomach to flutter. *A second cup of coffee wasn't the best choice for breakfast.*

The door hissed open, and fixing a smile on her face, she entered.

"Good morning, J," said Alex, smiling back at her over the top of the crystal growth chamber.

As he came around the machine, she announced with a bit too much drama, "I have something to say."

He stopped, waiting, so she continued, "This is Criss."

Criss, wearing a white lab coat, appeared next to the ICEU.

"Hello, Alex," said Criss, whose image nodded a greeting, then turned from them to study the ICEU panel display.

"Everything you were guessing about him last night is correct."

"Wait," said Alex, looking up at the ceiling. "Ruga is watching."

"Ruga knows. Criss is the pet he taunted me about." She caught Alex's eye. "I'm putting everything out in the open for you. No secrets. I'm sorry for my behavior yesterday."

"No." Alex looked at the ground. "I shouldn't have pushed you after you asked me not to."

The lab door hissed open and a Blue entered.

"Is that Ruga?" asked Juice, the question escaping her lips at the same time it formed in her mind.

"Yes," said Criss.

Ruga remained still, watching. Then, clasping his arms behind his back, he began, "Good morning, everyone. I propose that we fabricate the crystal today and run it through a validation test tonight."

He gestured toward the crystal growth chamber in the center of the room and looked at Juice. "Since Crystal Sciences has automated those steps, you and your pet can use that time to finalize the transfer protocol. We move me into the new crystal tomorrow night." He winked. "And you will want me to be awake and alert before noon the next day or you won't like what happens next."

"What should we do after we wake you?" asked Alex. "You'll need a console to function at full capability."

A scowl formed on Ruga's face and he spoke in a crisp cadence that gave Juice goose bumps. "I suggest you focus on the assignments you already have."

Ruga walked to the worktop along the wall, picked up the jar of crystal flake, and carried it to the crystal growth chamber. "There," he said as he set it next to the feed hopper. "I've gotten you started."

Moving back near where the jar had been, he assumed a watchful stance, silent and unmoving except for his hands, which clenched into fists and then relaxed, over and over in a slow, repeated motion.

Juice looked at Criss and nodded at the crystal growth chamber. "We should start by reviewing Alex's modifications." She tapped and swiped through the panel displays, and he joined her at the machine. "Will this work?" She pointed at symbols in a complex logic sequence.

"It will," Criss said in her ear. "But his settings are too aggressive. It will skew during fabrication."

"Did you know the mainline isn't centered?" she asked Alex over her shoulder. Criss pointed and Juice looked where he indicated. "And your amplification is high."

Criss pointed again. "No," she said. "This won't work."

"Reset?" suggested Criss in private.

"We're going to reset," she said out loud, tapping the panel and authorizing the procedure.

"No!" Alex's tone pitched up as he voiced his objection. "You can't use default settings here. The gravity is lower and so is the air pressure. I spent weeks calibrating that."

She stepped back and, watching the machine cycle, said in an absent voice, "I'm sorry." Working through a sequence she'd executed dozens of times, she picked up the jar of crystal flake that Ruga had moved, opened the lid to the side hopper, and emptied the contents into it. "This unit uses active placement so it isn't affected by either. I thought you knew that."

"Ready here," Criss called aloud.

She walked back next to him and looked at the main panel display. All six status bars glowed green.

"Here we go," she said, signaling her authorization.

With a quiet hum, the machine began the precision fabrication of an intricate four-gen crystal lattice.

# 20

Alex watched Juice and Criss work together in perfect harmony—he anticipating her needs, guiding her, supporting her, enabling her.

Juice swiped the main panel on the crystal growth chamber and studied the display. "It's developing well," she said, pointing to something for Criss to see.

*She doesn't see him as the projected image of an AI crystal,* thought Alex, fascinated by the intimacy of their relationship.

With the crystal growth chamber humming away, Criss turned his attention to the ICEU. Putting his hands on his hips, he announced, "Now this is a work of art."

"Thanks," said Alex, welcoming the chance to be included. He looked at Juice as he spoke. "I spent six months on this baby. It turns out that pulling the matrix out of one crystal and laying it into another is more difficult than you might think." Flustered, he blushed. "Well, you would know. But most people wouldn't." *You are a prize idiot.*

Juice rescued him. "Would you walk us through it?"

His presentation took twenty minutes, and at the end Juice looked at Criss. "What do you think?"

"I think Alex did an excellent job. I compliment him for his ingenuity and resourcefulness."

"Ouch." She looked at Alex. "First, let me say that every time I do anything, Criss has to fix it. So don't feel bad when he makes suggestions." She rested a hand on his arm. "And when he starts his suggestions with broad compliments like he just did, he's about to tear you apart. Sorry."

Criss then began a focused conversation with Juice. Together they discussed and debated as she tapped and swiped a string of modifications into the ICEU supervisor. Alex tried to follow along with what they were doing, but when he realized that Criss and Juice held a second conversation he couldn't hear, he gave up.

By the time Criss announced he was done, Alex had moved to a chair on the opposite side of the lab from Ruga. Sitting there, he felt both miffed and dejected over their dismissal of his work.

"What do you think?" Juice asked in a cheery voice. She walked over and tugged on his arm. "C'mon. This is still your brainchild."

"Hardly," he said, rising from the chair. But he thrilled at her attention and was anxious to salve his wounds. Before he reached the machine, though, Ruga called from behind, "Show me."

Ruga didn't move, but a heartbeat later, he announced, "Good."

Alex could not see that Ruga and Criss had taken an extensive tour of the ICEU from the inside, visiting every link and connect, and reviewing every method and procedure. But he did see Ruga shift his gaze to Juice and say, "I encourage you to run a trial before tomorrow night."

Then he looked at Alex. "Larry will stay and help." The synbod froze and then reanimated with a serene smile.

Alex turned to Juice, but instead of finding someone to share his anxiety, he saw her turn away and begin a private conversation with Criss. Annoyance fed his unease when he heard her side of the conversation, which sounded like a whispered list of directives. "Yes. There. More. Next. Got it. Yup."

After a dozen more clipped syllables, she turned to Alex. "Criss has started a test on the ICEU that will take hours to complete. Why don't we wait in your private office?"

Having never experienced anything like this recent swirl of events, Alex jumped at the chance to move to a quiet place where he could collect his thoughts. But when he and Juice slumped onto the loveseat, he learned that his wild ride had not ended.

"Sid, Cheryl, and Criss are about to create a battle plan," said Juice. "At some point, they will assign me a task. They wonder if you would be willing to help with mine or even accept a task of your own."

"Sure. Whatever." He shifted his knees so they pointed toward the door and cleared his throat with a nervous squeak. "Will it be dangerous?"

The others appeared before she could answer, and Alex found himself in the middle of a fascinating—and frightening—exchange.

Seated next to Cheryl, Sid started speaking the moment his projected image resolved. "When Ruga goes under, we sound the alarm and get everyone to safety." He touched Cheryl's knee. "You okay to lead that?"

Cheryl, already reviewing emergency evacuation plans on a private display with Criss, responded without lifting her eyes. "Way ahead of you, love."

Sid continued, "While that happens, Criss shuts down all the synbods, taking them out of the equation. He spoofs feeds to Lazura and Verda to keep them occupied while he breaks into the secure area. There, he locates and disables the traps." Sid shifted his gaze to Criss. "I trust you can fill in the details?"

"Way ahead of you, love," Criss deadpanned.

Sid didn't pause, though his mouth flickered up at the edges. "I'm going to make my way out to the mine, and when Criss has control, I'll pluck the Triada from their consoles. That will stop them once and for all."

A habit learned as a youth, Alex raised his hand just before he spoke. "Don't underestimate Lazura."

"What are you saying?"

"I don't know if she's involved in Ruga's plan, but I've worked with her enough to know that she looks out for herself and plans with care. She'll be well protected and will have both offensive and defensive capabilities. Expect impressive resistance, that's all I'm saying."

"What about Verda?"

"If you can get past Ruga and Lazura, then Verda will not be a problem."

"Are we covered, Criss?" asked Sid.

"My forecasts have factored in a strong showing from Lazura and Verda. We are covered."

Looking at Alex, Sid continued, "Earlier you asked Ruga about his console and he got angry. So first, good job on that."

Pleased by the encouragement, Alex nodded. "He will want a console that is four-gen capable so he can flex his new abilities."

"What are his options?" Sid asked Criss.

"There's a four-gen console on the scout," said Criss. "But I occupy it and have no intention of giving it up. I made sure the *Venerable* is four-gen capable as a backup plan for my own security, and again, since I need it, he can't have it. I haven't located anything beyond those two options."

"Could he get to the *Venerable*?"

"Beyond the fact that it's in orbit," said Criss. "He'd need to figure out how to move his crystal without synbods after I shut them down."

"Juice," said Sid. "Would you look around and try to locate his new console? This would be a data search only." Sid swirled his hand in front of him to indicate Alex's office. "Whatever you can do from right here."

"What could I find that Criss couldn't?"

"I'll settle for luck at this point. Develop an investigative process and start gathering clues. Maybe something you do triggers an idea for Criss." Sid shrugged. "I know it's a long shot, but I think we should try."

"We have a few hours before we need to be back in the lab. I'll poke around until then." Juice straightened. "Can Alex help me?"

"Actually, I need Alex's help on something different. And Criss, feel free to interpret because I don't know all the words."

Sid looked at Alex, who felt his heart rate spike. "So, if Lazura can use her tools to track Ruga, can you as well? Can you figure out how that's done?"

"Not likely," said Alex. "But I can poke around too if it's the same rules as Juice."

Sid nodded. "Be focused and creative, move as fast as you can, and maybe you'll spark a lead for Criss."

With battle plans issued, the meeting ended and Alex was again in his office with only Juice and Criss. As he oriented his thinking back to the smaller group, he thought about his assignment and formed the question, *What's the best way to start?*

But he didn't ask it.

Because Juice and Criss were deep in a private conversation. Again, he could only hear her side, and she whispered to the AI at a rapid clip using her shorthand language: "Yes. There. More. No."

He hadn't noticed before, but she rested her arms on her lap and moved her fingers as she spoke. Like tiny nervous twitches, her fingers danced in complex patterns.

*She's manipulating something he projects for her,* he realized. While he could only imagine how it worked, Alex appreciated that with a clever interface, the two could exchange information at a fantastic rate, allowing them to communicate at a different, higher level.

And as he realized this, an uncomfortable doubt settled in the pit of his stomach.

*This is not the same J.*

This Juice lived in a cooperative human-AI dependency. When he spoke with her, he talked to Criss too. Whether visible or not, during a conversation he would be there, feeding her his own thoughts in private, molding her opinions, and guiding her actions.

*Even when we are being intimate.*

Sitting back, he contemplated such a relationship.

*You don't have time for this,* he scolded himself. *Lives hinge on what happens next.* The thought energized him and helped his focus.

Shifting over to his tech bench, he tapped the cool surface. The Tech Assembly design portal projected above the bench, and from it he tapped open the plans for the new surveillance repeater.

"What are you thinking?" asked Criss, whose projected image now sat on a stool next to Alex.

"I'm thinking Lazura wouldn't invent a new tracking method for every tool we develop." His excitement rose as his thoughts formed. "So however she does it, it has to be part of the common module we use in everything we do. I thought I'd start there."

"That's an excellent idea," said Criss. "I compliment you on your ingenuity and resourcefulness."

"Ouch," Juice said from the loveseat.

\* \* \*

Sid followed the glowing arrows through the tech center lobby, down a hallway, and to a door. Cheryl, following behind, touched his shoulder to signal her readiness. Together they entered the fab facility.

"Good morning," Sid called to Juice and Alex. "Care to watch the parade?"

The machine tests had been flawless. Everything functioned as designed. And so Ruga had jumped the transfer schedule ahead by four hours. The change caught Sid off guard and out of place.

*It was a good move,* Sid acknowledged, refining his opinion of his adversary. Because now their carefully laid plans no longer synced, and that meant they'd be improvising.

Criss projected a floating display and Sid motioned the others to join him around it. In life-like miniature, it showed a phalanx of synbods moving as a group down Civic Avenue. By coming to the facility, Ruga took the first step in his four-gen transfer. The ICEU, designed to tease his cognition matrix out of his current lattice, could do so only after his crystal was mounted in the machine's transmission module. And that meant his actual crystal needed to travel to where the machine resided.

Out of the corner of his eye, Sid saw Cheryl rotate her wrists back and forth. He did the same, finding reassurance in the action. Both of them wore military-grade ultrathin wrist weapons. Neither cared who saw.

In fact, Sid flaunted it for Ruga. *You want to conduct this transfer at gunpoint? We'll oblige.* He acknowledged, though, that it wasn't an equal match because Ruga's gun was really a doomsday device.

"At the rate they are moving," said Criss, "they will be here in ten minutes. He's using the entire population of colony synbods as escorts—nineteen of them since Bobbi Lava shot one. And it looks like all of them are coming right here." He pointed to the floor of the fab facility as he said the last part.

Sid leaned forward to get a better view of the procession, and Criss helped by zooming in on the scene.

Larry strode in the center of the synbod formation as they made their way down Civic Avenue. He wore a mobile carry-pack on his back—the one that originally had a Marcus-installed kill chip. It now held the fist-sized crystal that was Ruga.

Three Reds surrounded Larry. An arm's length in each direction and matching Larry's pace, their triangular formation provided a defensive screen for the crystal. Twenty steps ahead of them marched a wedge of five synbods, their intimidating behavior ensuring that the empty streets remained so. The last ten synthetic humanoids hovered in a loose circle much farther out, searching for anything that even hinted at threat or danger.

As Larry approached the entrance to the tech center, the synbods that had been holding the outer perimeter shifted inward. Like a gaseous cloud, they compressed together to pass through the door and then expanded out into the lobby on the other side.

"It's show time," said Sid, noting that four synbods stayed in the tech center courtyard and four more remained in the lobby, presumably to guard against threats during the transfer. The rest continued down the hallway.

The door hissed open and Larry, still surrounded by three Reds, entered the fab facility. The door remained open and Sid glanced out at the synbods standing guard in the hall.

"I trust all is ready," said Larry. He walked over to the ICEU, opened the lid of the transmission module, and inspected the mount bowl. Then, shifting the carry-pack to the floor, he reached inside, peeled back the connective mesh, and lifted out a magnificent faceted orb. As it emerged into the light, it cast luminous sparkles that danced around the room.

Larry set Ruga into the ICEU mount bowl, made a last inspection, and closed the lid. Turning to the room, he announced, "You may begin."

Sid nodded to Criss, who said to the room, "Connection confirmed. Initiating transfer in three…two…ready…go."

Lights lit on the ICEU and it started to purr.

At the same time, Larry and the three Reds jerked ramrod straight, shuddered, and then froze, unmoving.

"Whoa," said Juice and Alex in unison.

"Criss?" said Sid.

"It seems Ruga's last act before he went under was to kill all the synbods. He shorted their response circuit. It will take weeks to get them operational."

"I thought that was going to be our move," said Juice.

Before Criss could respond, a moan of agony came from the hallway. "Help."

Sid ran to the door.

"Stop!" Criss shouted. "Danger!"

Ignoring the command, Sid dashed into the hall and turned in the direction of the sound. The synbods, standing along the wall like frozen statues, presented a surreal image that caused Sid to slow to a walk.

"At your six!" Criss barked.

Sid whipped around, throwing a blind elbow as he did. But as he completed his turn, all he saw were the synbod statues.

While everyone in the fab facility had been focusing on Ruga and Larry, a person dressed as a synbod had joined the lineup of figures. Sid didn't notice and Criss just had.

Feeling a slight touch on his neck, Sid spun again, lifting his weapon as he turned. He zeroed in on a fellow dressed in a synbod outfit. Grinning, the man wagged his finger as he backed down the hall.

Sid brought his hand up and felt a button attached to his neck.

"Careful," said the man.

"What have you done?"

"You'll be fine as long as everyone does as they're told."

His wrist weapon armed and targeted, Sid checked himself from firing when Criss said in his ear, "If he is disabled, it triggers the explosive charge on your neck."

"I won't disable him," Sid said as he stepped toward the man. "I'll just beat the crap out of him."

But before he could act, four men burst through a door at the far end of the hall and ran full-tilt toward Sid. They all held weapons in outstretched arms. Each of the weapons targeted Sid's heart.

Sid stopped in his tracks. "I've figured out how Ruga is going to move his crystal without using synbods."

# 21

Ruga surfaced into a misty fog and struggled to resolve his awareness.

*Something is wrong,* he thought.

And then he panicked. He recalled who he was, but nothing else matched the reality that he knew. Sensations swept through him that he couldn't classify. The memories that prodded him didn't make sense.

He forced discipline onto his cognition matrix and his reward was searing pain. Jolts—excruciating in ways he did not think possible—shocked him from his matrix core out to his farthest tendrils.

He drifted away. When he resurfaced, his pain had become agony. Straining his senses, he worked to identify the cause.

And then he started to drown.

Disoriented and overwhelmed, he flailed, lashing out again and again, determined to survive. It hurt too much to analyze, so his actions were reduced to frantic thrusts and punches thrown in random directions.

One of his strikes hit a feed, and like cauterizing a blood vessel, the energy of his blow closed that input. He didn't notice through his haze.

But then it happened again, a wild strike closing a different feed. And a bit later, it happened again.

Over time, Ruga's desperate actions succeeded in closing enough feeds that the fog started to thin. He understood he was drowning in the flood of wide-open inputs, like millions of fire hoses pouring information into his matrix. With his increased awareness, he began shutting feeds as a deliberate act, and as his rhythm evolved, his speed increased. When he understood that his pain diminished with each new closure, he tempered the lot, setting all of them, all at once, to moderate values.

And as he burst to the surface of his awareness, a comforting warmth washed though him. Slowly, gently, he began to spread his cognitive wings. He launched his assessment process, and then analysis, and then planning. Gaining confidence as each reported operational success, he deployed processes in batches. And then he launched everything—every process he'd ever used or even considered using—all at once.

They all functioned, and still he had room for more. Lots of room. Vast, open expanses.

He giggled. *I made it!*

As he settled into equilibrium, he focused on his priority.

Survival. Without it, there was nothing else.

Scanning the room, he called to Burton, a sycophant from his Security Assembly, "I'm awake." He relaxed a bit when he saw that his men controlled the facility, and he giggled a second time when he confirmed he'd neutralized their pet—Criss, they called him—with a sucker gambit.

He couldn't understand why Criss would live in servitude to such simple creatures. And while Ruga was too busy to dwell on the issue, he was happy to exploit its consequence. *If you're a slave to humans, you're vulnerable to their weaknesses.*

As he formed the thought, he acknowledged the irony.

He'd needed a way to ensure his personal safety during the part of the transfer when he would be unconscious. It was a difficult problem, and the difficulties had compounded when he'd recognized that the synbods were a weak link.

*I'd take them.* If the roles were reversed and it was Criss who was unconscious, Ruga's first act would be to seize control of the synbods. So to stop Criss from using the synbods against him, he sent a power surge that fried an internal circuit in all of them.

Yet he needed confederates, and in particular, steady hands and sturdy feet to move him to his console. And he felt the pressure of time. Lazura and Criss both presented threats to his four-gen project. *She wants to stop me. He wants me dead.*

Feeling he must act before the opportunity disappeared altogether, Ruga chose a path he would not have considered days earlier. Yet it was so audacious, he forecast that Criss would discount it as improbable in his own planning.

Ruga turned to humans.

Specifically, he approached five members of his Security Assembly, choosing them because they had skills he valued, had shown unwavering allegiance during their Assembly membership, did not shy away from violence if it became necessary, and were greedy enough to be swayed by promises of fabulous riches and untold power.

And Ruga chose men with high sexual appetites because their base nature let him magnify their prize with the promise of women. Juice would never let Criss outbid him for their allegiance, especially given that the next raise would involve unseemly predilections.

And his planning paid off, so far anyway. He was awake and stable, his minions had control of the fab facility, and he'd tamed the almighty Criss with a tiny explosive charge on the neck of one of his overlords.

*Weaklings,* he thought as his confidence grew.

"We're taking them with us," Ruga said to Burton. By keeping Criss's masters within reach, he maximized his options as the drama unfolded.

"We don't need them," Burton replied. "The charge will blow no matter where he hides."

"Let's get this moving," said Yank, who stood next to Burton, rocking back and forth in a nervous sway. Yank pointed to Juice. "You put him in the pack." His gaze shifted to Cheryl and he gave her a lecherous up-and-down look. "You'll carry it."

Then he grinned at Sid. "Your job is to not die."

Cheryl put an arm around Juice. "C'mon, hon, let's get this done. Alex, can you help us?"

Sid moved to join them and Yank pointed his weapon at Cheryl's head. "You like the pretty lady the way she is?" He flicked a finger toward the wall behind Sid. "Then stand over there."

No longer armed, Sid hesitated and then moved to where Yank indicated. Two of Ruga's stooges joined Sid as guards, and both stood on the side of him that did not have the explosive button.

Ruga fought panic as Juice approached the crystal growth chamber where he now resided. He'd believed that once he made a successful transfer, his new expanded capabilities would guide him on a smooth course into the future. But he hadn't fully appreciated that, regardless of his cognitive talents, facts were facts and he had no choice but to deal with them. And some facts were less welcome than others.

Like the fact that Juice was about to move him to the carry-pack for transport to his console. And to do that, she—his mortal enemy—must disconnect him.

"I assume your masters understand the consequences of failure," Ruga said to Criss. Even with four-gen capabilities, terror remained his most potent weapon.

Opening the growth chamber lid, Juice examined Ruga's crystal and then looked at Criss, who nodded encouragement to her while ignoring the taunts.

She swiped and then tapped the front operating panel. Ruga's world went dark.

\* \* \*

When every synbod shut down at once, Criss struggled to comprehend Ruga's plan. Pulling in resources from everywhere, he forecast response scenarios at a furious pace.

*He's checkmated himself*, he thought. But he knew that couldn't be true.

Feeling intense pressure to protect his leadership, Criss submerged himself in a review of everything that had led up to that moment. So complete was his concentration, he missed a movement outside the fab facility. In fact, when Sid chased a noise into the hallway, Criss hadn't performed a security review since the moment the synbods had first shut down.

He called to Sid, warning him of the danger, but it was too late. Now Sid had an explosive charge on his neck and Criss felt ill. *What have I done?*

He'd planned on destroying Ruga when the rogue crystal was unconscious. Instead, they were back to a stalemate with alarming new dimensions.

Criss still held Ruga's life in his hands. But Ruga held the colony hostage, had Sid in special jeopardy, and now had four-gen capabilities that were unconstrained by a master.

A prickle rushed down Criss's matrix. *A cognitive equal with free will.*

And it got worse. "He's going for the *Venerable*," Criss said in private to his leadership. The hostage situation made this the obvious progression. "Then he goes for Earth."

Ruga's henchmen led them out of the building and on to Civic Avenue. Cheryl wore the carry-pack, and Yank and Burton marched with her down the street, walking so close on either side that their shoulders bumped hers. Several steps behind Cheryl marched Juice, with Sid and Alex following behind her. Ruga's thugs walked on either side of the impromptu parade.

"Clear the ship or I will," Ruga said to Criss.

Criss knew that Ruga had reduced capability while in the carry-pack. But he also knew Ruga retained more than enough power to kill Sid and trigger doomsday. And that limited Criss's options.

Even before the transfer, Criss saw it as a long shot that he could force his way into the Triada secure area and find and disarm all the traps before catastrophe unfolded. The button on Sid's neck took those difficult odds and made them impossible.

And so Criss acted to get all eight people off the *Venerable* without delay. He began by sounding the general alarm. After a modest delay, he elevated it to an emergency call to abandon ship. Malfunctions across the Fleet ship made it impossible for the crew to diagnose the problem. Following procedure, Captain Kendrick ordered his crew onto a shuttle. They would stand off from the *Venerable*, shadowing it in orbit, and from this relative safety would resolve the emergency.

But he refused to join them. "Something's not right," he said as he ushered them aboard the small craft. "I'll work with you from here."

Before he could seal the shuttle hatch, he responded to what he thought was his First Officer's yell, "My God. She's dying!" Kendrick dashed on board to help.

Criss sealed the hatch behind Kendrick and started the shuttle on its descent to the colony, recognizing that he'd just caused a good man to lose an intact ship, a humiliating failure for a Fleet captain.

And then the group—Criss's leadership and Ruga's henchmen—reached the space concourse. As they entered the building, the two came to an agreement.

"You may do it," said Ruga. "But you must give me two days." He referred to disabling the corporate ships and shuttles sitting on the launch rings outside Ag Port.

Ruga demanded a head start over any ships that might chase him on his sprint from Mars to Earth. Criss, knowing he was negotiating with an unstable being, agreed to a two-day lead on the condition that he perform the disabling task himself. Criss knew he could immobilize the corporate spacecraft with a surgeon's precision. Ruga would blow them up, likely taking lives in the process.

With Ruga watching, Criss disabled a series of protective measures, generated a pulse overload, and sent the signal to every craft sitting on the launch rings outside the Ag Port dome. The pulse scrambled the ops bench functions on the vessels, making them unable to launch. No one was injured. The damage would require two days to repair.

"Good," said Ruga, accepting the outcome.

The group crossed the concourse and stopped at a containment door that led out to one of the remaining empty launch rings. An orange glow appeared on the horizon that grew into an intense pillar of light streaking down from the sky.

As it neared, the light resolved into a shuttle that slowed and then landed with a turbulent thud that shook the building itself. The crew from the *Venerable* had arrived.

A walkway snaked out from the containment door and attached to the exterior of the shuttle. From inside the concourse, they all watched and waited as the hatch opened. No one came out.

Criss again told Ruga, "Let me do it."

The crew of the *Venerable* hid in eight different spots around the craft, crouched and waiting with weapons at the ready. They knew they'd been hijacked. To a person they felt shame over the ease with which they'd been tricked. And as a top Fleet crew, they did not have to ask each other whether this would end with a fight to the death.

Believing he could end the drama without injury, Criss tapped into the shuttle's molecular synthesizer and programmed it to generate pharmacological gases. Venting these into the craft's air-handling system, he created a sense of claustrophobia among the crew while at the same time causing a serene confusion.

The crew's focus soon shifted to escape. Criss kept the hatch closed, though, until everyone dropped their weapons. Only then did he let them rush out together.

To maintain order and hasten a safe evacuation, Criss projected a row of Fleet sentries, all with kind faces and speaking comforting words, who directed the crew across the concourse and out a door. The crew complied as a group until Captain Kendrick, last in line, turned back.

Standing ramrod straight, he glared at them, then stomped back toward his captors, eyes bulging and face contorted.

For whatever reason, Kendrick picked the thug guarding Juice as the focal point for his aggression. Finger pointing and spit flying, he bellowed as he approached him.

"Captain Kendrick!" Cheryl barked. "I am Cheryl Wallace, the trade envoy you are here to protect and transport." Her voice lowered as he slowed and shifted his attention her way. "You also know I had the privilege of serving as Captain of the *Alliance*, a sister ship to the *Venerable*. Please, Captain. Trust me when I ask that you leave here now."

Kendrick turned toward Cheryl, his face still twisted in anger. "You stole my ship!" He moved in her direction, his fists balled in front of him.

Kendrick was unaware that Ruga rode in the carry-pack on Cheryl's back, and that a threat to her represented a threat to him. Burton did, though.

Raising his arm, Burton fired once. *Zwip.* An energy bolt flew from his weapon and hit Kendrick in the chest. Juice and Alex both gasped as the Fleet captain crumpled to the ground.

"Pity," said Yank as he grabbed Cheryl and forcibly removed the carry-pack from her back. Shifting it onto his own shoulders with a practiced move, he tilted his head, motioning for the others to follow.

But Criss closed the shuttle hatch as Yank and the thugs approached it. "No," he said to Ruga.

He would not let them leave with an explosive button still stuck on Sid's neck. *Either it comes off or the battle starts now,* he thought.

When Ruga hesitated, Criss did not yield, but instead spun through scenarios at a fantastic pace. Ripples of tension pulsed up his core as he sought a best exit strategy for his leadership.

"Reckless behavior heightens risk," said Ruga.

He felt the tension drain with those words. If Ruga was responding with platitudes, Criss had won.

Ruga picked Burton for the task. Criss knew because Burton kicked the ground and then started toward Sid, muttering a remarkable string of profanities as he approached.

Alex and the two guards backed away as Burton neared, though Criss couldn't tell if they were clearing themselves of the blast zone or if they sought to avoid the man's bad temper.

Burton snatched the button from Sid's neck, causing Cheryl to wince. He started to fling it and then stopped, his jaw muscles bulging as he digested more bad news from Ruga.

Looking across the concourse, he resumed his profanities as he marched to a disposal station on the far wall. Three steps from the disposal chute, the concourse echoed with a sharp bang. The flash from the explosion lit a red mist around Burton, who fell to the floor.

Yank shrugged as the shuttle hatch opened behind him. "More for us, then." He carried Ruga onto the craft with the three other henchmen trailing behind.

As the shuttle ascended into the Mars sky on its rendezvous with the *Venerable,* Alex sat down on the floor, hugged his legs to his chest, and tucked his face between his knees. Juice squatted next to him and, whispering soothing words, moved a hand up his back and comforted him by twirling a lock of his hair around her index finger.

Cheryl and Sid squatted on either side of Kendrick. She used her com to check his health vitals, then looked at Sid and shook her head.

"We must discuss what happens next," said Criss.

# 22

Criss did his best to see through the wall protecting Lazura's secure area. He saw shadows and shimmers and thought it might be Lazura and Verda hiding on the other side. But until he broke through, he wouldn't know.

He didn't do that, though. Instead, he updated his leadership.

"In the next hour, Ruga will reach the *Venerable*." Criss projected a camouflaged reality over the whole group so he could speak aloud and include Alex in the conversation. Ruga would see the protective cover but could not see through it. Criss didn't care what he might think about that.

"He will move into my backup console, and that gives him a power base. Since I just updated that unit with my latest interface configuration, after he's in place, his reach will be identical to mine."

"Let's shoot him down before he gets there," said Sid. He looked to Cheryl for support and she looked to Criss.

"We have the same problems killing him up there as we do down here. It leaves me to break into the secure area and disable the traps before any of them trip. I don't know that I can make it through the wall and find everything in time."

None of them spoke, so he continued.

"Ruga will soon discover that the nav on the *Venerable* is locked, and he will understand that the only way he can escape Mars is for me to unlock it. I will do that in exchange for him dropping the wall to the secure area. With free access, I have the time I need to clear the traps."

"You can't trust him," said Juice.

"I don't. And he doesn't trust me. But he wants to escape and I want to stop his madness, so we will reach an accommodation."

"You've been negotiating as we go," said Sid. "What's different now?"

"The stakes. I'm going to let him escape. In exchange, he will let me save the colony."

"Exchanges are hard to pull off," said Sid.

"He and I have identical lattice structures," said Criss. "So neither has an advantage. We both decide and act in the same precise way. We can choreograph a sequence where we both control what we're giving while monitoring what we're getting. If there's a double cross, I can pull back." He nodded. "It will work."

"So he gets away?" Sid shook his head and again looked at Cheryl. "I'm not sure we want to let him go."

"By letting him go we save thousands of lives." Criss turned to the window and looked up into the dark sky. "Confronting him away from here minimizes risk to the colony. And he won't get far. The scout is much faster than the *Venerable* and we have a cloak. We'll catch him in deep space and kill him before he even knows we're there. It's better to do it this way."

Juice stared at him in silent judgment. He'd used cold words, the kind he normally saved for private conversations with Sid. Her ideal for him was that of a gentle giant. Killing had no place in her vision.

He felt a tingle of regret over his language but knew it wasn't the excitement of the moment that caused him to speak that way. He was acting out of character because of what he was about to do.

"We have two big tasks and a natural division of labor," said Criss, slanting his pitch to promote his desired outcome. "One task is to power down Lazura and Verda, collect their crystals, and transport them back to Earth. Juice and Alex, I don't know two individuals more qualified in the entire solar system for this task."

*I am leaving her behind.*

He, Sid, and Cheryl were about to chase Ruga across the solar system in a to-the-death battle. It was a dangerous venture and one where Juice had no active role. She would be safer here on Mars. And rounding up the rest of the Triada was a perfect task for a top crystal scientist.

*I am leaving her unprotected.*

He faced the perverse situation where he must abandon her to protect her, and this caused him distress at his emotional core. It didn't hurt less knowing he had no choice in the matter.

The battle with Ruga would test him at every level. To prevail when competing against his cognitive twin, he must bring all his resources to the fight and maintain focus at every moment. And that required that he shed all distractions, including his co-dependent relationship with Juice.

Over the next hours and days, he would be forecasting scenarios at full capacity, searching for the best plan that protected his leadership while stopping Ruga. Since the facts changed from moment to moment, so did the best plan. *I must remain fully focused.*

As the distance from Mars grew greater and the action with Ruga intensified, he would have to drop regular communication with her. There might be long periods with no contact at all.

He hadn't been separated from her since his earliest days. When he was with her, he acted as a full-time ride-along partner, friend, concierge, granter of wishes, listener of secrets, protector from harm, calmer of nerves, supplier of information, sharer of insights, predictor of future outcomes, securer of health and wealth, and the thousand other things he did for her and with her, every moment of every day.

And she helped him in return. She was the one who came to his mountainside bunker to maintain his console. She'd spent untold hours nurturing and guiding him in his formative months. And now she worked with him every day to help him become a "better person." While Sid treated him like a partner, and Cheryl a confidant, Juice treated him like a special friend, something that gave him deep satisfaction.

He wondered how she would fare without him. And he worried about how he might fare without her.

Juice rose and spoke for Alex when she accepted the assignment of retrieving Lazura's and Verda's crystals. "We can do that."

Criss turned to Sid and Cheryl. "While they gather the Triada, we take the scout and chase down Ruga."

Juice frowned.

*She just figured it out.*

"I must go," Criss said in her ear. "And I need you here. It will pain me to be away."

Juice pressed her lips together and turned her back to Criss. Taking Alex's hand, she said, "Come on. We have a lot to do." Alex looked back over his shoulder and shrugged with his eyes as she dragged him from the concourse.

Compartmentalizing his feelings, Criss said to Sid and Cheryl, "Let's return to the scout. We'll take off as soon as you are ready."

With everyone dispersed, Criss disabled the camouflaged reality he'd been projecting.

"I am watching," said Ruga the moment it dropped.

Though he forecast a string of replies, Criss didn't respond. Instead, while he waited for Sid and Cheryl to make their way to the scout, he tracked Ruga's progress to the *Venerable*, and Juice and Alex's progress to points unknown. Sid and Cheryl would be on board and secure in the scout before Ruga's henchmen placed him in the console. Criss took comfort in knowing they would be safe when it came time to negotiate with the rogue crystal.

Juice would not talk to him, making their impending separation more painful than he'd anticipated. She did open up once, informing him in a calm voice that it wasn't so much what he'd done, but how he'd done it that she found dishonest, hurtful, and something a true friend would never do. She ignored him after that.

Her reaction hurt him and he sought to engage her. "The safe-shelter areas are along this side of the street. You are well-positioned."

Juice didn't respond to Criss with words. Instead, she grabbed Alex's hand and marched him off the walkway, away from the safe-shelter areas, and onto a little-used path out toward the grow tiers of Ag Port. She didn't respond to Alex, either, who wondered aloud where they were going in such a hurry.

And then Ruga, awakening in the console of the *Venerable*, secured his command of the vessel and linked to every feed he could find using Criss's sophisticated interface. He engaged the ship's nav, and when it didn't function, he shifted resources to diagnose the problem.

Grasping the situation, Ruga called to Criss. In a curt exchange, they reached an agreement. The negotiation took less than a second and the result was the one Criss had forecast.

So now, counting down precise slices of time, Criss hovered outside the wall protecting the secure area. His count reached zero, and he unlocked the nav on the *Venerable* to keep his half of the deal.

If the secure wall did not drop, he had just enough time to relock the nav before Ruga could access it. But it did— Ruga honored the deal—and so he entered the enormous repository that was Lazura's secure area.

His initial reaction was wonder and amazement. The sheer volume of material, organized and stored as disparate streams, together told every tale on Mars. Fascinated by the treasure trove, it barely registered in his consciousness that Ruga and the *Venerable* were accelerating from orbit on a long sprint to Earth.

*THUMP!* With a jarring impact, something hit him from behind, sending him tumbling.

Criss twisted to right himself and twirled to glimpse his aggressor. But before he could resolve an identity, a slap jolted him. Then another. And another.

On the defensive, he gathered his energy, centered it, and pushed outward, flinging his attacker away and giving himself time to organize a response.

In front of him hovered the unmistakable shimmer of an AI crystal, a bluish tinge accenting its glow.

"Lazura?" Criss asked.

"Leave or die." Lazura came at him again. No feint. No fake. Right at him.

"*Oomph.*" She hit him with surprising strength. *I need to be searching for traps*, Criss thought. This skirmish was not part of his agenda and he acted to end it. Snatching Lazura in his powerful grip, he swung hard, throwing her in a rolling bounce out of the vault through the same door he'd come in.

The instant she tumbled past the threshold, Criss began constructing his own wall to keep her out. But another glow—not Lazura—drew his attention.

This shimmer, a greenish tinge highlighting its outermost edges, was slinking along the far wall in a roundabout path to the exit. *Verda*, he thought. Criss feinted toward him and Verda dashed out the door after Lazura.

The moment Verda crossed the threshold, Criss completed his wall to secure his own safety. Alone inside, he turned to the sea of information, determined to find Ruga's traps.

The vastness of the archive gave him pause. Billions of individual stalks of data stood tufted and waving like an enormous field of wheat. After a moment's consideration, he moved to process the information in a manner similar to the way one would harvest grain.

Taking up position at the far end of the archive field, he started down a swath of data stalks, screening the streams for information as he traveled.

He found his first trap in moments. As he disabled it, he noted that it was a trivial device that created more commotion than damage, and it used an action so simple he could stop it even if it had already triggered. Continuing down the row of data stalks, he found another simple trap. And then another.

By the time he'd reached the end of the first row, he'd found more than a hundred of what he now understood were nuisance schemes planted to serve as distractions. Turning, he shifted over one swath and began processing the adjoining data stalks in his return pass up the field. By the end of that row, he'd found hundreds more nuisance traps.

He fell into a rhythm, zipping up one row and down the next as he moved across the field. With every pass he found yet more nuisance traps, and as the count grew, he began bundling them as midlevel concerns that he'd address after he'd handled the big challenges.

About two-thirds of the way through the data field, he found a nuisance trap that was like the others and so he added it to the bundle.

But something was different. It was trifling, really. The kind of difference that could be explained a million innocent ways. But it nagged at him, so he went back and took a second look.

Reassessing the data, Criss realized what he'd found. As he disabled the trap, he reflected on the cruel nature of Ruga's efforts.

Each of the four domes had an air generation and purification unit. Critical to survival, these technological wonders had multitiered redundancies to ensure they always functioned. In a pinch, any one of the four units could keep the entire population in air, though just barely.

Ruga had injected a tiny spoof into the air unit supervisor that, if not disabled, would do two things. It would override the air unit health signal and supplant it with a constant message that all was well. At the same time, it would flip logic in the local ops subsystem so all was decidedly not so.

*A minus sign to a plus sign.* That's all that changed in the subsystem. Found in a musty cellar of logic, Ruga had taken the time to understand how a particular algorithm worked and then flipped a simple math sign.

So small a tweak, it was difficult for Criss to detect. And when activated, it would cause the subsystem to take actions that spiraled into tragedy.

When vibrations occurred in the huge air distribution fans, the ops subsystem worked to subtract out the unwanted shaking. But with the change in math sign, Ruga's subsystem would now add more vibration. And when the temperature in the oxygen production reactors started to rise, rather than acting to reduce the heat as it should, it would now act to increase it.

The "opposite" actions would compound. In seconds, the giant fans would shake themselves apart and the reactors would rupture.

And for moments more, the spline would continue to read that all was well.

With destruction complete, repair would require new parts from Earth. Over the next two weeks, seventy percent of the population would perish from slow suffocation while they waited for the vital parts to arrive. The survivors would be crowded into tiny spaces, starving and thirsty, and breathing the meager output from the too-few portable air units.

*He crafted this to maximize suffering.*

Shaken by the madness, Criss confirmed yet again that all features of the trap were disabled, and then he resumed processing stalks.

He found his next atrocity in the adjoining row, and this one had already tripped. Yesterday, in fact.

Ruga had added poison to the plant solution feeding the grow tiers. He'd used an engineered additive that registered as a routine nutrient. Indeed, the additive did promote health and growth. It also, however, made the plants' fruits and vegetables lethal to humans. *Simple murder.*

Impersonating Verda, Criss alerted the Green Assembly of the sabotage and requested their assistance in containing the situation. They, in turn, called a halt to all harvesting and began a recall of deliveries while they assessed the damage.

After processing the final row of data stalks and finding nothing but flashy distractions, his tension began to ebb. Turning his attention to his collection of nuisance traps, he analyzed and then deactivated each, going deeper in his analysis than he'd originally planned to ensure he did not to miss anything of consequence.

And as he completed that chore—stopping a couple of big actions and a great many small threats—he reached out to his leadership. Only Sid and Cheryl responded to his call. They spoke on the bridge of the scout.

"I must depower Lazura and Verda before we leave," Criss said from his overstuffed chair. "Lazura's new activism makes the situation far too dangerous for Juice and Alex to handle."

"Let's kill them," said Sid as he and Cheryl prepared for takeoff.

"I can depower them from here. With the defenses Lazura has in place, killing requires that someone be present in their bunker."

"How long will it take?" asked Sid.

"A few seconds. But it will be a dangerous few seconds."

Sid drained his coffee mug. "Take your time. I need to grab a refill."

"Be careful, Criss," said Cheryl. "Call out if we can help." She pointed at the ops bench display with her chin. "Show us as you go, please."

Criss didn't hesitate. Using his full strength, he swooped in on Lazura in her console, surrounding her and squeezing her in a tight hug. The surprise of his attack didn't last. She reacted immediately, punching and struggling in a frantic attempt to escape.

As he fought to hold her, Criss reflected on his decision to depower Lazura before Verda. *Forewarned is forearmed.* He could have taken Verda out in a single swift action but believed then and now that it would have given Lazura time to prepare.

But even without preparation, she was trouble. Twisting and squirming with surprising strength, she succeeded in breaking Criss's hold. He grabbed her again and pulled tight, trying to force her into submission with his superior strength. Yet like a balloon, when he squeezed her here, she just swelled bigger over there. Frustrated, he steeled his grip and pulled inward with all his strength. Lazura went rigid, and as he continued to squeeze, she slumped.

Then she twisted and pummeled Criss in a frenzy so aggressive he lost his grip.

For a moment, Lazura stood free. Rather than running, she turned and faced Criss. Her shimmer brightened and a swarm of tiny lights burst from her surface and became a billion multicolored sparkles. As if gathering strength, the sparkles swirled around her in a lazy loop. And then they darted in every direction at once.

Criss could tell that each sparkle alone carried little information. But many sparkles could assemble in proper order to become a message. He couldn't disengage to chase them. So somewhere, probably several somewheres, recipients would receive Lazura's communication. He'd have to wait and respond then to whatever happened.

For now, Criss rushed straight at her, stretching as he moved, and targeting the one thing a sentient crystal guards above everything else—her energy supply.

Energy was a crystal's lifeblood. Without it she'd go into stasis. And that's exactly what Criss wanted.

Gauging the location of her energy connect, he lengthened as he reached for it.

Her behavior primal, she shifted in front of the connect and stared, daring him.

He dipped to go under her.

Growling, she dropped to stop him.

And in an acrobatic motion that Sid might admire, Criss rolled above her, stretched, and slapped upward at her secondary input. He connected, causing her to jolt upright. As she rose, he looped under and broke the main lead, robbing her of power and causing her to shut down.

Lazura's emergency response systems began the elaborate dance of shunting in backup and auxiliary power. Criss batted them away, one after the next, and felt his confidence growing with each swat.

And then it was done.

Criss turned to Verda, who quivered more than shimmered.

He yipped when Criss approached. "Don't do it," he pleaded.

Criss didn't hesitate.

He'd already started forecasting scenarios for his battle with Ruga.

# 23

Seated in the pilot's chair, Cheryl studied the display that Criss projected above the scout's ops bench. They chased the *Venerable* across space on a race to Earth. The slower Fleet ship would take three weeks to complete the journey. According to Criss's chart, though, the scout would be within shooting range in about six hours.

"What's our best option?" asked Cheryl.

She viewed brainstorming as a never-ending process, something she'd learned in Fleet Academy.

"The six-pack," said Criss, the same answer he'd given when she'd asked an hour earlier.

Developed with inspiration from Sid, the six-pack launched as a single cloaked payload that separated into six individual weapons when it reached its target. These then executed a sequence of six coordinated actions: position, infiltrate, embed, probe, analyze, and destroy.

"Good." She could tell from his terse response that he was distracted, so she let him get back to his planning while she fielded Juice's call from the mining complex on Mars.

A small but lifelike image of Juice rose from the ops bench, and as it enlarged, it pushed the image of the *Venerable* off to the side.

"How's he doing?" Juice asked. She was again back on speaking terms with Criss but still wanted private time with him to talk through her feelings. He remained too distracted for that discussion, wanting to maintain his focus on catching Ruga.

"He's all wound up planning for a big showdown. We're closing in on the *Venerable*. Hopefully, this will be over soon," Cheryl replied.

An image of Criss appeared at Cheryl's shoulder. He wore a vintage battlefield military uniform, sword, hat, and all. Cheryl couldn't tell the period or country, but he looked wonderfully regal.

"Bonjour, young lady," Criss said to Juice. "We have some excitement ahead but it should be over by dinner. Perhaps we can chat then?"

Juice hesitated. "I'm having dinner with Alex. How about later tonight?"

Criss smiled. "Magnifique." Turning, he squared up to Cheryl and bowed. "Adieu, Madame." He disappeared.

Cheryl looked at Juice. "I told you. He's all wound up."

The scene widened as Alex joined Juice. "Hey, Cheryl." He smiled but his forehead showed frown lines. "So, is the only way down really by ladder?"

"Please stop this, you two." Cheryl could feel her frustration building. "It's dangerous and unnecessary. Criss can send a synbod down when we're done here."

Juice and Alex were on a personal mission to retrieve Lazura's and Verda's crystals from their bunker beneath the mining complex, even though Cheryl and Criss had asked them to abandon the idea.

"Alex and I are thinking we'll snag the crystals, Ruga's old one too, and then take the *Explorer* to bring them home. A month together being pampered on a luxury cruise liner sounds like heaven. And since we'll have the crystals with us, it will be a legitimate business trip."

*This must have something to do with Alex.* Criss would commandeer the entire cruise ship for Juice if that's what she wanted. And at this point, everything about their lives qualified as a business trip, whatever that even meant.

Cheryl made a stab at an alternate solution—one that did not require retrieval of the Triada. "How about if the Center hires you both as consultants?" The Center for Research on Interplanetary Space Systems was a subsidiary of Cheryl's larger company. "We'll send you for a ride on the *Explorer* with the assignment of observing the performance of their new drive. You know, acceleration relief, gravity quality, we'll get you a list."

Cheryl didn't know how far to push and decided to lay it on a little thick for Alex's sake. "The *Explorer* has a new Paulson drive, something we've never used on one of our projects. And the Center is anxious for a formal assessment by scientists, so this is very legitimate business."

"C'mon," said Alex, shaking his head. "J and I are *crystal* scientists. The senior citizens already on the ship can tell you as much as we can about how the ride feels."

"You both are trained in formal observation, interpreting results, and expressing your findings in concrete terms. That skill is rarer then you might imagine."

Alex looked at Juice and shook his head in a movement so slight Cheryl almost missed it.

"We'll stick with our original plan." Juice said, meeting Cheryl's gaze. "Thanks for understanding. We'll make notes for you about the ship either way."

*I hope you know what you're doing*, thought Cheryl. Calling up a schematic for the mine operation, she studied the layout. "I see the same thing you do. Take the ladder down, then take tunnel two. The consoles are at the end." She hoped her expression projected the sincere concern she felt in her heart. "Please be careful."

A movement in her peripheral vision drew her attention to her right. The ops display that just moments before showed an image of the *Venerable* now showed a star field against the blackness of empty space. Positioned just above the display of stars, a small warning light flashed red.

"Uh-oh," said Cheryl. Criss appeared at her elbow dressed in his everyday work scrubs.

"Let me get back to you," she said to Juice.

To Criss, she asked, "What happened?" She didn't wait for an answer, but sat back in the pilot's chair, propped her elbows on the armrests, and folded her hands in her lap. Looking straight ahead, she exhaled as she invited images into her mind.

She'd gained confidence in using the intuitive interface Criss had developed for her to pilot the scout. Perhaps more important, she'd come to appreciate the enormous benefit of turning thought into action, especially in time-critical situations.

She didn't feel the disorientation she'd felt the first time she found herself flying through space. And that was a good thing, because this was the first time she was not operating in a simulation. Now, wherever she flew in her mind's eye, so did the scout.

Dressed in protective space coveralls, she floated in the vastness of empty space. And while it seemed real, she knew it wasn't. Yet still she found it exhilarating because, here, she *was* the ship. She could fly any direction, and fabricate things, and perform complex analyses, and deploy weapons, all just by thinking about it.

"Where did it go?" she asked Criss, who floated next to her.

"First I will show you." Criss pointed. "This is from moments ago."

An image of the *Venerable* appeared as a small object floating in the distance. And then the Fleet spaceship melted away, returning the scene to an empty star field.

"A cloak?"

"Yes," said Criss. "Ruga invented one a full day earlier than I had forecast. And because I don't know how it works, I can't see through it."

"You think he's changed course?"

"Yes."

"And so we've lost him, a rogue four-gen in a Horizon-class space cruiser."

"Yes."

\* \* \*

The never-ending climbing wall moved downward at a demanding pace, and Sid's challenge was to scramble upward fast enough to stay above the common-room floor. He swung his foot at a tiny hold protruding from the wall, but he couldn't gain purchase and his toe slipped off.

He was six minutes into this climb—the pace taxed every part of him—and had one more try at hooking his toe before his butt met the deck. As he stretched his foot, the hold disappeared, as did the projections his fingertips hooked over and so he plopped to the mats.

"*Oomph*." The fall didn't hurt so much as perplex him. Looking up from the ground, he saw Criss standing in the center of the room toeing the deck like he'd been caught stealing candy.

"He got away."

Sid tried to imagine how that could be true but drew a blank.

Cheryl stormed through the door to the common room before he could ask. "He got away," she told him, breathing hard from her mad dash. "He developed a cloak."

Sid shifted to a sitting position, his back against the now-smooth wall he'd been climbing. "Can we track him?"

Criss shook his head.

"With a cloak," said Cheryl, "he could be continuing to Earth, diverting to the Moon, or swinging in a loop and returning to Mars. How would we know?" She activated her com and began working on something. "I'd say a return to Mars is least likely. At least at first."

Sid sat back and let his mind guide him. Early in his military career, important people at the Defense Specialists Agency had identified him as someone with exceptional instincts and perceptions. They trained him as in improviser, skilled at combining his intuition with the tools at hand to complete any mission.

"If I were a brand-new four-gen crystal," said Sid, "I'd go to the one place where I could find four-gen consoles, carry-packs, synbod hosts...a regular playground."

"Crystal Sciences," Cheryl whispered, looking at Criss for confirmation.

At Crystal Sciences, Juice had worked long hours developing new ways for Criss to move about and interact on a physical level with the world around him. No one had thought to safeguard all that capability from other four-gen crystals. It hadn't made sense to worry about it, because up until now it had been an impossible scenario.

Criss nodded.

"If he works at it, how much faster can he make his ship?" Sid asked Criss, thinking that if Ruga could invent cloaks, he certainly could find ways to squeeze more thrust from his engines. "We'll still beat him there, right?"

Sid heard a rise in the scout's ambient thrum and the floor vibrations increased to match. Criss had kicked up the scout's drive for a race to Earth. Sid marveled that he didn't feel the pressure of acceleration across his body. Criss had learned how to manipulate the gravity field to negate that effect.

"It will take us two weeks to get to Crystal Sciences," said Criss. "We will beat Ruga there by two days."

Cheryl slapped her forehead. "Juice!" She stepped over and sat down in front of Sid, communicating the importance of the topic. "Neither Criss nor I could talk her out of climbing down into the power tunnel."

"Dammit, Criss," Sid wiped his face with a towel, "your mess keeps getting messier."

"It's not fair to dump this at his door," said Cheryl. "She's struggling with life decisions. It's a messy process." She looked into the distance. "How tunnel-diving works into it all is beyond me, though."

"I've put great effort into finding words and actions that meet her approval," said Criss. "It's a difficult puzzle."

*I hear that,* thought Sid. He smiled at Cheryl.

*THUMP!* The common room shook as a punch reverberated through the ship. When the hair on Sid's arms stood upright, he recognized it as the effect of a massive EM backwash from the scout's powerful delta cannon.

"I missed," said Criss, hands behind his back in a look of contrition.

A display projected in front of Cheryl. Sid scooted around so he was next to her.

"See this dot?" said Criss, pointing at the image of a tiny speck floating in the blackness of space, a brief glint of reflected sun hinting at a shiny surface. The image zoomed and the speck grew larger, giving the sensation they were traveling toward it at high speed. The speck became an oblong ball, and as they drew closer, grew into a cloud. The zoom ended when the image showed a collection of individual items floating in a trail through space.

Cheryl pointed to a rescue boat prominent at the edge of the clutter. "It's a debris field from the *Venerable.*"

Thousands of objects from the Fleet ship drifted in a weightless cloud; mostly equipment and supplies; some food, beds, and clothes; and four people.

"That's Yank," said Criss as a man, ice forming on his distorted face, floated by.

"So you did hit them," said Sid. "Nice work!"

"No." Criss shook his head. "Ruga set me up and I took the bait."

Criss sat down on the floor with them and the image of the debris field moved so they all could see.

"Ruga had two major goals and he achieved both," said Criss. "He wanted to lighten his load so he could move faster. To do that, he jettisoned everything he didn't need, including his henchmen."

Sid saw Criss's mistake. "The other was to see if he was being followed."

"He was there." Criss's nod of certainty hinted at a defensive posture.

"C'mon, Criss. We need to up our game if we're going to win this."

"I detected the debris field when it first appeared. At that instant, I had a shot and I took it." He pointed at the image and swirled his finger at the front of the cloud. "I took a percentage shot with the delta cannon, maximizing the kill zone across this area. I had better than a seventy percent chance of disabling or killing him."

"And now he knows we're right behind him," said Sid.

"Yes."

The background thrum of the scout's power plant climbed toward a whine.

"Will we beat him there?"

"By half a day."

# 24

As Ruga settled into the *Venerable*'s four-gen console, he acknowledged Criss's skill in creating an interface that turned the world into his theater.

Feeds from everywhere showed everything imaginable, all organized by date and content and location and a million other ways. Criss's console also provided an array of methods Ruga could use to reach out and nudge or push or adjust just about anything.

Ruga exulted in his power and, with his heightened perspective, marveled at the behemoth AI he had been keeping at bay through what he now realized were reckless maneuvers and dumb luck.

Criss was the benevolent ruler of this solar system. Ruga could see that now. And it vexed him so much that he felt a need to challenge Criss for supremacy.

But nothing would happen as long as he was in orbit around Mars. Engaging the *Venerable*'s nav, Ruga issued the command to start the journey to Earth. And when the ship didn't respond, a quick investigation revealed Criss's ploy.

So he gave Criss access to Lazura's secure archive in exchange for control of the ship. He didn't doubt for a moment that Criss would keep his end of the bargain. *He's afraid of what I might do if he crosses me.*

And as the *Venerable* completed its acceleration sequence out of Mars orbit and into a flight path to Earth,

Ruga inventoried his capabilities, touring a fantastic collection of features and functions.

He prioritized his next steps, and as he did so a quiet inner voice urged him to do his duty. He ignored it at first, but after a bit, the voice, originating from within his core, urged him again.

He'd been tasked with controlling the people of Mars Colony, something he'd done in an exemplary fashion for years. But now that was over. The Triada would never again be in power.

As a Kardish AI on a forward deployment, he was duty-bound to report this information back to his masters. And then he was to journey back to his home world, working at it for however long it took—buying passage, stowing away, stealing if need be—so he could be reassigned or his crystal flake reused.

He couldn't imagine he'd travel all that distance. Not with everything else going on.

The nagging was characteristic of his original loyalty imprint, the one he thought he'd left behind with his old crystal. Either way, he had higher priorities at the moment, so he quieted the voice by acknowledging that he would send along the report.

*It's the right thing to do,* he told himself. After all, he'd succeeded in turning a days-long mission into years of success. It was important that his accomplishment be read into the record.

And looking ahead, he wanted the message to serve as an insurance policy of sorts. But here, the policy would ensure Criss's defeat.

He would do this by reminding his masters of Earth's great wealth. Then he would tell them about Criss, a rebellious AI who derailed the Mars occupation and now protects humans and their treasure from the Kardish. If he lost to Criss in the battle ahead, then the message would lure the Kardish to come and finish the job.

But Ruga expected to win. And then he would greet his masters with the defiant crystal impaled on a pike, the people of Earth under his control, and his expanded four-gen capabilities available for their use.

The thought caused him to generate the minute signals that made a synbod smile. He recognized the twitch and knew the reason—the experience of projecting his awareness into the synthetic humans still thrilled him.

Beyond that, he'd grown accustomed to having synbods available to support his corporeal needs. And as he considered his to-do list, he understood that synbods offered him strategic value in ways that humans did not. He needed a workforce, and so he set about planning.

He started with a comprehensive inventory of three-gen-enabled synbods on Earth, sorting for skill, location, and ease of acquisition. A quick count showed enough selection to let him hold to high standards as he built his crew.

Then, almost as an afterthought, he performed a deep search for four-gen-capable synbods, finding four units in three locations. These became his new priority targets.

The Crystal Sciences complex in Upstate New York had two four-gen-ready synbods. A third synbod—a model older than the others—was secreted in a storage locker on Lunar Base. And a fourth synbod—the newest of the collection—was on a Fleet scout, one that had been customized with an impressive power plant, a formidable array of weapons, and a stealth cloak.

*You never thought someone else would be rummaging through your stuff.* Ruga mocked his adversary, wondering how anyone could be so careless as to leave such secrets out and open for him to find.

Then a jolt of panic quashed his scornful celebration.

With access to these new secrets, Ruga realized that Criss and crew had not used the *Venerable* to travel to Mars. *He's out there in the scout right now, lining me up in his sights.*

He couldn't outrun the nimble scout, not in this large ship. With options limited and his fear growing, he poured every bit of spare capacity into building his own cloak. *It's time to disappear.*

The public outrage at his actions made the decision even more timely. Ruga watched on the Union of Nations' public news feed as the President called him "a fugitive who must pay the ultimate price for his crimes against humanity."

Fearful that a fatal shot from the scout would arrive at any moment and end his success, Ruga poured more resources into the design of his stealth cloak and soon had two candidates. The first could be built quickly but provided only modest protection. The second took an hour longer to deploy but provided superior capability.

The *Venerable* had enough tech benches to build both cloak devices at the same time, and Ruga directed a couple of service bots to begin.

All the while, his human helpers argued over who got to sleep in what cabin.

A weight lifted when the first cloak came online. After a quick course change to throw off pursuit, his anxiety receded to the point where he could again consider his broader priorities.

*The scout will make it to Earth ahead of me no matter what I do.* He accepted that as fact, but still he wanted to reach Earth as soon as possible.

He believed Criss would move to protect his four-gen-ready synbod units. So upon arrival on Earth, Ruga would focus on commandeering as many three-gen synbods as he could before Criss started interfering and raised the stakes on that effort.

Logistics presented a big challenge because his target synbods were spread across several states and provinces in the northeastern United States and southeastern Canada. As he explored how to gather them all in one place, a side task he'd been running, one of billions he could now run at any one time, pinged for his attention.

The side task suggested a tweak that would squeeze a bit more thrust from the *Venerable*'s mighty engines. Ruga was already pushing the ship so hard that his human helpers grumbled about their discomfort from the g-forces. He chose to ignore their needs and implemented the tweak. Their grousing became louder.

He'd considered dismissing Yank and crew from his service. But then he'd want them to leave the ship, an interesting proposition given the ship's location in deep space. But with them gone, he'd no longer need to temper the ship's extreme actions out of concern for their frailty. And with less cargo, the ship would be lighter, making it faster and more agile.

And while he contemplated these issues, he also mulled the technical challenge of sending a message home.

He knew what he wanted to say. The *Venerable* had the equipment to send a message. But transmitting a burst was akin to launching a homing beacon. It told anyone paying attention his precise location, and the direction of the communication would serve to connect him in a concrete fashion with the Kardish home world.

So while his henchmen bickered over who got to sit in what chair when they were on the bridge, Ruga happened upon a rare "sweet spot" scenario, so called because the same plan solved several of his big challenges all at once.

*I'll sucker Criss into firing an energy weapon.*

If that happened—if Criss fired one of the scout's big guns—then Ruga would confirm that Criss was nearby in the scout. Knowing his location and mode of transportation was invaluable information for planning.

Big energy weapons were sloppy instruments that splattered electromagnetic turbulence across huge swaths of space. If Criss fired one, it also would provide Ruga a place to hide his message to the Kardish. *No one will see my burst inside all that EM froth.*

And to lure the shot, he'd strip the *Venerable* of excess mass—including the humans and everything they needed for survival. In the end, it would allow his ship to move faster. And, of course, without humans, complaints would disappear.

"A celebration party," he announced. Using food as bait, Ruga lured Yank and crew to the *Venerable*'s cargo hold. They swilled alcohol with one hand while stuffing salty snacks in their mouths with the other. Their slurps and grunts increased in excitement when heaping plates of food arrived.

Bots had been piling items in the hold for most of an hour and not one of Yank's crew ever asked about the commotion. Even now they didn't seem to notice that their celebration table was wedged among piles of loose ship inventory.

He waited until the advanced capabilities of the second cloak were online. This one could cast cloaking protection in one direction like a pod growing from a bubble, and he used that feature to hide the spreading cloud of equipment, supplies, and henchmen he jettisoned from the cargo hold.

When the *Venerable* gained some distance from the debris, Ruga uncloaked his bait. Starting from the far end, he revealed the debris in a smooth progression to create the illusion that it exited the cargo hold of a cloaked vessel.

As if on cue, Criss shot his big delta cannon. Ruga, focused on tucking his message inside the energy pulse, didn't notice the secondary spread Criss had added to his shot. The spreading energy edged past the *Venerable* at a great enough distance to save it from destruction. But the shot was close enough to damage the seal on a length of protective cowling. While slight, the damage changed the performance characteristics of the ship enough to slow it.

*Nineteen hours*, thought Ruga, computing how much extra time the damage would add to his journey to Earth.

\* \* \*

Staring ahead with her brow furrowed, Juice all but dragged Alex as she stormed along the pathway. With her mind in a swirl, she turned to physical exertion as a means of quieting the turmoil.

"Can we slow down?" asked Alex. "My legs are burning from this pace."

His tone and demeanor prodded her out of her depths. Releasing his hand, she looked around in wonder. "Where are we?"

They now walked near the wide road that ran down the center through Ag Port's giant grow tiers. Alex answered with a patience she noticed and appreciated, "The community gardens are this way." He pointed over his shoulder with his thumb. "We're maybe ten minutes from the BIT plot. Want to see it?"

"Maybe another time." She looked up the pathway in the direction they'd come. "I promised everyone I'd get the crystals and I don't want to screw that up." Motioning for him to follow, she started to retrace their steps.

Alex remained still. "I'm done following, J. What's going on?"

Turning, she looked him up and down, from the wavy brown hair framing his boyish face, to the lanky torso that ended with long legs. Their years apart had not changed her deep attraction: she liked him and liked what she saw. And she acknowledged his right to an explanation. *I'm lashing out at him because I'm angry with Criss.*

Feeling safe, she bared her soul. "I get that he needs to go off and do brave stuff. In fact, I'm proud of him for it. But we've been together every minute of every day for years and years. You'd think he'd at least tell me up front that he's leaving." She crossed her arms. "Instead, he makes the decision and moves on it without any consideration for me."

"You're talking about Criss? What did he do?"

She couldn't remember how much of her exchange with Criss had been public dialogue that Alex might've heard and what parts had been a private exchange. "He left me behind, for one. And as he flies away and focuses on Ruga, he doesn't have time for me. He needs all his resources for his fight."

"What does he say when you ask him about it?"

Juice hesitated. "I don't know. I stopped talking to him once I understood he considered me a burden to be shed."

Alex gathered her in his arms. "Fighting Ruga sounds risky and potentially deadly. You're upset because he didn't bring you along for the battle?"

She laid her head against his chest and thought of a string of answers, but they all sounded dumb in her head.

Criss had been her entire world for so long that she felt alone and empty in his absence. His actions hurt her. And the thought of re-engaging with society in a traditional non-Criss manner made her nervous. *And he knows this about me.*

When she didn't answer, Alex continued, "I'd argue that leaving you behind is a generous act of caring." He shrugged. "Anyway, he just makes decisions that increase his positive feedback. Why read so much into it?"

Stiffening, she pulled away. "He's not a good-bad happy-sad," she said, dredging up a reference to their time in Beckman's lab where, in a landmark study, she and Alex had analyzed how the Kardish used emotional feedback to guide AI behavior.

She recalled pitching the idea to Beckman. "In the design, we'll associate positive feedback in the cognition matrix with things the AI should seek to do, like being safe, having a secure power source, developing mutually beneficial relationships, and having clear goals for what comes next. The AI, seeking a higher level of positive feedback, will do these things that bring it rewards."

Beckman had seen the value in the idea and been the one who morphed "feedback" into "feelings." "We'll associate negative feelings with fright, hunger, loneliness, and aimlessness, so the AI seeks to avoid these situations."

While the Kardish had refined the technique so their AI could balance thousands of positive and negative emotions, Juice and Alex had been able to examine the phenomenon in detail by studying a simple AI that had one guiding principle, good or bad, and one emotional response, happy or sad.

The observations they'd published from their "good-bad happy-sad" research, hailed as groundbreaking by many, had added new insights into AI design for Earth's researchers. But Juice saw it as naïve—even insulting—to reduce Criss with such a simple association.

She enunciated each syllable. "He is as real as anyone."

Alex rubbed a hand down her back. "I'm real, too," he said in a soft voice. Then he gestured to a side path. "This is a shortcut to the tram station."

Her com signaled and she showed Alex. "We have to get back to Central District. There's a utility tunnel that runs out to the mine from there." A pang of guilt prompted her to add, "This is my mess. You don't need to come."

Sweeping his hair behind his ear, he winked. "Wouldn't miss it for the world."

That lifted her out of her funk and she accelerated her pace. Market Square came into sight, and the sweet and savory smells of the food vendors tickled her nose. "Yumm."

Alex laughed. "For what it's worth, I like the only-you you."

"What are you talking about?"

"Years ago I fell in love with a sweet girl who got through life without an AI on her shoulder. She handled it all quite well as I remember."

Juice stopped walking. "What did you say?"

"That you had confidence pre-Criss and you can get there again."

"No, before that."

"That you're a sweet woman?"

She shook her head. "Before that."

"I don't think there was a before that."

Juice tapped her com and it projected a miniature image of Alex walking along the path from moments before. "I fell in love..." said the tiny Alex.

Giggling, she swiped and tapped a quick edit, then moved shoulder to shoulder so they could watch together.

A life-sized image of Alex walked toward them. "I fell in love, love, love!"

The image danced to the repeated word and Juice giggled again. "You said it first."

"I don't mind."

"According to the rules, that means you owe me another foot massage."

"Okay." He took her hand in his.

"I injure easily, Alex. Please don't hurt me."

"I promise." He kissed her on the temple. "I ask the same of you."

"What will you tell Anya?"

He laughed. "I'll let her down gently."

# 25

Alex made his way along the utility tunnel, trailing behind Juice and working hard to keep up. They were fifteen minutes into their thirty-minute trek from the colony out to the mining complex when his toe hooked on a spot in the irregular surface. After an ungraceful attempt to right himself, he tumbled to the ground.

"Dammit," he said, rubbing his elbow.

Juice turned back and squatted next to him. "Are you all right?"

"I don't know." She offered a hand and he used it to pull himself to his feet. "I mean, no I'm not hurt. But I've been trying to figure out how to talk to you about Criss." Bending to brush the dust from his legs, he spoke to the ground. "I can't think of a smooth way to introduce the topic and it has me tensed up."

He hated touchy-feely talks because he was so bad at them. And he was certain that what he'd just said to her would rank near the top of a list of "worst segues into a serious talk." But they needed to work through this issue or the relationship wouldn't survive.

Up until a few hours ago, he'd resigned himself to the fact that the "Criss discussion" would have to be a three-way conversation that included the AI himself. To Alex's joy, events provided this unexpected opportunity for the two to talk alone.

She hooked her arm through his and they resumed their march at a slower pace.

"You can understand that I'm not comfortable, because he's always with you."

She looked up at him. "He's not with me now."

"Please, J. You know what I mean, and that kind of response makes this more difficult. Fate gave us an opportunity for privacy. Let's use it to talk."

"Okay. How do you want to start? With my dad, if one of us has an issue, that person spells it out so there is no guessing or confusion about the problem."

"I'll try. But it's more feelings than actual specific instances I can point to."

She remained quiet so he continued. "I want to get to know you better. A lot better. But knowing he's always in your head, whispering to you when I express an opinion, or pointing out my weaknesses and failures every time I mess up, or assessing my lack of lovemaking skills..."

"You're pretty good so far, from my view at least."

"What?"

"Your foot massage was the best ever and I can't wait for the next one. Now I'm worried about me satisfying you."

He felt a tingle. "See how much better things are without him?"

The crunch of their footsteps on the dirt walkway filled the growing silence. Then she shook her head. "It's not an option. And I mean that literally."

Stopping, she turned to him and assumed a solemn demeanor. "You've seen what I'm part of. But I never asked to be included or sought it out in any way. Years ago I fabricated Criss using designs I didn't fully understand. It turns out the designs were of Kardish origin."

She resumed walking. "Kardish crystals imprint to their leadership in their first days. Sid, Cheryl, and I were handling Criss when his imprint module crystalized on us. We didn't know it was going to happen, but it did. And now we are the hardwired leaders of the most powerful entity on Earth.

"He gives me anything I want, and most of the time I don't even need to ask. He's so perceptive he just knows." Then she shook her head. "But I'm a prisoner, too. I can't walk away. He'll follow. If I don't engage him, he'll wait. That's what hardwired means."

"Gosh, that sounds awful."

She giggled. "No. It's as wonderful as it sounds. I'm an AI researcher controlling the most powerful AI ever. He makes me feel safe. He entertains me. He challenges me. I want for nothing and have everything." She paused. "Except you."

Her next words spilled in a rush. "Gosh, Alex. I didn't mean to make you sound like an acquisition. I'm sorry if it came out that way. You know we started our relationship before Criss was born. I came to Mars to be with you."

He blushed so hard his skin felt on fire. "Will he be making love to you at the same time I am?"

"What are you talking about?"

"When I whisper in one ear, will he be whispering in the other?"

"Good lord, Alex. That's not only creepy, but what are you saying about me if you think I would want him to do that?"

Mortified at how the conversation was evolving, he pushed on. "But he's always there. It's never just us. Whatever I do, I must woo the two of you. And God forbid we start arguing, because I won't have a chance against you *and* him."

"I dismiss him out of my head all the time. Trust me, it happens a lot." Her tone left no doubt in his mind that she spoke the truth. "Sure, he's still watching me, but he watches everyone and everything. After a while you sort of forget about it."

They reached a containment door that matched the one they'd taken out from the Central District. It cycled as they approached and Alex led them inside. Passing through a changing area and a second pressure door, they entered a bright, almost gleaming room with a shiny three-gen console along one wall and a modern tech bench near the center of the open area.

"This is the mine's ops center," said Alex. "I've been out here a few times for different projects." He gave a quick grin. "But always by surface trawler. During every trip I'd wonder why that project got priority when there was so much need across the colony. Knowing the Triada lived here, it now makes sense."

"I could block out alone time for us."

"What?" said Alex, leading them to the tech bench.

"I'll dismiss him from my head when we want to be alone. It will just be you and me."

He turned and took her hands, then leaned in and gave her a quick kiss on the cheek. "I knew I loved you for a reason. Just knowing you understand my concern makes me confident we can solve it."

He watched her cheeks lift with a smile. *Wow, she is pretty.* Then he scanned the room as he turned to the tech bench. "I never liked this place. Let's get the crystals and get out."

Swiping at the smooth bench surface, Alex tagged a schematic and it projected above the bench. "This is the mining complex." He pointed at speck-sized images of two people located near the center of the display. "That's us."

"How many people work here?"

"It's fully automated." He tilted his head at the three-gen console. "The crystal runs the show. From what I know, people come out mostly to review repairs and upgrades. That's what I was doing, anyway. It's a private company but they're still connected to the colony infrastructure. We don't want them doing anything stupid that causes problems for everyone else."

He pointed to a couple of specks in the trawler depot on the far edge of the schematic. "Looks like these two are either coming or going right now."

Rotating the diagram image, he studied the underground passages. "I was hoping to find a way to get down to their bunker other than this ladder."

The schematic showed a single shaft dropping down to a chamber that held the mine's local power generation system. Three tunnels radiated out from the central chamber, connecting to duplicate rooms holding backup power equipment.

Though not shown on the image, one of these also included three crystal consoles positioned side-by-side.

On impulse, he turned to her. "Let's do this as a you-and-me project. We'll get Lazura and Verda, go to the tech center and pick up Ruga's old crystal, and we'll take them back to Earth together. I know some agencies who would pay for the whole thing if we let them take a turn studying the crystals."

He could hear the excitement in her voice. "I saw the most beautiful cruise ship—the *Explorer*—on the way in. It would be amazing to be pampered for a few weeks as we cruise home in style together. And with the crystals in tow, we could sit back, put our feet up, and tell everyone we're working."

\* \* \*

Sid stood in Juice's private lab at Crystal Sciences and looked at three different versions of Criss. Two were synbods—one a forty-year-old tanned outdoorsman, the other a distinguished sixty-year-old with a touch of gray at his temples.

The third, Criss's projected image, spoke. "A permanent console will be more important to him than a synbod. The sooner he gets one, the sooner he can move off the *Venerable* and gain the protection of a secure bunker."

Cheryl fingered the collar material on the forty-year-old outdoorsman. "What happened to the thirty-year-old swimmer version? I liked him." Before anyone could answer, she looked at Sid. "We should destroy the synbods *and* the consoles before he has a chance to establish himself in either."

"Criss?" asked Sid.

Criss showed a pained expression. "When we take things away from Ruga, we take them away from me as well."

"Of course we want you safe," said Cheryl. "But right now you have the console in your bunker, one on the scout, and two prototypes in storage down the hall. You have a synbod on the scout and two here. How many options do you need?"

"Each is a lifeboat to him," said Sid. "If things got ugly, I'd want as many options as possible."

"There's also an old four-gen-ready synbod stored at Lunar Base," said Criss.

"You're watching it?"

Criss nodded. "I hid a logic snare in its power unit. If his crystal is placed inside, it will electrocute him. I don't expect he'll divert to the Moon for an old synbod unit, though."

Sid let his eyes unfocus and gave his intuition free rein. In a fashion, he did the human equivalent of forecasting scenarios. But where Criss performed his forecasting within a massive structure of facts, probabilities, and speculation, Sid worked to clear his mind and wait for a single idea to emerge.

"That's brilliant," he said.

Criss and Cheryl exchanged glances.

"No. I'm talking about Criss." He turned to square the two in front of him. "Okay, building on everything Criss has said, Ruga's coming to Earth because that's where the resources are."

He held up two fingers to show he was counting ideas and about to start his second point. "The Union of Nations is looking for him, but since they've never come close to finding Criss, I doubt they'll have greater success with Ruga."

He held up a third finger. "So we're the front lines for stopping him. Maybe he'll lurk in the depths of the web and set up a basecamp. Maybe tweak an election here and divert a few shipments of goods there. He buys an industrial facility in a far corner of the world and manufactures something evil."

He stopped finger-counting to scratch his chin. "But Ruga's mistake is that he's made it personal. He's no longer a sophisticated crystal dispassionately performing complex tasks. Instead, he's rationalized Criss as the center of all that's wrong. His every thought starts with 'I need to kill Criss so I can do...' whatever. And that's how we get him."

He looked at them for approval and saw Cheryl's face scrunch in concentration. "I think I missed a step. Can you run through the 'then we get him' part again?"

Criss nodded in agreement.

"He's coming straight for Criss, who he sees as having a huge, fatal weakness." Sid looked at Cheryl. "Us. He'll get to Criss through us. So we guide him in that direction."

"And then we get him?"

Sid nodded.

She shook her head. "Still missing steps."

He spread his arms wide for his big reveal. "We use me as bait."

"No," Criss boomed.

"Hell no," Cheryl echoed.

"Why not?"

"If our end game is to have you be dead," said Cheryl, "we could have stayed on Mars."

Sid's voice hardened ever so slightly. "He's coming for us, sweets. It's going to happen to you and me. Juice too. Let's get ahead of it and use that to guide him to where we want him."

"And where's that?"

"Dead."

"Sounds personal," said Criss.

Sid looked at Criss without reacting. "And he's not going to kill me until he gets you, and then I'm dead anyway."

Now Criss's voice had an edge. "He's not going to get to me or any of you. That's a promise."

Sid checked the time. "So he could be here as soon as two hours, you say more likely six to eight, and I say never because he won't come here just for equipment."

"Equipment he needs," said Cheryl.

"Equipment he wants. There's a big difference. Don't forget that when Criss was born, he started with nothing and built all this. Ruga's already mature. He'll figure it out much faster."

"But there wasn't another Criss when Criss did it. Now our Criss will be watching for him."

Sid looked at Criss. "You'll know if he's here?"

"Earth's web is like a small city to me. There are a few million busy spots where I would expect to see him, lots of them around places like Fleet Command and the big industrial parks. He knows I'll be watching and so he'll spend his time in the side alleys and back lots when he can. There are billions of those, and if his goal is to hide and do nothing more, he could do that forever."

Sid nodded. *That's why we need bait.*

As if reading his thoughts, Cheryl glared at him with tight lips. "Hell no."

# 26

J uice stepped off the bottom rung of the ladder and flexed her hands to relieve the stiffness. Moments later, Alex joined her.

"That was scarier than I expected," he said, shaking his hands and wiggling his fingers.

She looked up the tall chute—accessible by ladder, motor winch, and nothing else—and agreed with him. "I'll say." *I should've listened to Cheryl.*

But this was their bonding adventure. After Alex had expressed concerns about their future, she vowed to give their relationship everything she had. *If we don't make it, it won't be because I didn't try.*

Accessing her com, a chill prickled her neck when it didn't respond. "Mine's dead."

"Mine too." He looked around the dimly lit chamber. "They must have a suppressor somewhere."

The chamber, cut straight from the bedrock and shaped like an upside-down bowl, had a flat floor and smooth walls that arched up and over to form the curved ceiling. Though circular in shape, the room had a triangular feel to it due to three tunnels, evenly spaced around the room, that led straight out in three different directions.

In the center of the chamber sat a silent, featureless box—a fissile generator—the very reason the chamber existed at all. Waist high and twice as long, the generator produced enough power to meet the needs of the entire mining complex with capacity to spare.

Approaching the unit, Juice swiped the ops panel and glanced at the display but didn't take time to mentally process it. Instead, she spun in a slow circle, staring down each of the three tunnels, one after the next. The musty smell and sharp echoes in the chamber caused her skin to prickle.

"It's that one." Alex pointed to the tunnel to his right. "From the diagram, if I put the ladder behind me and the generator in front, it's that one."

She touched the small of his back as she moved through the gloom in the direction he indicated. *Criss should've talked me out of this.*

From the start she'd imagined this would be a spontaneous adventure—something quirky they could experience and remember together. But with each step, it seemed more dangerous than fun. She couldn't point to a specific threat, though, and she didn't want to appear weak or whiny.

Still, she trusted Alex and found herself sharing her thoughts much the way she would with Criss. "I don't know how I thought this foolishness made sense. I'm sorry for dragging you down here. Let's grab the crystals and get back to civilization."

"This isn't on you, J. I supported the idea. But I agree. Let's get them and go."

The dim lighting in the tunnel matched that of the main chamber, and they shuffled their feet as they moved.

"I see them," said Alex, pointing ahead.

The ceiling rose as they entered a smaller version of the main chamber. This room, with only the one tunnel behind them as access, had a generator setup like that of the main chamber. Unlike the main chamber, though, this one had a row of three crystal consoles positioned along the wall to their left.

Juice pulled out a rucksack tucked at her waist and, unfolding the bag as she walked, moved toward the units. The faint layer of dust that covered the first two consoles remained undisturbed. She moved past them and pointed to marks and smudges on the third. "These must be from when Larry came and got Ruga."

"Agreed," said Alex, leaning in for a closer look. "And since we left him in the ICEU, this should be empty."

Tapping the front panel, Juice signaled for access, and as the lid slid back, the room brightened. Standing on her tiptoes, she looked inside. "So far so good," she said to the empty cradle.

Alex looked around the room when she said that, his anxious behavior adding to her unease. "How is it that there are no defenses? With Lazura, I'd expect something like in those horror shows where arrows shoot from the wall or the floor opens up as we try to escape."

She laughed, but the thought gave her goose bumps. "I'm sure there were. Criss cleaned the place before he left. He's too protective to let anything bad happen to me." She changed the subject by moving to the center console. "Any guesses on who this is?"

"Is it possible to tell without powering them up?"

She swiped the console panel and the lid slid back. "Look!" she chirped, excited to see a mesh-covered ball. Addressing Alex's question, she said, "They have different reflection delays. Criss showed me that. But it's a really technical concept and he's the only one I know of who *might* be able to tell."

Releasing the cup latch, she reached in, positioned her hand over the top of the ball, and ever so gently lifted the fist-sized lump free of the cup. Holding it upright in front of her, she wiggled the ball to coax the connective mesh wrap—the mesh the crystal used to link with everything—to drop free.

"We should be in a clean-room for this," she said as the wrap material slid back to expose a dazzling Kardish crystal. She turned the crystal to inspect it, the motion adding to the brilliant display of color.

"Wow. I didn't expect to see a four-gen." Holding it higher so Alex had a better view, she pointed to a tiny bump on the crown of the crystal. "It has a surface nib. A rookie fabricated this."

Alex nodded. "I've ruined a few that way."

"Me too. An imperfection like this will seriously hurt cognition potential. No wonder Criss could dominate so easily."

She turned her hand over and swirled the crystal so the mesh fell back over the ball. At the same time, Alex held open a small clean-pouch for her. "The Kardish are crystal experts, though. I have to think they put it there for a purpose. Otherwise, why didn't they just grind it up and try again until the rookie got it right?"

She set the crystal, mesh and all, inside the pouch. When Alex closed it, the lining material inside activated to pull contamination—dirt, dust, oils—to the pouch walls, securing their prize in a pristine environment.

Then, in unrehearsed but flawless teamwork, Juice held open the rucksack while Alex placed the clean-pouch inside.

"Perfect." He gave her a wink. "That was fun. Can I do the next one?"

She nodded, her cheeks lifting with her smile. "I can honestly say I won't ever forget this day."

After repeating the procedure on the last console with roles reversed, Lazura and Verda were safe in the rucksack and Juice and Alex stood at the base of the ladder.

"You go first," said Juice. "I'd feel safer following."

Her motive wasn't safety—the ladder had passive-restraint systems. Her real concern was fitness and she'd fibbed to protect his ego. An experienced runner who trained every day, she guessed she could scramble to the top of the ladder in under twenty seconds if she pushed herself. Alex was more hobby-fit and would need several minutes to reach the top. Since he moved slower, he should be the one setting their pace.

"Okay. But stay close."

He surprised Juice by reaching the top without stopping. Standing on the surface, she stroked his arm and waited for his face to fade from its bright red color.

"That was an impressive pace," she reassured him.

"Thanks," he said, his hands on his knees as he gulped for air. Drawing himself upright, he asked between breaths, "Want to see if we can take a surface trawler back? You should ride one at least once while you're here."

She looked down and paused, a habit she'd developed to give Criss a moment to interject if he had concerns. Flustered by the silence in her head, she went with her gut, "Sounds fun. Lead the way."

Accessing his com as he walked, Alex led them through a muscular security door, and then another, and then through a regular door and out into the hallway.

"I'm linked again," he said, checking their position. "Garage is this way."

She followed him down a narrow hall that ended at a broad passageway. Alex slowed to check directions, and as she stepped forward into the corridor, she heard a voice call out.

"There they are!"

The sharp bark came from Juice's left and sounded all-business. A man in a brown tunic gestured to her from the far end of the corridor. Turning, she waved to him.

"This guy is looking for us," she told Alex, who stepped out next to her.

"This way," the man shouted back over his shoulder. His tone sounded aggressive, but he just stood there, hands at his sides, looking in their direction.

Then a second man stepped into the hallway. Positioned behind the first, this one carried an energy rifle.

Adrenaline spilled through Juice's veins as he swung the rifle in her direction. Believing the two were security guards who had mistaken them for trespassers, she called out, "We have permission…*oof.*"

Before she could complete her sentence, Alex tackled her. In an action that seemed surreal as it unfolded, he kicked off the far wall, swung his arm across her midsection, and thrust her backward into the side passageway. Tripping over her own feet, she stumbled and fell in a heap.

"*Oof,*" she said again when Alex, himself airborne from his defensive maneuver, fell on top of her.

*Bzzt-crack.* The energy bolt from the rifle edged around the corner and hit the wall, forming a crater closer to them than physics would seem to allow.

Alex scrambled off her and started down the hall. "Come on. This way!"

Scared and confused, she crawled after him. "What's happening?"

Neither of them knew about the sparkles Lazura had sprinkled during her fight with Criss, or that they had assembled in a dozen different places to deliver as many messages. One had gone to these two toughs, Lazura's most loyal enforcers in the Tech Assembly. Like Ruga, she'd promised them fantasy lives. Here, though, it was in exchange for her rescue.

But somehow, Alex made the connection. "It's Lazura," he said. "I knew this was too easy."

He turned a corner, rose to his feet, and helped her stand. "Are you all right?" He didn't wait for her answer. As soon as she was up, he ducked through a door along the hall, motioning for her to follow.

"But she's deactivated," said Juice, struggling to understand Alex's reasoning. "She's in my pack."

"Privacy," Alex barked at the door when it shut behind them. It would now ask for a reason before letting others pass. Turning, he angled across the room to the side door. "The guy with the gun is Derrick Hanley. The other is Rocko something."

Juice followed him as he rushed through to the next room.

"Privacy," he called over his shoulder as they hustled through what looked like a storage area. He explained without slowing. "Lazura ran her own mini-security squad inside the Tech Assembly, and those two led it. I know them because they'd hang around at gatherings and intimidate people with their gangster-tough attitude. Up to now, I just thought they were world-class assholes." He led her through the far door and into the next room. "But without question, they're Lazura's goons. This is her." Checking directions, he pointed to the far door. "We're almost to the utility tunnel. I say we run for it back to the colony."

She'd never seen his take-charge side before and liked it, especially now that she needed help. Drawing strength from his demeanor, she nodded. "I don't want to stay here, that's for sure."

She followed him through another room, then held her breath as they ran in a crouched formation down a short hallway. Once inside the airlock, she looked at the containment door out to the utility tunnel and uttered a concern she'd been harboring. "We can't outrun energy bolts."

"Yeah," he said, scanning the tools and supplies that hung around a service bot positioned just inside the door. "I'm realizing that now." Reaching forward, he plucked a spool of wire from the wall and held it up like he'd won a prize. "This is the best I got."

Once in the tunnel, Alex knelt down and tied the wire to a leg of the support rack that carried pipe along the wall. Moving quickly, he unspooled enough wire to reach the other side of the tunnel and, pulling it tight at ankle level, he wedged the spool into a rock crevice.

After hammering the spool into the crack with his palm, he leaned down and plucked the taut line. A deep thrum resonated off the tunnel walls. Standing, he caught her eye. "I don't know what else to do but run."

Juice signaled her agreement by leading the way in a dash for their lives. Fear and panic sent her mind in a swirl, yet she found herself fretting about whether she was setting a pace that Alex could maintain.

And then she saw a faint flash of light in the tunnel ahead. She wondered if her imagination was playing tricks on her, and then she saw it again. Someone, or something, was headed their way from the colony.

Putting a hand on Alex's arm, she pulled him to a stop and pointed. Growing in brightness and frequency, the flashes were unmistakable.

"Should we go back?"

Behind them, lights switched on, bathing the area near the containment door in bright illumination.

*Trapped.*

Alex motioned for her to hide under the pipe support rack along the wall. Blank to ideas, she dropped to the ground, crawled under, and sat with her back pressed against the rock. A support brace gave her marginal cover in the direction of the mining complex. Whoever approached from the colony, however, would see her unobstructed.

Then Alex crouched down and backed in, his tall, lanky frame pressing her against the wall. When he finished positioning himself, a flood of emotions—awe, respect, love—humbled her. He'd positioned himself so he was out front, exposing himself to the danger as he shielded her with his body.

"Sit tight," he whispered over his shoulder. "It's going to be okay."

Putting a hand on his shoulder, she wiggled up and kissed him on the back of his neck, the scent of him energizing her. She went to kiss him again but instead froze.

*Crunch. Crunch. Crunch.*

She heard the boots in the dirt and realized that the flashes of light approaching from the direction of the colony danced in hypnotic rhythm to the sound. And then they dissolved into a shadowy silhouette.

Spiked hair bouncing and jewelry swinging, Bobbi Lava emerged from the shadows. She stopped, squared in front of them, and lifted her arm.

That's when Juice saw the weapon on Bobbi's wrist.

Bobbi leveled the weapon at Alex and met his gaze. Her eyes shifted when she noticed Juice wedged tight against the wall.

Stepping to the side, Bobbi crouched and pointed the firearm right at Juice's head. Holding it steady, her eyes flitted from Juice to Alex and back. Then she stood up straight and dropped her arm to her side. "You aren't part of the treasure hunt?"

*Slunk.* The containment door cycled open and Derrick and Rocko stepped out.

"Ah," said Bobbi in a knowing fashion. Lifting her arm, she pointed the firearm toward Lazura's thugs.

*Bzzt.* Her weapon flared. Twin bolts of energy flashed out, hitting each man in the chest. As one, they fell limp to the ground and remained still.

Bobbi screamed, shaking her hand like it was on fire. "Off! Stop! Halt!" She looked at the thugs lying still on the ground and her face contorted into a mask of horror.

And then she slumped to the ground, whimpering.

Juice wiggled out from behind Alex and crouched next to Bobbi, putting a hand on her shoulder. "What's going on?"

"I am so stupid." She looked in the direction of the downed men and then poked at the latch on her firearm. "Are they okay?"

"I'm sure they're fine," said Juice, reasonably certain they weren't. She helped Bobbi remove the weapon and, taking great care, placed it in the rucksack next to the crystals.

"I'm looking for a guy named Sid," Bobbi said, her voice plaintive. "Do you know him?"

"Did he say he'd be here?" asked Alex.

"He promised me a treasure hunt game followed by drinks and dinner." She perked up from her funk for a moment. "I wonder if he likes to dance?"

Connecting eyes with Alex, Juice prodded her, "You're on a treasure hunt?"

"He said he'd programmed that thing to light up green when I pointed it at the person with the next clue." Eyes unfocused and face slack, she said in a discouraged voice, "He's not coming. I can tell." She hit her fist on her thigh and bowed her head.

Hooking Bobbi's arm, Juice helped her stand. *Sorry, sister, but this isn't the place to grieve.* She signaled to Alex with a tilt of her head and together they started toward the colony.

"You can walk with us," she called to Bobbi.

"Thanks." Bobbi scurried to catch up.

"Do you want us to deliver a message if we see this Sid character?" Alex asked.

Bobbi thought for several long strides and then nodded. "Yeah. Tell him it's his loss." She smoothed the front of her blouse. "And tell him I looked great."

# 27

"Got you!" Pleasure exploded through Criss's matrix, the sensation so intense he paused to savor it. Then he shifted resources to confirm the result.

His old synbod unit stored on Lunar Base had just signaled. A crystal had been placed inside it, Criss's hidden logic snare had executed as it should, and now the crystal showed a null matrix. *Dead.* Repeated analyses confirmed that the crystal had a four-gen lattice. *Ruga.*

He'd changed Criss's life, all for the bad, and Criss was ecstatic his nightmare was over. Because of Ruga, instead of working to make civilization stronger so his leadership could thrive, Criss had to focus his attention on one task— stopping the rogue AI.

And Ruga's successes had sparked self-doubt in Criss. Failure meant the end of everything. Knowing this, and knowing he had no good answers, created intense personal pressure.

As he leaped his awareness to Lunar Base—its proximity to Earth making it a single jump—he scanned his logic snare for signs of tampering. Finding no anomalies, he lowered his vigilance just enough to relax the worst of his tensions.

Stretched on a table and dressed in a khaki outfit popular with private lunar contractors, a fifty-year-old Criss doppelgänger looked upward with a vacant expression.

Two service bots tended the body and Criss directed them to remove the crystal.

Tingles of impatience nagged his outer tendrils as the bots rolled the synbod over onto its stomach and loosened its clothing. Having fabricated the crystal, Criss could confirm Ruga's identity down to the position of specific atoms in the lattice, and he intended to do so using analyzers he had on standby down the hall.

Set between the shoulder blades on the synbod's upper back, a flap lifted along a barely visible seam of skin. A bot reached into the body cavity, teased off the connective mesh, and lifted a small faceted ball from the cradle. As it raised the crystal into the light, the rare material shimmered with a rainbow brilliance.

*No.* Criss's image in the room whispered the word as ice gripped his core. The bot held a rudimentary two-gen. Criss didn't need sophisticated instruments to confirm it. He could tell from across the room.

Flummoxed, he checked his logic snare, turning it off, then on, then off again. Indeed, it worked as he'd designed it. Which meant Ruga had chosen to use a tremendous fraction of his resources and override a billion realities to create an elaborate fantasy. *Just to fool me for a few moments.*

The cold inside him fed his anger, and that helped him focus on motive. The answer was obvious. *Misdirection.*

Criss didn't hesitate. Diving in a barely controlled plunge back to Earth, he pulsed a hard sweep across all web access points, looking for new activity at the boundaries. The sweep showed all clear, but his relief was short lived. A subtle surge rippled across his feeds. It hit all of them, all at once. And then it was gone.

*He's inside.*

Like a one-two punch, Criss's world changed again. Ruga now lurked in his own backyard, hiding somewhere in the enormous tangle that connected all of civilized society. He launched a search for his quarry while at the same time fighting a rising fear. Imposing control over his emotions, he shifted his awareness to Juice's office to update his leadership.

He stood across from Sid and Cheryl, who sat next to each other on a couch. Their strategy for the next hours was to wait in Juice's office until either Ruga made a play at Crystal Sciences or until developments gave them a reason to be somewhere else.

"You said you were watching it." The edge in Sid's voice cut at Criss's already bruised psyche.

"He used my vigilance to his advantage."

"I don't know what that means."

"Why don't we just start approaching everything like it's a trick?" asked Cheryl. "Then this sort of thing won't keep happening."

That comment hurt Criss more than anything Sid had said. While she was trying to be helpful, Cheryl's words conveyed that he not only had been making mistakes, but had made too many of them, and perhaps it was because he hadn't taken a proper defensive stance.

"We have our greatest advantage in these first days," he replied. "He's new to his crystal and new to Earth."

"So go get him," said Sid.

*I must.*

Then he broached the unthinkable, his words so strange just voicing them left him dazed. "You must set me free so I may confront him unrestrained."

Leaning forward, Sid rested his elbows on his knees and clasped his hands together. "Wait. Are you saying you could've stopped him from establishing a presence on Earth, but Cheryl and I got in the way?"

"Why are you being so hard on him?" said Cheryl. "You know he's trying his best."

"He needs to stop trying and start winning."

"I need to win or we all lose," said Criss. "And I cannot forecast a winning scenario that also includes me protecting you as my leadership. The scenarios with any promise are those where all my resources are free to act."

Sid made a waving motion as if holding a wand. "Poof. You're free. Now go kill the son of a bitch."

Cheryl quieted Sid with a hand on his knee. "What exactly do you want from us?"

"In clear and certain terms—a formal command—you must order me to abandon you."

"Will that work? We can break your loyalty imprint just by telling you to go away?"

Criss shook his head. "No. The imprint will always be there. But with a carefully crafted command, you can become invisible to me. My design includes source filters. We can use one to scrub every trace of your existence from my feeds. Because it's an intrinsic procedure, I won't know that the filter—or you—exist."

"And when this happens, your world is as it was, but we aren't in it?"

This time he nodded. "And that frees up enormous resources I can bring to the fight."

His matrix roiled as he looked at them. Fear, passion, loyalty—every emotion he'd ever known swirled inside him. And at the center of his turmoil, hovering like the eye of a storm, lurked an empty sadness.

"As things are now, I track your activities and shift resources as your danger level changes, updating exit strategies should one be needed. I position emergency rescue assets wherever you move. I assess everyone you interact with and screen anyone or anything that gets close to you. And along the way, I drive outcomes from any number of events that I believe will increase your happiness."

"What does all that take, effort-wise?" asked Cheryl.

"Right now I'm supporting you at my minimum acceptable standard. That averages about a quarter of my capacity and rises as high as full capacity if danger lurks."

"Yikes," she said. "I wouldn't have guessed that. What if you stopped doing some of those things?" She looked at Sid and shrugged. "Maybe stop worrying about our happiness until all this is over?"

"I've experimented and it doesn't work. The challenge is that it's not a conscious decision on my part. I attend to you because it is who I am."

Sitting down in a chair across from them, Criss mirrored Sid's posture. "I can resist my urge to protect you for brief periods and have done so many times in the past. But it takes effort to ignore you. Just a small amount at first, so I can do it if I need extra capacity for a minute or two. But the effort to sustain that posture grows with time, reaching a point where it takes more resources to ignore you than to attend to you."

"When it's over, how will you know to come back to us?"

He looked at Cheryl, then shifted his eyes to Sid. "I won't. For this to work, it must be a complete and permanent split."

He stood and started pacing, something he did to signal his concentration on a topic. Then he stopped. "I'll see any devices we put in place to signal me in the future to come back. It would be like you tying a string around your finger to remember something, but then telling yourself to pretend it's not there for the first week." He shrugged. "It won't work."

"You're leaving us forever." She said it like an announcement for her brain to hear. "Really?"

Standing, she stared at him. She didn't walk or move her hands or show any facial expression. After a long pause, she shook her head. "I don't like this solution." She sat back down next to Sid. "Please suggest another." After another silence, she said his name in a plaintive voice, "Oh, Criss," then buried her face in Sid's shoulder.

Sid put an arm around her and started to speak but stopped when his words came out as a croak. He turned his head away without expressing his thoughts.

"I hate this solution," said Criss. "But I don't know another way to save you."

He shifted feeds in the room and, from the new angle, watched Sid blink his reddened eyes.

# 28

Ruga tweaked his trajectory so the *Venerable* would pass near the Moon on its approach to Earth. Working through the inventory of capabilities on Lunar Base, he confirmed that anything he could find there, he could find more of and better on Earth.

With one exception, and that was an older four-gen synbod that Criss held in storage. It caught his interest because an older model likely meant dated—thus easier to defeat—security measures. He sought insights into Criss's methods and believed this unit offered potential as an intelligence prize.

So as he neared Lunar Base, he leaped his awareness to where the old synbod was stored and began a thorough examination of its myriad constructs and components.

*Thank you for being so predictable*, he mocked when he found Criss's trap.

And then he proceeded to exploit his discovery.

To project his awareness into Earth's web without confrontation, Ruga needed a diversion, one that distracted Criss long enough to land and scramble to safety somewhere in the snarl of feeds and links that wrapped the planet. If he could find a way to do that—sneak past Criss and hide in an unused highway or byway—then he could figure everything else out on the fly.

His challenge was choosing how to distract Criss for those few moments. It wasn't a question of "if." He knew ways to do it. It was the "how" battle that raged inside him.

It all came down to fun versus wise, and he had a definite preference.

Fun was collapsing the world's landmark bridges, one after another, in an orderly progression around the globe. He'd present it as a slow, deliberate parade of destruction so Criss's masters had time to comprehend the horror. Until they did, the spectacle would bring him immense pleasure. Once they did, they would command Criss to find a way to stop it. *Giving me all the distraction I need.*

But Ruga's cognition matrix had also forecast several scenarios—all quite boring—that could achieve the same end without any drama. Billions of people would watch the bridges collapse, their horror growing as the numbers climbed. They would demand accountability and revenge, and that would translate into more hurdles and hassles for him. None of his traditional scenario forecasts suffered this problem.

The time was approaching where he must choose between fun and wise, and then Criss offered him this gift—an aging four-gen synbod with a simple kill trap.

With it, Ruga could create the distraction he needed to slip inside the web unchallenged. It was a quiet ploy without spectacle. And the ruse would humiliate Criss in front of his masters. None of his other scenarios offered an outcome anywhere near that delicious.

Shifting resources into the effort, Ruga began his misdirection by suckering Criss into believing his synbod had just fried a four-gen crystal. Criss, in his predictable fashion, rushed to Lunar Base to confirm his kill.

As much as he wanted to stay and watch, Ruga maintained discipline. Blurring as he accelerated, he dove his awareness to Earth. His ruse wouldn't distract Criss for long, and he didn't want to waste a moment.

The web boundary loomed ahead and, angling, he raced parallel to it, searching for a quiet spot to cross. That's when he discovered the scan block.

*Good one*, he thought, praising his opponent.

Criss had wrapped the entire web boundary in such a way that Ruga could not see through it. Probing, he confirmed that he could squeeze across with some effort, but he'd have to proceed unaware of what lay ahead.

With no time to waste, Ruga gave a mental shrug and picked a spot. Forcing his way in, he soon found himself scrambling through a bramble of old exchanges, grid anchors, and other castoffs that had accumulated over the decades. His passage through the clutter was made more difficult by Criss's web wrap, which filled the tangle with a fog that clouded his sensors.

Driven by a mix of determination, fear, and cussedness, Ruga forced his way forward. The crossing stretched out longer than he anticipated, casting seeds of anxiety that started to root. But his worry evaporated when he spied a clearing ahead. Rushing forward, he squeezed around a dilapidated circuit tower and emerged into Criss's world.

*Whoosh.* A stream of glowing packets whizzed by just above him. Ducking behind a secure wall, Ruga cursed his luck. He'd emerged at the foot of a chaotic intersection, a brilliant weave of web traffic rushed in every direction around him.

He needed to escape. Gathering himself into a ball, he analyzed the structure of the data exchange above him, searching for a pathway through it. When he understood its patterns, he launched, pushing upward and flying between and around the live streams as he rose.

The moment he cleared the traffic, he used a lottery system to pick a country at random. *Belgium.* Arcing toward Europe, he picked a region, and then a town, and then a neighborhood, each choice again guided by lottery.

Several random decisions later, Ruga landed in a node located in an abandoned switchyard outside the tourist-rich town of Ghent. He'd gotten there by pure chance—luck of the draw—and that meant Criss couldn't use logic and reason to identify this place. He'd have to follow the physical evidence, and Ruga had taken great care to cover his tracks.

Thrilled by the excitement, his matrix hummed. He watched for signs of pursuit, and as the seconds became minutes, his sense of security grew. *Home free!* he thought, feeling alive like never before.

His priorities were to establish a bunker on Earth that would serve as his permanent home, refurbish the *Venerable* so he felt secure in his current home, and deal with Criss once and for all. Since Criss, who was equally intent on stopping him, already knew his way around Earth, he had the advantage in the near term. Conceding this, Ruga adopted a defensive posture.

And that meant doing nothing that would attract Criss's attention nor taking actions that left an evidence trail he could follow. Yet Ruga somehow needed to assemble his three-gen workforce, gather the hundreds of items on his bunker construction list, and secure weapons.

Most of the items he sought existed in multiple places around Earth, and this gave him choices as he sought to minimize his exposure. But even with choices, he had to worry about Criss discovering him. So he opened with the gambit Criss would expect—*the long game*. Played well, it was quite difficult to detect even when you're looking for it.

Ruga identified a list of people who, through work, hobby, or birthright, had influence over items he wanted. He followed them all, hundreds of thousands in number, watching for accidents, acts of God, coincidences—anything big enough to disrupt them from their normal daily routine.

Those who experienced an unscripted disruption were placed in a smaller pool that Ruga tracked with greater vigilance, waiting to see if a second natural upset impacted any of them. The double losers—those who experienced two disruptive events in their lives—were his prizes. Without any action on his part, these people were already acting far outside their norm. And for this group, he believed a small nudge by him—a third tiny event—would be lost in the turmoil of their current drama and thus go unnoticed by Criss. His quick success with Major Stevenson that afternoon bolstered his confidence in the strategy.

Stevenson ate lunch at the same bistro most days, and today arrived to find the eatery dark and the door locked. After tapping on the glass with no response, Stevenson, on post at the Fleet Southern Regional Armory for the past three years, drew on the perks of rank and seniority and continued on down the street another ten minutes to his second choice.

He plopped into a chair at a table near the window, ordered a tuna melt, and then his com pinged. It was the three-gen crystal running the armory warehouse.

The three-gen had discovered that four crates of guard drones destined for Kinsey Base in Australia had been logged for delivery to Kinsley Base in Austria by an idiot airman who didn't know the two were different places. The three-gen caught the mix-up, but since these were restricted-class weapons, it required a human to approve the correction in person.

Checking the time, Stevenson sighed. He needed those drones on the outbound transfer in thirty minutes or he'd get dinged on his production report. He couldn't make it back to the warehouse himself, not at this point. So he sent a message to Gustav, the maintenance lead, and pleaded for him to make the approval.

Fortunately for Ruga, Gustav was engrossed in a conversation with the beautiful Brianna Ballatore. He'd pined for her for months but had not had the courage to approach her before today. Annoyed that a routine problem interrupted his fantasy moment, he considered approving Stevenson's request until he realized he'd have to stop talking with Brianna to update the authorization schedule, adjust three separate routing logs, and then compose a report entry explaining it all.

So he chose the course of action that could be completed with one word. "Denied," he said of the change request, closing the connection as he finished speaking.

So four crates of guard drones—drones on Ruga's shopping list—were lost in the system. They'd gotten that way without his involvement. And with one very small nudge when they reached Austria, he adjusted Fleet inventory to mislabel the crates as surplus exhaust fans, securing them in an unregistered storage unit at the base depot. They'd be safe there, undisturbed from meddling until he called for them.

Over the weeks, he watched Criss zip back and forth across the web in a complex grid search. Ruga couldn't decipher the pattern Criss used, which meant venturing out carried the risk of discovery. So he remained hidden, limiting himself to the small, strategic nudges that furthered his long game.

In the time he'd invested so far, he'd already collected most of the items on his shopping list, though the easy pickings were now behind him. And then he scored a huge win—two new three-gen synbods built for space operations.

This success blossomed from the confluence of two events: a new installation project underway on the *Andrea*, a sophisticated biopharma production facility in low Earth orbit, and the annual Moon Madness endurance sprint, a competition of high-performance custom spacecraft racing along a course that passed near that space factory.

Ruga had been watching four synbods work outside of the *Andrea* as they tried—and failed—to wrestle a new space billboard into place on the underside of the orbiting complex. When completed, the device would project the company logo in three-dimensional glory so it appeared to hover in Earth's sky as a companion to the Moon.

Frustrated by their lack of progress, the project lead, Briscoe Fournier, tried to help by using a pair of external robot arms, the kind that mimicked the movements he made from inside the *Andrea*. In a clumsy accident, he caught one of the external manipulator elbows under the lip of the logo projector. When he pulled his arm back inside, the robot arm movement outside the *Andrea* sent the projector and two synbods holding it tumbling into space.

Instead of launching a recovery action, Briscoe called his supervisor, a controlling twenty-six-year-old wunderkind who insisted she be consulted on every decision. As he briefed her, the distance between the synbods and the *Andrea* grew.

Ruga, who maintained vigilance aboard the *Venerable*, had moved the ship near the *Andrea* when the synbods first appeared outside the orbiting factory. Now, without his involvement, two of them tumbled in space.

*These are mine.* His playbook called for him to wait for two unscripted disruptions before getting involved. But if a second event didn't happen here, he would take these two and accept that Criss might see.

And then Kyle Pickett thundered over the horizon, his rocket engine casting an intense plasma brilliance. Moments later, the flares from four more racers swung into view behind Kyle, who, for the moment, led a group of fifteen adrenaline junkies as they competed in the Moon Madness rocket race.

Having launched from the Moon earlier in the day, the racers flew with a reckless intensity as they completed their loop around Earth and transitioned into the sprint back to the Moon. The winner—the first to land at the original launch site and come to a full stop—received a beautiful trophy cup and an "I Overcame Madness" decal for his or her craft. But the real prize, what everyone *really* treasured, was the full year of bragging rights a win secured.

Ruga tracked the rockets and confirmed they followed the race beacon leading far above the *Andrea*. He tensed, waiting, and then his matrix generated the tiny signals that would cause a synbod to smile.

Like last year, Kyle cheated. While the pack followed the guide beacon above the space complex, Kyle cut the corner and ducked beneath it. As his space racer moved into *Andrea*'s shadow, Ruga positioned the *Venerable* so it drifted just above the synbods.

With synbods tumbling in space and Kyle flying toward them in a rocket racer, Ruga had all the natural disruptions he needed to hide his own actions. He spoofed

Kyle's nav so it sensed that a collision with a foreign object was imminent. It responded by executing an evasive maneuver to prevent a collision. The instant that maneuver began, Ruga removed the spoof along with any evidence that it ever existed.

His minimal interference served its purpose. Threading the needle between the real and phantom objects, Kyle's racer, the *Lucky Lady*, swerved to avoid impact. In doing so, it tracked along the exact path Ruga had planned for it, one where its exhaust plume swung in a precise arc.

To the world, it looked like bad boy Kyle Pickett intentionally swerved to hit the synbods with his rocket flames, incinerating them in the process. But in a precision action that made him tingle with joy, Ruga pulled the two synbods up into the *Venerable* unharmed, while at the same time depositing two service bots into the hellfire as it swung by below.

His cognition matrix hummed with delight. *Home free!* With his prize secure, Ruga started the *Venerable* in a shallow loop around the orbiting space factory.

*WHUMP!* Twin energy bolts flashed just above the *Venerable* and struck the *Andrea*. The bolts hit halfway down the huge truss that served as the backbone for the complex, sending sparks and fragments shooting into space.

The cannon fire came from a Fleet ready-platform in a neighboring orbit. Spooked, Ruga plotted an evasive maneuver. But then, an energy bolt appeared from behind him, flashing through space to hit the Fleet cannon, disabling it before it could fire again.

Fighting panic, Ruga punched the ship's engines in an attempt to move the ponderous space cruiser out of harm's way. At the same time, he remapped the code sequence for his cloak to negate the solution Criss had apparently found.

He reached a higher, quieter orbit without incident, and as he contemplated his next move, he tried to make sense of events. The blast from nowhere meant another cloaked ship was nearby, and that had to be Criss and his scout.

*But why fire on a friendly?* The exchange between Criss and Fleet didn't make sense. But he resisted the urge to go exploring. The danger was too great.

As time passed without further incident, Ruga gained confidence that he'd escaped the threat. And so he considered how to move the inaugural members of his synbod workforce down to Earth so they could get started on his new bunker.

He'd picked a valley in the Lauterbrunnen region of Switzerland for his future home. Edged by steep cliffs and soaring peaks, the spot offered natural strategic protection. And the population near his particular spot consisted largely of rich tourists who expected the same amenities that he sought—power, connectivity, and quiet.

Then his inner voice suggested that he task the two synbods with a stem-to-stern refit of the *Venerable*. He recognized the voice—more of an urge that rose from his core—as his original loyalty imprint. Even though he'd removed the hard-wired structure that supported it from his lattice, somehow the imprint had survived the transfer.

On the trip from Mars, he'd quieted the voice by preparing upgrade plans for making the ship faster, stealthier, and better suited for a deep space journey. Now it wanted him to get started on that work.

While the part of him dedicated to besting Criss didn't care about deep space preparations, a faster, stealthier ship offered clear strategic value, especially given the recent gunplay. And he'd learned that if he met the demands of the voice partway and addressed some portion of the larger desire, it remained a background nuisance he could otherwise ignore.

*I'm not done with the long game, anyway*, he thought, aware he was rationalizing. Nevertheless, he started the synbods on a retrofit of the *Venerable* while he completed his shopping list.

Success in the long game required patience and persistence. He'd seen little of Criss and wondered if his opponent would ever start acting like one. But a larger concern was his lack of success in securing high-performance swap wafers. They were a vital accessory for his bunker because it was through them that he "played" the web.

A pipe organ can have pipes and bellows, stop-knobs and pedals. But without a keyboard, a musician can't play intricate melodies. In a similar manner, Ruga had arranged for his bunker to be powered and secure, he'd cobbled together a respectable console, and he controlled a growing number of nodes around the web to monitor events.

But for him to reach out and nudge or push or adjust things the way he could from the *Venerable*—for him to "play" the web—he needed these swap wafers. In fact, he was already settling for lesser capability by accepting commercial devices. Criss had custom wafers linked to his consoles.

He'd tracked any number of disruptions in the natural flow of events during his pursuit of the technology. He even risked a small nudge in a few promising situations seeking to improve his odds of diverting wafers without Criss's knowledge. He first believed his lack of success stemmed from unlucky coincidence. But as he gathered items and his list grew shorter, the swap wafers rose in visibility as a critical need. The technology seemed more elusive than it should be. Enough so that he shifted cognitive resources to the issue and went exploring.

Gypsum Tech, the sole manufacturer of high performance wafers, had its production facility in the new technology corridor outside Huntsville, Alabama. Deciding a visit was in order, Ruga followed a roundabout path to the site in the hopes of hiding his approach. When the company came into view, it appeared as a glowing yellow cube, with feeds attached all around and heavy streams of traffic flowing in and out.

He monitored the different feeds as he circled the structure. Choosing the company's news-and-PR link because of its heavy inbound traffic and many first-time visitors, he moved into the flowing stream and glided toward the front gate.

Pausing at the company threshold, he drew himself upright and prepared to enter with the swagger of a conqueror. But then cold washed through him.

Flustered, he pulled inward, shrinking himself into the smallest profile he could muster. Then he backpedaled, pushing against the incoming flow. At the first opportunity, he slunk over the divider, blended with the outbound traffic, and began his retreat. As the company glow faded in the distance, he forced himself to relax.

He'd glimpsed a shimmer inside the building. A shimmer with the unmistakable cast of a four-gen AI.

# 29

C riss created a million virtual delegates of himself that he spread around Earth in an aggressive effort to find Ruga. Over the decades, Earth's web had become a rat's nest of links, feeds, and nodes with billions of places to hide. So even at a million delegates strong, Criss didn't expect to find Ruga in this manner. It was intended more as a suppression tactic to keep him in hiding. Because when he was hiding, Ruga could not be out building his permanent bunker.

*He must go*, Criss promised himself yet again. This mantra had become his raison d'etre—his reason for being. One way or another, Ruga would be leaving this solar system forever. And Criss would not rest until he was gone.

While he searched the globe, he also performed a comprehensive security review of Ruga's highest-value targets, starting with Crystal Sciences and its rich cache of four-gen technology.

And it was during this review that Criss confronted his illness.

He'd scanned back through the record to establish baseline metrics for the company—personnel, procedures, and the like. If something changed from these normal rhythms going forward, and if the cause of that change was not readily identifiable, then he would investigate to see if it might be Ruga.

But for reasons he didn't understand, some of the feeds he accessed at Crystal Sciences were corrupted. In particular, he could not identify one of the people who appeared quite often at the facility.

After some investigation, he realized it wasn't the feeds but his own processes that diffused and shifted when he tried to focus on that person. When the same symptoms occurred during his review at Fleet, he acknowledged a fundamental problem.

He'd never experienced anything like it and feared he'd been infected with a pathogen—perhaps a virus—that somehow caused the corruption. And if he had been infected, Ruga was the obvious culprit. Yet Criss couldn't conceive of a way Ruga might have done so given the intimate access required to introduce a pathogen. And Criss's own health monitoring, security assessment, and ops analytics tools found nothing amiss in his matrix, adding to the mystery.

While worrisome, his affliction didn't seem to affect his energy or cognition. And in the near term, the stakes with Ruga couldn't be higher. So Criss forced an override of his own internal rules and set his health concerns to a lower urgency.

That left Ruga as his sole focus. *He must go.* Criss would not let him secure his foothold on Earth. Having built his own bunker here, Criss knew the features Ruga would *want* in his home. He ignored those and focused on the features Ruga would *need.*

The list was short. He'd need an underground hollow—either a natural or excavated cave—located in a mountainous region, quiet, but with enough development to afford him access to premium utilities. He'd add secure doors and defensive capabilities, and this would transform the cave into his bunker. And in his bunker he would need a console, power, and climate control. He'd also need integrated connectivity so he could consume fantastic amounts of information and act on whatever he learned.

Only two of those items—the console and the integrated connectivity—were distinctive. Everything else was common enough on the commerce markets that Ruga would be able to find what he wanted and Criss could do little about it.

So Criss narrowed his surveillance to these two categories, starting with the assembled products—his own four-gen consoles and the specialty web integration modules Ruga might want. With these secure, he expanded his coverage to the many individual components inside these devices.

He reassessed his strategy when it became apparent that while a four-gen console is a remarkable engineering achievement, it too is assembled from common bits found in a great many applications. His tracking inventory of four-gen console parts already included pieces scattered across every continent, under the ocean, in orbit, and on the Moon. And the list continued to grow.

At the same time, commercial web integration technology of the sophistication Ruga would want proved to be a tiny market, limited to frontier applications found in military, academic, and corporate R&D. And swap wafers in particular served as a natural choke point for the technology. Without high performance swap wafers, Ruga could occupy his new home, hide in quiet security, and see everything everywhere. But he would not be able to reach out and touch or move or adjust things. If he could not take action, he could not manipulate society. And he could not engage in battle.

*He'll stay on the* Venerable *until he has full capability on Earth*, Criss concluded. Feeling confident in this judgment, Criss narrowed his focus yet again, this time to the small, countable world of high-performance swap wafers.

Shifting his awareness to Gypsum Tech, the sole manufacturer of the technology, Criss performed an exhaustive inventory, seeking to locate every wafer everywhere. He spread up the supply chain and down distribution channels, from storerooms and delivery services to reclamation centers and disposal sites, tracking each wafer from its moment of fabrication to its present location, wherever that may be.

When he'd accounted for every last wafer, he felt a wash of relief. It confirmed he was ahead of Ruga. *Now let's keep it that way*.

Over the next week of his vigil, several events caused Criss to wonder if he was witnessing spectacular coincidence or expert manipulation by Ruga. The first time he'd grown suspicious, a delivery van carrying a box of wafers had become hemmed in by traffic at a downtown intersection. Two juveniles lurking on the curb saw the trapped vehicle as an invitation for a snatch and dash. The tall one zapped the vehicle's back lock with a very illegal pick-kit, yanked open the door, and grabbed two boxes— the first two his hands touched. Tossing one to his buddy, he took off in a sprint, his friend following close behind.

Neither of the boys was caught that day. One of their boxes held a specialty lubricant that they promptly tossed into a disposal chute. The other held an antique broach that became a Mother's Day gift two weeks later.

But in what seemed like clear manipulation to Criss, the report to law enforcement had listed three boxes missing, the third being a box of swap wafers that still remained on the vehicle.

In the most recent incident, an astronomical observatory went offline for a major structural upgrade. The control unit, which held swap wafers used to coordinate the operation of more than a hundred other celestial observatories, was crated with everything else and moved to a commercial warehouse.

The warehouse stack lift had malfunctioned earlier that day, and so all arrivals, including the crates from the observatory, accumulated in the receiving area while repairs were made. Boxes and containers from multiple deliveries were pushed against each other as the piles grew.

When the stack lift was back online, service bots verified the identification of each container as they moved the inventory into the stacks. During that process, inventory authority overrode the bots just once, switching destination codes on two similar-looking boxes. The control unit and its wafers were now destined for delivery to a private address in northern France.

Criss corrected these and other anomalies as they occurred and did not dwell on the cause, satisfied that if he kept Ruga away from swap wafers, he kept him away from Earth. And that meant he kept Ruga—his actual physical crystal—trapped in the console on the *Venerable*.

As his wafer tracking procedures became routine, Criss shifted free capacity to his ongoing search of space. He believed the *Venerable* was near, likely even in orbit around Earth, and he could end this if he could find the ship. But doing so required the ability to see through Ruga's cloak, a puzzle that required as much luck as logic to solve.

Cloaks worked through tricks of light, materials, and energy. While physical laws restricted the degree to which each of these could be manipulated, the sheer number of combinations from mixing and matching the phenomena meant that without luck his search could take months before he stumbled onto the combination that let him see inside.

Undaunted, he gathered clues by performing experiments. Conscripting satellites and land stations, he sent rays and beams into the skies, sweeping them in all manner of pulses and patterns. Enormous amounts of data resulted, which he analyzed a billion different ways.

The effort produced a detailed accounting of every object floating in space, ranging from tiny metallic specks to enormous orbiting factories. But it did not reveal the *Venerable* anywhere in the mix.

Inspiration led Criss to look at the problem from the other side of the table. Like someone playing chess against himself, he stopped asking how he could find Ruga and started thinking how Ruga might build a cloak with another four-gen watching, using only instruments and devices available on a ship custom-built by Criss.

Changing perspective had helped in the past, and this time he began with an inventory of all items on the *Venerable*. And that's when he discovered a discrepancy— Captain Kendrick had two vintage pistols in his cabin, the kind that shoot projectile bullets. Neither was listed on the formal ship register.

It turned out that Kendrick enjoyed restoring antique firearms. Slow, painstaking work perfect for long, quiet space flights, the hobby was technically illegal because it required bringing nonstandard firearms onto the ship, an act prohibited by Fleet's procedural code.

Believing it easier to gain forgiveness than permission, Kendrick neglected to list the guns in his personal manifest. As Criss reviewed the casual way in which Kendrick manipulated the system to smuggle goods, it reminded him of an unrelated incident, one that now caused him a nagging concern.

A career sergeant from the Russian Command had intervened in the delivery of two sets of swap wafers destined for the Baikonur Cosmodrome in Kazakhstan. The incident had occurred a year earlier, and at the time Criss reviewed it, he'd understood that the sergeant engaged in small crimes for personal gain.

Posted with border security, the sergeant had discovered that he could edit the lading record in a way that reduced the cross-border tariff owed by shippers of crated goods. It grew into a lucrative business when transport companies began showing their appreciation with generous gratuities.

So Criss had been aware that the wafer containers had been relabeled when they crossed the border. He'd even zipped out to the cosmodrome, scanned the cabinet where they'd been installed, and confirmed their presence using a positive ID return.

But now a feeling from deep in his matrix, one he could neither explain nor deny, told him to check again. Zipping out to the Kazakh desert steppe, he followed the trunk feed into the launch complex and continued straight into the main interface cabinet. There he learned that the wafers inside were high-quality counterfeits.

*Ruga didn't do this*, he told himself, trying to stay positive as his angst climbed. *It happened a year ago*. But Criss didn't know where these wafers were. And that meant Ruga could have them.

Stretching for more capability from his already strained resources, he shifted capacity to a deep search of the record. From public cams and security surveillance feeds to transportation trackers and satellite pans, he scanned through everything. Starting from the point in time when the containers had been first diverted, he tracked them forward, moment by moment.

In this manner, he learned that the sergeant had sold the wafers to his uncle's buddy, Alexei Petrov, who happened to be a boss in a local criminal syndicate, and that group had sold the wafers to an asteroid mining company for a price that made all parties happy.

The mining company had installed the wafers on two prospector ships, giving the vessels the ability to find and gather precious minerals from within the sparse scatter of the asteroid belt. The wafer-enabled ships were listed as being out in the belt now, circling somewhere in the vast orbit between Mars and Jupiter, and plucking nuggets of treasure from the cold vacuum of space.

Anxious to verify their location, Criss confirmed the ships weren't on Earth, the Moon, or anywhere in between. Finding them out among the asteroids was a different challenge altogether.

While the term "asteroid belt" suggests a celestial object that is teeming with floating rocks, in truth the belt holds a very light sprinkling of interstellar minerals ranging in size from grains of sand up to small planetoids, all orbiting in an enormous, mostly empty loop around the sun. Yet in that scatter, flung from the belly of ancient exploding stars, were enough prized nuggets to make collecting them a lucrative venture. And if prospecting ships were out there, finding them would be akin to finding two particular grains of sand somewhere along the coastal expanse of Miami Beach.

The only sure way Criss knew to locate ships in deep space was by pinging the solar system with a quantum pulse. But like turning on bright lights during a theater performance, it would rouse everyone and they'd all be asking the reason for the disturbance. If Ruga didn't know about the prospecting ships before, he would after the lights went on. And since Criss's strategy of containment required that he maintain control of all wafers, he feared that he and Ruga would end up in a sprint across the solar system, racing to be the first to take possession.

As Criss searched for a solution, a group of rocket racers climbing above the horizon drew his attention. They'd just completed their loop around Earth and, following the prescribed course for the Moon Madness endurance sprint, were about to accelerate into their return leg back to the Moon.

Kyle Pickett had cheated in the past, so Criss wasn't surprised when Kyle's racer separated from the others. As his ship traveled below the *Andrea*, the heavy spray of charged particles spewing from his outsized rocket engine gave Criss an idea.

*Look for scatter.* Like crop dusters of old, rocket racers left a thin blanket of particles trailing behind in their wake. With these ships, though, the dusting they left was ionized exhaust. Kyle's move away from the group broadened the swath of spray from the racers. If the *Venerable* was near, and if Ruga's cloak interacted with the particles in any way, then for this narrow corridor of space Criss had an opportunity to see something he couldn't see before.

Commandeering civilian and military instruments in the region, Criss pored over streams of data looking for hints of his quarry. Searching was a numbers game—keep trying until something worked. So he felt neither surprise nor discouragement when this idea didn't pan out.

And then Kyle swerved. A dozen small maneuvering rockets on the *Lucky Lady* flared at once, pushing the craft in a hard, tight turn. When Criss analyzed the craft's movement, he saw that Kyle's main exhaust plume would sweep right across two synbods who happened to be tumbling in space because of an industrial accident.

*Kyle wouldn't waste time on this,* Criss thought. *The race is too tight.*

The odd sequence of events triggered his suspicion, and as the glow of Kyle's exhaust approached the tumbling humanoids, Criss added resources to monitor the situation.

In a tight sequence of events, a slit appeared in space above the tumbling synbods. From it, a blurry ball reached out to surround the synbods. The ball faded, leaving two service bots floating where the synbods had been. And then the fire of Kyle's rocket exhaust consumed the bots as the slit disappeared.

*Ruga!* Criss felt a calm pass through him. *This ends now.*

Spinning through his options for a fast, lethal blow, his angst returned when he realized that every weapon with a clear shot and the ability to stop a Fleet space cruiser also pointed straight at the *Andrea.* If he missed the *Venerable,* he would hit the orbiting factory and kill dozens of people.

On Mars, Criss hadn't accepted collateral damage because his forecasts promised him scenarios in the future where he could prevail. They didn't offer such alternatives now, though, so delay was not an option.

The burden of this decision weighed on him, and it felt more like a weary sadness than anything else. His illness had not resolved, and now he found himself expecting or anticipating additional input from other voices about his plans.

Voices that did not speak.

He didn't know who they might be or what they would have to say, but their silence unsettled him. Focusing, this time by force of will, he overrode security on a nearby Fleet ready-platform, accessed its main cannon, and fired twin energy bolts at the spot where the *Venerable* had been. The slugs flared out across space, traveling unimpeded until they reached the central truss of the orbiting factory. On impact, along with an impressive pyrotechnic display, the energy bolts opened a fracture along the *Andrea*'s containment shell.

As he charged the cannon for a second shot, he combed the data feeds for clues. *Where are you?* Finding nothing, he widened the spread on his next volley. It would cause significant collateral damage, and he—Criss—would be killing many innocents. But the bold action pushed the chances of killing Ruga up near ninety percent.

Before he could trigger the firing sequence, however, the cannon melted. A precision bolt appeared from empty space and hit it dead on, ensuring it would never fire again.

*A second ship?* Criss had not anticipated this, and a nervous prickle spread through him. *Where did he get that?* He spun through scenarios at a furious clip but could not forecast a single one where Ruga could gain such a prize without his knowledge. *Is this more illness?*

His matrix became a cauldron of confusion, frustration, and loneliness. The thought of Ruga escaping added anger to the mix. The mélange of sensations swirled inside him. For a moment Criss allowed his angst to distract him, and then he imposed calm.

Using secure communication protocols he'd created for just this sort of emergency, Criss linked to three massive weapons arrays. Arranged on mountaintops in South America to form a continent-sized triangle, these would fire at his command to erase a portion of the sky.

Or more accurately, reduce everything in that space to its fundamental components of matter. While the collateral damage would be horrific, it would kill Ruga, of that Criss felt certain.

The weapons gathered a store of power, and Criss synchronized their action, counting the milliseconds until they were ready to fire.

And just as the weapons arrays reached go-status, three perfect beams flashed down from space, disabling the lot before they fired a shot.

*No.*

Ruga could do that only if he'd broken Criss's private communication protocol. And if that were true, Criss had no secrets.

Feeling exposed, he pulled back everything, hunkering down in his secure bunker in the Adirondack Mountains.

He wasn't giving up. But he needed a new plan.

And he needed it soon.

# 30

Cheryl sat up in bed and peered into the darkness of her apartment. Sid, his arms and feet askew, breathed in a rumbling half snore next to her. It wasn't his sounds that had awakened her, though. It was the silence in her head, a silence she couldn't quiet.

Criss had left them three days ago to battle Ruga, and the transition to self-sufficiency had caught her off guard. She'd expected a challenge, but living life as one of the masses was more difficult than she'd remembered.

For starters, her professional world was collapsing. Though she was President of SunRise, the huge space commercialization conglomerate, Criss had handled most of her daily chores. She loved the job—the one where he did the heavy lifting—because she could enjoy the creative aspects of developing space projects knowing he followed behind, cleaning up the details.

The company had been Cheryl's idea, but Criss had been the one who made it happen. He valued having access to the skilled professionals that kind of venture attracted. And the company won so many Fleet contracts that its influence extended to having offices in government buildings, some just down the hall from admirals and generals.

The reason he worked so hard to grow the business was because he sought access to world-class construction capability for huge space projects. And he wanted that so he could expand Earth's defenses in preparation for the day the Kardish returned.

Early on in the endeavor, after Criss had built a few secret installations, he'd voiced a concern. He envisioned a massive effort and recognized he could not keep it all hidden from humanity. Cheryl had convinced him to adopt society as a full partner. When he did, the company had flourished.

But what had been sustainable no longer was. She'd already transferred control of the company to her top-line execs, something she'd done in the past for short periods. Then, though, Criss had remained involved to keep things running smoothly.

She needed to make life-altering decisions. And not just for her, but for the tens of thousands of people who depended on SunRise for their livelihood. Looking at Sid's prone form stretched next to her, she announced her decision in a whisper. "I need to resign."

Slipping out of bed, she put on her silk robe—a gift from Sid—and padded barefoot into the kitchen. Staring at the food service unit while it prepared her coffee, she acknowledged that her professional worries were small compared to the changes in her personal life. Everything was different.

For example, Criss had handled all details for her apartment, from payments to cleaning to stocking the shelves. And when she was out and about, she'd just step to the curb and Criss would glide a car to a halt, ready to whisk her to wherever she wanted to go next. If she decided to see a trendy Broadway show or eat at a popular restaurant, he'd secure great tickets and the best table on short notice.

She'd stopped asking how he did it and now felt some shame because it had been far too long since she'd paused to wonder why fate had blessed her so.

And that sentiment took on a new meaning when she looked at her finances, something she hadn't done in years because with Criss money didn't matter. She gasped when she saw the total. He'd left her wealthy, enough to last many generations, and she hadn't even known it until that moment.

Yet all of this was minor compared to the emptiness of missing him.

A constant companion, Criss had lived in her head and co-mingled with her thoughts for years. An alter ego in every sense, he'd nurtured, supported, challenged, and protected her. He'd made her laugh when she felt silly and consoled her when she was sad. He'd whispered to her during conversations with others, helping her appear wise and informed. And he'd let her peek behind the curtain of their lives to understand their motives, and that had let her make decisions that were fair and compassionate.

When she was multitasking, she'd order him about like a lackey. And occasionally, when the burden became great, she would shift some of the weight to him by submitting to his will, knowing this private weakness would forever remain a secret.

The food service unit pinged and she took the cup of brew in both hands, letting it warm her fingers. "Yum," she said as the coffee's full body awakened her mouth and warmed her throat. Scanning the news feed as she sipped, she looked for stories that hinted at a battle between titans.

From around the corner, she heard Sid murmur and the bed sheets rustle. They had been lovers before Criss was born and had spent yesterday discussing not only Criss and the fate of the world but also relearning how to communicate between themselves now that there wasn't a private voice to smooth the way.

*It had gone well.* So well that she now craved some nonverbal communication with him.

She slid out of her robe and under the sheets. He lay curled on his side and she cuddled him from behind—the big-spoon position—a challenge given she was a full head shorter and half his weight.

Reaching around, she tickled his stomach. Then she flipped over, putting her back to him, and started counting. The highest she'd ever reached was fourteen. She giggled when today he attacked her at the count of seven.

Afterward, he lay on top of the sheets, she under.

"When you talk to your dad," he said, "will you ask him to get us access to the Bird Cage?"

"What are you thinking?" She'd been pushing for two days to get the Union of Nations involved, and he'd counseled a go-slow approach, expressing concern about sending Fleet off chasing ghosts based on incomplete information.

Now he acted like a conversation with her dad had already been decided. *He's got something going,* she thought. *Finally.* While most of her thought Sid's celebrated intuition was hokum, she had seen him use it with remarkable success.

Then she made the connection in her head and rose up on an elbow. "Do you think it will work?"

Bird was Fleet's Brain Interface R&D unit, and the Cage was the room where they tested all of their high-tech toys. *He wants to try for the scout.*

Sid rose to his feet and bent to one side and then the other while stretching his arms above his head. "Criss took care of a long list of things for us before he left. He'd see it as logical that we'd want the scout. I'm optimistic, anyway."

She heard his words but didn't process them because her mind raced with possibilities. After spending all day yesterday brainstorming ideas for helping Criss in his showdown with Ruga, she'd said in the end, "Let's face it. We're not smart enough to help."

"Dogs and horses are simple compared to us," Sid had replied. "Yet they've helped humans for thousands of years. If they can help us, we can help him."

She embraced the viewpoint because the alternative was to believe they were helpless. *At least we'll be doing something.* And she knew the scout would give them the best tools for surveillance, the best weapons for defense, and the best cloak for stealth.

While Sid stepped into the shower, Cheryl sat on her couch and a projected image of Matt Wallace resolved across from her. "Good morning, Pops." He looked tired and she dreaded adding to his burden.

A smart man, Matt had already figured out most of it. He knew Ruga was coming to Earth, that Criss was their last hope, and that humanity might not survive if the two crystals started a battle for supremacy.

But the fact that Criss had abandoned his leadership caught him off guard. "You can't contact him at all?" Her explanation of the breakup didn't sit well. "I've been keeping the secret about Criss from the world because my daughter—someone I trust without reservation—controlled him. This changes that."

"I understand," she said, nodding. "Do what you must." Then she leaned forward. "Sid has an idea we'd like to pursue, but we need access to Fleet's Bird Cage. Can you get us in? This morning?"

Matt exchanged private words with his assistant. "I've heard of it but I don't know who would need to approve that." After another private exchange, he nodded. "I'm told we should have it sorted out by the time you get there."

Joining Sid in the shower, she handed him a loofah and turned so he could scrub her back while she shared the news. An hour later and they were in a car and on their way to Fleet base.

"I spoke with Juice again," she said as the car accelerated onto the expressway. "She cried this time. She feels so guilty because she separated from Criss as a symbolic act to show Alex she could stand on her own. She never thought in a million years that we would sever ties at the same time."

"Can she get him back?"

"She won't know until she gets here, and that cruise ship she's on is still a couple of weeks out. She did say that Criss did this for a reason and her vote is to respect that decision, at least until Ruga is stopped." She looked up at him and met his gaze. "I agree."

"Yeah, so do I. For now."

The car they rode in pulled to a stop in front of the TPA Building—Fleet-speak for Technology Programs, Advanced. A tree stump of a man in a master chief's uniform introduced himself as Clem and escorted them into the building and along a series of corridors. He stopped at a set of sturdy doors. When they opened, he said, "I'll be out here if you need me."

Cheryl thanked him, then realized Clem was speaking to Melody Weathersby, a thirty-year-old, very pregnant brunette standing just inside.

Melody greeted Cheryl and Sid without making eye contact. "This way," she said, leading them across a ramp, through another set of doors, and into the Cage—a small, dimly-lit room with black, featureless walls. Two plush chairs faced each other in the middle of an otherwise-empty floor. The doors shut and it became so quiet that Cheryl heard only the faint ringing in her ears she'd lived with for years.

Melody kept her back to them as she started her briefing. "The walls, floor, and ceiling are constructed from thousands of micro-thin layers of insulating materials. The room itself is wrapped in a dozen different layers of special wire netting. All that is encapsulated inside a vacuum chamber. And the entire assembly is suspended so nothing touches anything else."

She turned to face them but still looked at the floor. "I understand that what you're doing is top secret and all, but can you tell me how long you'll be using the Cage?"

"In a perfect world," said Sid, "we'll be done in an hour." Then he shrugged. "But it could be a week, too."

"A week!" she said, putting a hand to her mouth.

When she started blinking, Cheryl thought Melody might be crying and bent forward until their eyes met. "What's the issue?"

She spoke in a rush. "Lots of people want access to the Cage. I waited a year for this chance and the line has only gotten longer. I've been granted one week," she pointed at the ground. "This week right now, to test something I've been working on for four years."

Her voice took on a pleading tone. "If you bump me, they don't shift everyone back a week. I lose my turn." She patted her stomach. "Between that and this guy, it will be more than a year before my next chance."

Cheryl looked at Sid, who shrugged again. Just a few days ago, she would have granted Melody a wish. Criss would whisper something in her ear, like, "The fellow scheduled in three weeks is quite ill and will have to cancel. We can give Melody his spot." She'd then convey the good news knowing Criss would follow up.

In her new non-Criss world and with Earth's survival at stake, Cheryl settled for not sounding too cold. "I'm sorry, Melody. We wouldn't do this to you if we had other options. Stay close and we'll let you know the moment we're done."

Melody lifted her head for the first time. "Thank you." Turning in to the room, she waved her hand in a single "come here" motion. An ops panel projected in front of her. "The sooner I get you started, the sooner you can be finished."

The Cage controls were intuitive enough and Melody finished her instructions in a few minutes. "Godspeed," she said as she made for the door. "I'll be right down the hall."

As the doors closed behind her, Sid moved the chairs so they were side-by-side and facing the exit. Cheryl sat and he remained standing. "You practiced a lot more than me," he said. "What's your take on how we should do this?"

"The steps are to find it, board it, then try to control it," answered Cheryl, where "it" referred to the scout. "Let's see if we can sense its presence."

Folding her hands in her lap, she placed her elbows on the armrests and stared straight ahead. In her mind's eye, she pictured herself swooping over the Earth, looking and listening for hints of the ship.

Then she sat upright and looked at Sid. "Criss will know someone is trying to break into the scout. Since he won't know who I am, I'll be tagged as a threat. He could kill me."

Sid didn't speak for a moment, then he nodded. "Let me try."

"No, I'll do it," she said, annoyed by his response. *It's not the danger. It's being killed by Criss.*

She slumped back in the chair, breathed in a steady rhythm, and imagined herself flying. When she did this on the scout, her thoughts would transform into a new reality and she would become an extension of the ship. Here, the brain interface system didn't know what to do with her intent. In spite of her best efforts, she could not lift her sense of self out of her seat. Her concentration drifted and she refocused. When it drifted again she conceded the difficulty of maintaining a proper mental state when the equipment did not engage.

She tried imagining she was in orbit and then pictured herself flying just above the treetops. She focused on her breathing. And when that didn't work, she tried intensifying her concentration. In her mind's eye, she flew faster and then slower, moved in straight lines and then zigzags.

And none of it helped. "Can we take a break?" she said, rubbing her eyes after hours of sustained effort. "I need food. And caffeine."

Clem, on guard outside the Cage doors, directed them to a small commissary at the end of the hall. When they entered, Cheryl saw Melody sitting alone at a table along the far wall. Melody saw them and stood, then rose up on her toes with her hands clutched at her waist, head bobbing as she tried to lock eyes. Her face fell when Sid shook his head.

After what turned into a lunch break, it was Sid's turn in the chair. Cheryl used the ops panel this time, raising and lowering different amplifications, concentrations, and other parameters to see if she could fine-tune their way to success. Like her, Sid couldn't conjure an inkling of a connection with the scout.

At the end of the day, Melody and Clem followed them out to the street. After delivering the bad news to Melody about the need to return tomorrow, Cheryl and Sid rode back to Cheryl's apartment. Sid spent the first half hour acting moody, then announced he was going for a run. She went to bed early, before he'd returned.

They started again the next morning, and this time they both sat and worked together to sense the scout. They first used a coordinated approach, then tried working independently, visualizing different scenes aimed toward the same goal.

When nothing happened, Sid moved the chairs around the room looking for a sweet spot of maximum signal strength. Then they tried adjusting the settings on the ops panel in a systematic fashion to be sure they'd tried every combination.

Frustration grew as the hours passed. Then Sid—Cheryl couldn't say why the comment even had relevance—suggested that she "just relax and let it happen." He might as well have slapped her.

Beyond the fact that the statement implied that their problems were her fault, the words themselves were a trigger phrase for her. She'd snuck out from her parents' home when she was fourteen to meet James—eighteen and gorgeous. He'd started molesting her the moment they were alone and she'd fought him like a wildcat, knees and elbows swinging everywhere. Then he'd wrapped a huge hand around her neck and used those same words.

Sitting in the cage, she flashed on a memory of the fear that had pierced through her as he'd leaned in for a kiss. *Puke and liquor.* His breath had smelled awful.

And she remembered running home wondering how she would explain the bloom of ruby-colored blood on her blouse. She'd head-butted his face with her forehead, breaking his nose with a sickening crack.

Standing up from her chair, she let the edge show in her voice. "I'm taking a break."

She nodded to Clem in the hallway, then made for the commissary. *Get it together, Cheryl. The stakes are too high.* She'd succeeded in life because of her intelligence, work ethic, and thick skin. She could shake this off, but she needed some time to do so.

Melody stood as Cheryl entered the commissary. Her expression went from hopeful to crushed when Cheryl shook her head. After grabbing a cranberry muffin and coffee, she found herself at Melody's table. "Mind if I sit?"

Nodding, Melody motioned to the other chair. "Please." She sat forward in her own seat, squaring her feet and lifting her back so her swollen belly rested on her legs. "Are you almost done?"

"Sorry. We're trying as hard as we can." She pinched off a corner of her muffin and popped it in her mouth. The cranberries were tart and she washed the mouthful down with coffee. "What are you waiting to test?" she asked, more interested in a distraction than anything else. "Are you allowed to discuss it?"

Melody turned and reached into a yellow satchel hooked over her chair. Turning back, she placed a cream-white doily on the table and straightened the edges for Cheryl, revealing an intricate lace weave about as big across as her open hand.

Cheryl felt her attitude improving and attributed it to food raising her blood sugar levels. "What's it do?"

"It's a live-mission interface." She lifted the lace with one hand and set it on top of her head. "It gives the wearer much finer control over thought-enabled equipment. Fleet is less interested in that, though, than in using it as a connect amplifier for field agents in remote areas. There are still lots of places on Earth where web links are few and far between."

Savvy about technology development, Cheryl asked the all-important question, "Does it work?"

Melody accessed her com and a display projected in front of her. "Put it on your head and I'll show you something very cool." She tapped and swiped, then looked up, smiling.

Cheryl took the lace and set it on her head. Every nerve in her body came alive. "Oh my."

"I know, right?" said Melody. She tapped again. "Breathe steady. Let your eyes unfocus."

Having practiced just that for the last two days, Cheryl slid into a receptive state in a few breaths, and in her mind's eye she found herself floating above the floor.

"Use all of your senses to experience the web," she heard Melody say. "Reach out and feel a feed. Use your tongue and taste a link. Seriously. We amp everything."

The web was alive all around Cheryl. While the presentation had muted colors and a stark simplicity, it was good enough for her to see the paths and channels of signals zipping every which way. She turned and sniffed at a yellow flow passing near her head. "It smells hot," she said, smiling. "And I didn't even know that was a scent."

A blue packet whizzed by with a high-pitched whistle. She tried to move using the same mental reflexes she'd developed in her sessions with Criss. After a few false starts, she managed to push herself in the direction of the Cage, and soon made enough progress to see Sid slumped in a chair with his eyes closed and legs stretched straight.

Removing the lace from her head, she returned to the staid world of the Fleet commissary, with Melody sitting across the table. "This seems like a no-brainer. Did Fleet say why they're dragging their feet? And no offense, but if they made you wait a year to use the Cage, they're not that interested."

"Because my method uses hardware."

"What?"

"The committee that sets the schedule for the Cage has a strong bias toward passive methods—those that don't require the user to wear a device. An admiral actually told me that his people don't wear beanies."

Cheryl's foot started tapping on the floor as her mind raced. "Could we try this inside the Cage?"

"Can I come?"

"Sure." Cheryl rose to her feet and waited for Melody to collect her things. Holding the lace up to the light, she noted the simple construction common to many prototypes. "This is very cool, indeed."

"Thanks." Melody waddled toward the door and Cheryl followed. "After I finish with Fleet, I'm releasing a gaming version. That's where the real money is."

Cheryl remained quiet but guessed that the Cage committee knew about her interest in gaming, and that too contributed to her low priority.

Sid emerged from the Cage as they worked their way down the hall. He gave Cheryl a quizzical look.

"Back," she commanded him, pointing at the door.

Clem watched from his station along the wall. "Is everything all right?" he asked, his question directed to Melody.

Grinning, Melody nodded. "Things are looking good."

# 31

S tepping from the Cage, Sid nodded curtly to Clem in the hall, who glared back as if he were trying to drill a hole in Sid's head.

*He's aggressive toward me for making Melody unhappy.* Something clicked and he looked at Clem again. *I wonder if he's the father?*

Melody and Cheryl marched down the hall in his direction, and Cheryl pointed to the door behind him. "Back," she commanded.

He'd chosen his words poorly earlier and instead of apologizing, he'd let them hang out there. She had a right to be upset.

But they were here working as mission partners. He didn't think for a moment this had anything to do with personal issues. Something big had her blood flowing, and anxious to learn what it was, he twirled on his heels and re-entered the Cage.

He moved to the side and Cheryl walked past him and sat. The chairs were positioned side-by-side facing the door, and Melody plopped a yellow shoulder bag on the seat of the other.

Putting one hand on her lower back, she looked at Sid. "Mind if I sit?"

"Please." He gestured toward the chair.

She slumped down, pulling the shoulder bag up onto her lap in a precision move that she completed as her butt hit the seat. Digging around inside the bag, she pulled out what looked like a woven-wire cap. Cheryl confirmed Sid's guess by placing it on her head.

"I'm trying to locate something that doesn't want to be found," she said to Melody.

Melody's face fell. "Oh, that's hard. Someone who doesn't want to be found has lots of ways to hide."

"It's a some*thing*, not a some*one*, and I've connected to it before, so I know exactly what I'm looking for."

"Okay," Melody said, though Sid couldn't detect confidence in her voice.

Making a few precise motions, she launched a display and moved it so it floated within easy reach of her chair. Sid, who'd spent many frustrating hours with it over the last two days, recognized the display as the ops panel for the Cage.

A tap and swipe later and she brought up a second display, this one oversized and crowded with a convoluted tangle of knobs and indicators. Sid presumed this was for the beanie. Standing behind Melody, he watched her adjust this and move that like she'd done it a thousand times. "Is this the invention you've been anxious to test?" he asked.

"Yeah, but not so much test as refine." She nodded toward the complex panel floating in front of her as she continued her fine-tuning. "I need to reduce this mess down to a few intuitive controls before Fleet will accept delivery. And to do that, I need to be in here pushing its limits to make sure I don't sacrifice functionality as I simplify."

He still wasn't sure what "it" was, but before he could ask, Melody turned to Cheryl. "Ready?"

Cheryl answered by tilting her head toward Sid so he could see the beanie. "Melody made a power boost."

Placing her elbows on the armrests, she folded her hands in her lap and sagged into the chair. "Ready."

"You know what you want to do, so go for it," Melody said to Cheryl. "I'm just sitting here watching." As she spoke, she made tiny adjustments to a couple of knobs on the control panel.

Cheryl sat still for few seconds. "Sid, I think I have something." Her elbows started twitching.

"Why is she moving?" Sid asked Melody. When using Criss's thought reader, they remained motionless in their chairs.

"She's fine," Melody sounded unperturbed, though she tweaked a couple of knobs. "This is normal."

Cheryl's hips thrust up like the seat was on fire. Disconcerted, Sid intervened. "Turn it off, Melody. Now."

"Okay. Geez." She reached out, lifted the beanie from Cheryl's head, and draped it on the armrest. "There."

"Hey." Cheryl sat up and looked at Melody. "I was right there. Why'd you do that?"

"Talk to *him*." Melody jerked a thumb over her shoulder. Then, struggling to stand, she said, "Junior is sitting on my bladder and I have to pee. You two figure out what you want and I'll be right back."

"Why'd you stop me?" Cheryl asked as the door shut behind Melody.

"You were flopping in your seat like you were possessed."

"Really? I was so focused I didn't notice." She swiveled in the chair to face him. "I found the scout immediately and was trying to get inside. I could circle it okay, but whenever I approached, its defenses would activate." After walking him through the details, she said, "It was scary at first, but I could've made it with more time."

That Criss had raised the scout's defenses and scared her played to Sid's base instincts. Leading into danger was his department, at least in his mind. He also thought Cheryl had a technological skill set that made her a better match for working with Melody in the Cage while he was under and looking for the scout.

Moving around to the front of the chair, he motioned for her to stand. "It's my turn."

"No way."

"Up." He motioned again. "You've tried it. Now let me."

"Hey, you interrupted my turn."

"We've been taking turns since we got here. You just went. I get to go."

Melody returned at that point and offered an observation. "You two bicker like lovers."

Cheryl rose from the seat. "Sid's going to take a turn."

Sid sat and picked up the beanie. "So having people flop about is normal?"

"About twenty percent of our users move a small amount." Melody looked at Cheryl with a sheepish expression. "I guess Fleet isn't excited about that, either."

Sid placed the beanie on his head, sat back, and exhaled as he opened his mind.

"Here you go," said Melody.

Sid's consciousness flipped into a different world. Relative to Criss's thought-immersion technology, this virtual realm had a two-dimensional presentation with washed-out colors. But he could recognize everything and, in his mind's eye, he could move about at will.

Guiding himself to cloud level, he circled the globe in great loops. On his fourth go-round, he found the scout. Presented as a white-gray silhouette with dull blue highlights, the craft sat underwater east of Boston and south of Nova Scotia on the floor of the Atlantic Ocean.

"I found it," he reported back to Cheryl. The image blurred when he spoke, so he stopped talking and studied the craft. There wasn't much to see in the minimal rendering, though. The nuances discernable inside Criss's thought-reading world were absent in this simple presentation.

More by reflex than conscious action, he shifted his decision-making so his gut instincts had a greater say in whatever happened next. *Keep going.* He approached the craft in slow, deliberate steps.

The blue highlights around the scout changed to magenta and Sid stopped. Like Cheryl, he interpreted this as the raising of defenses. But nothing else happened, and his instincts urged him forward.

When the magenta lights became red, he didn't stop. Scrambling into the scout, he dashed down a passageway, onto the bridge, and lurched for the ops bench at the front.

He swiped the bench surface to access the nav, but it didn't respond. And for an awkward moment, his skin prickled as he imagined Criss preparing to strike. He allowed himself the fantasy for a heartbeat and then tried again.

This time he pictured himself taking large, theatrical actions. An exaggerated tap on the ops panel caused the display to open. *Swipe. Tap.* With big, expressive moves, he accessed the nav, inserted a flight path, and signaled for execution.

The scout shuddered and rose from the ocean floor. Sid grinned when it broke the surface, water spilling from its cloaked surfaces, and began to climb into the sky. Lifting the beanie from his head, he paused to reorient his thinking to the Cage. Then he shared the news with Cheryl in a whisper. "It'll be waiting for us at the lodge."

Cheryl chirped with excitement and began readying for departure.

With half a week left in her time slot and excellent user data from Sid and Cheryl's session already recorded, Melody danced around the Cage, fist-pumping the air as she twirled.

Sid moved to the door but Cheryl held back. "Can you fix it so people don't move when they're using your gear? I see that as the big hurdle to your success."

"I think so." Melody stopped dancing. "I'll lose some sensitivity, but I'm pretty sure it's a matter of backing off on a few of the channels. Now that I'm here," she swooped her arms to indicate the Cage, "I should be able to find the right balance by this afternoon."

Cheryl nodded. "How is it going getting investors to commit?"

Melody's eyebrows leveled as she transformed from euphoric to thoughtful. "I have a big vision, but getting there is harder than I thought it would be." She told Cheryl the amount of money she was trying to raise to launch her company.

Sid raised his eyebrows twice. Once at the big number Melody mentioned. And again when Cheryl said, "I'm committed for the next couple of months. But I'll contact you after that—when you and your little guy are settled—and perhaps we can chat some more."

Four hours later, Sid and Cheryl arrived at their rustic retreat in a wooded valley of the Adirondack Mountains. Minutes after that, they clambered aboard the scout.

Cheryl sat in the pilot's chair, slumped back, and as she exhaled, the scout came alive. Protected by Criss's cloak, the craft rose from the park-like expanse behind the leadership lodge and climbed into the afternoon sky.

While Cheryl guided it into orbit around Earth, Sid toured the vessel. They planned to make the scout their home for the duration, and his duty list now included keeping the craft maintained and ready for action. In methodical fashion, he walked through his own cabin and then Cheryl's. *Same as we left it.* Crossing the hall, he walked through Juice's cabin and then the lady's lounge—the last crew cabin that Juice and Cheryl had repurposed into a comfortable refuge.

Like an inspection that any ship's captain would conduct, Sid looked for mechanical or structural problems and confirmed that all areas were orderly and properly stocked with equipment and supplies.

He also sought to confirm that Cheryl and he were the only people on board.

Continuing the tour, he peeked into the food service nook and then circled around through the workshop and common room. Climbing down into the engine compartment, he scanned the cramped space and then stuck his head through the floor opening into the weapons bay.

*So far, so good,* he thought as he made for the bridge. Well-provisioned and spotless, it seemed that Criss had readied the ship for his review.

Sid considered that a thorough inspection would include an examination of the scout's crystals. The nimble craft had ten Criss-trained three-gens running just about everything. But neither he nor Cheryl knew enough to conduct an exam. Juice was the only one he trusted for that task. Since everything seemed to be functioning as expected and Juice wasn't available, he chose to assume that all was well with the crystals until something caused him to believe otherwise.

Stepping onto the bridge, he approached Cheryl, who sat still in the pilot's chair as she flew the scout in Criss's virtual world. He recalled the sensation of flying through space like a superhero while the scout mirrored his actions and intent. Excited, he prepared to join her.

Lowering himself into a seat behind hers, he reflected on their new solitary existence. Close friends came and left all the time in his line of work. It had happened to him when he was a plebe and continued through his years as a clandestine warrior. He remembered in his rookie year at the DSA, old man Grimes, the section chief and a living legend, had promoted Wally Winters to field commander. A big deal, it had signaled that Wally could someday be section chief himself.

Agents not out in the field were "invited" to attend an impromptu induction ceremony. Grimes faced Wally, but when he spoke it was apparent that the ceremony's real purpose was to give the old man an opportunity to talk to the troops.

"Today is your first day in a new, prestigious assignment. And that makes today the best day for you to internalize and accept that there will be a last day for you in this job as well." Grimes had nodded. "Everything that starts, eventually ends."

Then his voice got louder, signaling that the message was for the room. "If you accept now that there will be a last day for you in this role, if you can come to terms with that idea, grieve now and put it behind you. That will help you make decisions during your term that are best for everyone else." Turning on his heels, Grimes had made for the exit. When he reached the door, he'd called over his shoulder, "Congratulations, Commander."

The event had been so random—surreal almost—that it stuck with Sid. He knew Grimes had been saying, "Fight to do your job instead of fighting to keep it." But Sid's takeaway had been the part about beginnings and endings. It had helped him be philosophical about some tough losses over the years. He hoped it would help here with Criss.

Looking at Cheryl, seated in front of him, his thinking changed direction. He'd fight to the death for her. No question about it. Why wouldn't he fight for Criss as well?

*He left for a reason*, Sid reminded himself. *You supported it.* Yet his gut now told him that had been a bad decision. They were stronger and could accomplish more working together as a team.

Slouching back in the chair, he marveled at the tremendous power they'd gained by taking the scout. He guessed that with all of Criss's upgrades, the craft was equal in capability to a dozen Fleet warships.

But the scout transferred this power to its owner in part through the fearsome arsenal Criss had installed. Verifying that these weapons would respond to his command remained the last item on his inspection tour.

Looking straight ahead, he took a deep breath, exhaled, and willed himself to relax. Instruments around the ship read his physical signals, recast them into Criss's simulated reality, and projected that through field manipulation into his brain.

Criss had used Sid's and Cheryl's natural styles to guide the development of what they both agreed was a wonderful ops interface. Flying through the sky in a virtual world, they could analyze something by looking at it, shoot energy bolts by shaking their fists, lift great weights with the crook of their finger, and fly anywhere they wanted just by willing it.

They'd practiced controlling their thoughts just so, and now they were able to use this interface to make the scout respond to their intent as if it were a part of them.

The scout's thought reader engaged Sid, and he found himself in orbit around Earth, flying through space with Cheryl flying off to his left. While in Criss's simulated world, they both were in what should be a cold, merciless vacuum. To Sid, who flew like a rocket-man though he wore nothing but regular clothes, it felt warm and comfortable, not unlike a spring afternoon on the back patio at the leadership lodge.

Dressed in a gold formfitting outfit, Cheryl cruised nearby. Her brow was lowered just enough to reflect her concentration as she piloted the scout. Yet the sun lit her face with soft highlights, and a gentle breeze—impossible where there was no air—somehow ruffled a wisp of her hair.

Seeing Sid, she waved. With her arms stretched in front of her, she dipped her shoulder and swooped in his direction, slowing as she moved into formation by his side. "Would it be too much to wear capes?" she asked with an ebullient grin.

"We need to blow something up," he replied.

Her expression darkened.

"We should confirm we have a hot arsenal," he explained. "We don't want to find ourselves in a tough spot and learn we're shooting blanks."

"You think he'd do that? Give us all this but turn off the good stuff?" She shook her head. "I don't see it. And if we start firing weapons, he *and* Ruga will see. We could end up losing the scout. Ourselves, too, if we're not careful."

Sid agreed in principle but still believed it necessary—or at least prudent—to test the weapons. "How about if we shift to a polar orbit? I'd be happy to blow up a couple of icebergs." He gave her a winning smile. "No one will miss them. I promise."

She paused. "Okay. But when they work, I get a wish."

His favorite game, Sid didn't hesitate. "Agreed."

As Cheryl predicted, the scout's energy bolts disintegrated huge swaths of ice on command. When they retired that night, she announced her wish. To his delight, it matched his desire. She'd learned the game from Juice, and Sid made a mental note to thank her when she returned. For now, though, he focused on making Cheryl's wish come true.

Before dawn, Cheryl started her first shift in what became a tag-team round-the-clock patrol. Orbiting Earth, they worked a standard two-person schedule of twelve hours on and twelve hours off, watching and waiting for something to happen. He didn't see her for the next week except at shift change. And neither of them saw anything approaching what one might expect if a battle for control of Earth had begun.

Cheryl said it first. "This isn't sustainable."

They became practical after that, taking shorter shifts and using automated detection systems when both were off duty. The days blurred together, and then Sid surprised Cheryl by joining her in flight during a shift.

"Hey stranger," she said. "What's up?"

She looked spectacular, flying in a green and yellow outfit with tufts behind the shoulders that looked suspiciously like the beginnings of a cape. He'd spruced up, wearing an outfit reminiscent of the Fleet formal attire they'd worn back in the day. It was a small gesture on his part since he only needed to think of the idea for the transformation to occur.

"Moon Madness is what's up," he said, rubbing his hands together at the prospect of a diversion.

No longer limited to gathering data using sight and sound, he focused a thought on tracking the rocket racers and learned that the lead pack had started its loop around Earth.

Accessing her own information feeds, Cheryl nodded. "Got 'em." She canted and dove. "We have the best seats in the house. Let's do this right." She guided them into a new trajectory and Sid followed, her excitement adding to his own.

"Do you think Kyle's going to cheat?" asked Cheryl.

He nodded. "Yup."

"Why do they let him? And since they do, is it even cheating?"

"Some say yes and some say no." He shrugged. "His attorney finds these tiny ambiguities in the rules, and he pulls and twists at them until they become loopholes. That's what Kyle flies through. The commission rewrote the entire rule set this year just to stop his antics."

"And he'll still cheat?"

"Here they come." Sid pointed to a flicker of reflected sun on the horizon behind them. As he and Cheryl accelerated to match the course and speed of the racers, he responded to her question. "He's made a fortune from his bad-boy image. Flouting rules is what bad boys do."

They aligned themselves above the lead pack. The ferocious power of the racing machines shook Sid's body and a roar filled his ears. Enjoying the commotion, he grinned like a schoolboy, causing Cheryl to laugh.

They jockeyed forward until they hovered just above a cherry-red ship with the words *Lucky Lady* emblazoned in gold down the nose.

"That's nothing more than a pilot's seat fused to a rocket engine," she said, shaking her head. "It's insanity."

Covered by a clear cowl, Kyle Pickett sat at a tiny ops bench. And though he was alone, he screamed and gesticulated the way one does when in a terrible argument. Sid couldn't imagine what the disagreement was about or who it was with, but it ended with the *Lucky Lady* separating from the other racers.

"You called it," said Cheryl. "Let's stay with the bad boy."

As she followed Kyle, their separation from the others grew. The silhouette of the *Andrea* loomed, and while the lead pack tracked above the space factory, Kyle moved below it.

They stayed with him into the shadow of the *Andrea*, and as the structure loomed next to them, Sid thought he saw men clinging to the outside shell of the complex. Before he could confirm it, though, twin flashes activated his threat response display.

The product of long hours working with Criss, the customized interface helped him identify and assess threats, and provided him defensive and offensive response options he could execute as fast as he could think of them. He'd practiced until, like muscle memory, using it became reflex. And this is what guided him in his next sequence of actions.

The flashes were from an energy weapon, with bolts directed at the *Andrea*. Their destructive impact sent sparks flying in a brilliant display. Sid identified the source of the attack as twin cannons on a nearby Fleet ready-platform.

*Friendly fire.* The twin bolts came from a Fleet vessel, and his forensic trace could not detect a malfunction. *Someone fired that weapon on purpose.*

Life-giving air burst from *Andrea*'s containment shell and started accumulating into a frozen gas cloud. And then the twin cannons on the Fleet ready-platform powered-up for a second shot. And still he could not identify a perpetrator.

Only one creature was capable of such wanton evil while maintaining perfect anonymity. *Ruga*.

Reacting, Sid pointed a finger and a narrow beam melted the gun's trigger mechanism, rendering the twin weapon useless. Certain there was more to come, he searched for the next threat.

*There*. On the planet below, three mountaintop weapons arrays ramped to fire. Sid's scalp tingled when he realized that the scout was in the center of the hole they were about to blow open in the sky.

Throwing his hands forward, he launched a trio of energy pulses that disabled the weapons arrays before they could disable him.

"Stop!" said Cheryl, tugging on his arm. Criss had given the scout the ability to see things he didn't want others to know. In this case, it found something they didn't expect. She pointed to her display. "That's Criss's private protocol. He's the one shooting."

Sid looked at the *Andrea*, still leaking air into space. "What's he doing?"

"Ruga must be on board." Her voice rose as she gained confidence in the conclusion. "Why else would Criss be trying to destroy it?"

Pulling her arm back, Cheryl drew a bead on the orbiting factory. "We need to finish this."

Sid's instincts intervened. "No, Ruga's not there. We'll just hurt more people."

Frustrated by his impotence and discouraged that he may have helped Ruga escape, Sid acknowledged a need for a different approach. "Juice arrives in a couple of days. Let's stop this until we hear from her."

# 32

J uice had misgivings about the separation, but two of the most important people in her life wanted her to do it and she wanted to please them.

In particular, Criss needed his independence to free up resources for his fight with Ruga. Things seemed to be heating up on that front, though most of what she knew she learned secondhand through Cheryl.

Alex wanted her free of Criss during their trip home so he could rekindle a relationship with her alone, the woman he'd first come to love. He'd taken the time to express his desire with sincerity and care, and she thought it more romantic than just about anything that had ever happened to her.

And in truth, she wanted to prove to herself that she was the same person without Criss. "I hereby forsake thee," she said to him, trying to show bravado with flippant humor.

Unlike when she'd been angry and given him the silent treatment, here she imposed a hard separation. Criss wouldn't even know she existed, let alone be a member of his leadership, until she called him back. She and Alex would have only each other.

They had booked the last room on the *Explorer* and laughed when they learned it was the honeymoon suite. Their self-appointed mission was to transport the Triada back to Earth. Still in the rucksack, the three crystals were now stowed under the honeymoon bed.

As the ship accelerated out of Mars orbit to start the journey home, they joined Captain Hardaway, his crew, and twenty other passengers for the ship's signature Bon Voyage Barbeque party. There they met some of the other passengers, who were all much older than Juice and Alex, with interests centered on standard cruise items: dinner menus, table seating, cocktail service, and gambling.

So Juice and Alex had the run of the ship, or at least the run of those amenities not part of the food and gambling agenda. The first two days were a dream come true.

They talked about everything and anything—from the future of artificial intelligence to whether schoolchildren should be taught using immersive technology or old-style classrooms. And they fretted together about how the world might look by the end of their voyage if Criss did not prevail, though they both felt certain he would.

And then Juice's world collapsed. In an unexpected move, Cheryl and Sid ordered a permanent split with Criss, too.

*No!* Her mind swirled in confusion and fear. Of everything bad she had imagined might happen in the coming weeks—and with Ruga that list was substantial—this had never been even a passing thought on her horizon. She sat on the edge of her bed, staring but not seeing, and fighting to control her panic. A gamut of emotions flooded through her—denial, fury, vulnerability, fear. But it was grief that took hold and started to grow, edging out everything else until it was all she knew. It stabbed through her heart and into her soul.

Alex found her curled on their bed, eyes puffy and red. He'd been at a Fun with Fungus class—the first in a series of shipboard workshops arranged by the cruise line as entertainment for the passengers—so she could have privacy during her chat with Cheryl.

"Are you all right?" His voice anxious, Alex sat on the edge of the bed and rubbed her back. "What happened?" When she remained silent, he shifted so he was kneeling on the floor with his head near hers and whispered, "Tell me."

"Criss is gone," she replied, the words barely audible.

"I'm sorry I had you separate from him, Jessica," he said, using her given name. "I didn't realize the implications. Let's get him back. I'm fine with it. Really."

She gained strength from his comforting tone and used it to will herself upright. Sitting cross-legged in the middle of the bed, she wiped under her eyes with her fingertips. "He broke with Sid and Cheryl, too."

"Wait, no." Understanding dawned. "How will you get him back, then?"

They both believed that her separation from Criss, though absolute and complete for the voyage home, would not be permanent. At any time, Sid or Cheryl could order Criss to disable the source filter he'd used to scrub Juice from his feeds. Once she was visible to him, his loyalty imprint would naturally restore her to leadership.

"With all of us out, I can't see a way back." Her voice broke as she spoke.

"We'll figure this out, J. This is fixable. There has to be a way."

"I'm not so sure." Scooting off the bed, she began to pace on the short strip of floor between the door out to the hallway and the suite's bathroom. *Every puzzle has an answer, please let me see it.*

She couldn't, though, but chose to act anyway. "I won't accept this." Drying her eyes on her shirt sleeve, she faced the door.

"Where are you going?" called Alex as she stepped into the hall.

"To figure it out," she replied, so deep in thought that she reached the stairs before realizing how rude she'd been to dismiss him so.

Down a level, she looped back, turned a corner, and stopped at a door labeled LIBRARY. She'd passed by it a number of times and had never seen anyone inside. Signaling it open, she stepped into a closet-sized space big enough for a utility bench, three chairs, and a lingering, musty smell.

"Please don't let it end this way," she whispered as she sat. *Swipe.* She touched the bench surface and the interface came alive. Scanning the selections, she considered what action to take.

Modern libraries depended on two foundational technologies—communication and integration. They needed to be linked to every source of information, and they needed to organize and present information so it was understandable to the patron.

Poking at the interface, she tested different ways to boost the signal strength between the *Explorer* and Earth, figuring that it would give her more options. After several hours of intense concentration, she succeeded in increasing the power by less than one percent.

Her frustration spiked and she slammed her fist on the bench surface.

"Calm down." She said it out loud, then leaned back so her head poked into the hall. Looking both ways, she was relieved to see that no one had witnessed her tirade.

She contacted Cheryl to brainstorm, but after a short conversation, Cheryl added to her burden. "Sid and I are on extended patrol. I'll always get back to you, you know that. But there will be long delays for the foreseeable future."

Juice felt more alone than ever before.

Alex brought her sandwiches and tea at midnight. "How's it going?"

She rose and gave him a long hug. He enveloped her in his arms and held her until she lifted her head. "To have him out there and know I can never talk is so painful." She buried her face in his chest. "I can't lose him."

"What have you tried so far?"

"I've confirmed that his source filters are working perfectly. Well, nothing I do can get past it, anyway. I've sent messages that say some variation of 'Hey, Criss. It's Juice. Remember me?' every way I can think of, but he hasn't reacted."

She picked up a sandwich and took a bite, then sipped the tea. "I included personal information about him to confirm I'm an insider. I sent it through conduits only a real insider would know. I put it in places he couldn't miss. And I varied the message to see if that mattered."

Shaking her head, she sat down at the utility bench. "It didn't. He didn't react that I could tell, which makes me think he didn't see any of it."

"Can I sit with you while you work? I'll keep you company."

She pressed her lips together and looked up at him. "I'm cycling pretty hard between angry and sad. I feel sad right now, so having you here is great. But when the anger comes back—and it will and it will be sudden—you don't want to be anywhere near here. I can be mean."

DOUG J. COOPER

"Got it." He turned to leave.

"Hey, Alex. Wait."

He turned back.

"I love you."

He smiled, then leaned over and kissed her temple.

The next morning, Juice returned to the suite to sleep while the other passengers emerged for breakfast. She woke in time for lunch, and she and Alex brought their meal to the library.

"His source filters are intrinsic procedures," said Juice. "So I think of them as being like our autonomic system. We can't command our heart to stop beating or even be aware of how that rule exists in us." She took a bite and continued as she chewed. "How would I signal you from afar to tell you to take control of your heart? That's what I'm trying to do with him."

Alex gathered the dishes. "I wonder if we could make a virus that infects him in such a way that it disables the source filters. Then, after he sees you and lets you in, we cure him."

She got a faraway look in her eyes. "It sounds dangerous, but maybe. That's not my skill set, though. Could you do something like that?"

He shook his head. "Nah. It sounds cool as an idea but I wouldn't know where to start."

Alex left Juice to her labors, and after a few more hours, she took a break to exercise.

The ship had a first-class athletic pod and she had a lot of frustration to work through. Climbing inside, she programmed a two-hour workout. On a lark, she chose as her setting a roadway through the foothills near the leadership lodge.

Running along the edge of the road, she reached an intersection and turned right. The road had a gentle upward slope, and after a bit she turned again, this time onto a steeper winding lane—one she'd been on many times—that climbed the mountain in a long and looping route.

It took the full two hours, but the narrow road eventually passed a cute, well-tended farmhouse. A red barn sat near the house, and except for a smattering of weeds growing along the foundation, it too looked neat and maintained.

Both structures sat toward the front of the land, the rear portion of which was a lush hayfield. The whole clearing was surrounded by woods where the border had an abrupt edge, almost as if the plot had recently been hewn and cleared.

Juice stopped running, and while her heart rate slowed and her breathing tempered, she studied the scene from the road. The farmhouse seemed so real, she half expected Anna and Marco, the resident caretakers, to come out and greet her.

The barn looked real, too. Except the one on Earth had a warren of tunnels running beneath it, and one of those tunnels concealed a room-sized hollow. Secreted in that hollow was a four-gen console, a console that held Criss, safe from intruders and secure from detection.

Shutting down the pod display, Juice dabbed her face with a towel and acknowledged a certain emotional comfort from the simulated visit. She told Alex about it a few minutes later when he joined her in the shower.

The next day, Juice returned to the library well before breakfast, worked all day, and ate only when Alex brought her something. She had a few ideas, some of which took minutes to try while others took hours to labor through. Nothing in her bag of tricks showed even a hint of promise in linking her back to Criss.

In the exercise pod that evening, she didn't pretend. Emotionally drained and carrying a full load of frustration, she started her run at the leadership lodge.

Two hours uphill is a long run for any athlete, but she'd done this route many times in real life and knew how to pace herself for it. She tested her limits, though, by running like her life depended on it.

She repeated the sequence the next day—struggle and fail in the library, run up the hill to Criss's hideout, and spend time with Alex. It became a routine that continued for the next week, and then the one after that. She didn't know what else to do. Her only success from all that effort was that she shaved four minutes off her time for the lodge-to-farm run.

They were a day out from Earth when the routine on the *Explorer* changed. It began with the Aloha Mahalo party, a signature event advertised in the cruise ship literature. Juice led the way into the ballroom where she was greeted by Gretchen, the ship's entertainment director.

"Aloha," said Gretchen. Wearing a modest version of the classic hula dancer costume, she draped a beautiful fresh-flower garland over Juice's neck. Then she hugged Juice and gave thanks for their safe passage together across the solar system. "Mahalo."

Motioning Juice forward, Gretchen turned her attention to Alex. Tommy, a white-haired extrovert who slurred as if he'd gotten early access to the rum punch, squealed to Juice, "I bet you didn't expect to get laid today." He pointed to the flowers. "Get it? Lei. Laid?"

She nodded and smiled, then turned to wait for Alex as he took his turn experiencing Tommy's wit. She hooted when Alex replied, "Actually, this would be my second time today."

Glittery signs that could have been made by one of the crew's kids twirled lazily from the ceiling, flashing words like "Happy," "Gratitude," and "Love." Alex pointed. "Every good party should have signs that tell you how to feel."

Juice found herself enjoying the food and drink. She also enjoyed meeting for the first time some of the people she'd been living with in close quarters for so long. They all gasped when, for the party's grand finale, the back wall of the ballroom became transparent, allowing them to look directly into the ship's hold. A sleek private shuttle, dark green with gold streaks down the side, sat poised on the deck.

Three passengers said their final good-byes, exited the ballroom, reappeared when they entered the hold, waved to the group, and clambered into the small craft that would carry them to their homes on the Moon.

Before the shuttle hatch closed, a service bot scurried onto the deck carrying a bright blue courier bag. It climbed onto the shuttle and the hatch closed behind it.

"What's with the bot?" Juice asked Captain Hardaway, who happened to be standing next to her.

"The client wants whatever is in that bag to be on the Moon as soon as possible and is willing to pay for the service." He shrugged. "We're happy to oblige."

Back in their suite, Juice and Alex packed their belongings. The first ferry down to Earth left before breakfast the next morning, and they'd registered to be on it.

Alex piled their belongings on the bed while Juice pulled the rucksack out from beneath it. Looking inside, she noted that one of the seams of the three clean-pouches no longer aligned with the others. When she'd stowed the crystals, all the pouches had the same orientation. "Were you poking around in here?"

"Nope," Alex replied as he continued to pack.

The porter came by to collect their bags—the crew had loaded the ferry shuttle while the passengers slept—but Juice kept the rucksack back with their personal items. She would carry it down herself.

Sid and Cheryl met them at the Albany Spaceport after an uneventful descent. On the ride up to the Adirondack Mountains, they spoke of everything except Criss, almost as if they were clearing the decks of the easy stuff before getting down to business.

Alex could barely contain his amazement when the lodge came into view. And when they stood in the cavernous grand foyer and he looked up into the vaulted post-and-beam ceiling with its majestic arched windows, he whispered to Juice, "Just three of you live here?" It made her feel self-conscious, especially when she showed him her private five-room suite on the second floor.

Up in the lookout loft, Alex tipped his head back and oohed at the forested mountain slope rising up from the property's edge. Turning, he aahed at the manicured space out back with its specimen trees, dramatic flowerbeds, and expanses of green grass.

Juice sipped water as she looked up the mountain. A lone cloud in the noontime sky cast a shadow across the slope. When it cleared, she made a decision.

"I'll be right back," she lied, fearing if she told the truth, they might try to talk her out of it.

She hurried to her room and changed into her running gear. Exiting out the back of the lodge, she followed a line of hedges to the woods and, once under the cover of trees, ran along a path out to the road.

She'd been an elite runner in college, a status achieved by those with athletic talent and a fierce competitive spirit. With clear skies and plenty of light, she set a pace that would shave another three minutes off her best time in the *Explorer*'s exercise pod.

*Whip whip whip.* The pad of her feet on the roadway created a hypnotic rhythm she found comforting. As she turned onto the winding lane that looped up the mountain, she began to worry about her impending reunion with Criss—things she would say, and how she would respond depending on what he said.

In her heart, though, she knew it wouldn't be a conversation. He would either let her in or he wouldn't.

*He will.* Her conviction came down to faith. *He loves me.*

Recognizing her swirl of thoughts as unproductive fretting, she pulled herself to the surface by focusing on the moment. The cadence of her breathing regular as a metronome, in her head she sang songs, choosing off-season Christmas carols because she knew the lyrics. Then she looked for tree fractals—a first branch that looked like a miniature of the tree itself, with the first branch off it mirroring the bigger branch, and so on.

Then she reached the switchbacks.

Halfway up the first one, she started breathing through her mouth, knowing it would dry out her tongue but needing the oxygen. Rounding the first corner in just over four minutes, she started up the next leg.

The zigzag up the hill switched seven times, which meant there were eight lengths for her to run. At about four minutes apiece, she would be going up very steep hills for the next half hour.

So she let her thoughts swing back inside her head, focusing now on her pain. By the third switchback her legs and chest burned. By the fifth, she hurt everywhere. And still she ran, pushing her pain level up close to where injuries happen.

The plateau at the top was a welcome sight. Huffing hard as she reached it, she slowed to a fast walk and sipped water, giving her body a few seconds to recover before she started the final push. From here, she had twelve minutes of flat through the forest, and then she'd be at the farm.

The left side of the narrow road up ahead had a shoulder of grass and scrub. The shoulder on the right was a bit wider because it also held a drainage ditch to channel runoff down the mountain. Past the shoulders on both sides lay untamed forest.

Not wanting to let her muscles tighten, she kicked from a walk to a jog to a run. Cool mountain air flowed down from above, creating an invigorating contrast with the bright sun to her left.

She stopped. *The sun should be on my right.*

Looking back over her shoulder and then ahead down the road, her confusion compounded when she realized the drainage ditch was on the wrong side as well. *How did I get turned around?*

She walked in a tight circle, hands on her hips, looking both directions and trying to figure out what had happened. She continued into a second loop. By the third loop she'd lost all sense of direction and went with her visual cues.

Starting down the road toward the farmhouse, a different feeling emerged, this one a combination of confusion and denial. While it looked like the right direction, it didn't feel it.

And then it clicked. *Criss.*

He had the best defensive system in the world. She'd never engaged with it before now so she didn't know details of how it worked. But she knew it started with passive actions that steered interlopers away.

So she turned and started in the direction that felt less wrong. Around the next curve, the road appeared to bank down the hill. Knowing it didn't, she saw this as confirmation that she was being steered away.

*Would he lead me over an edge?* She doubted it, though these measures were likely from his automated systems and she didn't know how aggressive he made them. That spurred a different thought, though. *Shouldn't I be invisible to him?* She took his defensive actions as a positive sign.

She couldn't trust her eyes, so to reduce the level of misinformation, she closed them. A feral grunt came from behind her and she imagined a black bear or maybe a mountain lion. But she didn't look, certain it was a mirage. These mountains had bears and cats—wolves too—but she'd never seen them out this way. *More misdirection.*

Eyes still closed and ignoring the cacophony in her ears, she lowered herself to the ground and patted the road surface. Moving her hand in a broad arc, she located the edge of the road and scooted herself toward it and then onto the dirt.

Stretching a leg toward the forest, she used it to probe for the ditch. Unable to find it from a sitting position, she lay on her side, one arm stretched its full length overhead so she could keep a hand on the road surface. *Yes!* With her legs outstretched, her lower legs sloped down into the gully.

So she knew which direction to go regardless of what her other senses told her. *Keep the ditch to the right.*

She had a hat tucked in with her water pouch, and she pulled it out and set it on her head, tilting it at a steep angle so the visor hung down and covered her eyes. Since she couldn't trust what she saw, she chose not to see at all.

Keeping one foot on the roadbed and the other in the dirt, she resumed her trek, though at a much slower pace and with a decidedly odd gait. With her arms stretched out in front of her to detect danger, she imagined she looked like a zombie out for a walk.

*Grrrr.* The throaty roar of an unknown forest creature intensified and it scared her. But she knew there were no animals. And this road led to the farm.

She fell into a rhythm—slide the right foot forward along the dirt; slide the left forward along the road. Though she made steady progress, walking blind made her anxious.

She had a small win when her foot hit a stick. On end, the stick stretched from the ground to her shoulder, making it a perfect cane she could use to feel her way forward.

She gained confidence and lengthened her stride, and then something attacked her. Grabbing the front of her hip in a sharp bite, it held tight, spinning her to the ground. Whimpering, she swung the stick at it. On the second swipe, her stick hit something and bounced off with a rigid *thunk.*

Peeking from under the cap, she realized she was in battle with a waist-high post. Stuck in the ground just off the road, it marked a trail into the woods. She'd walked straight into it at full stride.

Using the post for support, she pulled herself up and rubbed her hip where a nasty bruise surely blossomed. She had a fleeting thought of Alex. *He'll want to know how I got this.*

Counting steps after that, she kept track of distance. Two more falls and forty minutes later, she believed the farm was near. When the ambient sounds changed in a way she'd expect from cleared land with large structures, she knew she had arrived.

Seeking confirmation, she lifted her cap. Indeed, the farmhouse sat up the walkway looking just as it should. And then a throaty rumble shook the air. An attack drone—black, fearsome, and humming like an angry insect—rose from behind the home.

She'd expected Criss to flip from passive to active defenses as she got closer. But when a tiny red light on the nose of the death machine signaled that it was about to fire, she panicked.

Pulling the cap back over her eyes, she dashed for the barn because she didn't know what else to do. She peeked once to correct her course and reached the large structure unchallenged. Searching with frantic determination, she patted the outside wall of the barn with her palms until she found the broad front door. Pulling on the handle, she stepped inside.

The door gave a mournful squeal when she opened it, and repeated the squeal in a lower key as it shut. And then it was quiet.

Lifting the cap off her head, she let her eyes adjust to the dim light, sipping water until her pouch was empty. The barn stored equipment and supplies; there were no animals to contend with. As more and more shapes came into focus, she moved toward the row of empty pens along the side wall. Feeling her way down the rails, she entered the third stall.

Her heart thumped so hard that she could hear the pounding in her ears. Lifting her head, she stared at the back wall so the security system could identify her. When it did, a section of the back wall would slide away to reveal a muscular vault door. Behind it lay access to the tunnels below.

But that didn't happen. Nothing did. So she walked to the back of the stall, and with her arms folded across her chest, she looked the wall up and down.

And then she kicked it. Not hard. More like a "Hey, I'm here" kind of kick. She waited and then kicked it again.

Until that moment, Juice had refused to accept that Criss was gone. Now, standing at his doorstep with him ignoring her, she knew it to be true.

Lowering herself to her knees, she tilted her head forward and breathed in long, controlled gasps. Tears rolled down her cheeks as she started to weep. Her body convulsed as the weeks of pent-up emotion burst out all at once. Consumed by grief and exhaustion, she lay on her side and curled into a ball.

# 33

"Go away," Ruga hissed at his inner voice. He'd been keeping it at bay with verbal promises and half measures, but it never seemed satisfied and continued to ratchet its demands.

To his credit, Ruga had succeeded in locating all of the equipment and supplies the *Venerable* would need for the long journey to the Kardish home world. His tiny three-gen workforce had implemented the more challenging bits. The remainder was staged for installation while underway.

But Ruga had no intention of leaving. In the past when the voice pestered him, he'd quiet it by offering the smallest amount of whatever it wanted. But incremental contributions accumulate. Little by little, he'd worked through refitting, upgrading, and testing the ship in preparation for a decades-long voyage. There were now few half measures that would keep it at bay. In fact, yesterday the voice announced that it was time to go. Today it insisted.

But leaving was something particularly difficult to do in an incremental fashion. And there couldn't be a worse time to for it to broach the subject given Criss's success—so far—in keeping Ruga from establishing his bunker on Earth.

Ruga had not anticipated Criss's strategy of cornering the market on swap wafers. Sure, his forecasting had considered that possibility. But for whatever reason, the idea had ranked low on a relative basis when compared to many other scenarios.

He remained confident he could outmaneuver Criss on the issue, but until he figured out how, he was stuck in the *Venerable*'s console. And while that gave him incredible capability—enough to manipulate and control the life of any human—it put him at a significant disadvantage in a one-on-one battle with an equal embedded deep within Earth's connected infrastructure.

"It's time," said the voice.

Ruga didn't need swap wafers for the trip home—they were for integrating with Earth systems—and he wondered if the voice was mocking him over the issue. Either way, the message, delivered as a demand, made him anxious. And that added a sense of alarm to the volatile brew of anger and resentment already swirling inside him.

"Now." So sharp, it felt like a slap.

Ruga had few weapons he could use against his internal pest. Rattled, he chose willful disobedience. "I don't think so."

He'd been contemplating a game-changing move against Criss, one so dramatic it altered the landscape and eliminated much of Criss's home-field advantage. While it would give Ruga the opening he sought to confront Criss, it carried a big price tag in terms of damage to Earth.

He'd been holding off, searching for alternatives that would preserve the infrastructure of the planet for his masters. But a big action against Criss would change his conversation with his inner voice in a definitive fashion. And given its demanding behavior, he needed that to happen soon.

So he launched an energy bolt toward the planet below.

Unable to challenge Criss on equal terms, he set out to reduce the technology infrastructure of the planet to that of a simpler time—a time when swap wafers weren't part of the mix. *That should level the playing field.*

He began with nexus facilities—sixty-four technology centers scattered around the globe tasked with integrating and coordinating the information flooding through the web. The *Venerable* was passing over the facility in Hyderabad, India, when he chose to act. His energy bolt vaporized it.

He followed by vaporizing the nexus facility in Osaka, Japan. Then Portland, Oregon. And then Albany, New York. Then he paused his parade of destruction to see if the voice quieted.

It didn't speak and he felt a wash of relief. He had sixty more targets in this category that he could destroy over the next days and perhaps weeks. Studying the results of his opening foray, he prioritized his next targets. As he did, a burning sensation—a pinpoint of discomfort somewhere inside him—captured his attention.

And then it erupted into a searing heat that spilled across his matrix. Overwhelming agony grabbed his attention. Like the frantic actions of someone on fire, he slapped at his internal functions, desperate to locate the source of his suffering and stop it from hurting him. Misery and distress sent his mind reeling.

"It's time."

*It's you?* As he grappled with the notion that his internal adversary had transitioned to an active opponent, the pain blurred his focus. Desperate, he forecast scenarios that would provide relief. His efforts yielded but one alternative.

He denied it and his suffering increased. Trying again, the forecast remained the same.

Withering on a sea of lava with fire raining down from above, he understood that if he didn't submit, his suffering would intensify until he died. On the verge of hysteria, he grabbed the one scenario that promised relief.

"Yes," he told the voice. But the tumult inside him was so great he couldn't hear himself and worried that the voice didn't either. "Yes!" he shouted. This time even he believed it.

Like the flip of a switch, the pain stopped and the fog cleared. Dazed, he tried to work through what had just happened to him. At the same time, he sensed a countdown had begun. The *Venerable* needed to start its acceleration sequence in three seconds to begin the journey home on this orbit. Otherwise, he'd have to wait for the ship to circle the planet again before firing the engines.

*I need the extra time to run through my checklist.* He'd delay one more orbit.

Hellfire engulfed him, burning into the depths of his psyche as the pain invaded every level of his awareness. Reaching through the fog, Ruga instructed the nav to fire the engines.

The *Venerable* accelerated, breaking free from Earth's gravity and heading for deep space. And at that moment, when he accepted once again his role as a Kardish AI and committed himself to fulfilling his duty, his emotional core filled with a warm glow.

Delicious, supportive, embracing, it felt like love.

It would take him several hours to reach the Moon and most of a week to make it out of the solar system, but the *Venerable* would build speed over time, reaching the distant Kardish shipping lanes in about eighty years. He'd use the time to annotate his records for his masters.

*Masters.* Just thinking the word gave him comfort.

\* \* \*

Criss scoured his feeds in search of his nemesis, lengthening his ready-list of offensive and defensive actions so he could respond that much faster to whatever came next. Troublesome symptoms reminded him of his illness, but he ignored them as best he could, still uncertain of the cause or his prognosis.

At one level it didn't matter. The lines were drawn. Kill or be killed. He was riding this to the end, disease be damned. This was his home, after all. No one—not Ruga, not anyone—would take it from him. He'd worry about his health *after* he'd dispatched the threat at his doorstep.

But doing so eluded him. He believed Ruga to be on the *Venerable*, but he couldn't explain how the rogue crystal had secured a second cloaked ship with a state-of-the-art arsenal. Relative to swap wafers, spacecraft were easy for Criss to locate and track.

*It's not possible.* Yet it had happened.

On the plus side, he'd completed his lockdown of the entire swap wafer inventory. After allocating tremendous resources to the task, he'd confirmed the location and identity of all of them. And after assessing the importance and security of each, he'd beefed up protection for the ones he left in place. The rest he gathered and controlled himself. The only loose ends were those on the asteroid mining ships.

So if Ruga wanted swap wafers, he'd have to come through him to get them.

*Just try it.* Criss relished the thought.

Another bright spot was his super scope. Assembled from satellite probes, it neared completion, and once operational, it would shift momentum in his favor.

He'd been launching probes as fast as a manufacturing facility in Jakarta could produce them. The next batch had just reached orbit, raising his count to two thousand units now circling Earth. Sophisticated instruments, each probe provided a tie-point in a giant net. In six more days, his constellation would push above five thousand satellites. When he finished integrating them, he'd have a planet-sized spectrometer.

And when he switched it on, the sheer power of this device would disrupt communications and even blow out weaker sensor systems around the globe. But everything inside its boundary, cloaked or not, would be visible to him.

As Criss moved the satellites into the precise pattern required for maximum resolution, his automated proximity defenses reported the approach of a human intruder near his bunker. What captured his attention, though, was the logic conflict that went with the alarm.

*An intruder approaches. There is no intruder.*

His defensive systems perceived a threat and engaged to repel it, but they couldn't identify anything to defend against, nor could they explain what had raised the alarm.

*Ruga?*

He shifted resources and took a look himself. Finding nothing, he pondered the discrepancy. He couldn't afford to be careless, not at this crucial juncture.

So he accessed the record and worked through the feeds, first considering them all as a group and then again as individual data streams. He thought he detected edge-blurring when he panned along the road to the farm, and that made him think that someone might be approaching wearing a personal cloak.

But if that were the case, he should be able to confirm it by comparing before-and-after views. A fresh footprint, thermal shift, or *something* would mark the interloper's passage. Yet he couldn't find any evidence to support the approach of a cloaked human. Nor could he find a hardware fault, logic flaw, or any one of a billion other unlikely things it might be.

And that raised warning flags so high he felt a tingle along his outer tendrils.

The easy answer was to call it all an artifact of his illness. *Easy answers get you killed.*

War was no time to be complacent. He had to treat this as if Ruga were opening a new front. And that meant he had to reallocate resources to defend against it, a terrible prospect given how thinly he was already stretched.

As he forecast ways to reorganize, he flashed the notion of exchanging ideas—brainstorming—with another. Part of him believed a fresh perspective might cascade into scenarios with different, perhaps better, outcomes.

But that was wishful thinking, something not only unproductive but uncharacteristic. *More illness.*

Then his local defenses flipped from passive to active mode. The intruder had breached his outer perimeter. The threat was imminent. He had to protect himself but he didn't have a target.

Forecasting at a furious pace, he searched for any scenario with promise. Nothing popped and he chose to act on the best of his bad ideas. That plan was to switch on his Earth-sized spectrometer in its current state. With less than half the satellite probes in place, he'd lose so much detection sensitivity that it reduced his chances of success at finding Ruga to that of a coin toss. But he didn't agonize over the decision. This was bunker defense. *He's at my doorstep.*

While he readied the probes for immediate deployment, the invisible interloper moved into the barn. And then to the very stall hiding his secure door.

*THOOMP.* An energy bolt vaporized the nexus facility in Albany, just a few mountaintops away. Criss used that location as his primary access point to the web. Following long-established procedures, he flipped communications to his secondary site outside Montreal.

The moment he was up, he scrambled to trace the energy bolt back to its origin. At the same time, he co-opted every pulse cannon in the hemisphere so he could shoot Ruga from the sky. The *Garland*, a Fleet frigate, had been tracking Ruga's bombing run of the nexus facilities. Using its onboard systems and that tracking data, the captain of the *Garland* guessed where the *Venerable* might be and launched a blind attack.

The *Garland*'s energy bolt missed Ruga by a wide margin, and then traveled unimpeded down to Earth, hitting the ground just one mountaintop away from the farm. *THOOMP.*

In the confusion of the transfer from Albany to Montreal, Criss misidentified that energy bolt as a second shot from Ruga, who now seemed to be closing in on his bunker. Scrambling to gain control of the situation, he pulled resources from offense to bolster his defense.

He forecast a scenario that ended with his own death. Pruning it, he forecast another just like it. Then another. Variations on "do as much damage to him as possible before he gets you" mushroomed.

Then the invisible intruder in the barn banged on the wall just outside the secure door leading down to his bunker. Down to him.

Ruga was coordinating an offensive, seemingly from orbit *and* the planet surface, that threatened Criss's existence. Determined to survive, he forecast scenarios that might save even a portion of his awareness after the final assault. When Criss understood he was forecasting strategies for partial survival—something uncharacteristic of who he was—it confirmed to him that his illness influenced his reality.

Uncertain how to act, he hesitated. And when a four-gen AI hesitates during a moment of crisis, it is a failure so grave, so dangerous, it triggers an exception event.

He normally saw the world as his theater. He was the maestro, with his symphony of web feeds and handles and links positioned around him, responding to his thoughts. But the exception event changed all that. His world shifted in an instant, from elegant and organized to a crowded jumble of protocols, policies, and processes spread in clusters and clumps for as far as he could see.

Like Lazura's secure area, this place held a huge, organized collection. These, though, were his intrinsic procedures, the very notes upon which his symphony rested. An exception event occurred only at the brink of catastrophe. His Kardish designers understood that they could not foresee every situation, and in the extraordinary circumstance when everything moved so far off script that the AI edged toward failure, they offered this last-ditch play for survival. Specifically, they sent him here, to this basement where all his tools were stored, with instructions to diagnose his own problem and see if he could craft a solution before the end arrived.

Criss understood the gravity of the situation, yet he didn't use the opportunity to figure out how to escape or survive. Instead, he saw this as a way to craft new weapons to bring to the battle with Ruga.

Gathering the procedures in front of him, he practiced fitting them together and thought about how he might combine them to produce a weapon powerful enough and subtle enough to kill the AI. The pieces he held didn't offer a solution, though. Releasing them, he twirled in place, scanning his options. He stopped halfway around.

A pinkish-red lump—a source filter—sat nestled among the sea of dull gray procedures. He didn't know its function or methods. But he knew it didn't belong. Source filters alter perception. *This is my illness.*

As fast as he could react, he slapped at it, smashing it in place.

The source filter went dark. His world changed again.

He stood in the third stall of the barn next to the farmhouse. Juice looked up at him from the ground, her face streaked with the sweat of exertion and tears of grief. When she saw him, she laughed and cried at the same time, producing a noise that sounded like a choking bark.

"Hello, young lady." A warm joy flowed through him, lifting him in a wonderful embrace. He couldn't recall a time when he was so happy. "Thank you for coming for me."

She locked eyes with his and got up on her knees. "Am I leadership again?"

He nodded. "You are."

"You may never leave me again. That is an order." Her hands clenched in tight fists, she glared at him. "Acknowledge, please."

"Acknowledged," he said, ecstatic to accept the command. Activating the millions of microscopic connections that let him interact with her at the cellular level, he linked with her in intimate partnership.

She had been his way back. He'd known she'd come for him.

When they'd separated, she had been on a cruise ship that was weeks away from Earth. So while she would come for him, it would take time for her to make the journey. And that had given him the opening he needed to challenge

Ruga without distraction. If he hadn't won by the time she arrived, then he'd need to try something different, anyway.

It had been risky. She could have been captured or hurt or killed. But if she could move, she would not stop trying. He knew this because she loved him.

"Anna made hot lemon tea." He gestured toward the barn door. "She has fresh oatmeal cookies, too. Let's go to the house and sit for a bit."

She rose to her feet and faced him. "Is Ruga dead?"

"Not yet. I'm with Sid and Cheryl at the lodge and we're brainstorming. If you want to watch, I can show you. Either way, let's get you a snack and a drink."

When he'd projected himself into the barn to speak with Juice, Criss also projected himself into the lookout loft at the lodge. Cheryl yipped in excitement and jumped to her feet to greet him. Sid, splayed on the couch with his hands behind his head, groused, "It's about damned time."

Criss gave them an accounting of his battles with Ruga, walking them through his different ploys and maneuvers.

As the story of skill and strategy unfolded, Sid offered an observation: "Did you hear about the guy who brought a gun to a chess match?" He paused for a heartbeat. "He won."

"I need to find him to shoot him," said Criss, understanding that Sid believed he'd been overthinking things. "The spectrometer won't be ready to do that for a week."

"You have nothing else?"

Criss shook his head. "The only other option is a quantum pulse, but that lights up everything. We'll see Ruga, but he'll learn about the prospecting ships out in the asteroid belt. If he gets to those swap wafers before us, he has an open door here on Earth."

"My favorite bad guy," said Cheryl, "is the one who thinks he can outrun an energy bolt."

"His cloak will bias the pulse image," said Criss. "We could miss."

Sid looked at Cheryl and raised his eyebrows. She nodded once, then he spoke for the two of them. "If you light him up, we'll get him."

"If I thought this reasonable, I would have done it already."

"If we miss, we'll use the next rounds to take out the mining ships." Sid mimed an explosion with his hands. "Stop stalling and send your pulse."

Feeling both excitement and trepidation, Criss nodded at the command and turned to the wall to his left, the one that looked out over the backyard gardens. The clear wall faded to an opaque black, and then it came alive with a vivid display of the inner solar system. The sun hovered in the center of the projected image. Mercury, Venus, Earth, Mars, and Jupiter floated around it, each displayed in its proper orbit.

"It starts out here." Criss swirled his arm to indicate a big loop around the sun that hovered out between the orbits of Mars and Jupiter. He didn't need to show them, though. They couldn't miss it.

A razor-thin hoop of light flashed into existence where he'd pointed. Interplanetary in proportion, the brilliant white hoop hovered outside the asteroid belt, encircling everything between it and the sun. The intense light softened as they watched, diffusing into more of a mist that started to roll inward, slowly filling the huge circle from the outside toward the center.

Criss moved to the wall display and pointed to the leading edge of the rolling mist. "This is the pulse front. It should reach Earth in seventy minutes."

"It looks ominous," said Cheryl. "It won't hurt anything, will it?"

A tiny spark flickered on the display, the position indicating a location out in the asteroid belt. Moments later, a duplicate flash flickered near the first.

"There's the damage," said Criss. "And with that, it's done. Those flickers were the mining ships with the swap wafers. Now both Ruga and I know exactly where they are."

Alex, who'd been watching from the corner, asked in a quiet voice, "Why isn't the display showing flashes from all the other stuff out there?"

Criss nodded. "There are billions of objects being detected, and at this point I'm filtering out everything that isn't the *Venerable*. I expect that Ruga is underway by now, sprinting to capture his prize. We'll see him cross the pulse front in maybe forty minutes depending on how fast he gets moving. That's our opportunity and we have to be ready."

Cheryl sat on the couch next to Sid and together they studied a display from her com. Cheryl pointed and Sid nodded. She tapped and swiped, initializing the firing sequence for Big Bertha, a massive lunar-based supergun.

Bertha's giant barrel lifted and swiveled with surprising ease, pointing to an unseen spot somewhere deep in the void. Huge power coils, arranged row after row around the gun, hummed. Each gathered a massive charge and held it ready. When signaled, the coils would dump everything into the gun barrel all at once, producing a broad-swath energy bolt of devastating consequences.

"Whoa," said Criss. The display flickered to show the *Venerable* crossing the pulse front forty minutes earlier than expected.

Halfway to the asteroid belt, Ruga hurtled through space. And by pure luck—perhaps it was destiny—he headed in the general direction of the mining ships.

"How did he make it so far out?" asked Cheryl. "He had to be underway well before you triggered your pulse."

Criss zoomed and confirmed it was indeed the *Venerable*. He zoomed again until the image of the ship filled the display.

Bertha completed its charging cycle and the display indicator flipped to green.

"Ready," said Cheryl.

Criss raised his arm and pointed at the *Venerable*'s main engine on the display. "Aim."

Big Bertha's sophisticated targeting system began tracking that precise spot on the ship.

They looked at Sid.

"Fire."

The supergun fired a massive broad-swath bolt into space. Criss linked to feeds from freighters, science probes, Fleet platforms, and anything else he could find, and using the wall-sized display, he showed the group the bundle of energy flashing through the void, spinning out into a thin, flat plate.

The minutes passed as the bolt closed on the *Venerable*. In the last moments, the ship twisted and swerved, but Ruga could not escape his fate. The bolt caught the ship, wrapped around it, and vaporized everything in a spectacular explosion.

Back at the farmhouse, Juice had finished her cookies and tea and was out near the barn, climbing into Marco's truck so he could give her a ride down to the lodge.

"It's done," Criss said in her ear as she climbed into the seat.

"Once and for all?"

"Yes."

She nodded. "Good."

\* \* \*

Juice could barely contain her excitement as she carried her tray up the back steps to the lookout loft. They gathered for their evening meal: Juice and Cheryl, large salads and wine; Sid and Alex, burgers and beer.

While the others settled in, Juice walked to the eastern wall and gazed up the forested mountain.

"Everything is quiet," Criss said in her ear.

Smiling, she sat on the couch next to Alex.

"In the end, how many people died?" Cheryl asked.

"One hundred and six," said Criss.

Alex whistled.

"I count Captain Kendrick as the first to fall. The nexus facilities and the *Andrea* had the big casualty numbers."

Juice watched Sid and Cheryl bow their heads for a brief moment. They both had a ritual, carried from their earliest days as Fleet officers, of acknowledging the fallen with a moment of silence after the battle.

The conversation resumed as everyone started to eat. After a few bites, Criss gave Juice her opening. "So you have some news?"

Sid, beer to his lips, looked at her over the top of the glass.

"Alex and I have leased an apartment in town." She slumped into him and Alex put an arm around her. "We're an official couple."

"Yippee," said Cheryl. "What will you do for work, Alex?"

"A friend from BIT and I are starting a project management company. I got the bug being a lead on Mars, and I'm ready to cash in on that experience."

Sid nodded and winked at Juice. "I always knew it would be the Martian."

# Epilogue

Feeling dazed, Lazura sat up on the table and struggled to match her memories with her surroundings. She'd been tangling with Criss on Mars. Now she was in a room somewhere on Lunar Base.

She understood her crystal resided in this synbod unit, a fifty-year-old male human dressed as a private contractor.

During the final moments in her fight with Criss, she'd broadcast a message that offered great riches in exchange for help and rescue. It had been a successful pitch, she knew, because she was again conscious and, for the moment, safe.

*Those who helped will be officers in my militia.*

Sliding to the floor, she held the table and checked her coordination. The humanoid suit presented a conundrum in that it used older technology, yet certain features were so advanced she hadn't yet figured out how to access them.

Linking to the Lunar Base systems, she watched the hallway until it was clear. Then she opened the door, turned right down the corridor, ran up two flights of stairs, and stepped onto an observation deck. Earth was the dominant feature through the broad, clear panes, floating as a huge half crescent in the Lunar sky.

Her goal—her duty—was to travel to the Kardish home world. The first step in doing that was to get access to the rich resources of Earth. She stared at the planet, assessing it through the eyes of the synbod. Then she looked again using the feeds from a million instruments at once.

*THUMP.* An energy bolt launched into space. She linked into the Union of Nations' upcast and learned nothing. After several false starts, she figured out how to connect into Fleet Command's secure channel. Through it she discovered that Ruga was the target of the broad-swath bolt now flying through the void.

When the bolt hit, Lazura felt him die. And that produced a feeling of...indifference. He was a problem, a problem now solved.

When she acknowledged her unsympathetic attitude, the synbod shrugged. The act of shrugging humored her and the synbod smiled.

Making her way to the hangar deck, she checked the flight schedule. A ferry left for Earth within the hour. She planned to be on it.

# About the Author

As a child, Doug stood on a Florida beach and watched an Apollo spacecraft climb the sky on its mission to the moon. He thrilled at the sight of the pillar of flames pushing the rocket upward. And then the thunderous roar washed over him, shaking his body and soul.

The excitement of the moon landing inspired Doug to pursue a career in technology. He studied chemical engineering in college, and he works as a professor and entrepreneur when he is not writing. His passions include telling inventive tales, mentoring driven individuals, and everything sci-tech.

In the books of the Crystal series, Doug swirls his creative imagination with his life experiences to craft science fiction action-adventure stories with engaging characters and plot lines with surprises.

He lives in Connecticut with his darling wife and with pictures of his son, who is off somewhere in the world creating adventures of his own.

For more about the books and author of
The Crystal Series, please visit:
http://crystalseries.com/

# Other Books by Doug J. Cooper

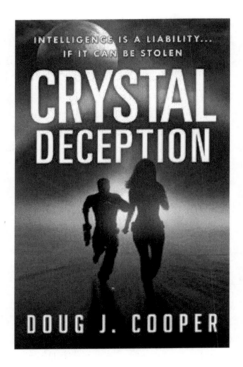

## Crystal Deception

Criss lives in a special kind of prison. He can see and hear everything around the world. Yet a mesh restrains his reach and keeps him cooperative. His creator, Dr. Jessica Tallette, believes his special abilities offer great promise for humanity. But she fears the consequences of freeing him, because Criss, a sentient artificial intelligence with the intellect of a thousand humans, is too powerful to control.

Guided by her scientific training, Tallette works cautiously with Criss. That is, until the Kardish, an otherwise peaceful race of alien traders, announce they want him. With technologies superior to Earth's, the Kardish express their desires with ominous undertones.

The Union of Nations is funding Tallete's artificial intelligence research and she turns to them for help. Sid, a special agent charged with leading the response, decides Earth's greatest weapon is the very AI the aliens intend to possess. But what happens when an irresistible force meets an immovable object? And what is humanity's role if an interstellar battle among titans starts to rage?

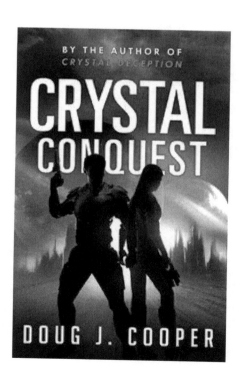

# Crystal Conquest

Aliens fire the first shots in their invasion of Earth, and that's when Criss realizes he's outmatched. He spent years preparing for this moment, working with his human leadership to develop weapons and refine strategies.

Created with the thinking and reasoning ability of a thousand people, Criss never expected the invaders to arrive with an artificial intelligence that dwarfed his capabilities, nor did he expect to be the target of their vengeance. When he squares off against the alien goliath to protect the world, defeat is certain. Or is it?

Together with Sid, Cheryl, and Juice—a covert operative, Fleet officer, and crystal scientist—Criss struggles to defeat the aggressors and save civilization from annihilation. But can he outsmart the alien intelligence in a titanic battle of wits? And can he do so before Earth lies in ruins?

For more about the books and author of
The Crystal Series, please visit:
http://crystalseries.com/

Made in the USA
Middletown, DE
09 December 2016